A Safe Haven

Book 1: Prepare For the End Series

Rina Lynn

Copyright © 2023, Rina Lynn

I0691516

Total Freedom Publishing

`A Safe Haven

Copyright © 2023, Rina Lynn

All rights reserved. Printed in the United States of American. No part of this book may be used or reproduced in any manner whatsoever without written permission, except in the case of brief quotations embodied in critical articles or reviews. It cannot be transmitted in any form or by any means, electronic or mechanical, including photocopying, recording, or by any information storage and retrieval system, without permission in writing from the publisher.
This book is a work of fiction. Names, characters, businesses, organizations, places, events, and incidents depicted in this book are products of the author's imagination or are used fictitiously. Any resemblance to actual events, locales, organizations, or persons, living or dead, is entirely coincidental and beyond the intent of the author or the publisher.

Unless it's book references, or easily recognizable people in the public arena (used as fiction) I have mentioned; or information cited from my research, it's all a story.

Contact Info: **www.rinalynn.com**

Front Cover Design and Author Photo by:

ISBN: 979-8-9894053-1-2

(paperback)

Library of Congress – Registration

First Edition: October 2023

987654321

All Bible quotations are taken from the Thompson Chain-Reference Bible, Fifth Improved Edition, Copyright © 1988 by B.B. Kirkbride Bible Company, Inc.

Table Of Contents

Dedication

I dedicate this book to all God's Men & Women who fight the good fight. To those who have a calling on their life and listen daily to that 'still small voice' that directs our path. I think of those who have come along side me and been that support, that prayer team, that voice of encouragement.

I especially think of Pam Van Meter, who's been a rock in my life. Amanda Mullens, who's read every page, and given her godly wisdom and insight, and so much encouragement.

Sharon, Lori, and Suzanne, and all the others from my support group, who helped put me back together when my life was ripped to shreds. They encouraged me when God told me to 'write it out' and read all my early poetry that spoke to so many of us. I may have been the one He tasked, to write it down, but it was for all of us; and they shared that with me so many times for so many years.

I appreciate every word, every insight, every request that led to a new piece and another layer of healing for each of us. Thank you, Cooter for your support and words of life. They are why the later books will be able to be written. I've met so many people walking the path of healing from things it would seem impossible to heal from.

I think of a ministry friend from my former life, who studied with me, prayed with me, and for me; and ministered together with me so many times. You'll never know how many times I've thought of you through the years, or what your words have meant. Thank you, my brother.

Robert Lamm, of Arkansas State University, whose words of encouragement about my writing ability helped bridge that last gap of confidence to finally 'just get it out there, Rina.'

To all the hurting people I've met who have shared some of the most unbelievable stories of pain, destroyed lives, and how you made it through. So many of your stories will be seen in this series. You all deserve a medal for allowing me to use what you've gone through and learned. May God richly bless you and keep you.

And, my two beautiful children, Katie, and Joshua. Love for them kept me going, when the road seemed impossible to find.

A SAFE HAVEN

May you see your mother's heart and passion in the words the Lord has given me to tell His wonderful story of healing, battling the enemy, and restoration of relationships that looked like all was lost.

A special thanks to Memori Ruesing for allowing me to use a picture of her beautiful home, the Walker-Manor home, for the cover. My friend and I spent a delightful afternoon having tea in the home, and Memori is now a friend.

To my readers:

Thank you for trusting me to lead you on a journey of love, drama, pain, healing, learning to stand when it seems the enemy is too big, too powerful, and too dedicated to your destruction. Most of all, learning to lean on and trust the only one who can bring us through it—Jesus

Fight the good fight with courage and determination.

The day of reckoning is coming. Our Savior Sees, Hears, and is even now saying… "On my way…"

SIGN UP FOR MY AUTHOR NEWSLETTER

Be the FIRST to learn about Rina Lynn's new releases and receive exclusive content for both readers and writers!

WWW.RINALYNN.COM

Preface

This book came into being due to my having a life experience that clearly showed me that some people love to do good, and care for other people, and some love to hate and hurt others. In my journey to heal and move forward, I learned lot about hearts, souls, and why people do the things they do, and met many people with stories of hardship, pain, and loss; and their effort to heal and grow through it all.

As I pondered it, I wondered… what if this were taken to the extreme… and on one hand you had those who truly followed God, and on the other those who were completely dedicated to the enemy. I'd studied the story of good and evil for most of my life, trying to 'rightly divide the word.' I couldn't get away from it. I'd meet another person, and hear another story, and I understood, this isn't something new. God began to lay a burden on my heart to let it play out and see what it would be like.

There is a kingdom war in the heavenly realm. It's battled out in the human realm as well. What happens when one group of families' is determined to follow God and do good things, and another group of families are dedicated to the old gods, the fallen ones, the demons of old. How would that play out in our modern world, where righteous people are bound to follow the laws of God and man, and the pagans follow no law, but to 'do what thou wilt' and indulge in every sensuous pleasure they can?

What if the pagans knew who the members of the Godly families were, and have targeted them and their children for over a century; but stay hidden in the shadows, and behind righteous and upstanding 'facades,' while waging a continuous war upon their hated enemy?

What if you were a member of the righteous family, and had to be on guard, alert, 24/7, never knowing what direction the attack was coming from, or who was behind it all? Where bodies are found mutilated, or never found at all. Where satanic ceremonies set off a series of events that you have to stop, or someone you love will die. How far would you go to protect your loved ones? What if even law enforcement, and the employees at the local hospital were infiltrated by the enemy? Where would you turn to for safety, solace, or help? Who do you trust against an enemy that will cross any line, no matter how heinous?

Join me as I begin a series that tells the tale of good vs evil in today's world, with today's laws, and God's forever rules of engagement. Watch how the men and women of God are pushed to the wall time and time again. Watch how they peel back layers in themselves and grow as they fight the good fight on a scale most of us will never experience.

Hint of Darkness

Chapter 1

MAGGIE WAS WALKING AND thinking. It'd been a tough year. The inky night surrounded her as she walked, trying to soothe her troubled mind. *How do I get through this year… year, heck… how do I get through this month?*

Commission is a tough way to make a living at any time, but lately it seems all I do is work and worry. What is God's plan for me to make it through this crazy time? He has to have one, but I can't seem to find it. Soft footfalls, regular and even, beat the tempo of her relentless pacing.

Balmy winds blowing against her face and arms, blowing her hair around as her strides took her on her silent patrol; thoughts coming as fast as the leaves flying about, with the rising gusts detaching them from the branches that'd been their home since the spring; their crackling brown color and large size so different from the tiny pale green that was their appearance just a few short months ago.

As the breeze picked up, turning into gusts that almost knocked her down, the wild feeling that pre-storm gales always generated deep in her soul increased, tapping into the innate courage that'd always been so much a part of her. The determination set in, and a feeling of hope and trust began once more, to grow, as she leaned upon the one who'd been with her through so much.

How many years have I spent walking and praying? Some years it seems like all I've done…but this year…it's such a part of my daily and nightly ritual; it's like my body brings me out here without my brain even having to issue instructions to my feet.

2021…to a woman that grew up in the 80s, it still sounds so futuristic to say it's 2021. I can still remember the day my dad said he'd never live to the year 2000. I laughed at him; "Good grief dad, that's only 15 years away". I can still see him sitting there, smoking his cigarette, totally at ease, speaking of his own demise. The very next day he'd brought a woman from the funeral home with him so they—along with her—could plan his funeral.

That was one unbelievable conversation as she was determined to have no part in it, but he'd prevailed, and a short five years later how utterly comforting it had been to just make a phone call and implement the plan they'd devised; as her sister lay sobbing in the hospital chair, totally useless. No arguments, no debate, no money having to be found.

Just a quiet call, the papers signed, and it all went off without a hitch; with no one able to do a thing about what they would have done differently. Her dad's unique signature on the bottom line ended every attempt at trying to preempt the choices and make it into something he didn't want.

Step, step, step. Arms swinging, blouse blowing, breaths in and out, in and out. *What I wouldn't give for one more conversation with him right now. In my mind I can hear his wonderful, enjoyably irreverent, hilarious tirades against government officials and their ability to screw up a solid steel block. I can almost smell the pungent Sulphur of the match head as he lit his next smoke. Too bad I didn't have a better relationship with him; but still, at least we had something.* She still felt such pain at not having one with her mother, or her sisters.

She'd worked so hard to keep her business intact throughout this nightmare year. Working so many more appointments for so much less income. *Do I go get another job? Do I try to work even more hours? Is there anyone, anywhere, I could live with?* As usual, that led to quickly suppressed sadness at being so alone in the world, where each day the news seemed darker than the day before. *Thank God for Jake, Sharon, Rachel, and Sarah. What would I do without them?*

She once again spun scenarios in her mind as to where she thought it was all going, and how fast it was going to take to get there. And, in the middle of it all, she had to make a living somehow. *Lord, please tell me what to do to get through these horrible times.*

Walking felt so good. It relieved the tension built up from sitting in a chair all day and all evening, trying to convince clients they needed to protect their family. It's a hard sell when their business is either gone or doing as little as her own, or they were still laid off from the lockdown. She felt lucky in spite of the lesser amount of income, because a lot of businesses had already gone under.

It's almost as if I can push back the evil as I walk. It can't touch me if I keep walking, keep praying. Her mind went over her prep list one more time. Extra food, check; extra water, check; extra toilet paper, check; new puzzles in case the next lockdown is announced; check. Defense; check. Someone to watch her back; *nope. Crud. Buck up girl. Face it. It's you and God.* Well, that's not totally true. She had her prayer group, the alliance, and Jake and his family. She once again realized she didn't know what she'd do without their friendship. They were the family she no longer had.

The thought of being in her house for weeks or months, completely alone again, made her sick. The thought of thugs coming into her neighborhood sent a pang of fear through her middle. *When will it end? Will it end? I'm totally convinced it never will. We're too far in; too invested in the lifestyles we've chosen in America.*

God has to judge us—as Ruth Graham once stated—or apologize to Sodom and Gomorrah. Thank God, for Jake's friendship. If I couldn't call him, or look down to see the phone light up with his name shining in bright blue letters, and his smiling face, I think they'd of, had to put me in the looney bin already.

Her mind went back to her interrupted prayer: *"God, I know you're there. I know you see and hear. It looks so dire right now, but your Word says you'll never leave me nor forsake me, unlike so many in my life. Your Word says: 'My God shall supply all my needs according to his riches in glory, by Christ Jesus.' I can't see how we're going to get thru this financial devastation; right now, I need so much just to get out of the end of the year. I can't see a way Lord, but I trust you to keep your Word. Please show me the way.*

Provide in abundance. Make a way where there is no way. Show the enemy, and the people who follow him, that he can't take away my provision, because you are the one who provides. He can't steal my joy forever. He can't destroy any more than you allow. God help me find the right path. Show me, every single step, as if I'm a child. Make a way. Thank you once again... my true father... I'll just keep working and helping families, and watch you create a path through the mire."

She began to silently pray the other prayers God heard so regularly; the ones for a life's companion that was true. The ones for her family. The ones to not be alone in such a hostile world with so many evil men and women. Her thoughts went to Jake... wishing... but he'd never wanted more than a friendship, and being his friend was so precious to her...

And once again she heard that still, small voice, whisper.... "I've got this... you keep doing your part, and I'll do my part... watch it unfold... I've called you to a work that will be difficult, but I'll send a helper... soon you will begin to understand why all this is happening. You will know true fear, but don't be afraid. You will see things that astound you, but stay calm. Guard against deception; things aren't always as they seem. Let me show you the real enemy. Let me use you to make a difference. Let me lead you to the calling I placed upon you so long ago. Are you willing? Are you ready? It's time."

A chill went up her spine. She could have sworn she heard a sharp intake of breath from someone just behind her, in fear at the words that still seemed to linger in the night air. She turned to look and see who was there, but the night held nothing she could see. She 'felt' a presence, but it wasn't visible. Like so often lately, she could 'feel' the darkness becoming more palpable, and sense that something was coming to an end—and something else was about to begin. She smelled a stench that seemed to permeate the air around her. It was like nothing she'd ever smelled before.

All her life she'd felt a calling. A 'knowing' that there was something she was supposed to do. The hunger to understand, leading her to endless hours of bible study, conversations with others who loved the word; the countless sermons, and podcasts she'd listened to for as long as she could remember. Absorbing. Learning. Wringing every possible nuance, she could, from each phrase, each individual word, each scholarly voice as they taught in their sphere of influence. Studying. Thinking. Praying. Preparation for she knew not what, just that she had to continue to strengthen her heart, mind, soul, and spirit. And above all…to be ready…

As the wind around her began to pick up, the sound whistling through the tree limbs increased exponentially. She heard shrieks, wails, and moans that were more than human; not animal; not nature; but unmistakably there. When she unexpectedly turned toward the house faster than her usual pace, she caught a glimpse—for just a fraction of a heartbeat—of a face that was almost human, but with something completely wrong. It was such an infinitesimally short a sight, that it was shocking how it imprinted itself into her brain; seared forever into her memory so that she would always be able to describe it, to the minutest detail.

It that heartbeat of time she read the look in a way that could not be her understanding alone; Holy Spirit intel showed her fear, anger, malevolence, and a determination to stomp her out of the picture in the most vicious way possible…. but also, the clear knowledge that it knew it could not touch her… yet…

Preparation Acceleration

Chapter 2

JUST AS SHE REACHED the house, the rain hit. It was as if the bottom of the ocean of another world, just above ours, opened up and began to drain. It rained with a fury she'd seldom seen. It came down unbelievably fast; it rained sideways; it bounced so hard it seemed as if it rained from the bottom up; She wasn't too sure it wasn't raining in circles. *I feel like Noah watching the beginning of the deluge.* It turned blacker and blacker, and the howls she'd heard earlier were multiplying with each drop of water.

She sat in the dark on her glassed-in porch watching it all; eyes continuously examining every inch of the night to see if 'it' was still out there. She sensed that it was; like a sentinel sent to keep watch on her. She wondered who 'it' reported back to, then she laughed… *the name doesn't really matter... it's the headquarters of the enemy. I'm sure of that.*

Ok, God; I get it. 'It's time'... really means... it's time, 'now.' Are you sure I'm up to the task? Am I ready? Do I have the courage, the steadfastness, the rock-solid faith in my calling? Have I learned enough? I haven't memorized scripture. These last few years have weakened me. I don't have the strength I used to have."

"My daughter: I've layered more into you than you can even imagine. You've been through endless repeats of exercises. Your 'spiritual muscle memory' is effortless. You do some things so naturally that you don't even notice. There are areas that you can only learn and grow through *in* the battle. So much depends upon you staying close. Trusting. Obedience will be the deciding factor. Leaning on your training. Never going it alone. You are multifaceted. Some areas are a warrior well trained for battle, but untried on the bigger battlefield. Some areas are—and must be— a small child listening to the voice of her father leading her

6

where she can't see. You will stumble, but if you will listen and instantly obey, you will not fall. As you've already seen, the enemy grows bold... and close...

The enemy is evil beyond anything you've ever even considered. He is relentless. He knows his time is short; and he's on an all-out—do or die—campaign to destroy my greatest creation, take over the universe, and ultimately sit on my very throne. You've read the book. This will never happen, but scripture has to be fulfilled.

He knows he will be thrown down very soon, and his angels with him, and he is totally insane. In his mind he must win. He knows his fate. It's win or be locked away forever. In his narcissistic absorption, in the perfection of his original state of creation, he cannot grasp how fallen he truly is. He was the highest; the most beautiful; the wisest; the one just under the godhead. He was created to rule; he is the anointed cherub who covereth... perfect... until iniquity was found in him...

Mirrors only show him the past, never the present. Most of the time he and his fallen ones can't even see their own reflection in mirrors. They see their desires, they see their original face, and they see their 'win.' It's the mark of a true narcissist. They can ever only see themselves as the greatest—unable to see the true nature of their soul—that's been forged through an endless series of selfish, hateful, sinful, choices and deeds.

They grow bold. Like vultures gathering around the battlefield looking to gorge themselves, they are on the earth in ever increasing numbers. Stay vigilant, but do not fear, don't even be anxious. Occasionally, like tonight, you may get a glimpse of them. This is to create fear, which is their greatest asset in manipulating humans, but it wasn't intended tonight for you to see; his fury made him careless. They operate in darkness, hidden—stalkers—the lot of them.

Know this, even if you can't see them, my holy ones are here as well. They surround my children; watchful guardians and messengers. You have your own personal guardian, and others that are assigned due to your calling. Prayer is the currency in my kingdom; but don't pray to them. Pray to me, and I will send them. I will instruct them.

I will arm them with heaven's finest weapons of defense; but pray for offense also. Far too often my children are on the

BOOK 1: "PREPARE FOR THE END" SERIES

defense, retreating before the attacking ones. That is not my way. Offense. Kingdom warriors who push back the hordes of hell. We hold the title deed now. They know that; unfortunately, most of 'my' human family does not."

As the silence settled in, she knew the instructor was going to be silent for the night unless she needed him again. It wasn't often she heard his voice quite as clearly as she did tonight. But she'd learned through the years—that in times when she needed Him the most—it was almost like talking to a visible person and hearing an audible voice. What's that they say in testimony services...all but audible...that was what this reminded her of...but even more...it's like His very words are written on my heart. Engraved forever to ponder, consider, hold close, and have comfort in.

She realized, that although the rain was still as hard as before, the howls had ceased when the Holy one was speaking; and the presence of the evil watcher was gone. She didn't guess; She knew. That spirit of discernment He'd given her so long ago was even sharper now. She knew her gifting had been increased again, and was here to stay. Each time the father gifted her, she instantly 'knew' and it was like it had always been there, never to leave, or lessen. She left the porch and passed the night watch to the one who never sleeps, knowing she was as safe as a babe in his mother's arms.

She went to bed with a clear heart and mind, knowing her father truly did 'have this.' She slept well and deeply, with dreams of being clad in the shiniest armor she'd ever seen, holding the sword she'd grown so familiar with through the years. She may have been elevated to a different arena, but her weapon was the same as it'd always been...the never changing Word of God...which is, always has been, and always will be, our true sword.

Morning Reflection

Chapter 3

THE BRILLIANT SUSHINE flooding around the edges of the blinds woke her. It was like the rain of the night before had never been. She stretched, enjoying the morning feel of the sheets, like pure silk under the weight of the comforter. The movements caused the sunshine to bounce off the shiny golden squares stamped on the soft covering; each enhancing the other; combining to shimmer across the beige walls like the lights reflected from a glitter ball at a high school prom.

It never failed to make her smile and fill her heart with delight. *I swear, I'm worse than a kid.* The only thing that rivaled it was lying in bed reading, with the twinkling Christmas lights she'd strung close to the ceiling instead of putting up a wallpaper border, plugged in. The colored lights reflected off the golden squares as well, making it as if the bed itself were decorated. With the lights twinkling on and off, it was like being inside a 3-D Christmas globe. Again, it was one of her more childish moments, but it was also done during one of the deepest healing times in recovering from child abuse.

She'd never gotten to just be a child; or choose, or to delight in a choice. She was learning to do something just because it made her happy; a very difficult concept for someone whose happiness had never been factored into the equation. It was very challenging to ferret out little things that made her happy; and the elements of that journey still surrounded her in her home, in the eclectic choices, each purchased in the moment, independent of the others, that she'd began to indulge herself with for quite a long time now.

She'd finally figured out her 'style,' but it took a while. Through several years of trial and error, letting go of lack of confidence, trying to watch others or read magazines, to see what was 'right,' she'd finally learned to just notice what instilled delight in herself. You can look around my home now and see things I would never have bought before, but now seem such obvious choices.

Shiny metals; unusual wooden pieces; glittery glass; things a bit 'funky' (like the crazy 'ugly' chickens that are a bit on the side of abnormal); chalky pottery; and florals. For a woman who had been her dad's 'boy,' who only used to choose denim and t-shirts—which she still loved—she'd found florals, lace, and just beautiful, feminine, flowy fabrics, were really what made her feel beautiful.

She smiled thinking of the song she wrote during that period of exploration, 'Demin & Lace.' *I'll always love that song! One of my forever favorites is the plaque on the kitchen wall that says 'it's never too late for a happy childhood.' I still send pics of that to people just starting the healing journey I've walked so many years. Some things you can't get back—but some things you can—if you're willing to reach out and take it.*

One more stretch and she threw back the covers, making her chihuahua, Annie, yelp, and dart back under the pile. She laughed at the hilarious morning routine. Annie hid until the last possible moment before she jumped off the high bed, running as fast as she could to the door to be let out. Their morning routine seldom changed no matter the time they woke up.

Me, up first; to the kitchen to push the button on the coffee machine, that brewed the nectar that made life doable; back to the bathroom for teeth brushing and other necessities; then let Annie out, and in, getting her breakfast—the coveted peanut butter rollup and doggy cookie—pour up the cup of heaven-on-earth, then my recliner to spend time with my God, his Word, my wonderful furry 'kid,' and just get comfortable in the new day.

As she sat nurturing the second cup, her mind went back to the brief glimpse of the face from the night before. Reflecting in the morning light it seemed so fanciful, and she wondered if she'd imagined it in the wild feel of the storm approaching. *Am I really called by God to do something in these end times? Or am I just so caught up in bible history, and the vignettes into the lives of the ones written about—there for us to pattern ourselves on; whom I love to study about so much—that I think I too have a place in the saga of the great kingdom war? Do I just want to be like one of them enough to believe it can be just like that for us today?*

Contemplating brought back that still small voice, and the words He spoke. She'd walked with Him long enough to know His voice. All, of a sudden, she felt the gravity of the times and could feel the mantle once again settle down around her. Familiar, well-fitting, like a starched uniform in the hush before leaving for a mission. I know from his Word what's coming, but the particular details are always revealed in the moment. She heard the barest whisper in the depths of my soul, 'trust me... just trust me.'

Noticing the position of the hands on the clock, she startled Annabelle by suddenly flipping down the footstool of the recliner, and standing up. "Gotta make the donuts." Annie's tiny tail waved back and forth at the daily statement, totally oblivious in her doggy world to the throwback reference of a long-gone commercial.

Hair, makeup, dressing, then making breakfast, was the second part of the routine. The same for many years now of living alone. It used to be leaving for work then, but now it was going to her desk for a long day of phone calls, zoom meetings, and paperwork. The great covid-19 lock down had changed the world for millions. She rather liked working from home; able to do laundry and other small tasks in between meetings, and having occasional naps when someone no-showed her. Being able to talk to friends on the phone, off and on all day long, was nice also; but being in her home alone so much, also accentuated the aloneness and loneliness of her life. She filled the solitary spaces by listening to podcasts or videos of the great men and women of God speaking of end-time timelines, and prophetic fulfillments, and the medical experts who explained the truth of the covid lies.

These mandates make me feel extremely unsettled in the depths of my being, especially knowing I still have to make a living. It's me. Just me. I need a place to live, but I also am certain that taking that shot would be an incredible mistake, both physically and spiritually. As each doctor revealed even more damage being caused by the jabs, she became more determined to not take it, no matter what.

My God shall supply all my needs is my constant mental refrain, she thought. *As the anxiety grows, I sometimes have, to make myself say it, other times it comes easily*; but the anxiety and underlying uncertainty of what was coming, and how imminently it was coming, made her feel an insecurity that was hard to deal with. *I feel a darkness approaching.*

She, and her like-minded friends, often asked each other, "What do you think is really happening?" "What have you heard lately?" "How much time do we have?" "Are we in the tribulation, or still the birth pangs?" and always reminding each other: "Jesus is coming soon; we have to be strong."

It always looped around to God's voice, "Just hold on. Just do your part. Listen to my Word. Do my work. Preach the word; save the lost; heal people; cast out demons; DO NOT BE DECEIVED." It seemed so easy while among each other; but dealing with clients, who were totally absorbed in the worldly habits and the main-stream media fear-inducing hysteria, was a different story.

She sat down after another such session. A nice couple, not highly educated, but ok. She was walking them through signing the paperwork when the lady passionately said, "I just can't understand why people won't get the vaccine!" Maggie had looked at her in surprise, thinking: *"I know not everyone listens to the podcasts of speakers that I do all day, or has studied end time events for the number of years, and to the extent that I have, but to me there is simply no excuse to not understand this shot is bad.*

She'd worked with people long enough, and seen enough close-minded people—without a 'teachable' spirit—to know the woman could not hear the truth; especially, as it was so obvious, she and her family had taken the jab, but Maggie knew she had to speak up for those who were a bit wiser.

She said, "I'm on the other side of that; I've studied quite a bit about this shot and the effects it's having on people. I've heard many doctors, including the world's leading virologists, speak about the damage they are doing. I live alone, and cannot afford to have that happen to me." Maybe it wasn't what she needed to hear, the truth that it is killing people across the world, and could be a pre-curser or an essential element of the mark of the beast, or that it is a bio-weapon designed to kill us all, but it was the kindest thing she could say in the moment.

She had already seen that she could not really change her mind; and the people would not study to prove to themselves what she could have told her. And the truth is she really couldn't handle the knowledge that her entire family had just signed their own death warrant, or at the very least shortened their lifespans; or that those years would most likely be filled with a plethora of medical issues. It felt too unkind to try to force the harsh truth on someone who had already rejected it.

Maggie had seen the woman's husband shoot her a look to shut her mouth. I was one of '*those*.' A thought crossed her mind that in the coming days, if interrogated about knowledge of anyone un-vaxxed, that they would turn her in to keep themselves safe. *It's unbelievable in America to have to worry about such a thing; but I've read the book. Even family members will turn each other in; strangers certainly will, especially to gain food or personal safety.*

And, people who've been jabbed, may have opened doors to a demonic spirit with a complete lack of compassion for those who've not, especially when they begin to see the jabbed dying, while we live. I believe it will begin to bring out a hatred and jealousy that will retaliate in its fury. Once again, she saw the two kingdoms, the difference in each, and the coming kinetic war, along with the ongoing spiritual war, being set up between the increasingly different beliefs of the members of humanity.

She had another worry also that was more personal. In selling life insurance, she got paid with advances of a percentage of the first-year premiums, before the client pays those premiums; so, if the people cancel or pass away in the first year, she had to pay her paycheck back.

She'd already had numerous 'chargeback's when so many people were locked down last year and losing their job. She didn't mean to be callous, these are humans made in the image of God, but she did secretly wonder how these mass deaths, if the doctors were correct, would affect her financially. She wrote a large volume of business to support herself. If a great many of them were to pass away she would go under fast and lose her home. The thought of homelessness was an ongoing anxiety, that covid inflated quite a bit as this whole thing has unfolded.

She could sense a long sleepless night ahead; praying; anxiety; possible scenarios spinning, while she tried to mentally prepare for each one. *Oh, how I envy women with a godly husband, a close family, and a place in the community where they are not so alone.* She had a moment of longing... and a regret that it wouldn't be...

She'd begun to sit there each night pondering, listening to her nightly array of podcasters, praying, and trying to get calm enough to sleep. Jake would often call and talk, but when he didn't the night got long. After one last trip outside with Annie, she picked her up, setting her on the bed so she could scoot under the blankets, showered, brushed her teeth, and climbed in, exhausted and shocked by the clock hands.

I gotta stop doing this. But, as usual, my routine did it's intended work, I'm so tired, I think I can actually fall sleep, rather than laying in anxiety through the night. One more day in the can. Life alone in your home is not really living, its existing. I so miss being out among people, freely interacting; mask-less, effortless living; doing whatever you wanted, whenever you wanted, and money being a bit easier. How I wished I could believe, like so many, that we would soon get back to 'normal.'

If God's word is true, it will get progressively worse and the calamities will be progressively larger, harder, and scarier. If you read the book of Revelation about the number of people who will die, it's going to get bad. Without people to work them, factories will be shut down, food will not be harvested, truckdrivers will not bring anything to stores, and people will be abandoned to fend for themselves; not to mention, those who don't take the antichrist's mark will be hunted down and slaughtered; as the devil and his angels have their few short years of total reign.

Exterminating those made in God's image is their ongoing desire. Our current governments, as evil as they are being revealed to be, are just a token of what's coming when the ones they serve are visibly and physically on this earth to do their worst.

...and I'm supposed to sleep like a baby, with no anxiety; not fearing, and totally at ease, knowing God has this...I've never felt so unworthy of his love and sacrifice in my life than I

have since the lockdown, and the revealing of those so incredibly determined to kill us all...... 'fear not' seems a bit hard to manage.

God, surround me with your holy ones. Guard my yard, my home, my bedroom, my children, and grandchild, and help me be an asset to the kingdom. Keep me safe through the night," she prayed as she drifted closer to sleep.

More and more I'm beginning to understand Revelation 22:20.

"He which testifieth these things saith, surely, I come quickly. Amen."

"Even so, come, Lord Jesus!"

Prayer Meeting

Chapter 4

"HELLO MAGGIE," JAKE GREETED her, as she let herself into his home for the monthly prayer meeting. He was her best friend. They'd been teaching small groups together for quite some time. He loved to study the bible as much as she did; and since so few did nowadays, it was inevitable that they'd become friends years ago, while meeting for coffee and sharing the minutest details of what they'd ferreted out from their current area of interest. They were known for microscopically examining a passage of scripture, and discussing it for hours, born out of sheer love of the Word.

The volume of study they each performed, consistently made them light years ahead of a lot of people they knew, and each had often seen the glazed-over look on the face of others as they caught themselves going on and on, somehow expecting everyone to get as excited as they did. It never ceased to disappoint Maggie to know that others truly didn't have the love of reading the old, old story the way that she did; and Jake was the balm of Gilead that healed the wounds that unkind, condemning—sometimes scathing—remarks had inflicted.

Sometimes you just needed to discuss, debate, or marvel with someone at the deeper meanings as they opened up to you. God had sown in so much for those willing to study to show themself approved unto God, a workman that needeth not to be ashamed, rightly dividing the word of truth; as 2nd Timothy 2:15 stated. They were part of a larger group that worked together to push back the darkness, but in this particular bible study, they were the ones people looked to for answers.

"Jake, I'm so glad you are willing to allow us to start up again. It's hard when you live alone and can't get out to be with other people. I love talking to you, and our calls keep me sane, but I'm so excited to share with the group tonight. I've been keeping up with the scientific evidence coming out about this so called 'vaccine.' We've got to get the truth out. This jab is not what people think it is. I'm so happy we're meeting to discuss it all.

"It's been hard on me too, out here all alone. At least I can get out and walk in the woods around the house without being subject to people's ire," he agreed. "If you and Sharon, and Matt and Rachel, didn't come out, I'd go nuts. I'm used to being on campus with lots going on. We get to open the classroom at the college next week. Some students will still be remote though. I'll have to adjust my lectures accordingly. How about we have Matt and Rachel over on Friday and we can cook and play monopoly?"

"That's wonderful. I think I may work some in my office in town too. It's time. Who's going to be here tonight?" Maggie finished, with a look of inquiry. "I've been trying to figure out who will chance it, and who will obey the TV 'talking heads' for the rest of their lives."

"The usual. Mr. 'I think I'm a scholar.' Ms. 'I got my hair done this week, isn't it dreamy?' Aunt 'Honey, I brought a pound cake; things go so much better with sweets.' Brother 'I just want to do my part. Do we need to paint the church again?' and the ever-present, lovely, Miss 'Of course I'm a Christian, my Momma went to this church;' came the quip that was the newest version of a never-ending, constantly changing answer, to that monthly question.

"And let's not forget Mr. 'I'm a stand-up comic," Maggie shot right back. Jake didn't have a mean bone in his body, but he could take one facet of a person's life and make a verbal caricature as good as any artist could draw one.

"Ouch," Jake pretended to be wounded, even staggering back a few steps, and doing a perfect imitation of someone taking an arrow to the heart. "Oh, you got me... help... I'm injured... I may not recover...." he gasped; while wrapping his hands around the invisible arrow, mouth trying it's best to open in a silent scream, while losing the battle to twinkling eyes and snickers of laughter. "I think Ms. 'Calls it like she sees it' just used me for target practice. Again."

Cracking up, Maggie began to make the coffee, and add fresh milk to the small creamer pitcher on the silver tray Jake had set on the counter. It was lovely the way the highly polished metal reflected the blues and greens of Jake's kitchen, along with the cedar toned cabinets, and now the color of the rich white milk. The light from the lamps above the counter made bright spots that sparkled like diamonds on the shiny silver as she moved around, and the brilliance faded the other colors into an interesting background that made the artist in her want to start mixing colors and capture the look.

She had to smile. She'd been making coffee in Jake's kitchen for so long, and thinking the same thoughts almost every time. The smell of the muffins, mingling with the fresh coffee aroma, made her hungry. Food just seemed to be so much better with other people. She'd always loved spending time with him doing simple mundane things. It may have been a while since she'd been here, but some things just felt comfortable; and the simple pleasure she got every time, seeing the reflections change with whatever was nearby, was a part of her happy world. She used to scold Jake about using the good silver for every day, until he'd finally shared with her why he did.

He'd grown up watching people give his grandmother lovely things and seeing it hidden away in the box or in the closet, because it was just 'too beautiful to use for everyday;' and he was sad when she passed, that it was all still in its original wrappers. She even had a chest-of-drawers filled with the most beautiful linens: sheet sets, towels, hand-knitted dishrags, specialty towels for bread baskets, a bag of hand-tatted lace; you name it, it was in there—in the plastic it left the store in—or the gift bag she'd received it in.

He'd often caught her opening the drawers and running her hands over it, a bittersweet enjoyment on her face as she shut the drawer, relishing ownership of such finery, but never willing to use it; but he had not one single memory of her enjoying using it; or sharing it with the people who'd gifted her, showing each her gratitude; or having the fun of pleasing someone who'd indulged her love of beauty and fine things.

As he'd dismantled her home, he'd unwrapped each piece, imagining her doing so, and having a special coffee time with her 'hen circle' as he'd liked to call her friends. Or, having the beautiful towels hanging in the bathroom, to make her feel pampered, as the giver had planned. She had many silver pieces; a large cutlery collection; a gorgeous set of rose floral China, that she'd admired for 30 years before being presented with it on her 50th birthday, after they'd divided up the purchases among them; drawers full of colorful linens; and even a pair of boots that had been in the closet, unworn so long, the leather had rotted.

The giver, his cousin Sharon, had often shared her outrage at the money she'd spent being thrown away because Grandma was so backward in her thinking. It'd become the family joke; who could buy the best 'closet treasure' for her to hide away each year. For years they'd annually held award ceremonies—behind Grandma's back of course—with a long-since hammered-out set of criteria to judge the merit of each 'treasure.'

Those memories were the real treasures to Jake. The laughter, the comradery, the unique way of psychologically handling the—incomprehensible, to them—refusal to use the treasure they so loved to give her. How they had longed to see her use it, and share in the using, to bring everyone pleasure.

About 10 years back, Jake's brother, Russell, had devised a challenge. They created a jar of cash that each of them added a small amount to each year, that would go to the one who could—stealthily—convince grandma to finally use a stashed item. *Ahh... families... and their quirks... that's the stuff that sets us apart and makes us different from every other family. All families have them.*

It makes the best stories, the hardiest laughter, and the fondest soft places inside, when the person is no longer here. He wouldn't trade those precious memories of his grandma for anything; but he refused to keep the hoard intact when she was gone. After the funeral they'd all gone to eat—fully funded from the prize money that had never been claimed—though they each had tried. Those stories were all hilarious too.

After the dinner, they'd gone back to grandma's house and decided what to do with all her belongings, including the accumulated cache. Each writing on a slip of paper their name, what they truly would like to have and why, what they'd bought, and if they wanted it back. They'd read them out loud, awarded the prize to whomever it was decided was the most deserving, and divided the treasure so that each could have a few special pieces to remind them of grandma, her peculiarities, and the closeness the experience of it all had brought to each of them, individually and collectively.

They all used their liberated inheritance daily, or with close friends and family at special times, determined to make living memories, instead of stored dreams that were never truly realized. It was a normal part of each extended family home that made grandma never completely gone, and each felt grandma's sanction, as she wouldn't want them to have the regret of unused blessings.

Instead of 'grandma's closet treasures,' they now called them 'godsent daily treasures,' or, more often—still poking fun at her—'Babushka's Pirate Plunder.' Babushka was the Russian name for grandma, which Jake's cousin Rachel had learned one summer while reading, and they'd called her that off and on from that time forward.

One thing about Jake's family, their sense of humor and ability to laugh at themselves, and each other, made them easy to be with; and guaranteed a hilarious enjoyment, whether it be a moment at the post office with one of them, or an entire evening with them all. *I wish I'd grown up like that, and had a family that was so much fun, and so close.*

As Maggie poured the steaming coffee into the silver samovar, Jake added a lump of smooth yellow butter to the antique silver-plated dish sitting on a second tray; laid the silver serving knife beside it, and filled the sugar bowl, adding the matching spoon. He pulled the batch of fresh baked zucchini muffins out of the oven, transferring them into a woven oak bowl lined with a bread towel, then folded the cross shaped pieces across the muffins to keep them warm.

"Just like momma used to make," he said. She smiled at the hand stitched daisies Jake's mother had so carefully sown, while creating another gift for her own mother, that was now enjoyably used by Jake,0 as he fondly remembered his mother sitting by the fireplace, carefully placing each stitch. His parents were gone too, and he loved making the food his mother used to make.

Maggie picked up the stack of clear glass plates and the stack of beautiful handmade napkins, setting them on the edge of the platter. They could hear chatter outside as they placed the silver trays on the table, just as the first of their group walked onto the porch, and it wasn't long before they were all assembled for their weekly gathering. It had been disrupted for a time when this whole mess had begun; and as the lockdown lasted much longer than anyone anticipated, they'd missed the meetings too much.

Since Jake lived out in the country, his home located a mile or two down a private road with a locked gate, surrounded by trees; they'd recently decided to carry on, unobserved by the 'covid police,' as they liked to call the busybodies who kept up with who complied with the CDC's rules, and who didn't.

They prayed over the simple sandwich and desert meal, poured the coffee, made their plates, and began to eat and fellowship, which was how they always started out. They'd known each other for years, and at each get-together they picked up pretty much where they'd left off the last time. Then they completed another chapter of the bible, as they had each week before the lock-down. Reading, discussing, and sometimes strongly debating—some might say arguing—over what it meant; trying to apply it to their current lives, and always encouraging one another; eating and drinking the strong hot coffee as they did so.

"Oh, Jake, these muffins are to die for!" Maisie said, with a look of pure rapture on her face. "It's been simply ages since you've made them. "

"Why thank you Maisie," Jake replied, while shooting a private smirk at Maggie, who instantly had a 'coughing' spell, trying to cover her laughter at the confirmation of how cleverly he'd pegged Maisie earlier. "It's my mother's recipe. She made them once a month for breakfast. I love to make them too.

It's even more fun to share them with people who can truly appreciate them," he added, knowing Maisie was oblivious to the earlier quip, which did nothing to stop Maggie's coughing. She held a napkin over her mouth to hide the grin, but tears were beginning to run down her face as she almost choked over the remarks. Jake, knowing the truth of her laughter induced coughing, continued without pausing.

"Why Maggie, my dear, are you ok?" "Do you need a glass of water? I'll be happy to get you one," he said with exaggerated concern. At that, Maisie opened her eyes, and noticing Maggie's coughing and tears, hurriedly put the muffin back on her plate.

"Maggie! Are you alright?! Did you swallow something down the wrong pipe?" she said, genuinely concerned. "Jake, go get the water!" she commanded. "Maggie's seriously in trouble!" She got off the couch and headed toward Maggie's chair, "I know the Heimlich maneuver! Get up so I can pop that sucker right out!"

Maggie, trying desperately to contain the—by now, gales of laughter—exacerbated by the crumbs hanging off Maisie's chin, made the mistake of looking over Maisie's shoulder at Jake. He was standing there with a look on his face of almost pain, as he suppressed the need to let out his response to the slapstick comedy playing out before his eyes; trying to look 'oh so innocent' while knowing full well he'd set the whole thing off; with both his humorous assessment of everyone as they prepared, and his playing on the earlier fun by adding those seemly simple responses to Maisie's appreciation of a good desert. His twinkling eyes were not helping her at all.

He hurriedly turned and headed for the kitchen, leaving Maggie to try to get herself under control while the entire room went into panic mode at her distress. With Jake and his expressive face gone for a couple of moments, she was finally able to remove the napkin; and wiping her eyes, she smiled and waved them off, nodding that she was ok.

"Oh, excuse me everyone," she managed, while accepting the water Jake was now handing her, "I don't know what got into me. I haven't been that choked up in a while." At the double meaning of that, aimed square at him this time, Jake had to turn around to hide the instant need to laugh again.

This wasn't the first time Jake and Maggie had been aware that they communicated on a level that often escaped the rest of the group. They'd been friends so long, they could almost read each other's mind, and Maggie often accused him of having a demented sense of humor. He then reminded her she was as bad, and besides, she totally 'got' it like no one other than his family, or Matt's, ever had before. They were both quick witted and loved witty repartee and bantering, and could turn a simple phrase into something that would put most comedy writers to shame.

They regularly practiced making the other lose it, while staying self-possessed to any onlookers, using their incredibly rich vocabulary to sail banter completely over the head of those clueless of what was really being said. They didn't have a mean bone in their body, so it wasn't with a sense of superiority, but sometimes a high IQ and reading tomes acquiring knowledge, just made them aware of words most people seldom encountered, and double meanings were easy.

They could shoot a look across a room and speak volumes to each other without saying a word. He was the master of arching one eyebrow, conveying various types of additional information, and it set her off every single time he did it. When their ridiculous funny bone got triggered, it was all bets off. At least one of them was going to succumb, and the other instantly became the straight man who kept making the most guileless sounding remarks, that totally slayed the one who was trying to suppress the—oftentimes, inappropriate for the moment—mirth.

Missy, who was aware of Maisie's love of a good bakery delight, and had taken part in some good-natured tongue-in-cheek joking about it herself on occasion, had caught most of it; She was quietly enjoying the banter, said, "Jake, your house is so comfortable. I'm so glad to be a part of this group." She spoke, in part, to get the focus off Maggie, but also in genuine gratitude.

"Me too," Jason chimed in. "I love studying with this group. I learn so much, and feel as if I have so much more to add to conversations whenever we go into another new topic. Maggie, if you're sure you're ok, I'd like to get started, so we have plenty of time to discuss our issues."

Jake and Maggie knew 'plenty of time to discuss' meant Jason wanted plenty of time to try to argue his own brand of theology, based on opinion, church doctrine, and what his momma thought about it. Try as they might, getting him to rightly divide the word by being a good Berean was an ongoing uphill challenge.

Still, Jason was a good man, a good Christian, and loyal to the bone. He was a good addition to the group; and often in deconstructing and explaining—in great detail—a passage, while debating with him, it seemed to add just the clarification the other members needed.

They constantly reminded themselves, and each other, to not fall into the sin of spiritual pridefulness, because they simply had studied deeper and longer. A few years back they were just like most people, until God called them to be deeper students. But it was frustrating, when they saw it so clearly, and had a calling to raise the bar of knowledge to those around them. Jason refused to study more, but wanted to have a reigning voice in the discussions.

"Well," Maggie began, "I've been doing a lot of research on these shots we're being told we have to take. I'm very disturbed by the information I've come across. Have any of you been looking into it?"

"Why should we look into it?" Louise retorted. "We need to take them. We need to do our part to keep everyone safe, don't we?"

"I haven't been doing any real looking," Jason chimed in, "but I'm not about to take a shot just because some government official says I have to."

"Well, I've got an appointment this week to have mine," inserted Missy. "I just want this to all be over so I can get back to my life. I haven't had a night out with my friends in months." *Except for meeting Billy at his house a few times.* "Sneaking over here for this meeting is about all I've gotten out for, unless you count the grocery store and work. What have you found out? I need to know fast, if it's something important."

Missy had been to the bible studies long enough to understand that Jake and Maggie really cared about what God had placed in the Bible for them to study; and she trusted them to do the work she knew she wasn't going to spend the time to do; but when it came down to it, she was going to make up her own mind about all of it.

They grew up in a different era and sometimes didn't understand why she and her friends lived the way they did. *After all, we grew up in the information and computer age, and we don't sit out in the country wondering what's happening here and there; if we want to know, we can just google it*, she justified her view.

Maisie, who had picked up the tongs to serve herself a second sandwich, said "Some of my friends think it's the mark of the beast. Have you ever heard anything so crazy? It ain't even a mark. It's a vaccine. We've been taking vaccines since we were a kid. What's one more?"

Maggie exchanged a look with Jake, who stepped into the conversation. "I've been listening to a lot of the front-line doctors and other scientists that say it's not really a vaccine. It's a gene-therapy experiment. Taking it will alter your DNA, and that will change you from being 100% human to something less. I'm not sure what the change is yet, but that doesn't sound good to me," he added to the info Maggie had started with.

"Less than human?" Louise scoffed. "How could we be less than human? I think you've been watching too many of those Sci-Fi movies again, Jake. God made me human, and I'll be human till the day I die, no matter what. What about people who lose a body part, or have a heart transplant. Does that make them less than who they are?"

"Well, no," Jake began, "but there are some very interesting studies on people who've had transplants that suddenly start liking things they've never liked before, and later find out the donor of the organ did. I've been doing some reading on that off and on for years."

"And this is something entirely different from that," Maggie smoothly interjected to keep them from going down that rabbit trail. "My understanding is, it has nanotechnology in it, and it has coding like a computer operating system. Some scientists believe it's going to be used with the new 5G towers to control people. All I'm reading and hearing is very concerning."

Missy was smiling with amusement. She'd grown up with spiderman, X-man, and hulk movies, and she understood how introducing new genes into the body could make unexpected alterations, but believed it was just in the movies. "Do you really think someone would make something like that?" she asked. "And do you really believe no one else in the medical world wouldn't catch it and stop it? Doctors everywhere have recommended we take it. It can't be something so bizarre."

"They've been doing gene therapy for several years now," Jake explained. "It's been mostly therapeutic, but some of it has bothered me. For instance, once you introduce a gene to someone, it goes to every cell of the body, and even if it wasn't a positive outcome, you can't undo it. Once it's introduced, its

BOOK 1: "PREPARE FOR THE END" SERIES

permanent. Sometimes people are worse off than they were before. And then it can be genetically passed down to your kids and grandkids.

A lot of doctors are speaking up against it; that's our point entirely. Missy, what if this isn't what we think it is? Then, it's in your body and you can't get it out. Wouldn't you prefer to wait a while and make sure it's helping others before doing something you can't undo?" he asked.

"This is the first time something like this has been mandated, and it hasn't gone through the usual trials for safety," Maggie stated. "I don't feel comfortable with the lack of known safety. They've had some bad medicines in the last few years that harmed people and it had to be recalled.

The most popular manufacturer, especially, has been fined repeatedly for harmful drugs. The package doesn't even have an ingredient list or safety insert included; each one has a message that says 'Left Intentionally Blank.' That makes me very uncomfortable. I agree with Jake; we need to give it some time, keep researching, and wait to see if it stops the virus; and more importantly, how it affects people. Surely a few months will begin to show that."

"I agree with that," Jason rejoined the conversation. "My mother lived by a woman who took that thalidomide back in the 50's or 60's. Her son was born with stumps for arms and legs. I was always grateful my mother never took that drug."

Missy, growing uncomfortable with the memory she had of watching a documentary on TV about that, began to question whether, or not, she should keep her appointment to get the jab. Maybe they were right. Waiting didn't mean she couldn't take it; it just meant she might prove that it was safe, and when she did take it, she wouldn't have to worry about it. Maggie and Jake looked at a lot of different info, and she had learned a lot from them during the last year. She knew they would keep up with the research and tell the group.

But, darn it, she'd waited on the list a while now to be able to go get the shot. If she canceled her appointment, there's no telling how long it would take to get it rescheduled. Oh, well. She didn't have to decide right now; her appointment wasn't till

Thursday. Maybe she would do some research of her own, and today was only Saturday.

Louise, who'd been sitting quietly, listening to the exchange, surprised Maggie. "You said a computer operating system, Maggie; If it's an operating system, what's it operating, and who is the operator?" she questioned, with—unusual for her—insight.

At that, Maisie began to nod her head. "Those are good questions, Louise. I don't think I thought about it like that. That's kind of scary if it is true. With all we've been learning about the illuminati, the brotherhood of darkness, and the kingdom of darkness taking over to prepare for the antichrist, that kind of sounds like one of end-times scenarios you taught us about. I think I may wait too," she concluded.

Maggie, smiling in relief, said "exactly my point Maisie. It's too early to tell if this is the mark of the beast, but I suspect it very well could be a part of the set-up. I say we make a pact to wait on the shot, research to see what's really happening, and pray for God to show us what we couldn't know without His Holy Spirit intel."

"Perfect Maggie," Jake took up the conversation. "Only God knows where this is going; and it's really going to come down to where we are on His timeline. The Word tells us we are in the end-times, but sometimes the minute details aren't given until they are needed; and often the people in the bible didn't see what was right in front of them, like the birth of Jesus. Only those who were watching and praying and staying in the Word knew it, like Simeon and Anna; or those who were told, like Mary and Joseph.

Daniel was told to seal up the knowledge until the end. John was shown more, and was able to write about it. We may very well be in the days they were shown, but we were warned over, and over again to 'be not deceived.' I think we need to be very vigilant about anything that could possibly change our DNA. After all, that's what the book of Enoch says caused the great flood to destroy the earth. Only Noah, his wife, sons, and their wives were genetically pure and were saved by God," he finished.

"Yes," Maggie harmonized, "from the beginning, this virus has bothered me. How quickly our entire nation—shoot, the entire world—was shut down, despite the crashing of so many economies. I've studied this stuff for decades, and it completely took me by surprise how the world could so entirely change from one day to the next. My 'Spidey senses' have been tingling off the charts.

We've understood for a while now that we are in the 'birth pangs' and I believe, like I've shared before, that September 2019—if we stay in the birth process analogy—we entered what doctors call 'transition', which means it's on now; there is nothing that will stop labor until the baby is born. In prophecy, that translates to: we have entered the very last, last days, period of time. Prophecy/Revelation, will be fulfilled. Nothing can stop it now until Jesus comes. Just saying that 'feels' right," she completed her thoughts.

"And don't forget, we were told to watch for THE lie," Jason inputted. "Maggie, we all trust your gift of discernment. It's panned out again and again. I think I may be getting one too." he shared. "When you said that just now, I felt like God himself was telling me it was truth. Sometimes it's like He's standing right in front of you giving a confirmation; like when a preacher is preaching, and you just know in the depths of your soul, it's from the Holy Spirit himself."

"Ok." Maisie, ready to move forward with the plan, clinched the agreement; "Let's pray now. I don't want to mess up. I can wait and see. What about you Louise?" she inquired of her friend.

"Oh, I'm in." Louise acknowledged, standing to her feet. "I'm in. There's too much weirdness going on right now not to at least pray about it. Watching the news, it's like up is down, and down is up. Black is white, and white is black; right is wrong and wrong is right."

Looking at Jake and Maggie, she went on, "I'm sure you two know a verse or two that says that in a better way; I may not study like the both of you, but I can sure see there's something more than business-as-usual going on right now." She clinched the thought in their mind that, in spite, of her refusal to do much self-study, she was a good choice for the group.

Missy stood up to join the others. She still wasn't sure what she wanted to do about the vaccine, but she was sure she wasn't going to let a group of other people, even bible-study partners, make the choice for her; even so she resolved to at least, look, into the pros and cons of getting it this week, or at all.

They joined hands and Jake led the group in prayer. "Father, a lot is going on right now. As your children, and your hands and feet in this world, we need your guidance, as always. This is a very crazy time in our world and it looks as if it's shaping up to fulfilling what you've warned us of so long ago. We don't want to try to hammer events into forcing them to fit prophecy, but we don't want to miss it either.

Most missed the signs for your first coming, and we sure don't want to miss the signs of your second coming. And we don't want to fall under the spell of the evil one, or the man of sin that your Word says is coming. Please give us eyes to see, ears to hear, and Holy Spirit Intel to understand the times we are living in. Show us, and the world, the truth about these shots, their true purpose, if they really contain something that changes us from being created in your image to something else, and what you'd have us, individually and collectively, to do. Go with us as we leave this place, and give each safe travels, and a week that is blessed by you. Thank you, Amen."

"Amen" was heard around the circle as each added their agreement to Jake's plea. Most knew there was a lot riding on knowing the truth. All but Missy, were in their 40's - 60s. Missy was only 22, but had started coming after her mother passed away a few months back.

She missed her mother. She'd long been a member of the church they used to go to; and although she never really did more than occasionally attend, she'd started coming to the bible study group shortly before her death; and Missy came by invitation after losing her mom, to be close to people whom her mother admired.

Sometimes she wished her mom had been more like Maggie, but her mom had a hard life and Missy believed she'd done the best she could to raise her. Church was a place she liked to go, but it seemed as if church never really changed her from the person she'd always been.

Maggie, Jake, Jason, and the other ladies were different in a way Missy couldn't quite grasp. They'd accepted and included her, but deep inside Missy knew that she too, was different. She understood most of what was taught, but intellectually only, and couldn't seem to muster the faith to wholly believe that it was all 100% truth, because of what seemed like inconsistencies, especially in the Old Testament.

Maggie said some things could only be spiritually grasped by being filled with the Holy Spirit, but Missy couldn't quite believe you could read the same words and some 'spirit' helped you to see things that others couldn't see.

She'd envisioned holding a piece of red cellophane over a printed page, and words you couldn't see without it, popping into vision, like the books her mom bought her as child. She'd actually gone and bought some red cellophane right before the lockdown, holding the plastic over pages of the bible Jake had given her, to see if she could see anything new.

Of course, she could not, and she laughed at her silliness as she threw it in the garbage can. Obviously, as nice as they were, they told you those things to keep you anticipating some new ability, like the proverbial carrot on a stick to keep you coming until they could make a true convert out of you.

Missy laughed as she drove home. Try as shy might, she loved her life, her friends, her freedom, and having a good time with her boyfriend way too much for that to ever happen. Still…something inside her longed to be what they seemed to be.…

Change Is In The Air

Chapter 5

"WELL, DIANE, THE TEST is positive. It looks like you're going to be a mother," Dr. Stella Maven stated, with a smile on her face. "We'll need to get you started on prenatal vitamins and schedule you for bloodwork. In a few weeks we can do a sonogram, and see if we'll be having a pink baby Launch or a blue baby Launch, but either way a new human should be 'launched' about 7 months from now."

"Oh, no; not another pun at my expense," Diane groaned while she laughed. Her last name was Launch, and Stella, her doctor since high school, was famous for being able to make a joke about anything. "Wait. What? A pink or a blue Launch? Are you saying what I think you're saying?"

Dr. Stella laughed the rich laugh that everyone in their small town could identify from a mile away. "Yes, ma'am. I told you to stay away from that Launch boy. But no, you just had to marry him, and now look what he's done; I told you he'd get you in trouble someday."

"Dr. Stella! We've been married for 8 years! You know we've been trying to get pregnant for at least the last 5," Dianne laughed, trying to take it all in. "Are you sure? Are you really, sure? Did it finally happen?" She asked questions in her excited new awareness so fast, that Stella couldn't answer any of them before the next one came.

"Yes, yes, and yes. This explains the nausea, the tiredness, and the irritability. Rest a bit more than usual, take the vitamins daily, drink lots of water, and try to stay off ladders. That husband of yours can get a ranch hand. We don't want to tempt fate."

Seeing the look on Diane's face, she laughed again; "Women have been having babies since Eve had the first one, but I like to be careful the first few months. Don't worry, I haven't seen any issues, I just know you. You can exercise within reason, go out on the ranch with Frankie, and garden all you want next spring; just skip the acrobatics for the next 7 months, ok?"

Diane smiled with joy at the long-awaited news. "I can't wait to tell Frankie! And my mother. And Candy. My brother will be excited too," she almost sang the words, with a wonder-filled acceptance, as her eyes teared up. "I just can't believe it's finally happened."

"Oh, it's happened all right," Dr. Stella asserted. "You'd better 'happen' to get some big old jeans with some stretch elastic. And I hear there's a store over in Cartersville with shirts big enough to make an outdoor umbrella. You might want to think about laying in a supply of those too. Everybody knows the Launch family is filled with twins," she teased.

Diane was wiping tears and giggling at that. "Twins?! You can tell that just by the blood test? Maybe you need to quit doctoring and go into fortune telling; sounds like you're already predicting the future; you might as well get paid for it," she teased right back.

"Oh, honey, I'll be gettin' paid. Don't you worry about that. You best tell Frankie to start thinkin' about selling off a few of those calves; I've going to charge him big time. And if it's twins, I'm going to charge him double; cuz with him being involved they'll probably decide to come into the world at 3 AM, and I'll miss my beauty sleep. Shoot for that, the nurses may charge him triple just for having to look at me the next day." She was having way too much fun with her witty repartee to stop. Dana, her nurse, was laughing too.

Gathering up her things and walking toward the door, Diane, smiling at the ribbing, replied, "Stella, I'm so glad you're my doctor and my friend. This new adventure just wouldn't be the same without you. I'll see you next month."

Getting in the truck, she called Frankie. "Honey, are you still over at the feed store?"

"Yeah," he drawled in that Texas voice she so loved. "What's up? Everything ok with your check-up?"

"Of course. I just wanted to see what time you'd be home. I'm headed to the grocery store, then home to cook, and I want your dinner to be hot when you get there," she answered. She couldn't wait to tell him he was going to be a father, but not over a cell phone. She wanted to make a memory they could cherish for a lifetime.

"Well, I'm going over to Tractor Supply and picking up another feed trough for the new calves when I leave here, but I'll probably be home by six." She could tell he was busy, so she said "fine, see you then," and let him get back to his man shopping. He didn't come to town unless he had to, and just liked to get what he needed and head back to the ranch.

She quickly finished her own shopping, secretly buying a pink pacifier and a soft baby blanket with pale yellow ducks that she hid beneath the package of toilet paper, telling the check-out lady—who was one of her mom's friends—that it was for a friend's baby shower. She'd picked up a gift bag and card also, to stave off questions, because in a town this small, it'd be all over the news before she was ready to tell people herself.

On the ride home the world looked just a little bit brighter than it had on the drive in. If, happiness was the color yellow, she'd be sitting in a puddle of liquid sunshine. A smile of pure satisfaction mixed with anticipation spread across her face, and you couldn't have wiped it off with the best cleanser on the market.

Humming, she unloaded the groceries, straightened up the living room from the carelessness of the morning, and started cooking spaghetti—Frankie's favorite meal—except for grilled steaks. She didn't want to have to wait for him to grill. She couldn't keep a secret that long if she had to. She thought about chilling a bottle of wine to go with dinner, thought better of it in her new-found condition, and made a fresh pitcher of lemonade instead. Life would be different from now on. She had to start thinking like a parent. Protective already, she didn't want to do anything to jeopardize her child's health and well-being.

The timer on the stove was just starting to ding when Frankie walked in. In response to its insistent chimes, he headed for the back of the house. "I'm just going to take a quick shower and I'll be right back," he said as he passed thru the kitchen.

"That's fine," Diane returned, as she finished cutting up the tomatoes for the salads she was making to go with the spaghetti. She completed the salads, finished setting the table, and was just taking the bread out of the oven as he walked in.

"Yum. It smells wonderful in here. You haven't made spaghetti in ages. It's just perfect for this fall weather. I can unload the truck later; I missed lunch in town because I had to go to three different vet clinics to get the horse wormer. They said everyone was buying it to treat covid. I told Hank I didn't have covid, but I did have horses that need wormed," he shared, as he grabbed the lemonade pitcher and filled their glasses.

Listening to him share his day, along with the tinkling sound of the ice chunks as the liquid swirled them around inside the glasses, made Diane smile. This was just a perfect moment of happiness. She anticipated his joy as he learned they were going to be parents. She finished dishing up the food and putting the plates on the table, sat down opposite him, and they reached across to hold hands as they blessed the meal.

They didn't really practice Christianity, but both had grown up in homes with Christian parents, where grace was said without fail. All four of their parents were staunch Christians, and held out hope they'd go back to the way they were raised, so it was part of their nightly ritual. Tonight though, Diana felt like thanking God. She knew he was real, and maybe it was time to start reading the bible so she could share it with her children the way her mother had with her.

"Lord, please bless this meal. We ask this is Jesus' name;" Frankie said the words his father always said. "I may just unload the trough, feed the calves, and take an early evening tonight," he went on, with barely a pause. "I'm tired. It's been a long week."

"That's good," Diane agreed. "I'd like to just snuggle up and talk. We haven't had a lot of time for that the last couple of weeks. Getting a ranch ready for winter takes a lot of work. I'm ready to hibernate."

She let him finish his dinner, although she was dying to tell him about the baby, but she didn't want to spoil the moment by rushing it. He worked hard and always relaxed as he ate. She wanted him relaxed and undistracted, so she could have his whole attention, and he could be able to just absorb the news the way she had. She thought about waiting until he was through feeding the calves, but she couldn't manage to contain herself that long.

As he wiped his mouth for the last time and placed his napkin beside his plate, she set the plain blue gift bag in front of him, trying to hold back the grin that wanted to escape. "What's this?" he asked. "It's not my birthday."

"Nope," she agreed.

"We haven't had a fight in a while, so it can't be an apology," he teased her, noticing the excitement in her eyes. He stopped and just looked at her for a moment, taking in the pure joy shining from her; puzzled, as he tried to figure out what set it off. "What's up?" he asked, realizing it had to be something big by the look on her face.

"Just open it," she encouraged, afraid she might blurt it out before he could see the items inside.

Still looking at her, he reached inside, and feeling the soft blanket, he looked down, pulling it out, not quite sure why she'd bought him a blanket with ducks on it. Mystified, he reached back in and pulled out the pink pacifier. He looked it, then remembered her check-up was her yearly gynecology visit. As comprehension seeped in, he looked at her in complete shock. "What?! Are you sure?! Oh, my gosh!! When? Are you ok?!!"

Giggling at how much he sounded like she had earlier with Dr. Stella, she finally released the held-back grin. "That's exactly what I sounded like when I was in the doctor's office," she shared. "I just can't believe it."

"We're going to be parents," he marveled. "I'm going to be a father. I can't wait to tell our dads, and Tucker. But, Di, you bought the wrong color pacy. I'm having a boy," he emphatically stated, while thumping his chest with his thumb.

"You're having whoever is in here," she countered. "We said we didn't care, as long as it's healthy; and even if there's issues…it's Our Baby!" the Cheshire cat grin grew wider. She knew he didn't care; but a man had to want a son. It's required.

He stood up, and coming around the table, he pulled her into his arms and held her close; kissing her tenderly, and she knew he as pleased as she was. It'd been hard on him too, waiting eight long years; while their friends—except for Nate and Candy, who only had one—all had two or three each by now. At each shower, birth, and birthday party, they'd done their part, and were truly pleased for their friends, but they'd felt left out and sometimes she wondered if that's why Frankie had gotten so reluctant to leave the ranch.

It felt good. It felt 'right' to know they were finally going to become parents. She also wondered if it would be a boy or a girl, but really, she didn't care. She'd wanted to be a mom for so long, either would be completely loved and accepted, warts and all. She loved her brother Tucker, and knew he'd love it too. She knew Frankie would be a good dad. He was kind and patient, and loved their friend's kids, always ready to teach them a new skill, listen to their stories, and hold them. They all loved their 'uncle Frankie' and couldn't wait to show him their new toys.

She felt so safe and loved with him, and the thought of extending that into a growing family made her heart content. She cleaned the kitchen as he fed the calves, then they settled down to watch a movie, share the joy of the news of their baby, and just let the reality that it had finally happened, seep into a new normal. They went to bed, tired but happy, and prepared for a whole new world.

A Chance Meeting

Chapter 6

MAGGIE DROVE UP THE dirt road increasingly slow as she neared her destination. It'd been a while since she'd been out here. The restrictions were being more and more lifted, and larger numbers were starting to come out, almost like they'd been before the lockdown; but people still seemed to stay close to home, work, and the basic-necessity shopping places. They were going to restaurants again, but it seemed as if people, as-a-whole, were subdued, like there was a collective underlying depression or anxiety. Some people acted as if it was all over and—almost too much—behaved as if they were just waiting for everything to return to the way it used to be.

Maggie knew that was not ever going to happen. She'd studied end-time events enough to know the world was on a fast-track to Armageddon. As the holiday season approached, she often caught herself bracing for the coming New Year and the acceleration of deaths. She'd decided to run out here today and spend a few moments; partly doing her duty, and partly needing the comfort of familiarity of life.

She parked outside the gates, looking at the newly mown grass, already beginning to be covered with fall leaves again. The normal, but abnormal, look of bright florals against the dull browns, and the last of the faded grass, made her laugh. Cemeteries this time of year always drew her attention with the incongruousness of bright colors standing out from barren nature. The place was old and had been here at least 200 years. She wished she'd asked Jake, Rachel, or Sarah to come with her. It'd been a long drive alone, but she really needed out.

With the older tombstones leaning at crazy angles, dark with the patina of centuries of grime, it was like a horror movie scene—cut with shots of the psychopath, alternating with his clueless victim, accompanied by bright carnival music—in a twisted humorous moment right before the killer pounced; only done silently, with color and granite, instead of sound. She even looked around to see where the bringer of death was standing.

"Oh, good grief," she caught herself. "I've been out here my whole life. This is the safest place I know, even if it is out here so far from town. If it was May, the sunshine would be too bright, the grass would be sprinkled with tiny lavender flowers, and I wouldn't think a thing about the bright flowers, or be worried about being murdered before I can get back to my truck."

Maggie's creativity and active imagination was second only to her humor, and between the two, she could dream up all kinds of scenarios. She laughed at herself, but suddenly felt uneasy as she went through the gate in the chain link fence. It squealed loudly when she pushed it open, and she didn't remember it ever doing that before.

Aloud, she offered greetings to the names on the newer stones of people she'd known in her life that were now here. She noticed the bright red poinsettias, and even some garland, as she walked across the field, staying in the avenues between monuments; walking back to where her mom was buried by the far fence. Funny, how we need to normalize death by decorating even the burial grounds, she thought, as she wove her way deeper into the enclosure.

Normally an enjoyable trip, her fanciful notion as she came in the gate seemed to want to linger; and the peace she had on the drive out, had somehow turned to a tense edgy feeling, that put a damper on her visit. Arriving at her mother's place of rest, she sat on the bench placed there for times of remembrance and contemplation. She arranged the fall mums she'd brought in the granite vase attached to the side of the stone that had her mom's name and the dates carved into it.

She felt closer to her mom here than she ever had in life. They had never had a close relationship; and, try as she might, Maggie could never get her mom to open up, or create the connection she so craved. She'd learned so much after her mother passed that filled in the blanks of a lot of unanswered questions; and worked hard with her therapist to overcome the neglect she'd been raised with. But here now, after dealing with the anger and grief, she finally felt a tranquility that was never there before. *Momma, I'm sorry you had to go through what you did, but taking it out on your own child was wrong.*

She'd even dealt with the anguish of knowing her mother had died unsaved. Maggie had told her about Jesus, over, and over again; but her mother refused to ask God for forgiveness, due to some things from her own childhood that she was determined to blame on God. Maggie wondered just how many people out here had tried and convicted God for things evil people had done. It was so sad, and exactly how the enemy worked; the consummate narcissist who did diabolical things, and then 'flipped the script' to pass the consequences onto the person who had long been a victim of it all.

So many wasted lives. So many damaged people. So many of God's creation that would miss the wonders of eternity with him. Once again, she determined to be different. To assign fault to the culpable party; and to live a life that celebrated others, while making them feel loved, wanted, and special. But to also stand up against those who deliberately hurt others.

Evil always enjoyed stirring up a mess and the chaos that ensued. Long ago she'd stopped accepting what was handed to her, or staying silent about it. *Lord, help me to always show another person love and grace, but also be unafraid to speak up against evil.*

One thing she couldn't stand was to watch someone leave someone else out, or make them feel diminished. She may not always defend herself; but if you picked on others around her, especially those who were already wounded, you had a mad red-head with no back-up button on you. The warrior in her just came out; almost like a paladin, invisible until necessary, then— instant combat soldier—then back to normal Maggie, when the aggressor had been dealt with and the fury subsided.

She'd also learned to quit apologizing a day later. Sometimes anger, and what the Word called 'harshly rebuking' people, was exactly what the situation required. There is no apology necessary for stopping abuse; no matter who the perpetrator is. The bible said 'be angry and sin not;' not, don't be angry.

One of the best lessons she'd learned in the past few years was from a very humble pastor, who'd shared with her that when abuse entered a relationship—especially in the context of a marital relationship—it broke the covenant just like adultery; and not only were you free to leave, you ought to. That lesson brought so much needed healing; and offset a lifetime of pastors telling her to 'be a more dutiful wife,' while living in appalling circumstances.

Out here with her mother, it seemed as if her thoughts had gotten offtrack, but Maggie knew very well that the abuse she'd accepted as a wife, and the misunderstanding that she had to keep taking it, was born, and bred, right here with her mother and father; and the early training they'd given her that she had no value, and deserved whatever anyone else decided to dish out. *If you had treated me with love and respect, I'd have known what it looked and felt like, and I'd have never lived with that abusive piece of garbage for so long.*

The therapist had the hardest time getting her to understand and accept the truth that she'd had no part in the failure of these relationships. She was the family scapegoat, whom the weight of everyone else's sin was laid upon, so they could walk off guilt free.

For a person who'd continuously been blamed for the abuse heaped upon her, understanding she was a faultless victim of others evil cruelty was a difficult concept; especially in this day, and age, where the term 'victim mentality' was thrown about everywhere. She understood what people meant by it, but preferred if they would use the correct term 'playing the victim.'

That *was* prevalent in our society, and she'd watched her mother, sister, and ex play the victim many, many times; but the incorrect term thrown at someone who truly was a victim, not only made being a true victim a crime, but greatly intensified the wrongful guilt and true pain of the one so falsely accused.

She thought about the lesson she'd taught to her group not too long ago: The word victim was created for a purpose: to describe a person harmed, injured, or killed, as a result of a crime, accident, or other event or action; targeted and damaged by another party, while doing nothing to bring it on or deserve it; or a person being hoaxed or duped. *I was all three; both growing up, and in my marriage.* And 'victim shaming' someone who'd been so abused just trapped the pain and anguish inside, and kept them from being able to heal by owning, then sharing, their story. It kept them broken and ashamed.

Becoming able to share your story released the shame created by having to hide the pain, horror, and insult of the abuse. Being told you are the perpetrator of your own pain because you can now speak of it traps you in grief and loneliness; thereby allowing the abuse to continue by proxy abusers long after the abuser has moved on to another victim, or passed from this life escaping earthly punishment for their crimes. *So many condemning voices heaped more and more pain upon me, until I learned to see it for what it is.*

Part of the abuse was trapping you in it, by telling you they will kill you, your family, or your children if you tell; or that no one will believe you and they will instead hate you. This is often the case due to a true psychopath being a total angel around others, or a counselor, while the true evil is only experienced by their chosen target, or prey. You help them hide what they are doing to you out of fear of more humiliation or to protect others. They convince you that the whole family will be destroyed and that it will be your fault. *Not telling, made me look like the liar, after years of him setting up his alibi made of lies. When I did tell, no one believed me, not even my own children.*

They won't escape the judgement seat of God though. He'd shown her that repeatedly in her healing journey. Her ex-husband was a well-known businessman, and people had believed his lies about her the entire time she'd been married to him.

Sitting there, she was amazed anew at how far she'd come. She was no longer a victim; now she was an overcomer. And even beyond that; she'd become a champion for victims everywhere, running a Narcissist Victim Abuse Meet Up group, and counseling abuse victims everywhere, showing them the path to true healing.

She often wished she'd heard someone speak about their own healing journey years ago, so that she would have had an understanding, and a path to follow to growth and healing. She chuckled, as she remembered when she'd begged God to heal her from all the pain; and he'd told her he would, but she'd have to take 'the scenic route.' She knew now that if he'd healed her instantly she wouldn't have had even half the growth.

The journey had been brutal and she suffered much in the hellish quest for wholeness; but it had forged a strength, courage, and sense of individuality that led to finally feeling like a functioning adult for the first time in her life; and given her so much to offer to others. *No one can guide you over the mountain like someone who's already walked the path and made it over. No one.*

She let the glory of God's spirit wash over her as she felt gratefulness for his wisdom in allowing her to take the harder path, and all he'd given her in the process. *He really does have our best in his heart and decisions, even when we can't see it from inside the fiery furnace.* He'd stayed right beside her through it all; and she was left with the dross having been boiled to the top and scooped off, far more able to reflect his image than she ever would have been without the excruciating process.

Having fulfilled her intention, and finding the place of peace she sought, she stood up and began to make her way back across the stone and flower filled obstacle course. She was less than halfway across when she caught a glimpse of a very weathered gargoyle type face peering at her from the tree line that started just beyond the back fence on the farthest side of the grave yard. The anxiety ratcheted back into a desire to leave at the fastest pace possible. *What is that? That cannot be human! What is it? a demon?*

As she watched, it began to move toward her, and she knew she'd never make it to her truck in time. *Oh, God. It's headed toward me!* Watching the face while she hurried—as a sense of malevolence enveloped her—she tripped over a small bench and went down, crying out as she twisted her ankle. Panic filled her mind as she cried out to the Lord, "help me!"

"Of course, I'll help you," came a soothing voice just behind her. She looked around, staring at the gentle old man reaching down for her hand. "You shouldn't run in the place of rest, you know," he admonished her, as he helped her up. "There're too many stumbling blocks. You wouldn't want to hurt yourself out here all alone," he continued; "It's a good thing I was here and saw you fall."

"But... but... where did you come from?" Maggie sputtered, totally non-plussed at his sudden and unexpected appearance. "You weren't here just a minute ago."

"Oh, my dear," he good-humoredly chuckled. "I was here, you just couldn't see me. I was behind the tree over there," he pointed in the opposite direction from the gargoyle that'd been coming toward her. "I like to come out and take care of things often, so it's ready when we get visitors, such as yourself."

Maggie had been here many times in the past and had never seen the man before. "Who are you?" she inquired.

"Oh, people just call me the gardener," he humbly returned. "Here, sit and let me look at your ankle." He led her hobbling to a larger concrete bench that she did not remember seeing on her path across the busy field. The pain was intense. Without him she wouldn't have made it.

Pushing up her pants leg, he pulled her wool sock down a few inches, then began to run his hands up and down that portion of her leg, speaking softly in a language she couldn't quite catch. "What are you doing?" she asked. *I don't even know this man; should I allow him to touch me?*

The pain at his touch caused her to gasp, and she knew she should be entirely uncomfortable with a stranger touching her in such a way, but he seemed to know what he was doing, and had exhibited such kind helpfulness, that she wasn't at all worried. Funny, just a couple of minutes ago she'd been almost terrified.

Remembering, she turned her head to scan the far tree line, looking for the earlier presence. "Oh, you won't be bothered here again by him," he spoke with quiet authority. "This place is safe. Come here as often as you like. That's what the fence is for."

"You saw it too," Maggie questioned. "I was beginning to think I'm nuts." *Thank God, he saw it too.* Relieved at not being alone and helpless while being stalked, and that she had a witness, she continued with her curiosity. "I've never seen you here before, or whatever that was. I thought it was coming toward me. It seemed as if it would harm me. That's why I fell. What is it? Have you seen it before?"

"I'm a heartbeat away whenever you need me. Just call, like you did just now. If you call, I'll come, and you will be safe. Now, if you're finished here, let's get you to your vehicle," he said, with that same gentle authority. "You need to rest for a day or two and the best place to do that is at home. Hopefully you can navigate your house without tripping," he teased.

"I'm not sure I can navigate to the parking spot," she retorted. At that, he began to pull her up. "Come on, it's not broken. I think you can do it," he encouraged. *I hope he's right, otherwise I'll never get home.*

Anticipating the pain again, she put her weight on the other foot, but as they began to move, she put the injured foot down from force of habit. She had taken a step, like always, before realizing it no longer hurt at all. She carefully took another step, then another, marveling at the lack of pain. "What did you do?" she searched his face as she spoke. "It's like it never happened."

He chucked again. "I told you it wasn't broken. I just used an old technique to move the tendons back inline. They were stretched a bit and may take a few days to heal. If you rest and be careful, it shouldn't hurt, but if you overdo it, it may ache a bit," he cautioned.

He helped her as she navigated the rest of the enclosure, then up into her truck. Once she was seated inside, he told her to drive safely, and as she put the key in to start the engine, he smiled, then shut the door. She looked again at the tree line, then back to where he was standing, to thank him once more, but he was not there. She looked toward the gate, twisted in the seat to look toward the back of the truck, then the other side, and finally the rear-view mirror.

There was simply no place he could have gone, but gone he was. She sat there another minute or two, perplexed, then put the lever in gear and began to back out of the spot she was parked in. A movement in the fenced-in area caught her eye. He was disappearing back around the tree he'd told her he was behind earlier. *How'd he, do that?*

Astonished at how quickly he'd gone through the gate and walked that far without her seeing him, she silently thanked God for her helpful hero and drove home, pondering at his timely interference in what she suspected may have ended rather differently if he'd not been there. She wondered what the creature was that she'd seen, and why it was there at all; and more importantly why it had come toward her with such determination. High strangeness. That's what one of her favorite speakers would say, and it seemed to fit today very well.

Wiped Out

Chapter 7

BZZT……… BZZT……... BZZT………

Missy slowly became aware the cell phone on the table beside the bed was buzzing, while the vibration sent it dancing around the wooden top. "Ugh," she groaned. "Who is calling me this early?"

She pried open one eye, grabbed the phone, and brought it close enough to check the time. "Oh no!" she groaned even louder. "Nine o'clock, crud. I'm late for work." She hit the decline option, set it back on the table, and even as she began to move her legs to get up, she fell back asleep; not waking again until after 11:00.

Her eyes opened more easily as she woke naturally this time. She blinked at the light in the room, knowing instantly she was in trouble with her boss, but unable to care. *I must have fever*, she thought. *I haven't felt this bad in ages. Maylene is gonna kill me.*

Her body felt heavy and unwilling to move, and her eyes kept trying to close again. It was like she was drugged, but she knew she hadn't taken anything. Her lungs felt labored with each breath. She had to go to the bathroom, but just couldn't make herself go. Moving her legs under the smooth sheets, she felt so comfortable, she wanted to just stay there all day.

Finally, unable to put it off any longer, she pulled the covers aside, sluggishly swung her legs off the edge, attempted to stand, and almost fell. She sat back on the bed, feeling nauseated, as her head swam. She felt like she was moving while sitting still. "Vertigo," she thought. "It must be. This is exactly how I felt two years ago."

She sat there hoping it would settle down, but the longer she sat there the more the bile rose. She barely made it to the

46

bathroom, upchucking until she had nothing left, but still retching. When she was in control, she wiped her face, sat on the toilet for a bit, then brushed her teeth, trying hard not to start gagging again. *Good grief. What is wrong with me?*

Moving gently, she shuffled to the kitchen, hit the button on the coffee maker, put sugar in a cup, grabbed a spoon, sat it beside the appliance, and then started looking through the medicine drawer for the bottle of aspirin she kept in there. Her head was pounding, and she didn't have the strength to keep standing.

She found the aspirin, twisted off the lid, and shook two tablets into her hand, then almost dropped the bottle while trying to put the lid back on. She finally managed to get it closed and placed it on the counter. The coffee maker started chiming to let her know the coffee was ready, and even that noise, usually barely noticed, amplified the pain around her eyes, making her wince. *Oh... make it stop... I can't stand it.*

She poured a cup of coffee, stirred in the sugar, picked it up by the handle, took a drink and swallowed the aspirin, burning her mouth in the process. She then shuffled into the living room, and dropped into the recliner, feeling like a pile of limp clothing. Slouching to the side, she placed her head on the pillow she always kept there, unable to even sit up straight. Another wave of nausea overwhelmed her.

She knew there was nothing left in her stomach, and she didn't have the energy to walk back to the bathroom, so she put both hands over her head, then lowered one to hold her nose, and breathed deeply through her mouth until it calmed; a trick the ER nurse had taught her the last time she had the stomach flu. It lasted for about ten minutes then she ran back to the bathroom, and threw up, off and on, for almost 30. She brushed her teeth again, then dragged herself back to the chair.

After a few moments, she flipped up the foot rest, causing the chair to lean back, and closed her eyes. This was going to be a sleep day. It was all she could manage. She dozed, in between sups, of coffee. The hot liquid felt good on her throat, which, along with the entire sinus area of her face, felt inflamed.

Ears, throat, sinus, chest, and stomach. Was this the flu? "Oh crap." She just realized she'd listed all the covid-19 symptoms. She'd heard horror stories about the covid testing swab. Everyone said they rammed it almost into your brain and it hurt like the dickens.

Remembering the discussion a few nights ago when Maggie spoke about it breaking the barrier close to the brain, she knew she didn't want to have it done to her. She still wasn't sure she bought that the vaccine could do all they had explained, but she didn't like pain, and really didn't like the thought of things shoved up her nose. *How did I catch covid?*

Suddenly, in the fogginess of her thinking, she remembered how many people she'd been around. The bible study at Jake's house, and the next day her boyfriend Billy and his friend Erwin. She'd been off work the last couple of days due to the rotation, but she'd worked the 5 days before that. If it was covid, she knew she may have been contagious several days, but couldn't for the life of her remember what the incubation period was. *Oh well*, she thought. *It doesn't matter now. I didn't know, and what's done is done. The only thing left to do was inform everyone, and then get through it.*

Then it occurred to her that if she was contagious, and a lot of other people got sick because of her, they might hold her responsible for medical bills, or—suddenly thinking about the deaths Maggie had spoken about—sue her, if a family member caught covid from her and died. *I sure don't have the money for that.*

She thought it over for a while and made the decision to hide the truth and not tell anyone she may have covid. After all, she hadn't tested positive and there was no record or proof. She would have to call Maylene soon though. Maylene was the owner of Mac's Café where she was a waitress. Maylene had been good to her and she didn't need to lose her job.

What do I tell her? she wondered; *I'll probably need to be off for several days. If I tell her I have the flu, she'll want me to get tested. If I say a stomach virus, she may still want me to get tested. If I say car trouble, she'll send someone to pick me up.*

It wasn't the first time she'd had to come up with a reason she wasn't at work, but that was usually just one shift here and there, not several days. She then remembered she only had today's shift, then she was supposed to be off again for the next 6, and then work doubles for 7 days in a row. She'd swapped with Amy, who was leaving for her sister's wedding next week and wanted to work all she could before she left, to have extra tip money for gas and food.

Missy hadn't cared. They often swapped days so they could do things. 3 days early in the week, or 3 days later made no difference; Mac's was so busy, even with reduced business, that she could always count on $50 to $75 in tips, and more on evenings.

She realized it was time for her monthly cycle, and even though it hadn't begun yet, she was known to suffer severe cramps. She quickly concluded that she had her reason to call in. She picked up the phone, and called Maylene. She used to have the same problems; she'll never be angry over menstrual pain. Telling her she'd taken her antispasmodic meds last night and overslept, she said she'd call Amy.

Maylene informed her Amy was already there. She'd come in for her check, and finding out Missy was late, she'd just stayed. She didn't mind the extra money for an additional day's work; and Maylene was used to them swapping and didn't mind either.

She told her to get a heating pad and go back to bed; it was covered. Missy thanked her, hung up, and was very glad she worked for Maylene. She was so forgiving. Maylene had helped take care of her since she was kid; she'd forgive Missy almost anything.

She refilled her cup, found some Nyquil to go with the Aspirin, smeared some Vicks VapoRub on her chest, and settled into the recliner for the day. Young people didn't seem to get too sick from this and she hoped to be better before she had to go in. She had seven whole days now; surely, I'll be well in seven days. *At least I hope so. Right now, I feel like I'd have to get better to die.*

She was back asleep before the first 5 minutes of the movie she'd settled on played.

Arrangements of Life

Chapter 8

"HELLO," LOUISE'S BRIGHT voice matched the multicolored blouse she wore, as she answered the store phone. "Kaleidoscope of Petals; how may I help you? Of course; let me grab a pad. Fall mums... yellow, gold, or red? We have large pots or smaller ones. What did you have in mind?

The large is in a copper pot, has 38 stems with about 4 blooms each. The smaller is about half the size, in a square ceramic bowl. Both have ribbons and come with the card of your choice. Either can be kept thru the fall season, then planted;" she answered the questions posed by the caller, then asked one of her own. "What are you ordering it for?

A funeral? We currently have several we're doing arrangements for. Who is it in honor of?" she inquired; thinking to herself that it'd been a long time since they'd had four at once to do flowers for.

"Who was that? Jane George? Oh, my; I hadn't heard she'd passed. I'm so sorry to hear that. You worked with her? I see. Yes, she'll be greatly missed. Which funeral home are we delivering to? Yes. I can have it there today. We're going over there before noon to deliver several others, and if I get started now, I can take it along with those." *Oh, Lord, how will we get another one done today?*

"The large one in the copper pot? That's $58.99 plus tax." Quickly adding on her calculator, she went on, "$4.86 for tax, for a total of $63.85; Now, what would you like on the card?" She wrote the message exactly as it was given, on the order form, took the client's name, the company credit card information, and phone number, and concluded the call.

"I swear, this is as bad as prom, valentines, or even Mother's Day," she stated to her assistant Ellie as she wrote out the card in her beautiful script. "Five funerals in two days. We better call in

Alice. We're going to need her. I'll get started on these mums, if you'll try to reach her." She picked up the order pad and started to the back and the phone rang again.

"I'll get it." Ellie said, while reaching for the phone. "Kaleidoscope of Petals, how may I help you?"

It rang twice more. As soon as she rang up the orders and ran the credit cards, she called Alice. "I know we discussed possibly needing you just for today, but you'd better plan on the rest of the week. We have five funerals, and I just took an order for someone who's dad is in the hospital with covid; and it's looking bad enough her friends are already sending flowers. Looks like we may have six or more before the day's out. It's short notice, but can you come now?"

Knowing they could count on Alice, she joined Louise at the preparation table, taking a moment to straighten up from earlier, refill the ribbon rolls on the large dispenser rod, and finally, going to the side storage room to bring in another stack of pots. The phone started ringing again as she sat them down, and as Louise began to take another order, she grabbed a pre-printed wholesale order form and began a quick inventory of flowers, ribbon, baby's breath, and containers.

They were going to have to do a mid-week order to replenish supplies, and the way it was going they needed a big order, and she didn't want to miss anything they might run out of. They didn't ordinarily keep a lot of stock on hand between Homecoming and Christmas. This many services in what was normally a less busy time meant they had to do a quick adjustment of what they would normally order.

Completing the form in record time, she reached for her cell phone, and while doing so, noticed the jar of plastic card holder floral picks was down to just a handful. She checked off the box for another thousand, grateful she'd needed the other phone. She knew she'd averted a possible disaster. Every arrangement needed a pick, and she'd forgotten to include them the last few times they'd called in an order. I've got to keep my head in the game. That's a critical omission.

She could hear "Kaleidoscope of Petals, how may I help you?" as she hit speed dial, and the bells above the door as she was hanging up. She hurried to the front, praying Alice would get there soon, and thinking she needed to call her son to make deliveries. It was going to take all three of them to keep up with the florals and calls, and they couldn't spare anyone for the time it would take to drive both ways, unload, and set up at 3 funeral homes. *What is going on in this town?*

What's In a Name?

Chapter 9

MAGGIE FINISHED CHECKING HER underwriting requirements, was just about to take a break when her phone rang. "Good morning, Albright Insurance. How may I help you?" she professionally answered.

Maggie, this is Bob. I have a question," a well-known client began.

"Of course. I'm sure I have an answer," she laughed, as she gave her usual reply to his usual opening. Bob was always pleasant. She had several policies for his family and he was usually the contact. He called periodically and knew if she didn't have an immediate response, she'd find the information and get back to him. It was a friendly business relationship.

"If I die in an auto accident, does my accidental death policy pay?" he questioned.

"Yes, that's why you bought it, remember?" Maggie reminded him. *I wonder where this is coming from?* "I can send you the brochure again if you'd like, and you can read the coverage."

"Are you absolutely sure? Because if not, I want to cancel it," he pressed; somewhat insistently.

"I'm sure. Why do you ask?" Maggie could tell he wasn't his usual affable self, and sensed something was wrong. *This is more than a casual inquiry.*

"My best friend's daughter was just in an auto accident. They made it to the hospital with her, but she died in the ER. After she was dead, they did a covid test, said it was positive, and put on the death certificate she died of covid. Now his insurance company says they won't pay because it wasn't ruled an accident.

She bled out from her injuries from the wreck right there on the table, in front of them all, and that's all the coverage they had on her. Now they can't pay for the funeral and I'm not going to pay for something for nothing," he explained. "I'm thinking about just canceling everything."

"Calm down, Bob," Maggie soothed her client. "The company goes by what is put on the death certificate. If the doctor put down that she died of Covid-19, that's a medical issue, and an accident policy doesn't pay for deaths by a medical issue, only accidental death."

"That's what I'm saying," Bob replied. "If a doctor can say anything they want and now it won't pay, what's the point of, having it? Everyone, even the ER nurses, said it was injuries from the accident. She bled out on the ER bed from the open wounds, with her parents watching. She didn't even have symptoms of Covid. She was fine, left for work, and wrecked. Then died from the wreck injuries. They don't even have the money for a funeral because they were off work so long. He was let go because the whole crew went down, so he lost his life insurance from work."

Oh, my! Maggie had heard they were calling anything they could a Covid death to inflate the numbers, but she was stunned. *Hiding a pneumonia, or congestive heart failure, or kidney disease was bad enough, but bleeding out in an ER in front of the entire room full of people with her parents watching, and calling it a Covid death, is simply outrageous.*

"Well?" pressed Bob, "say something. He's about ready to sue the insurance company and his agent. I like you Maggie, and you've always done us right, but I need to tell you, I'd do the same thing. I done told him that, but I told him I'd call you first and see what you have to say."

Maggie looked around her office, trying to choose her words carefully. As his agent, she knew she was supposed to protect both him and the industry, but as a regular person she was as outraged as he was. And frankly a bit worried too. If all deaths were going to be called Covid, or even illnesses for that matter, a lot of people would be questioning their coverage, including her. And not just the accident policies, but the ones with the living benefits too. It pays for cancer, heart attack, stroke, end-stage renal disease, but not Covid injuries. Calling it Covid for everything means it wouldn't pay out for a lot of things.

"Bob," she began, but before she could say another word, he interrupted. "Maggie, please don't give me a load of 'insurance agent' bullshit. These are real people, unable to bury their daughter. I have a real family as well. Just tell me, as a mother, what would you really do if this was your child? You know what happened to us," he reminded her.

Maggie could hear the pain in his voice.

"Bob," Maggie started again, "I'll answer that question as honestly as you asked it, but first you need to understand something."

"Ok. What's that?"

"I'm taking off my 'Maggie the insurance broker' hat, and putting on my 'Maggie, just another person' hat, speaking to you as one regular person to another. One parent to another. One family member to another. Do you understand what I'm saying?" she quietly stated. "As an agent, I represent my business, my agency, and the companies I write for, my clients, and our state law, put in place by our state commissioner; and anything I say under that hat could make me liable. As a regular person chatting with another regular person, it's simply my opinion I'm giving you. Do you get me?"

"I hear you. Just shoot me straight," Bob handed the ball back to her.

Lord, help me to choose my words carefully. "As a mother, not an insurance broker, just a real mother who would also need to bury her child, and would need to use the accident policy that I also pay for each month, I would be just as outraged as you are; in fact, I am now. But, as an insurance agent, I understand the insurance laws.

Let's walk thru this logically. If I were the agent who wrote that coverage, I would have written it in good faith. I would have walked your friend point-for-point thru what that policy did and did not cover, just like I did with you. I would have mailed him a copy of the brochure, and a copy of the policy, both which state it will not cover a medical death, only an accidental death. Just like I did with you when I wrote your policy.

So, if someone sued me because it did not cover a death that was stated on the death certificate as being caused by a so-called virus, there would be no way to win because there could be no coercion, no fraud, and no intent to fraud. I was just doing what agents all over the country do every day.

As her father, so was he; a man buying a family insurance policy in case of an accidental death; an everyday, usual, in good faith, insurance contract. As the agent, I don't write what the policy does and does not cover. I present the facts from the life insurance company. I can add or change nothing that they don't offer. There would be no liability.

If he sued the insurance company, he would also lose the case. The brochure and the policy both are very clear about what it pays for, and what it doesn't pay for. It's any injury that results in death, within a year, except for what I stated earlier. Virus, pneumonia, the flu, or any other medical reasons for death, are not covered. If a death certificate was sent in with a medical cause of death, it's not covered. Period. So, there would again be no coercion, no fraud, and no intent to fraud. Right?

So, where was the fraud, and/or the intent to fraud, done? Who did it? What was the purpose? Was there monetary gain? Who made that decision? Who signed off on it? Who signed the death certificate? Who received the ill-gotten gain? In other words, who benefited from putting the wrong cause of death on the form?

Bob was beginning to nod his head, comprehension dawning in his eyes. "I get it," he said. "He needs to sue the doctor who made the decision, and the hospital that gets to charge their medical insurance for a 'Covid-19' death, instead of just an ER bill?"

Maggie—needing to drive home the point—not just as an insurance agent protecting the industry, but to really make him see where the fault really was, added, "This is going to get bad. The greed and the cover-up will hurt millions. They will soak the medical insurance companies for tons of money in overblown claims, damage the life insurance company's reputations, and make millions. That way they can fill the hospital coffers, while shifting blame for the lawsuits that will inevitably follow to someone else. It has to stop. There will be many families like your friend, Bob. We have to stand up against this from the start.

If it were me—and remember, I'm wearing my 'Maggie, everyday person' hat here—I would sue the doctor who treated her, the doctor who signed the death certificate, the hospital administrator—by name as an individual accomplice—and the hospital itself. I would include—by name—any nurse, or other individual, that is involved in the coverup. If I were a nurse, or hospital employee at all, who was coerced into agreeing to a medical fraudulence of any kind, I would in turn sue the hospital. Let them use that money to turn around and pay the families who are truly losing; instead of filling their coffers.

I would specifically state that it puts my entire family in a financial emergency, and adds enormous additional pain and suffering, on top of watching my child bleed out in the ER and having to deal with her death, while not even being able to afford to bury her; due to a misrepresentation—at best—or an outright criminally premediated decision—at worst—to lie to obtain insurance money funds; while cheating a grieving family from collecting the funds they have been paying premiums for, to bury their daughter and pay the property damage and final hospital bill AT THEIR OWN HOSPITAL."

"And Bob; if you still want to cancel your coverage, I truly understand, and I'll submit the paperwork now, but I really feel as if that's not the answer. You need the coverage. I need the business to be retained, and the insurance company doesn't need to suffer for doctors and hospitals fraudulent actions. I say, take the lawsuit to the perpetrators of the crime and don't upset the applecart of the innocent.

Another thing. Start calling other friends and create a fund for your friend. Put it on social media. Put it on a billboard. Let it be known exactly why they need it. Create public outrage to put the pressure on the doctors and hospitals to stop these criminal acts now. I'll help. I'll call the flower shop today and put $50 toward a spray for the top of the casket."

"Maggie," Bob smiled thru the tears starting to drip down his face, "that's why we come to you. You aren't the usual insurance agent just out for a buck. You really care, and you give good advice. That's why I tell my friends about you. I'll going to start making calls as soon as I get off this one. I'll keep my coverage for now. You're right. Thank you."

He then shared, "I know what it's like to deal with hospitals after a child's wreck and the devastation that follows. We didn't have to fight for our insurance. Charlie's hospital bill was paid. I

BOOK 1: "PREPARE FOR THE END" SERIES

can't even imagine how my friend feels right now, but I'm going to raise that money. And he will know who paid for the flowers for his little girl."

"That's not necessary," Maggie protested.

"That's just like you, to not even want to take credit, Maggie," Bob sputtered. "Most business owners would be advertising it to get noticed. You always do good and always behind the scenes. I admire that."

After he ended the call, Maggie sat back in her office chair for a moment, then laid her head down on the desk. Her mind went back a few years to a memory of holding a little pink blanket, rocking the sweet baby girl one more time, before having to surrender her to the nurse, in exchange for a death certificate. No parent should have to ever lose a child; and no one should have to fight with a hospital or insurance company in order to bury them. Her heart ached in a way that was familiar, but it had been a while since the pain had felt this overwhelming.

She knew this was just the beginning. Evil was rising and there would be many parents burying their little ones, and many children burying their parents as well. *God give me the strength to make it through these dark days ahead*, she prayed. *Please show me the path you've laid out for me and what you would have me do. Let me never turn back or betray you. Help me, to be, a reflection of you, and be a comfort to all I encounter.*

Growing Awareness

Chapter 10

"... AND THAT IS WHY I NEED to run to town," Frankie finished his explanation. "I was too busy with getting the last of the pumpkins to the school in time for the annual pumpkin fundraiser, to get the rest of the shot gun shells for deer season. And I just realized I'm out of Peppe's."

"Peppe's?" Diane inquired, with a puzzled look on her face.

"You know, the stuff I use to keep my shotgun cleaned and oiled," Frankie reminded her. "It's a kit I keep in that zip pouch in my ammo bag. It has a bottle of cleaner, oil, another lubricant, and even includes the cleaning patches. I usually have 2-3 scattered around, but for some reason I'm out of it all. I may just pick up a few packs to make sure I have some for as long, as I need.

All these supply chain issues have gotten me thinking that maybe we need to make a list of things we use, and start getting extra items now to store for a while, until those supply ships off the coast of California are finally cleared to dock. I'd hate to run into a wild boar or a rattlesnake and be out of ammo.

"Do you really think it's that bad?" Diane knew Frankie spent a lot of time listening to podcasts while working on the ranch. He kept up with the state of the nation, and listened to all kinds of farm reports and economy experts. She trusted his knowledge and now her mind started automatically creating a list.

"I've been watching the baby supplies when I go shopping and I've noticed that the shelves don't seem as full as they used to be; they also don't seem to have the large number of choices I thought they used to. I mean, I've never had reason to be in that part of the store, except for shower gifts, but it still caught my attention. I've been meaning to ask you if you thought I'd be rushing things if I started buying a few diapers, blankets, and wipes each week. We'll probably have a good baby shower since we know everybody in town, but I just keep getting this urge to gather up stuff."

She suddenly laughed, but it came out strangely. "I know this sounds crazy, and really it may just be a 'nesting' thing kicking in, but I just can't help but feel the need to have articles of clothes, shoes, even toys bought already. I don't keep up with the same information that you do, but Frankie, I watched two women arguing over the last package of medium diapers the other day, and I remember Candace talking about how many they used when Will was a baby. For some reason I just worry we won't be able to get enough when our baby arrives."

Suddenly she looked sad. "Frankie; I can't believe our country is in a shape where that sentence just seriously came out of my mouth." All at once Frankie saw her beautiful blue eyes fill with tears and brim over. "And I've been thinking about this shot everyone's been talking about. Do you think they will make me take it when I go to the hospital? What about the baby? I heard that guy on TV the other day talking about vaccinating five-year-old kids. Frankie, I'm hearing all kinds of weird things about this shot. I don't want our baby to have it, and I don't want us to have it either," she stammered through her tears.

"Come here honey," Frankie gathered her in his arms for a hug. "Baby items is part of the items I've been thinking about too. Let's go shopping in Waco this weekend. We can get a few things here, but I also feel like we need to spread it out. Don't make it seem as if we're getting a lot. I keep some extra cash, and I'll get some more when I run to town. You start getting $40-$50 cash every time you go to Wal-Mart or the grocery store.

I don't like the thought of what they might be putting in the baby food either, but we may start picking up some of that as well. My mom made our food from what she grew, cooked it very soft, and put it thru a food mill. She always said that way she knew what was in it, and that it had no preservatives or extra salt or sugar. Let's watch for one of those too. In fact, let's get 2-3. I don't know how long they last, but I just feel the need to start getting things we may need and not be able to get for a year or two."

Realizing, he was serious, Diane grabbed a sheet of paper. "Hang on, let me make a quick list. I'll go in with you today and get groceries. I'll add some extra salt, pepper, sugar, and flour. And remind me when we get back. I'll get online and order some extra jar lids from Talman's. You can get a case there. And I know we raise cattle, but do you think I need to order some cases of canned meat too?"

"That's a good idea. It would keep longer than us canning it in jars, but let's get some extra jars today also. I used to help mom can meat, vegetables, and fruit. It wouldn't be a bad idea to start preserving food. If we're being silly, we can always eat it, but if things are going to get as bad as I'm hearing, it may be what keeps us alive.

And order a water filter and a dehydrator. Some of the guys I've been listening are always talking about certain brands that they to seem to think are the best. I'll look up their website and give you the names. I think it's time we started putting some of the things we both learned growing up into practice. Learning we're going to be parents during this crazy time, and watching people fight over toilet paper last year, has really made me consider why my parents always grew so much of our food, and preserved it for the winter.

My mom always had enough for 2-3 winters. She said one bad crop year would make it hard on all of us. I'd rather have it and laugh at ourselves next year, then laugh at ourselves now, and be caught short. Especially where the baby is concerned."

"Let's get several sizes of diapers and clothes for the baby," Diane added. "And teething toys, bibs, and anything we think we'll need. I don't care if we waste a little money, although we don't have it to waste. Suddenly I feel like a hoarder, but it just seems like I'm not as anxious even just talking about it. And I'd better add some citric acid and bottles of lemon juice on the list; we'll need it to can tomatoes."

"Diane, about that shot; I'm not taking it and I don't want you too either. Remember Tom from the FFA program that I roomed with at the convention my junior year? His wife was expecting their second child, had the shot, and had a miscarriage the next day. I didn't tell you because I didn't want to upset you; but I just think since we live out here on the farm, we can gather up what we need, and make sure we can weather through for even a year or two. If we need to stay away from people, we can, so we don't need it anyway." He supported her thoughts on the matter.

"Let's get some medical supplies in Waco too." Diane added a column to the list.

"I already keep some antibiotics for the farm animals, but I can get some more Ivermectin and fish antibiotics from the Vet's office. I'd also like you to start listening to some daily podcasts with me. These guys really believe we may go to civil war and I'd like you to hear the things they are buying to keep their family safe. We need to talk about how practical it is, what we really think we need, and how hard it may to obtain if we do go to war.

I remember my great grandpa talking about the dust bowl. He and my grandparents always had a pantry that looked like a restaurant used it, but he said he'd never live buying on a weekly basis again. His family lost 3 siblings from starvation, and he had health issues his whole life from those days."

"My dad has bought a roll of silver dimes every week since I was kid," Diane reminded him. And ammo. I think he has a lot of gold too. You know he has it hid all over the farm. We had to memorize the places when we were teens. His grandfather went through the 30's too. He had my mom seal bullets in her food sealer bags, and he has a couple of barrels with ammo, guns, and even some grenades buried out in the woods."

"Oh, my god," Frankie said it low and shocked. "We're becoming our parents."

Diane cracked up. "Well, it's inevitable you know. Everybody eventually does. But at least we'll be prepared. I always said, if I could just get to mom and dad's place, I could take on an army and live to be 100."

"I know that's right," he laughed with her; "especially if your brother is there. Let's go. We have a few decades of prepping to catch up with."

History Repeats

Chapter 11

"OK PEOPLE, JAKE ADDRESSED his World History class. "Do the next 3 chapters. Read 'The Hypnotic Communist: The Satanic Seduction of America' by W. Calvin Fields III | May 17, 2021. You can get it on Amazon. You've been questioning the decisions being made by our current administration and the direction this country is going; I think this man's views will answer some of that. It's a timely written book that will contrast nicely with the views we've been reading up to this point, although it's not popular with most campus opinions.

I want a 15-page essay on Capitalism vs. Communism by next Friday, and the end of the section Quiz will be the following Monday. Any questions?"

Jake loved to pace as he lectured, and it was crimping his style a bit having to stay where the camera angles were, so the zoom students could keep up. He appreciated those willing to come to class in person. It was so much easier to gauge their reactions, and ask an 'on-the-spot' question, to see what they were thinking. His instant perception, fantastic peripheral vision, and lack of censoring different ideas, had led to many a lively discussion.

"Mr. Johnson, I don't believe in Satan. Why are we discussing anything religious in our history class?" a young man from the zoom meeting queried belligerently." *Oh, boy. Here we go.*

"Andrew, we've discussed this before. People's religious preferences—and the consequences of a particular religion being imposed by governments onto the populace—have always been a part of history. In this class we look at the 'book ends' and discuss the contrast, the reasons given by the governments involved, and the impact upon the people. Remember, it was religious differences that led to Rome's entertainment of allowing people to be ripped apart and eaten by animals, while they cheered in the coliseum; and it was also religion that caused many, many people to be sacrificed by the Aztecs.

Over 100,000 skulls have been found buried at one temple alone. In England, each monarch, imposed Protestant or Catholic Christianity on the entire nation; and this eventually led to people giving up their lives there to build the wonderful country we all grew up in. Every country has its history, of people following one religion's hatred, and slaughter of people with a different view.

This determination by elements of society to try to stamp out religion, or impose your own choices upon everybody else, is the reason we have political upheaval in several areas of the world right now. You all know that I come from a biblical worldview, so I would say if people would follow the teachings of the bible, and especially the New Testament ideology of 'love thy neighbor as thyself,' we could eliminate a lot of hatred, strife, and criminal activity. Others believe that taking what I've earned and giving it to someone who refuses to work is the answer to world harmony. That's why you will be writing on the contrast of different philosophies of government. Who knows? Maybe your generation will be the one to fix it all," Jake chuckled.

"I can't wait to read your essays, because I believe, in this class, we will have numerous different beliefs. Ask yourself, what's the creed you live by? Does it fit more closely with Capitalism or Communism? What will be the impact upon your children if one or the other is strictly imposed upon them? Don't just guess or give your opinion. Research actual countries where one or the other was imposed, and see what really happened.

I'll tell you what, let's add a bonus. Some of you could use it to get your grade up. For those who would like their opinion on it to be known, such as Andrew," the class laughed at that, because Andrew always liked to interrupt and argue against any Capitalistic or Christian views, "an additional 8-pages on what you, as an individual believe, why you believe it, and which political platform it fits with. Aaaand..." he drew the word out as long he possibly could "... you have, to come to class and present it in a 10-minute speech, and be prepared to defend it from those with opposing views in a Q&A after the speech.

It's an additional free 50 points; with another 50 possible, based on the merit of your delivery, the ability to convey the foundational facts your beliefs are based upon, and your ability to defend it logically—while respecting the beliefs of the opposing opinions. It will be good practice for defending your principles with neighbors, co-workers, and in public office, if any of you find yourself there one day. We'll do the speeches until the end of the week before Christmas break." He buttered up the gift, "who couldn't use an extra 100 points?"

Andrew once again spoke up, picking out the one sentence he could argue against: "why do you say especially the New Testament? Everyone knows that book is not historically reliable."

"Oh," Jake probed; then used his favorite question: "what facts do you rest that opinion on?" *Just what I hoped he'd say. I've got them now.*

"You, know," Andrew pressed, "everyone knows it's based on myths."

"Did you know that the New Testament is the most reliable ancient history book we have?" Jake pressed back. "If we throw out the New Testament, we'll have to throw out every ancient history book. And just so you know, there is more historical evidence that Jesus Christ lived, died, and was resurrected, then there is that Julius Caesar or Abraham Lincoln ever lived," he concluded.

At that, Andrew, and a few others, cracked up. "Prove it," he condescendingly baited Jake, with a sneer.

"I'd love to," Jake smoothly answered with a friendly smile on his face. He'd been watching for just such an opportunity, and it wasn't the first time he'd set up an 'Andrew' for just this purpose. He couldn't 'talk religion' in his classroom, unless the students brought it up and asked questions; but he could answer them when it happened, and he could examine the bible with them as a historical document.

"December starts after our quiz on Monday. Then, as previously stated, we'll listen to speeches, with this change in schedule. The week before Christmas break, we will examine

BOOK 1: "PREPARE FOR THE END" SERIES

the New Testament strictly as a historical document. Where did it come from, who wrote it, is there proof that what it says is true, and how reliable that proof is.

We'll compare it to other ancient documents and contrast the proof of authorship of each, the number of manuscripts preserved over the centuries, and are there other historical sources written around the same time frame that support or refute it. We'll use the same criteria that literary critics around the world use to verify any ancient document. That will keep any bias out of the evaluation. Thank you, Andrew for bringing this discussion to us. I'm sure the entire class will enjoy learning whether, or not, the New Testament is a reliable ancient document.

Andrew, so sure he could smash any 'proof' Jake could bring to the table, smirked into the camera, and said, "right on Mr. J; we can't wait to see your 'proof' for this 'ancient document' you believe can help us all be a better person," he said with a disrespectful slur. "We'll be here. I may just come to class in person for this one."

"Great," Jake warmly responded. "I love it when people are here. I miss being able to look out and see all of you, instead of just a few. In fact, Andrew, since you're so sure it isn't reliable and has no proof, why don't we just make it a debate, since you're coming to class anyway."

Jake knew, so much of communication is body language, and he couldn't wait to see the class members' face as they were exposed to the tremendous amount of historical evidence for the New Testament. He taught Apologetics in his home bible study, and people who'd not ever been told the truth about how much historical evidence there really is, were always amazed.

"Whoooooa...." Several students said. "All right Andrew!" And as a class they started chanting "Debate. Debate. Debate. Debate." Over, and over again. Andrew's face fell, but, since he couldn't lose face, he sneered again, "bring it Mr. J. Bring it."

"I'll let Dean Oakley know today we'll be having a debate. Ok, see you next week. Email me with any homework questions, as usual. Have a good weekend!" Jake dismissed the students.

He walked into his office and sank into his chair, then pulled up his schedule to see if he had time to walk over to the library.

It was only open at certain times of the week now, and he wanted to find a book he'd meant to order and had forgotten about. He was pretty sure he had time to order it and get it in on time, but he'd rather start reading it now and get his notes together for the first of the year.

Thank you, Lord, for once again providing an opportunity to teach the truth of your Word to a group of young adults. Please anoint each word, and provide a hedge of protection that keeps the enemy mute or out of the room.

Jake didn't teach the same rotating classes each semester. He was always teaching from ancient history to modern civics, and he especially loved teaching how today reflected yesterday, and people were people, that didn't really change all that much. He also wanted to impart to his classes that choices have consequences, and it affects more than just you; and when leaders make choices, it can affect entire nations.

He always spent time sowing into each young class how important our voting system is; and to investigate each candidate thoroughly and weigh the possible outcome of that person, or the people he may appoint to positions of authority while in charge of our country; before they cast their own vote.

"Mr. Johnson," he heard from the doorway, "do you have a minute?"

He looked up to see a student from the last class. "Sure Bridgit. What can I do for you?"

"We've never had a bible at our house," she explained hesitantly, while looking repeatedly out the door into the hallway. "My dad is an atheist, so I've never read the New Testament. I thought maybe I ought to before the discussion. I'm not sure how long it is, but I'm a fast reader. Do you have a copy I can borrow?"

Jake, feeling a pang he'd felt many a time, was moved, that in America so many had never heard the words of God from His book. "Of course. And if it helps, you can read nine chapters a day and read it through in a month. I've done that for years, although I usually round it up to ten. It's easier for me to keep up with ten. After several times, you'll know it fairly, well.

Since you have less than two weeks, I'd say you may have to read ten chapters in the morning, and ten in the evening, or spend quite a bit of time on both weekends. I know you're a fast reader and can assimilate knowledge well so you shouldn't have any problems. Another thing you can do, is download it, and listen to it as you do other things. I do that while I drive or work around the house."

He spun his chair around and pulled a copy of the King James Bible off his bookshelf. "Here you go," he handed it to her.

"This looks brand-new," Bridgit said. "I promise I'll be careful with it, and bring it back after we go through the discussion."

"No, keep it," Jake offered. "I keep them around to give to people. You're not the only one who's needed a copy. I buy them by the case for a class I teach and an outreach program I'm involved in. I'm happy to give you one. I think you'll find many of the principles you see me expound on in this class, and hopefully, see me live by. Feel free to call me with any questions you may have."

Bridgit smiled with gratitude. "Thanks, Dr. Johnson. I can't wait to see what causes Andrew, my dad, and so many others, to get so mad any time you bring it up. I'll see you Monday."

Jake watched her leave, then leaned back in his chair and prayed that God would remove any scales from her eyes, and illuminate His Word to her understanding, as she read the long-penned words of life. He prayed for each person that would read the book for as long as it was around. He prayed for Bridgit and her family and friends; for their salvation and calling into the service of the Master.

He'd given out cases of bibles through the years and prayed over each one. He prayed when he bought the bibles, as he gave each out and for the recipient, and prayed collective prayers over all the people they would touch over time. God said His Word would never return void, and Jake knew each copy could touch many lives.

He pulled a worn diary out of the bottom drawer of his desk and added her name and the date. He had a record of most of the bibles he'd given out and he used it to pray often. This one, like the ones at home, was almost filled with names. He put it in his

BOOK 1: "PREPARE FOR THE END" SERIES

briefcase. It was time to start keeping it at home with the others. The times were a changing and he wanted nothing that would point to specific students left at work.

He was just considering going to the teacher's lounge for a coffee when his phone rang.

A Friend in Need...

Chapter 12

MAGGIE DECIDED SHE NEEDED emotional support. It'd been a rough morning. Talking to Bob, then the conversation with Louise when she called Kaleidoscope of Petals to order the spray of flowers for his friend's daughter, had just kicked her in the gut. She picked up the phone and texted Jake.

Are you out of your class yet?

Yes, I just got out.

Are you free?

No. But my rental price is discounted today for friends.

Maggie smiled, in spite, of her emotional pain. She could always count on Jake and his humor to lift her spirits.

I see. And how much is an hour of your time, Sir?

That depends.

Oh.... and what are the conditions?

If you need home repair, it's $10 per referral, or you have to cook for me it I do it myself. If it's a book recommendation, $5 per title. If it's advice, I charge by the minute, with extra for personal confessions; and you'll have to sign a non-disclosure statement if I give details.

Maggie's grin was growing with each exchange.

How much for a coffee at the bookstore behind Kroger?

Will it require me listening to insurance stories?

... actually... yes....

Do I need to buy anything?

No. I can get the coffee.

How about a piece of pie?

Yes. I think I can throw in a piece of pie. But you can tip the waitress and clean the table.

Done. Meet you in 10 minutes.

Grabbing her keys, Maggie checked her schedule book one last time. She didn't have any insurance meetings until three, and the Narcissistic Abuse Recovery Meet-Up wasn't until 6. She'd been the leader of the meet-up for the last 3 years, but there were several new people tonight that only needed the initial information.

She was doing zoom meetings now, and sometimes just sent email info packets, if few could attend. So far few had messaged her they would be there, so she might just do that tonight and not meet in a zoom.

Since it was just now ten, she had plenty of time to meet with Jake, and come back and make dials to add to her income producing activities. IPA was her bread and butter, but one of the things she loved about what she did for a living was being able to take time out to have coffee or lunch with a friend.

The bookstore, called 'The Bookworm,' was close to the campus and Jake was stepping off the sidewalk into the parking lot as she pulled into the driveway, having walked over. She parked and met him at the front of the building. He opened the door for her, then followed her in. They put in their order, then walked to the farthest table back on the side with the windows, where they usually sat.

Jake assessed her face, noting the sadness in her eyes and the smudge of mascara she'd missed when wiping her eyes after her cry earlier. *Has she been crying?* He realized something had occurred beyond just needing out of the office for a break. He was about to ask her what was wrong when Kelly, the waitress, walked over with the tray holding their coffee and pie.

"I added ice cream to your apple pie, Jake," she stated. "I hope I wasn't too presumptuous, but in three years of working here, I've never seen you order apple pie without ice cream," she teasingly explained.

"Yes, Ma'am," Jake teased back. "Maggie's buying today and she's too cheap to offer ice cream. I was going to just suck it up and take it like a man."

"Jake," Maggie protested, laughing, "you could have added ice cream. You know I wouldn't have minded."

"Oh, no Ma'am," Jake, with the face of an overly innocent choir boy, ribbed. "A deal's a deal. Coffee and pie for an hour of my time. I would never take advantage of you by upping the price after the fact. But, to show my complete appreciation of

Kelly's attention to my personal likes, I'll pay for the ice cream. Kelly, please bring Maggie a dish too," he generously added.

Kelly, totally at ease with these two and their usual hilarious banter, walked off smiling while hollering back, "no way. The ice cream 's on me today. You two are always good for a sunshine moment and I appreciate those more than you know."

In less than a minute she returned, setting a bowl in front of Maggie that contained one scoop of chocolate and one scoop of pistachio almond, which she also knew was Maggie's favorite. The consideration—and just knowing someone cared—even after so many years of healing from her own abuse, touched Maggie deeply; and tears once again filled her eyes as Kelly walked back to the front.

Jake, still watching Maggie closely, noticed the glint of extra moisture. He'd known Maggie long enough to know something had triggered her old pain, and knew she needed both comfort and a listening ear. "What's up Mags? Did something happen?"

Maggie filled him in on her conversation with Bob, then added the information she'd received from Louise. There had been ten calls this morning from families arranging funerals. Louise had been in the middle of ordering flowers and supplies from four different vendors, just to get enough deliveries to fill the orders that were still coming in.

She'd had to call in two part-time workers and one retiree just to make it work. Louise was thrilled with the business, at a time when so many local businesses hadn't made it through the lock-down, but everyone was exhausted, with no sign of relief in sight; and knowing her clients were about to bury a loved one took its toll on her loving heart.

"Jake, everything we've been seeing and hearing about is happening. We've taught for years now that it's going to get bad; but, studying it and teaching, it is far different from being in the middle of it happening. I have to say, I'm feeling a bit vulnerable right now. I know I'm supposed to be upbeat and positive, and just trust that we will be ok, but I'm having a hard time doing that today," she confessed.

"Mags," he gently replied, "You don't ever have to worry about being 'upbeat and positive' with me. We both know that comes from witchcraft while creating thoughtforms anyway. I just want you to trust me enough to be honest with me, good, bad, or ugly. You know what I always say, "The truth isn't always pretty, but it's still the truth," they said it together, smiling at the many times they'd said it in unison over the years.

She'd heard him say that phrase so many times, she could almost predict when it was going to come out of his mouth, but today it was especially comforting. To know she had someone that understood, and didn't condemn her for telling the truth when she was at less than her best, was something she still found rare. "I just feel like I need to have more faith," she quietly whispered; not sure what his reaction would be.

I know what that's like, he thought.

"Maggie, no one has more faith than you, and even the 'greats' in the bible had times when they were in the crosshairs of the onslaught from the enemy, when they wondered if God was going to show up. It's our human nature. I've had my share of that. What's happening in this country, indeed the world, is at best concerning, and at worst terrifying.

We are living in a time unprecedented. Remember, 'men's hearts will fail them for fear of what's coming on the earth.' Even Jesus said if he doesn't return when he does, that no flesh will be saved. It's ok to be scared. It's ok to be sad. It's ok to worry about friends and family. It's true valid concerns.

Remember when we figured up the sheer number of people that will die in the opening days of the book of Revelation? Maggie, billions are going to die. We are witnessing the lead up into the very closing days of human history before God remakes the earth. It will not—and indeed cannot—be easy. But we weren't born into this time by accident. We have a purpose; and not the kind of purpose that kook wrote about; but a real calling from the God of the Universe; the Ancient of Days, the King of Kings, and Lord of Lords; to be His hands and feet, to speak the truth, to pray and fight the enemy. Our weapons of warfare are not carnal, but mighty through God to the pulling down of strongholds, Corinthians II 10:4 says.

Of course, the enemy wants us to be afraid and emotionally gutted. We were built to be in the garden, safe, walking with God himself. We were meant to have families and lead them in worshipping and fellowshipping with him. We were meant for eternal life; not to witness so much death and destruction. It will challenge everything we are and believe over the next few years."

They talked for a while longer, then he said, "I hate to leave you right now, but my next class starts in 20 minutes. Why don't you come out tonight and let me make you dinner? We can look up verses of God's miraculous provision, and what He would have of us in these dark days. Bring an overnight bag so you don't have to drive back into town tonight by yourself. I've got the spare rooms ready, and we can stay up as long as we want to.

I think we need to just spend a great deal of time in prayer. For intercession, for instruction, for comfort; to war against the enemies in high places; and to ask God for Holy Spirit intel for what to do, and how to reach the lost as this world falls apart. Tomorrow is Saturday, and we can sleep in, and study and pray more then, as well.

I'll call the study group and have them meet us around five. We can spend the afternoon and evening strategizing and upping our plans, and pray as a group. But, for some reason I believe we need to keep it small and only the older ones. If it makes you more comfortable, I'll call Sharon or Rachel to come also so you won't be alone with an old bachelor man," he said, while raising and lowering his eyebrows with a feigned look of a lecher suggesting something nefarious.

"Louise may not be able to make it," Maggie reminded him, but I'll let her know when I run by to pay for the flowers. I forgot my debit card this morning and planned to go home and get it and bring her a cold tea this afternoon. I may run by the bakery and bring them a box of cookies also. They'll probably appreciate a pick-me-up this afternoon, as busy as they are.

Thank you, Jake. I appreciate you so much. A night of prayer and digging into the Word is exactly what I need right now. And Jake, I know you're teasing me, and I know it may be more correct to have Sharon or Rachel be there with us, but I'm not worried; and right now, I need a retreat into His heavenly presence more than I need a chaperon. For some reason you and I are on the same page spiritually, and we've both known that for a while. It feels as if we are being called to prepare for a time of battle unlike any we've ever know. Will you be ok if it's just the two of us?"

Then, unable to resist the need to jest back a bit, after his eyebrow wiggling imitation of a wicked man compromising an innocent, "I promise to not assault your virtue," she added in a high-pitched voice, while wildly batting her eyes, in a complete farce of a Hollywood movie flirtation; totally flipping the role of just who was compromising who, in her effort to give as good as she got.

She hadn't yet told him about the weird happenings she'd experienced of late, but vowed to herself she would tonight, and she didn't want to share it with anyone but him. He would understand, others might not. *I hate that Jake's never wanted to be more than friends; but I know I'm safe with him.*

Jake laughed at her ridiculous attempt at appearing to be a coquette. Maggie was about as far from a flirt or loose woman as they came. In fact, he acknowledged to himself, that she was a beautiful, intelligent, witty, loving woman that any man would be privileged to have as a companion; and she'd never put him or herself in a compromising position; so, he knew she had a reason to request it be kept to the two of them.

He'd admired her for a while, and appreciated her friendship greatly, but suddenly he saw her in a completely different light. Interestingly feminine, and lovely far beyond any Hollywood starlet, he admitted; while filing this new awareness into a separate mental file, to be explored at a more fitting time; unable to even contemplate that possibility. *I don't know if I can ever go there again... even with her...*

"Mags, are you propositioning me?" he played along to her batting eyelashes. "Are you maneuvering me into a situation? Do I need to install a lock on my bedroom door this afternoon before you drive over, to protect my reputation?" he relentlessly bantered.

Maggie was laughing with sheer delight at his endless efforts at staying on top of their continued merriment. She knew she was safe with Jake. She'd trust him with her life, and the truth was, in today's world, if anyone even knew she was there, no one would think a thing about it. And as secluded as his place was, no one would know.

She suddenly remembered her Meet-up and decided to postpone it. She'd send out info sheets from past events for the new people, and prepare to build on it next week. Right now, prayer for instructions from the throne seemed the only course that felt right.

They parted in the parking lot after agreeing on a time. She'd run home and pack a bag, grab her bank card, go pay Louise, and invite her for tomorrow. Then, head back to her office and still have time to make a few dials, and be free for the 3:00 zoom meeting with her client, and leave for Jake's right after. She should be there by 5:30, possibly before. Jake's last class was over at 3, so he'd said he would head to the market, pick up a few things, and have dinner ready when she arrived.

It suddenly occurred to her that they sounded like two old married people coordinating their evening. She'd never looked at her relationship with Jake like that before. She'd wanted to go deeper in a relationship for a while, but Jake just didn't seem to want anything else. She'd never known why, and wasn't comfortable asking.

She didn't want to jeopardize their friendship by asking, so she secretly just enjoyed being the one he spent time with; and as she started the engine of her vehicle, she recalled all the times she'd arrived early to help him prepare for the group. They had always worked in tandem effortlessly to have everything ready for the other participants. They'd cleaned up each after each meeting companionly, discussing how the evening went, and then she drove home.

Jake was a great friend and a great guy. And while he'd never seemed interested in more with her, she'd often wondered why he was still single, and why he was always available for her. She realized if he found someone to share his life with, none of those things would be possible anymore. It was an uncomfortable thought. She pondered the possibility of what life would be like without her close friendship with him as she drove home.

She suddenly felt sad again, like a hole had opened that would never be filled, and realized she didn't want to lose his friendship—ever. She'd never had a friend in her relationship with her ex-husband. He was so difficult to be around, and it was a constant fight. He sneered at her religious beliefs, even to the point that if she wore a skirt, especially a long denim one, he'd say, in as mocking a way he could, with pure disdain and disgust dripping in his tone, "Oh, here comes the little Pentecostal lady, doing her daily good works, so she can get into heaven."

He ridiculed her constantly, and would never have studied the bible with her; much less pray, unless it was to impress the people at church. He often prayed big, pretentious prayers in church, while laughing in her face when she asked him to pray with her at home. In his words, 'Stupid; no one prays at home. That's just church stuff. You're crazy;' while stomping out the door, to go do God knows what.

He'd taught her children that she was a fanatic, and just going to church each week, and forgetting about it the other six days, was the normal way to be a Christian. It was part of why they refused to have her in their life now. That was a constant source of pain, but she refused to allow more abuse, even from her kids.

She realized once again what an incredible gift she'd received when he'd given her an ultimatum to do what she couldn't do, or leave. She hadn't thought so at the time. His rejection, after teaching her she was completely unlovable, and how lucky she was that he put up with her, had almost killed her, especially when she had to leave her children to keep them safe. She grew nauseous at the thought of what it would be like to still be his wife, instead of having her friendship with Jake; and it brought her full circle to her tears from earlier.

Her friend/client was filled with fury over the atrocity that his friend was rendered unable to bury his daughter, while Maggie knew she'd buried her beautiful baby girl because her ex had punched her in her extended pregnant belly four weeks before her due date. She'd never told anyone the truth, not even her doctor. She'd been too afraid and too humiliated at the time. That kind of imposed fear and humiliation, and how to overcome it, was what she needed to help the new-comers to her Meet-up group with first, she decided. Next week that's what the lesson would be on.

A quiet peace filled her heart as she realized she could finally tell Jake that awful truth. He was safe. He wouldn't ridicule her, or condemn her for being 'negative.' He would simply comfort her and hold her hand while she shared the long-carried horror of that time. A warm feeling began to spread through her, radiating out from the center of her being as she realized the depth of friendship Jake had offered her. *I'll always wish he wanted more, but at least I have his friendship.*

The studying, the humorous bantering, and the companionable activities, were soul healing; but were nothing beside the gift of knowing she could trust him to respect her, listen to her feelings and opinions, and offer the gift of allowing her to be her true self without censorship. She loved spending time with him; and the time they spent with his family, or just Matt and Rachel were precious to her.

They were the family that had replaced the one she lost. She felt another twinge, wondering what would happen if Jake ever dated someone else. The thought slammed into her gut, and hurt more than she liked.

She finished her day, and was filled with a sense of destiny as she made the journey to Jake's, somehow feeling as if she were on her way home. She quietly filed away the feeling in her heart, content with the evening's plans and knowing God would guide them to do His will.

Caught

Chapter 13

"MISSY, ARE YOU FEELING ANY BETTER?" Amy asked her friend and co-worker. She'd called after working a double once again. She was exhausted. She was both worried about Missy and thrilled with the tips she'd earned working five doubles in a row, not to mention the doubled hourly wage. She'd be able to go to the wedding with no financial worries or the hardship she'd anticipated having when she returned home.

"Actually, yes and no;" Missy's voice sounded as tired as Amy felt, when she answered. "I'm no longer coughing or wheezing, and I only ran a temp for one day. My lungs seem to be clear; but I'm still having trouble with fatigue, and my nausea won't seem to let up. Between sleeping and puking, I'm wondering how I'll survive a shift next week, much less doubles."

"Do I need to get Maylene to call in somebody else?" Amy asked.

"No. I need the money. Everything is due, and I haven't worked in over a week. I used to have a bigger savings account, but with the reduced tips the last few months, I've used most of it. I still have a couple of days off. I'm hoping I'll be well by then.

It's weird, I never throw up and now it's daily, almost by the clock. I get up, brush my teeth, walk to the kitchen to turn on the coffee maker, and run back to the bathroom. Then I sit in my chair for an hour feeling like death warmed over, drinking a couple of cups of coffee and I'm fine, except being so tired," Missy shared with her friend.

Amy looked at her friend with a perplexed expression, that slowly became a look of shock as she put two and two together. "Missy, did you ever get your period?"

79

"No. I think this flu messed my whole system up. I'm still very bloated and you know what, that may be why I feel so tired. I always get tired when it's that time."

"How late are you?" Amy chewed on her fingernail `as she kept on.

"About a week. Why?"

"Do you think you could be pregnant?" Amy wondered.

"Pregnant! Oh, my, I haven't even thought of that!" she exclaimed. Last time Billy and I were together I was out of birth control pills and he didn't have anything.

"Oh, how could I be so stupid?" she moaned. "Billy is going to kill me. He's said over, and over again, he's just in it for the fun, and he's not having any kids."

"Do you want me to run to the drugstore and buy a test for you?" Amy offered.

"Would you? I hope I'm wrong and it's just the last effects of the flu. I'm only 22 and totally not ready for this." She grabbed her purse and took out a twenty-dollar bill. She handed it to Amy saying, "Go by and get us a drink too. I need a fresh-fruit strawberry slush. Make it a route 44." I'll make us something to eat while you're gone, but you'll have to settle for chicken salad sandwiches.

I haven't been shopping in almost two weeks. I don't even think I have any chips or crackers." She was grateful for Amy and knew she would keep this between the two of them. Amy had a scare last year, and Missy had done the same for her.

The look on Amy's face told her she remembered what it felt like to sit here and wonder whether she was or wasn't pregnant. She picked up her purse and said, "I'll run by the grocery store too and pick up both, and some fruit and vegetables also. Do you need anything else?"

"I could use a carton of eggs and some coffee. Maybe another bottle of aspirin for the headaches. Thanks Amy; I've never had a friend I could trust like I do you," she offered her appreciation.

"I feel the same way. I've never forgotten how scared I was last year. And when you said we could move in together and you'd help me raise it if I was, it took away at least half the fear.

I'll help you the same way if Billy doesn't come through," she added.

Hugging her friend, she then quietly slipped out the door to run the errands. She was ready to just put her feet up and rest, but no way was she not going to be there for Missy the way Missy had been for her.

She returned about an hour later. Missy had made them both sandwiches from the chicken salad she'd put together while Amy was shopping; then, after she returned with the groceries, added a small vegetable salad and a few chips to each plate; setting one down in front of Amy on the small glass table, and then sat the other across from her, sinking down into the second chair.

Both were hungry and having not seen each other for several days, they chattered about everything while they ate, with Amy sharing stories of their usual customers, and some of the 'crazies' that came from the diner being located on the main off-ramp from the interstate. They'd had several nutjobs over the years and often tried to top each other's most off-the-wall experiences.

Finally, Amy picked up the box that held the pregnancy test and shooed her to the bathroom. "We need to know if life will go on as usual, or if you'll be getting an early summer surprise."

Missy looked up and Amy saw how nervous her friend was. She remembered that moment and how a night of partying had led her to the exact same fear. "At least you're dating Billy," she comforted Missy. "I barely knew the guy's name."

"I know." Missy patted her hand. "But look at the changes you've made. You'll never do that again."

She stood up with the box in her hand, and reached to pick up her plate. "I've got this," Amy told her. "Just go. I'll clean up and put the rest of the groceries away. Come back and we'll wait the 5 minutes together."

"Ok." Missy straightened her shoulders and started down the hall. She knew she had no one, but herself, to blame, if she was 'caught' as her mom used to call it. She followed the directions, set the test wand on the sink, and came back into the kitchen. She set the oven timer for 5 minutes and then sat back at the table, with Amy sitting down at the same time.

"Remember the game you made me play?" Amy, getting her revenge, demanded.

"Yes," Missy snorted; "but it was a lot more fun when it was you," she laughed. "Ok, I'll start. If it's a girl I'll buy pink dresses," she smiled.

"And if it's a boy, I'll buy a blue outfit and get a blanket with cowboys on it," Amy took her turn in the verbal game.

"And if it's twins," they spoke together, "we'll buy both; and if they're the same sex and look just alike, we'll paint one toenail on each baby a different color."

Knowing she wasn't in this alone, Missy was comforted; as she knew Amy had been last year as she made up the 'what if' game. Just then the timer went off and she shot Amy a look of pure panic.

"Do you want me to come with you, or wait in here?" Amy softly asked, while watching the expression on Missy's face. "Please come," was the panicky reply. "I need you."

Amy looked her directly in the eyes, silently offering strength and support, while she took her hand. "Come on." *We'll get through this... we'll get through this...*

She led the way down the hall, then stepped aside, letting Missy go in while she leaned on the doorframe; not in or out, just present, watching while Missy's trembling hand reached for the wand. She knew before Missy could speak the words. "It's positive. Oh my god; it's positive." She sank down on the closed toilet lid and rested her head on the sink counter. *I'm pregnant! Billy's going to kill me! OMG... I'm pregnant. Momma, I need you.*

Amy kept silent and waited, and finally Missy looked up. "What now?"

"Now, we go back in the kitchen and get down the fancy glasses. We'll put some fresh-fruit strawberry slush in them and celebrate. You're going to be a mother, and I'm going to be an aunt. Tomorrow you will make a doctor's appointment and get some vitamins. Then, when I get back, we will make a list of everything you'll need and when you know how far along you are—it can't be much—we'll divide the weeks, make a budget, and start buying things one at a time. I told you, you're not alone. I'm right here and I'm not going anywhere."

Missy took Amy's outstretched hand and followed her down the hall in a daze. She allowed Amy to push her down into the chair she'd been sitting in earlier. She watched Amy get down the champaign flutes and pour in the ruby red frozen drinks from the Styrofoam cups and bring them back to the table.

Amy then reached into the grocery bag and took out a box of special cookies with "Mother" written on them in soft green icing and got out the glass dessert plates. She sat two on each plate and brought them over and served them both. Tears began to overflow from Missy's eyes as she understood the depths of Amy's thoughtfulness. She missed her mother so much right now, but Amy was truly being the sister she'd never had and she would never ever forget this moment.

She knew, in that instant, that whatever Billy said; whatever he thought, or wanted, or didn't want, she was keeping this baby. Her mind went to the bible study group and how hard it would be to tell them, but she also knew she'd made enough sinful choices and it was time to grow up. *Lord, help me be the mother I need to* *be.*

A Cord of Three Stands Is Not Easily Broken

Moving On

Chapter 19

"HERE YOU GO," Missy sat the plate in front of her customer. "Runny, but not too runny, as usual," she smiled at Ed. He'd eaten breakfast here every Saturday for as long as she'd worked at the Café.

"Thanks Missy." Ed was a bit temperamental, but also appreciative that Missy always made sure his eggs were cooked the way he liked them. He was a man who needed routine and wasn't flexible enough to start the day with his eggs wrong.

He liked his coffee warmed up when it was exactly half full. Missy always knew when it was time. He liked strawberry jelly and would accept nothing else. He wanted real butter on his pancakes, and refused to eat syrup or grits.

None of his food could touch on the plate. He wanted his silverware set on the left side and his drink on the right. He didn't like any changes at all. He liked Missy because she didn't get huffy or rude with him. She just did it exactly like he liked. He always left her a good tip. Most waitresses enjoyed doing the exact opposite of what he asked for. She had never done that. Not once.

Missy walked over to the coffee maker. The pot was almost empty. She sat it to the side and hurried to make a new pot. It would have just enough time to brew before it was time to refill Ed's cup. She went to the kitchen to get another container of coffee. She'd used the last bit in the current canister for the prior pot.

As she came back into the room, the bell above the door tinkled and she glanced over to see Billy and Erwin walk in. She briefly smiled and then went to finish making the coffee. Then she grabbed two menus and headed to their table. She needed to talk to Billy, but not here, and not now.

"Good morning gentlemen," she sat the menus down before them, as she spoke the greeting. "Two coffees?"

"Yep," Billy looked tired. "We don't need the menus. Just the usual. Bacon, two eggs over easy, hashbrowns, and biscuits instead of toast. And Missy, bring us some grape jelly. I like that on my biscuits."

Missy looked at Erwin, who grinned. "Ditto; except make mine sausage, and add two pancakes, please." He was trying to figure out how to limit his time with Billy and not have to take part in anymore rituals. He wished Missy hadn't gotten mixed up with him. She was too nice, and nothing like the girls he usually dated.

"You got it." She went to get their coffee. She poured two, emptying the pot, and set them on a platter, added two glasses of ice water, a bowl with individual servings of butter and grape jelly, and silverware rolled in napkins. She picked the fresh pot of coffee up, walked over and refilled Ed's cup, right on time, then brought the tray over to serve her friends. As she passed, other customers raised their cup to show her they needed a refill also.

She walked around the room, refilling cups and joking with the regulars. Most were there each day, or each Saturday. It was a comfortable group, friendly, mostly easy-going, and patient when she got busy. Most tipped well and she appreciated that as much as they appreciated her taking care of them.

Billy watched her teasing with the other patrons, and his face soured. She looked up just as a dark look moved across his face. *Oh crap*, she thought. They'd been through this before. He didn't understand she was just being friendly, and in this line of business, that's how you got the tips. Missy was naturally outgoing, and having a good time with her regulars made her day.

Most people had their co-workers they saw every day. Missy saw the early work crews on their way to work; and the owners of the companies a little later in the day. More than a few business meetings were discussed over breakfast or lunch.

It was natural to be cordial and get to know people you saw regularly. When she was in their places of business, they all greeted her as a friend and helped her find whatever she was shopping for. Most, in this pandemic, knowing business was down, had tipped more than usual. It's how she'd kept her apartment and paid her bills. Both she and Amy gave good service, and it was repaid in the ability to have a place to live and a nice rapport that made the hard work of waitressing a pleasant way to make a living.

Billy was jealous, but he'd never committed to her in any way, and she wasn't about to become a silent rude person to keep him happy. She had just about been ready to tell him to hit the road, when she found out she was pregnant. She wouldn't even tell him at this point, knowing how he'd feel about it, but this was a small town, and he'd find out anyway.

Telling him was just a formality though; she'd already decided to keep it, and she didn't expect any money or help from him. He'd been more than clear he didn't want any 'brats' and she knew he'd paid for abortions before. For a moment she was sad that he wouldn't be a real father, but that's just how it was. She was really mad at herself for getting in this mess with him.

She'd been wooed by his amazing good looks and his charm, but the longer she'd known him, the more the charm had worn off, as the real Billy became known. She'd already realized he'd taken advantage of her grief, while in a tough part of her life.

She waited until Erwin stepped outside to take a phone call on his cell, then walked over to the table. "Can you come over at 10:00 tonight? I'm working a double, but I need to talk to you."

"Why?" he shot back. "Looks like you got a room full of guys to talk with already." His tone was disrespectful and his voice loud enough that most heard him. Several of the men looked over to see what was going on.

"Stop it," Missy quietly hissed; embarrassed by his rudeness. "This is where I work, and these are my customers.

They're in here often and I'm just being friendly. I just want to talk. Now, will you come over or not?"

Billy, who always enjoyed an audience and humiliating people, raised his voice just a tad more. "Ain't but one thing you'd want me to come over that late for, honey. I guess if you're begging for it, I can make it happen."

Missy couldn't believe he'd treat her this way while she was working. She knew he could be crappy at times, but he'd never deliberately humiliated her in public before. She felt diminished in the eyes of her usual diners, and hurt that he'd speak to the mother of his child that way, not that he knew of course. She felt her cheeks redden in anger as much as embarrassment, and her eyes filled with tears, "how dare you speak to me that way?" she was furious now.

"Honey, if I'm sleeping with you, I can speak to you anyway I want," he carried it even further, and spoke even louder. She looked at him in astonishment, her mouth falling open. "You know what?" she quietly stated, "forget coming by tonight. Forget coming by ever. We're done." She turned and walked back to the kitchen, eyes on her all the way.

As soon as she left the room, a tall older cowboy stood up. He walked toward Billy's table. "I don't know who you think you are son, but you're going to treat ladies with respect in this place. She's a nice girl. She's always friendly and kind, and there's no call for mistreating her."

"She's my girl," Billy sneered at the man. He had a headache and was in a mood to argue. He hated to be told what to do. He was used to having his way and he didn't like the man. Everyone knew Dan Blanchard from the Rockin' O Ranch. Billy had gone to school with his son Clayton, and Dan had never liked Billy. Clayton, like his dad, was a do-gooder, and Billy had made his life miserable in high school.

"That may be," Dan answered him with a calm manner, "But you'll treat her with respect in front of me."

Billy smiled a triumphant smile, "you're not in here every day, old man," he sneered.

"No, but one of us will be," another guy spoke up. "That's right," came from another table. Several men all stood up at once. "One of us will usually be here; and we'll look out for her." One spoke, and all nodded.

Erwin came in the front door, and Missy came from the kitchen, just as Matt Hench stood up, anger wrapped around each overly annunciated word, "we'll watch out for her, and she *will* be treated with respect. Do you *understand* me, Carter?"

Missy shot a questioning look at Erwin, who shrugged. He didn't know what was going on either. Erwin walked toward the table, already embarrassed to be with him, as Missy looked at Dan. Ed surprised them all. "Missy, if this man bothers you in any way, you call us. One of us, or all of us. We'll take care of you."

She looked around the room. Most of her regular breakfast crowd were standing. Most looked both mad and determined. She suddenly felt protected in a way she'd never felt. She looked at Billy and saw the fury on his face. She knew there'd be hell to pay later, but right now it felt good seeing him put in his place. "Thank you, gentlemen."

She continued to Billy's table, setting down the tray she had been holding with their plates on it. She silently sat a plate before each one, then just as silently walked back to the kitchen. Billy, knowing when he didn't have the upper hand, waved at the standing men. "I was just playing with her, that's all. You boys can go back to your breakfast. It was just a misunderstanding." He picked up his fork, dismissing them all as he took a bite.

"We're not playing," Dan Blanchard stated flatly, looking at him with a measuring look. "Remember that." He turned his back on Billy and sat back down, and the others followed suit, but all vowed to keep a watch on their favorite waitress. Matt continued to glare at him the entire time, while finishing his breakfast, severely wanting to knock that self-satisfied grin off his face.

Billy pointedly ignored them all as he ate his breakfast. Guys like Billy liked to fight, but usually only when the arena was in their favor. Billy, hating to lose face, was already plotting his revenge, but you'd never know it by the careless look on his face as he enjoyed his breakfast.

She'd been close to her expiration date with him anyway, but he'd stick around long enough to make her pay for putting him in this position. She'd learn who was boss, and to stop making him look bad in front of other men. As usual, he flipped the script, and blamed her for his own behavior, and the consequences it created.

He remembered the power that had filled him last night, and felt the importance of being chosen by so vast a presence. These puny little men, with their puny little ranches, had no idea the resources he had, and the spirits he could command. The spirits that always resided in him, stirred up by the confrontation, began to whisper dark things inside his head. He'd show them all, just wait.

One by one, or in groups, the men began to leave to get on with their day. Dan Blanchard and his foreman, Matt Hench, deliberately stayed; waiting for Billy to leave, so he couldn't harass Missy again. For the life of him, Dan couldn't understand why women fell for guys like Billy. Sure, he was good looking, but he was an abusive bully. Clayton had told him a lot about Billy, and the way he went through women.

He love-bombed them, then mistreated them, got a few pregnant and insisted on getting rid of the baby, then moved on to the next. It was a pattern. A cycle that was seldom broken by guys like him. Dan felt bad that a nice girl like Missy had gotten mixed up with the likes of him.

Billy, realizing he wouldn't get to speak with Missy alone, finally got up and motioned to Erwin it was time to leave. He threw a $5 bill on the table for a tip then walked to the register. Missy came over to cash him out. He handed her his debit card, and making sure the other two men heard him, he informed Missy that he'd be over at 10:00, as requested. She looked at him, considering whether to allow it or not, and decided she didn't need to tell him now.

She knew he was mad at being thwarted in his attempt to continue to humiliate her today, and she just wasn't up to whatever it was he'd dream up to punish her. She had seven months to tell him. He could wait. She was working doubles all week so Amy could go to see her family. She didn't have the energy or the desire to deal with Billy and his moods.

"No. I don't want you to come. It can wait."

"You asked me to come over," he insisted, "and I'm coming. You're my girl, and I decide when I come and when I don't."

"I told you I'm done. We've gone out a few times, but it's not like you've kept it exclusive, or we're an item," she countered. "I've been ready to move on for a while; and like you always said, it's just fun and games with no strings attached. I'm tired of fun and games. It's time to grow up and move forward into my life. Go find the next one, or visit the three or four others you've been messing with lately."

It was exactly what Billy wanted as well, but he liked to be the one to move on, leaving girls who thought they were the only one in his life, begging him to stay. Her making the decision just made him dig in his heels. He raised his voice a bit in his anger, reaching out to grab her wrist. "I said, I'll be over at 10."

"That will be enough," Matt stated with finality, standing right behind him. "Missy, has he paid his bill?"

Missy, looking angry, snatched her arm from Billy's grasp. "Yes, Matt, he has," she answered, as he saw the red mark left around her wrist.

Matt grabbed Billy by the back of the denim jacket he wore and escorted him out the door, shoving him ahead of him, as he angrily walked. In the parking lot, he let him go and pointed at Billy's truck. "The best thing you can do right now is get in that truck and go. Everybody in this town knows you have a string of short-term girlfriends all at once. Let this one go. It's obvious you don't care about her, but a lot of us think she's worth protecting from the likes of you. Just move on."

"Come on, Billy," Erwin urged. Dan and Matt did a lot of business with the hardware store Erwin worked at, and he had a friendly relationship with both men. He didn't want to get sideways with them because of Billy. He liked Missy too, and knew how mean Billy could be. He looked at Matt apologetically. Matt looked back at Erwin wondering why he was friends with such a loser.

Matt's family had known Erwin's parents and grandparents for years, and knew they were good people. Erwin's dad had died when Erwin was four or five, and his mom when he was about seven. He knew Erwin and Billy had been friends since they were kids, but figured eventually Erwin would grow up and find better friends.

His grandfather had worked for Dan's dad, and then Dan, for years, but had died a few years back, and his grandmother had raised him. He'd never had a man in his life, and he felt a pang about that, knowing that was partially his fault. "Just get him out of here."

Billy, excepting defeat, got in his truck. He started the engine and was already putting it in gear as Erwin hopped in and shut the door. They roared out of the lot headed to the hardware store. Erwin had to work, and Billy needed to pick up some stuff for his job.

Erwin looked at him. "Let it go Billy. You were through with Missy anyway. You've never stayed with any girl more than a year. It's time. There's no need to drag it out, or stir up a bunch of garbage. Most of those men do business where I work and I don't want to be dragged into a mess. Missy's, nice. You were being a complete ass and you know it."

All, of a sudden, Billy started laughing. "I know. I have a headache from this hangover. But it doesn't set well them ganging up on me like that. Did you see her, flirting with the whole room, right in front of me? It made me mad."

"She wasn't flirting, and you know that. She was doing her job. I joke with them all when they're in the store, too. It's part of customer service and friendliness. You do it in your business just like everybody does. It makes for good customer relations, and you know she lives on tips, not the lousy wage she gets."

"Yeah. I know," Billy acquiesced. "Sorry I drug you into a mess."

Back inside the café, Dan and Matt spoke to Missy. "I don't know how long you've been dating that boy, but Missy, you need to know he has a real bad reputation. He loves 'em and leaves 'em, and always dates a string of them at once. You're a nice girl. Let him go and find a nice guy. There's still a few around."

"It was just something casual," Missy admitted. "I've been meaning to break it off. Thanks for taking up for me today. I haven't had that happen often."

"Anytime. I've never liked that boy." Dan smiled, "I can send someone around to watch your house tonight around 10:00, if you want. Matt, give her your cell phone number. Missy, his cousin works with the police department. If you have any trouble, just call or text Matt. He'll get Ryan out there within minutes."

"Thanks Dan. I don't think he'll do anything, but it's nice to know someone cares." She accepted the paper Matt had written his number on, sliding it in her pocket.

"If you need anything," Matt said, "I mean anything, just text me. We all know your momma passed recently. I don't know if you have any other help, but I have a crew that can do pretty much everything, from fixin' a door to car repair. Call me before you pay for anything. I don't mind sending someone over.

And if that jackass gives you any grief, I'll take care of it. You've been good to us every time we've been in here. Maylene talks highly of you all the time. Tell Amy to call also, if she needs anything. I know her family doesn't live here. You two need a father or a brother. We can fill that role."

Missy had tears in her eyes at their generosity. "I appreciate that more than you know. Especially now."

"Now?" Dan asked, seeing the tears.

"It's nothing I care to share." Missy was reluctant to tell her news. "But it's time to grow up and live differently than I have. I may need to call for that help. Amy and I are thinking about buying a house together, and we'll probably have to get something older."

"My sister is a real estate agent," Dan said. "I'll tell her to start watching. In fact, I think there's one out by the ranch. I'll send her around, and if you need any help getting in it, just let us know. We can move both of you in an afternoon, and I'll have Matt check the house out before you buy it. We can get it in shape so you don't have to worry about repairs for a time."

Missy, surprised at their offer, felt a tear start down her cheek. She tried to speak but couldn't manage. Matt came around the counter and hugged her. "Missy, you aren't alone. We're here for both of you."

They paid their bill and left. When Missy went to collect their dirty dishes there were two twenty-dollar bills on the table, one beside each plate. She couldn't wait to tell Amy about their offer to help. Maybe they could get out of the apartments and into a house sooner that they'd planned.

Chapter 14

"HERE, LET ME HELP you with that." Jake had come out the back door, and walked to where she was parked, while Maggie was struggling with her suitcase; and startled her when he spoke while standing right behind her.

"AHHHH!!" she cried out as he reached around her.

"Maggie! It's me!" Jake started to laugh at her, until he saw the real fright on her face. "My, aren't we jumpy tonight;" came out instead.

"Jake Johnson! Don't you ever do that to me again!!" she screamed with a tremor in her voice. "Good grief! You know I'm in heart attack age, range, right?" she tried to not appear as frightened as she really was. With all the weirdness going on, and the sense of evil she'd been having, she had instantly assumed something was about to grab her when she bumped into him.

Jake was torn between wanting to laugh, and being disturbed at how much fear still showed on her face. *What's gotten into her today?* It just wasn't like Maggie to be so fearful. Assuming being triggered into tears earlier had made her more vulnerable than usual, he decided to err on the side of chivalry. "Come on, its cold out here. Dinner's almost ready. Let's get you settled in your room, and we'll eat and relax before we start our war on the denizens of hell." He just couldn't help himself, he had to have some fun out of it.

Maggie, in spite, of herself, began to giggle. She knew far more than he did that the denizens of hell were already gathering for the battle. But not yet having shared her recent experiences, she just wanted to enjoy the pleasure of being with him tonight, and not being alone in this suddenly changed world.

She relaxed as he carried her case inside; and she followed with her purse, bible, notepad, and schedule book. She wasn't planning on working, but had learned a long time ago, that people were always going to call and change their appointment date, or want to schedule one. She found it easier to just carry it with her.

They put her case in the spare room; and Jake went to finish up dinner as she unpacked the items she would need for the night, brushed her teeth, and washed her hands. Feeling much refreshed, she picked up her bible and notepad, and walked down the stairs to the kitchen. "It smells wonderful in here." She breathed deeply. "I could live on the aroma."

"I'm not quite sure which plate you serve aroma on," Jake quipped, while smiling. "Do you think I could pour it in a glass? Maybe I need a bong like the kids at school use, or maybe you could just smoke it like weed."

"Do you ever stop?" Maggie loved his sense of humor; he could turn anything into an instant come-back, and it was usually hysterical. Then she jumped right in, as she normally did. "Possibly we need to stick it in a nebulizer and I can breathe it right into my lungs. It would go to the brain much faster."

At that, Jake cracked up, smiling with amusement. "Oh, Maggie, what would I do without you to best me at my own game?"

He opened the oven and waved even more of the delicious aroma toward her face. "You don't need a nebulizer; just breathe my dear. It's BBQ chicken. I know that's one of your favorites. Mine too. I have homemade mac & cheese, broccoli, and for dessert, peach pie."

"Yum, Jake," Maggie said with admiration. "I can't wait. Are the peaches from your own trees?"

"Yep. They're the ones you helped me pick and freeze last August. The ugly ones I couldn't sell at the farmer's market and we chopped up and made into pie filling. You were very wise to make me add the spices right into the peaches and put it into 'pie sized' containers. All I had to do was sit it in the sink under running water for about 15 minutes and I poured it right into the crust. I didn't have to mix a thing.

I think I'm going to do that every year. It'd probably work with apples too. I didn't even have to make a crust; I cheated and bought a ready-made one when I stopped for groceries," he informed her, rather proud of himself.

"Jake, you constantly amaze me," Maggie awarded him praise. "No man in my life has ever cooked much, and certainly not as good as a woman."

"As good as a woman, huh?" he taunted with a grin. "I've known plenty of women that couldn't do anything but burn toast," he retorted.

"Well, I'm sorry you picked a harem of toast burners," she shot right back. "It's a good thing your mother and grandmother taught you a thing or two. Otherwise, you'd have had to learn to live on love and burnt toast."

All at once—for the first time ever—Maggie wondered how many women had been in Jake's life. She knew he'd been married once, long ago, but didn't know any details; only that they'd called it quits after a very short time. His cousins had once said the family had been relieved, and that Jake had never been willing to talk about it.

Sharon said that even asking him about it made him completely shut down; and he'd leave shortly after. Both them, and his brother's wives, had said he'd never been the same; and he'd never been as close to any of the family since he moved back. She'd never asked, and she didn't want to talk about her past either, so neither knew much about their prior marriages.

She wasn't sure thinking about Jake in this new context was a good thing. He was not only her closest friend, but the best friend, she'd never, before had. Someone she could talk to about almost anything; and besides Rachel, and sometimes Sharon, the only person she'd ever known that she could truly just be herself with, all the time. He was so easy to be with, and they could talk about almost anything, but neither spoke about their former marriages.

She wondered what he'd be like as a husband, but reminded herself, once again, he seemed content with what they had. She'd had to accept that's all it would ever be, and she wanted to do nothing to jeopardize having at least that with him. She couldn't help but wish it was different though.

She looked at him as he dished up the food. His tall frame, that was fit from hiking and his workouts; his twinkling blue eyes and dark hair were pleasing. As he was early-40s, it was just now starting to be salt and pepper, but the dark was still prevalent. She'd always said Jake was good looking, but now she saw it was more than just looks. Anyone could have a nice face, but it took years to build in the lines of character and humor that were etched into his visage.

BOOK 1: "PREPARE FOR THE END" SERIES

Even though he made his living teaching, he had man hands that were slightly roughened from work around the small orchard he kept up, and the vegetable patch he'd always grown. He also did all the remodeling and home repairs instead of hiring someone. *I wonder why he's not dated since his marriage?*

Jake had grown up in a family that, while not poor, wasn't exactly wealthy either. His father had taught all the kids to work hard and do things for themselves; and Jake just continued to live his life the same way, even though he could afford to hire it out. Jake was what people called 'solid.'

She noticed the way his jeans fit his long legs, and her artist eyes began to watch how the wrinkles moved with his steps, as he finished up the plates. The light reflecting off the top of the wrinkles and the dark shadows in the valleys intrigued her as they moved about, continually changing directions, with the stress put on them from the different angles as he turned and moved; and with his bending down getting pans out of the oven, hugging, then loosening around his body, as he moved one way, and then the other.

He looked up at her, and noticing the strange unfamiliar way she was watching him, he set the pan he was holding on top of the burner and took a step toward her. He searched her face for answers, and then looking into her eyes, seeing her lost in her thoughts, he decided to investigate this new look. "Mags, are you ok?"

She was watching the way his mouth formed the words, still admiring the lines in his face, and almost didn't hear him speak. "Mags," he said again. "Yoo-hoo… you in there?" He waved his hand in front of her face until comprehension finally came across her eyes.

"Oh, sorry. I was just thinking about something," she murmured back, worried he'd noticed her watching his jeans.

"It must have been a deep something," he returned. "You looked like you were a million miles away. Anything I can help you with?"

Maggie felt her face turning red as she moved back to the table. "Um… not really…." she managed. There was no way she'd tell Jake she'd been lost in admiring his face and hands; or God help her, his jeans. She'd never hear the end of it.

He caught a quick glimpse of the red rising in her cheeks as she turned. A bit surprised, he teased, "Mags, are you blushing?"

The red intensified, and Maggie was starting to get embarrassed. Jake took instant notice, and intrigued, shifted his stance to lean back against the counter. He folded his arms across his chest, crossed one leg over the other, and a slow grin started across his face as he watched her mortification grow. In all the years he'd known her, he'd never seen her so unsettled.

She heard his low chuckle, and dared a look at his face. His twinkling eyes almost did her in. *Good grief, Maggie,* she reminded herself, *this is Jake. You've been in this house hundreds of times watching him cook.*

He was highly interested now at the play of thoughts and emotions that were running across her expressive face. His grin widened, as he noticed the effect, he was having on her, but wasn't completely sure why she was so embarrassed; they'd been friends for years, and he'd cooked for her many times. Then he realized where she'd been looking. *Interesting…* "Mags, it's not too late to call Sharon. It's your call," he offered; still grinning.

Jake," Maggie, getting ahold of herself, started speaking; "We've already decided against that. I want to spend time in study and prayer, then I want to tell you some things. Just you. I need you to help me figure something out, and this afternoon I had an awareness that I'd like to share some other things with you as well; some things from my past that I've never talked about with anyone. Would it be ok with you if we didn't call her tonight?"

Jake was truly intrigued now. Maggie was always open and honest but she shared little of the details of her past. He knew her marriage had been bad, and her husband had eventually been diagnosed with co-morbid personality disorders. He knew she'd lost a child, but not the circumstances. He knew she had grown children that weren't presently part of her life. He knew she helped others who'd been through the same type of abuse and admired that.

He wondered what brought this time of revelation now. They'd known each other well for a very long time, and this was a first. One of the things he'd always been so comfortable with, was she didn't ask questions about his past either. She looked especially vulnerable tonight, and it brought out a tenderness in him. He hated to see people hurt. It brought back too many memories, and he always wanted to alleviate their pain.

He looked at her without speaking for several long seconds, feeling her vulnerability, as it tapped into his own. Maybe what she was planning on sharing was really embarrassing, and she'd been lost in thought about how to tell him what it was. Then, deciding to make it easier for her, he said, "sure, let's eat. We can talk while we eat, then get into the word. We can let the evening play out as it will. Prayer can be when we both know it's right."

Grateful, Maggie sank back into her chair as he put the plates on the table. She put her napkin in her lap and reached to take the hand he offered. They bowed their heads and Jake thanked God for the food, the fellowship, his friendship with Maggie, and His presence in their lives. He asked Him to watch over them as they read His word, and take them where He wanted them to go.

He asked their heavenly Father to bind the eyes and ears of the enemy and to keep them safe in every way. His prayers were always wonderful, but tonight Maggie felt especially comforted, as she knew the unbelievably surreal happenings, she was about to tell him; and for the first time, she enjoyed the warmth of his hand touching hers far more than she knew she should. He noticed her blush again, and saw how attractive it made her, and wondered what was different tonight.

They talked about the food, the people dying, and the meeting the next day. Jake shared with her the extra credit essay he'd assigned, and the unexpected opening he'd been handed to teach his students the truth about the reliability of the New Testament. He couldn't wait to tell them about how much proof there really was. She marveled at his adept handling of the situation.

They felt a new tenderness underneath the conversation and easy familiarity. They watched each other, noticing things they hadn't before, especially the attractiveness of the other one. Both knew something had changed between them, but neither was quite sure what to do about it, and neither wanted to risk endangering the ability to be open with the other. Both had been badly hurt in their pasts, and they'd each thrown themselves into their respective jobs, and their love of God and his word.

Each had been surprised at their unexpected friendship, and it had filled a place that had been empty for years. Neither of them had dated since their respective divorces, and meeting one another had given them someone to go places and do things with, while they were unable to move forward. It'd grown comfortable, and neither were willing to risk it by asking much beyond it.

Finishing up, they cleaned the kitchen together, like so many times before, then poured one last glass of tea, and headed toward the study. They sat across from each other in easy chairs and opened their bibles. Jake prayed once again, asking God to guide them to what He wanted them to know. The plan was to find verses about His provision to share with the group tomorrow.

After an hour or so, their confidence that God provided for His people in even the hardest of times, had been raised another notch or two, and they began to look at end-times prophecy. They'd studied the verses many times in the past, but right now it seemed like reading the evening news.

"It just amazes me how many people don't seem to have a clue," Maggie stated. "I mean, it's right here. It's like God had an open window into today and just wrote it down for us."

"He did," Jake chuckled, then reminded her: "They don't have eyes to see. 1 Corinthians 2:14 says it plainly: 'But the natural man receiveth not the things of the Spirit of God: for they are foolishness unto him: neither can he know them, because they are spiritually discerned.'"

"Sometimes I forget how blessed we are to be able to receive the things of the Spirit of God," she declared. "Jake, I hate knowing what's coming on this world and the amount of people who are about to die. Most of them will be lost."

"Me too, Mags," he agreed. "But, in all fairness to God, there's a church on every corner in America, and Christianity has been a part of our culture all our lives. People have had every opportunity to know. Many were raised in Christian homes and were taken to church. It's a choice."

"Yes, Maggie granted. "And now we're all about to see the results of those choices. In fact, we already are. I already see the sheep being divided from the goats. I'm just shocked at some that are being shown to be goats. It's frightening and disheartening."

She looked around the room and was comforted by its familiarity. Jake loved having his family and friends come, and it was arranged so that conversation was encouraged, and she loved the soft lighting with just the lamps lit. Each were placed so they could read the bible they were holding, and she looked up at him, noticing once again, his attractiveness, watching his eyes, and then his mouth as he replied.

That look from earlier went across her face again, and he watched it, intrigued again, while he spoke. "Yes, but also, people are waking up and becoming sheep that wouldn't have considered it a year ago," he countered. *I love talking to her like this. I wish I knew what has her so rattled today, and what she's thinking about right now.*

"That's true," she conceded.

They kept looking up verses, writing a plan for tomorrow to share with the others. Like everybody else that was watching this all play out, they couldn't quite decide if they were in the tribulation, or just very near it.

Eventually they decided it was time to pray; but before they did, Maggie stopped Jake. "Wait, I want to tell you something I've been experiencing. I want us to wait, and pray about it too."

"Ok. Of course," he leaned forward in his seat to focus his attention fully on her. "What's been bothering you?" *Maybe she's about to tell me what she's been thinking about all evening.*

She glanced at him with a look that transformed her countenance from total confidence in him, to something that seemed to alternate between reluctance, and determination. Once again, he was intrigued, but also a bit concerned. He'd watched students wrestle with trying to articulate a thought, while worrying about the class reaction, enough to know to wait her out; but even that awareness, and how it fit so well with the apprehension he was currently perceiving, slightly disquieted him. This was something big. Something unusual. He wondered if he'd offended her somehow and she felt the need to address it. *Geez, what did I do?*

Curiosity growing, he watched her look away, then around the room, briefly back at his face, then down towards the bible in her lap. She was silent, and the stiffness in her shoulders and the taunt cords in her neck, showed her sudden tension. *How do I tell him this? He'll think I've gone round the bend.*

"I'm here Maggie," he encouraged softly. "Just say what you need to."

She took a quick peek at his face, then looked up and seemed to scan it for any sign of rejection. Finally, taking a deep breath that seemed to relax the tension slightly, she very softly said, "I know. And I really appreciate that, Jake; I just don't know how to tell you what's been happening without you thinking I'm ready for the looney bin."

"This sounds interesting," he briefly replied, then waited again.

"Jake… I've had some… um… weird experiences, lately. I know they are real, and… I'm pretty sure what they are… but not why, exactly I'm having them, she started.

"What kind of weird experiences?" he probed.

"Well, I've been hearing things, possibly seeing things, and feeling things," she continued, still slightly uncomfortable with the subject she wanted to share.

It was his turn to scan her face, biting his lip, while trying to see if she was joking, or if maybe she was confessing that she needed some help for a suspected psychological issue. He didn't want to hurt her, or humiliate her if she felt like she needed help, but was certain he'd never seen any sign of psychological or mental illness.

He decided to err on the side of protective reassurance, while he allowed her to tell him what she was seeing, hearing, and feeling. "Ok," he calmly accepted her statement. "Why don't you tell me exactly what your experiences are, when they are happening, and where it's happening. Maybe I can help you figure it out."

"Well, you know I have this keen gift of discernment, right?" she asked rhetorically. "How sometimes I know things?"

BOOK 1: "PREPARE FOR THE END" SERIES

"Yes." He agreed. "You have one of the most unbelievable gifts of discernment I've ever seen."

"I think it may be part of that," Maggie explained. "I think God spoke directly to me the other night. And I also am certain I heard an agent of evil as well. I was given a warning to prepare for God to give me a work that will scare me, but I'm not supposed to be afraid. He said he would show me the real enemy and would use me to make a difference. He said this was my true calling that he placed upon me long ago," she added.

"I see," he said, his voice matching the seriousness of what she'd imparted. "Did he say anything else?"

"He told me he'd send a partner, and asked me if I was willing, and if I was ready; then said, 'it's time.' He said to keep doing my part and He would do His part."

He could detect a slight tremor in her answer. He wasn't sure if it was fear she was trying not to show, or awe at the fact that God had been so direct in His information. "Mags, did you really actually hear him, audibly? Did you see Him?" he questioned.

"I didn't see Him, but I felt He was right there. Right beside me. I 'heard' but not with my ears. It was as if He was truly speaking to me, but audible inside my mind. It was a conversation like He was right in front of me. That alone should scare me, since it's what abductees often say they experience from the aliens; but Jake, I swear, there was no fear, no doubt whatsoever. God was there and He spoke to me."

Jake heard the truth in her voice, and what he now knew was her awe at the experience. "Wow, Mags; did you answer him? Can you tell me everything?" he was truly fascinated now, and wanted to know everything while she was willing to share it. He grabbed his pen to make notes.

She was visibly trembling now, her face shining with the memory. "I asked Him if He was sure I was up to the task, if I was ready, if I have the courage and faith. Jake, I'm not the person I used to be. There's so much I haven't told you, but the last few years have weakened me," she confessed, while her eyes pleaded for understanding. *What if he wants to distance himself from me now, like people have others, who claim to hear from God?*

In that instant Jake also had an instant 'knowing.' He knew beyond a doubt that he was supposed to help carry the load—impart strength to her, and protect her—while she carried out the task she'd been assigned to, and he had a part in the task too; he was supposed to help do it, while protecting her. He 'heard,' in that heartbeat between understanding and speaking again, only one word, in that 'all but audible' voice, *"Yes."*

He looked at her with tears welling up in his eyes. "Maggie, God just spoke to me too, right now, as you revealed that to me. He's tasked me to help you; to help carry the burden, and to carry you." He paused for a moment to collect himself, then went on, now trembling as well. He held her gaze, and his eyes promised his fidelity; to the task, to the one who had given it to them, and to her, even as he spoke.

"I give you my allegiance, Maggie, in this task you've been entrusted with, and I've been entrusted to help with; just as I give my allegiance to the one who called us. No matter what it requires, no matter where it takes us, no matter what it costs."

It was one of the most profound moments in either of their lives; and sharing it, in that instant, created a bond that both understood would never be broken. It was such an earth-shattering cognizance that each would look back upon many times in the coming years; where a long-enjoyed friendship was forged into something more than the sum of the whole.

Jake stood up without warning and his bible slid to the floor. He picked it up and looked at the page it had landed on. "And, if one, prevail against him, two shall withstand him; and a threefold cord is not easily broken. Ecclesiastes 4:12." he read aloud. Again, he heard, deep in his spirit, *"Yes."*

"Jake, I can tell you word for word what God said next. It's etched into my mind," and she spoke the words:

"My daughter: I've layered more into you than you can even imagine. You've been through endless repeats of exercises for preparation. Your 'spiritual muscle memory' is effortless. You do some things so naturally that you don't even notice. There are areas that you can only learn and grow through in the battle. So much depends upon you staying close. Trusting. Obedience will be the deciding factor. Leaning on your training. Never going it alone.

You are multifaceted. Some areas are a warrior well trained for battle, but untried on the bigger battlefield. Some areas are—and have, to be—a small child listening to the voice of her father leading her where she can't see. You will stumble, but if you will listen and instantly obey, you will not fall. As you've already seen, the enemy grows bold... and close....

The enemy is evil beyond anything you've ever even considered. He is relentless. He knows his time is short; and he's on an all-out—do or die—campaign to destroy my greatest creation, take over the universe, and ultimately sit on my very throne. You've read the book. This will never happen; but scripture must be fulfilled. He knows he will be thrown down very soon, and his angels with him, and he is totally insane. In his mind he must win. He knows his fate. It's win or be locked away forever.

In his narcissistic absorption, in the perfection of his original creation—he cannot grasp—how fallen he truly is. He was the highest, the most beautiful, the wisest, the one just under the godhead. He was created to rule; he is the anointed cherub who covereth... perfect... until iniquity was found in him...

Mirrors only show him the past, never the present. Most of the time he and his fallen cohorts can't even see their own reflection in mirrors. They see their desires. They see their original faces, and they see their 'win.' It's the mark of a true narcissist. They can ever only see themselves as the greatest; unable to ever see the true nature of their soul, that's been forged through an endless series of selfish, hateful, sinful, choices and deeds."

"They grow bold. Like vultures gathering around the battlefield looking to gorge themselves, they are on the earth in ever increasing numbers. Stay vigilant, but do not fear, don't even be anxious. Occasionally, like tonight, you may get a glimpse of them. This is to create fear, which is their greatest asset in manipulating humans, but it wasn't intended tonight for you to see; his fury made him careless. They operate in darkness, hidden—stalkers—the lot of them.

Know this, even if you can't see them, my holy ones are here as well. They surround my children; watchful guardians and messengers. You have your own personal guardian, and others that are assigned due to your calling.

Prayer is the currency in my kingdom. Don't pray to them though; pray to me and I will send them. I will instruct them. I will arm them with heaven's finest weapons of defense; but pray for offense also. Far too often my children are on the defense, retreating before the attacking ones. That is not my way. Offense. Kingdom warriors who push back the hordes of hell. We hold the title deed now. They know that; unfortunately, most of my human family does not."

"We've known for some time we've been in a kingdom war. It's what we do with the alliance, and what we've worked so hard to teach to our small group and others; but what a confirmation," Jake acknowledged.

"And we've stressed obedience, and that God has his guardians among us, too," Maggie added.

"Did you actually see a fallen one?" he asked, the look on his face showing his concern. *No wonder she's been so rattled. I'd be terrified.*

"Yes," Maggie whispered. "Except I'm not sure if it was a fallen one, or a demon. It was most definitely one, or the other. It was stalking me. I only saw it for a split second, but it was shocked that I could see it. It looked almost as if it was afraid at having being caught, but also incredibly angry, and completely malevolent.

I'm positive he heard some of what the Ancient of Days said to me, but not all. Some was sealed for my ears only. I got the intense impression that I'm his assignment, and that he knew I had some 'task, of importance' before I did." *I can still see that hideous face...*

"Has there been any other occurrences?" Jake was relentless in his desire to know it all, and he'd furiously written down what she'd been saying.

Maggie filled him in on her trip to the cemetery, the hideous gargoyle creature, and how frightened she'd been when it started running toward her. He gasped in concern when she told him about falling and twisting her ankle, believing she wouldn't escape its attack. When she told him about the kind gentle man, the way he'd healed her leg, and that he said he was the 'gardener' he looked stunned.

He smiled a satisfied smile when she told him the gardener had told her she was safe there anytime, and grinned outright when she told him about how fast he'd disappeared. "Maggie," Jake quietly said, the awe back in his voice, "I think you saw your guardian angel; or, with him being the 'gardener,' possibly Jesus himself."

"You know something Jake?" Maggie—with a look of wonder on her face—uttered back, "I came to the same conclusion. It's been such a strange week. I've seen great evil, it's true, and been very frightened; but I've also heard the voice of God himself, and been rescued by Him; either personally, or by his guardian.

I feel like I can take up the mantle of my calling and know, that I know, that I know, that I know, that He will be there alongside me, keeping me safe from the enemy. And now, knowing you will be there too… well… there are no words to how much safe, and more capable, I feel.

Today, hearing about all the loss, and the pain in Bob's voice for his friend, brought back so much, I was overwhelmed. Just knowing I could call you for coffee was so very comforting. Thank you for your continuous friendship, your allegiance to the Kingdom of Righteousness, and for being willing to help carry the burden of whatever it is we are going to war against. Thank you also for allowing it to be just the two of us tonight. I can't share this with anyone else right now, or possibly ever; but the thought of carrying it out alone was absolutely, daunting."

"Now I know why you were so startled earlier out by your truck and why we needed to be alone Maggie," Jake offered. "I had to be tasked and take up the mantle also. I may have missed His voice if we'd had anyone else here with us. Some journeys have to be safe-guarded from others knowing. I believe this is one of those. I haven't yet seen what you've seen, but something tells me I will. I'll have to see; not to believe, but to protect you. And Mags…I WILL protect you. You can count on that.

Also, it just occurred to me, that if you've been gifted with the power of sight, and we've both been called to a greater battle, then the "dark side" must be ramping up. Somebody, somewhere close to us, is calling upon them for power, just as we are calling upon God for power. They too are being tasked for end time events. We both know what we've been fighting in this area for the last century. I feel deeply that somebody is in true trouble.

Now, I feel the time to pray is upon us. I know you want to bring other things to my knowledge, and I am very willing to help you bear that too, but we must pray to seal this… this… well, I can only call it a call to battle, and an acceptance to go.

Let's especially ask God to rescue anyone that we can; and for anyone really into the evil that is rising, but may not yet be totally committed, to have at least one more call from the Holy Spirit, so they can get out before it's too late. Will you pray with me?" he held out his hand for hers.

She nodded, eyes overflowing with tears at this extraordinary man God had gifted her to have for a friend. *Thank you, God—for him, and his understanding. Thank you for calling him too, so I don't have to fight this battle alone on this earth.*

They knelt down side-by-side, bowing on the couch together for the first time, instead of on the individual chairs as they normally did. They poured their heart out to the one who called them, accepting the tasks, offering their continuing allegiance, and praising the Ancient of Days for his love of humans everywhere.

As they worshipped, they were filled with His glory; and at some point, both, physically and spiritually felt the weight of an unseen mantle come down around them and rest upon their shoulders. The weight felt right; light, and totally as if they'd been dressed in shiny armor and surrounded with a shroud of responsibility; and that the King's 'colors,' and robe, swirled around them, marking them as His emissaries and warriors; ambassadors with the full authority to carry out His will.

People in this realm may not be able to see the mantle as in the old days, but both understood—with zero hesitancy—that those in the unseen realm, from either kingdom, could. Maggie looked over at Jake once, and God opened her sight again, and she saw he looked like a king with a robe around him, and she saw hands on his shoulders imparting something. *Yes…* She heard the voice of God again.

They were marked by the creator. They had a mission; and each knew the fury against them had been ignited in the mostly unseen enemy, and that the battle that had raged for millennia had come to earth in ways it never had before; or at least not since before the great flood, or the days that Jesus walked the earth as a man. Each knew it was a battle to the death with no quarter given.

During the prayer session, many new gifts had been bestowed, not the least of which was a new courage and boldness beyond anything they'd ever known. Each 'knew' the guardians were close, and would remain so. Each picked up their own bible and held it aloft to the creator and He showed them the sword it truly was. They wore the helmet of salvation, the breastplate of righteousness, the belt of truth, the shoes fitted with the gospel of peace, and they carried the shield of faith.

Unseen to them, the enemy's emissaries were right outside, furious at the union of two such strong warriors for their hated creator. Alone, they had a better chance of confusing, frightening, and weakening them. The guardians were always close. They'd tried many times lately to take out the female; but every time they had gotten close, highly ranked guardian warriors showed up just in the nick of time. These two were covered in armor, and knew who they were in Him, and therefore were dangerous to Lucifer's kingdom.

And now they'd taken a new pledge to the creator, together... the gargoyle shook with fury... and where two or more joined together... the power of the creator was exponentially greater; and He was... among them; the hated book was very plain about that. And, these two, could influence others, especially the small group they led, and the greater group they called 'the alliance.' Arrrggghhh...

They especially hated those with the gifting and desire to bring others to the savior, and to a higher understanding of the dark one's ways. It cut them to the core of their black, wicked, withered hearts every time they heard the words 'forgive me' or 'I surrender all' or the dreaded 'I forgive' directed to another human who'd wronged them.

It was a swift trip to Lucifer's throne in the center of the pit for punishment if you committed the most egregious crime in his kingdom, which was letting your assignment surrender to the King of Kings and Lord of Lords.

Arrrggghhh...just thinking those words made his ink black robe start smoking. He jumped around in a circle, batting the flames that had burst out on the robe until he got them all out, while enduring the cackles and hoots of glee from the hideous beings that were his brothers, all of which—like him—were the offspring of the fallen angels themselves, conceived with the mothers of the hated human race.

They discussed the members of the hated group, comparing notes on the weaknesses of each, then divided up assignments to break each one. They already had an opening in the girl, with her illegitimate child already conceived and, unbeknownst to her, about to be promised to them, and her love of partying. They could build on the pride of one, the greed of another, and the sense of superiority and love of being right in the last.

They looked into the more important influence of other people surrounding them, and several were chosen for targets, as they designed a campaign to take away everything, they could from each, and cast doubt and confusion. Humans were always distracted, and selfish, when they were battling their own issues. They knew just what to do.

They could poke their sharp poisoned fingers into the wounds of the team just forged in the house they watched, as each had places that had yet to be totally healed. Easy points to leverage for those who've spent the last 6,000 years manipulating and destroying the weaklings who the creator had chosen to bear his image. Oh, how they hated the ones who'd been offered salvation, when they had not.

They glared through the trees at the guardians who surrounded the home that held the warriors who'd just been promoted, and vowed to bring them down. If they couldn't get directly to those two 'chosen' ones, they'd get to them indirectly by taking down those they loved, or motivating them to take down these two. Humans had free will, but they knew how to manipulate human will. Lord Lucifer had demanded they be taken down by any means. Each trembled with fear at the thought of failure, knowing they'd have to face the serpent king just under Lucifer, if they failed.

They left to begin to brainstorm more intimate details, and create a plan to separate these two, no matter what it took. Each had old wounds they could begin to stick their sharp claws in. One, who went by the name 'misunderstanding' began to plot as he was silent among them. He grinned an evil grin. *I know how to separate them...*

Back inside the house, Maggie and Jake sat on either end of the couch with their feet beside the other, and talked long into the night, easy with their long friendship, and comfortable in their combined calling. They'd decided the rest of Maggie's revelations could wait until morning; tonight, was for planning how to create an offensive against the enemies of men's souls, how to reach others for Jesus in these end-time days, how to stand firm against the mandates coming down, and how to show people love.

They both worked in service industries already, and touched many lives, but they needed to figure out how to take it up a notch. Number 1 on Jake's list was to prepare to blow the socks off his class with the Apologetics of the proofs of the New Testament writings. Then, without getting reprimanded or fired, to parley that into discussions off-campus about the implications of the New Testament being an ancient history book, that has been proven authentic, never was proven wrong, was not refuted at the time of writing, and has more copies by far than any other ancient document.

And it says, Jesus was the son of God, who came down to be born of a virgin, live among us a perfect sinless life, performed many miracles, was killed on the cross of calvary for our sins, and was resurrected from the dead, seen by over 500 people, and rose into the air to heaven, while angels promised he'd return in like manner.

He knew he couldn't win them all; but each one he could reach would be one that escaped hell, and lived for eternity with a creator that loved him beyond all comprehension, and is preparing for us gifts that He says we can't even think up. It was worth every second of preparation, and that preparation began with more prayer by the two of them.

Riding the wave of glory already descended, they just kept praying, praising, talking, and worshipping in spirit and in truth; happy with one another's presence, instead of speaking over a phone. Each wondered what it would be like to be able to do this more often.

The Full Armor of God

Finally, be strong in the Lord and in His mighty power. Put on the full armor of God, so that you can make your stand against the devil's schemes. For our struggle is not against flesh and blood, but against the rulers, against the authorities, against the powers of this world's darkness, and against the spiritual forces of evil in the heavenly realms.

Therefore, take up the full armor of God, so that when the day of evil comes, you will be able to stand your ground, and having done everything, to stand. Stand firm then, with the belt of truth buckled around your waist, with the breastplate of righteousness arrayed, and with your feet fitted with the readiness of the gospel of peace. In addition to all this, take up the shield of faith, with which you can extinguish all the flaming arrows of the evil one. And take the helmet of salvation and the sword of the Spirit, which is the word of God.

Pray in the Spirit at all times, with every kind of prayer and petition. To this end, stay alert with all perseverance in your prayers for all the saints. Pray also for me, that whenever I open my mouth, words may be given me so that I will boldly make known the mystery of the gospel, for which I am an ambassador in chains. Pray that I may proclaim it fearlessly, as I should.

2 Corinthians 10:3-5, For though we walk in the flesh, we do not war according to the flesh, for the weapons of our warfare are not of the flesh, but divinely powerful for the destruction of fortresses. We are destroying speculations and every lofty thing raised up against the knowledge of God, and we are taking every thought captive to the obedience of Christ,

Mark 6:7, And He *summoned the twelve and began to send them out in pairs, and gave them authority over the unclean spirits;

Luke 10:19 Behold, I have given you authority to tread on serpents and scorpions, and over all the power of the enemy, and nothing will injure you.

The Ceremony

Chapter 15

"DID YOU GET THE BEER?" Billy said as he opened the door for Erwin. "You know we don't have time to go back. The rest of the guys will be here by seven. We're supposed to eat, then start the party. This is an important ceremony, and it's going to be a long one tonight."

"Yeah," Erwin slouched in the door carrying two 30 packs, and then went back for the rest. Coming back in, he sat several grey plastic bags, and one paper one, on the kitchen counter. "I got the chips, dip, pretzels, and I picked up a bottle of Jack Daniels and vodka too."

"What brand?" Billy was already looking in the bag.

"McCormick's."

"Oh, good. I hate that crap Alex always gets. I get sick every time." Billy shuddered at the memory.

"Let me grab the ice out of the back," Erwin started back out to his truck. "Hold the door; I got four."

"Hang on a minute. I forgot to get the ice chest out of the garage. I'll be right back." Billy followed him out, and turned right into the attached garage to get the container.

Carrying the extra-large cooler into the kitchen, he held the door for Erwin. "Let's put in a couple of bags, then put the beer in and add the other two on top, then grab that salt and give it a good sprinkle of that too; it'll get cold faster that way," he instructed. "That gives us an hour for it to chill, till Leroy gets here with the pizza—he better be on time too—I'm starving."

They got the beer on ice, while rescuing a couple of already chilled ones from the smaller Igloo in the back of Erwin's truck. Billy popped the metal ring on the top and at the 'psk' sound, he grinned. "I've been waiting all day to hear that." He threw back his head and drained about half the can with the first drink, then grinned again. "I'm ready to party," he shouted.

"You get the other stuff?" Erwin leaned against the counter, drinking deeply from his own can, dreading the evening. It was starting to lose its appeal, as they descended into greater levels of witchcraft. He was having a harder time going home to face his gran after.

"Oh, yeah." Billy's voice was cocky and the look on his face excited. "I got the candles, the incense, and a new bowl for the offering. I have the idols. They're solid silver. I picked up a new athame last month. This one is cool. It has a black blade, curved like a serpent, with the symbol of Hecate on the cross bar. It's wicked sweet."

"I have a picture of my grandmother also. You know she worshipped Jezebel and Molech, and was the high priestess for years with the older generation. She left the idols to me before she died. They've been handed down in my family for generations. I was chosen by her to be her spiritual heir. It's a position guaranteed by the bloodline and the idols. I'll be the high priest when I fulfill a sacred ritual obligation, but they haven't told me what that is yet. All I know is, it's coming up soon."

"Your grandmother scared me to death the first time I saw her," Erwin confessed. "We were what— under ten years old— the first time I went over there with you?"

"Yeah," Billy sniggered. "We rode our bike out there bringing her groceries from Doc's. You should have seen the look on your face when she stepped out from around that bush by the back of the house."

"Good grief," Erwin exclaimed. "She was wearing all black; her hair was coming all out of that bun she had it in, and she had a butcher knife in her hand with blood dripping off it. And that cackle... omg... I thought she was some crazed witch that escaped from a movie, that was about to kill us and eat us. She looked as bad as Freddy Kruger." He shuddered at the sudden memory.

Billy, openly laughing now, said, "she did, didn't she? I was used to her cleaning rabbits in the backyard in that black dress. She wore it because it didn't show the blood stains after she washed it. I just saw my grandma. I never really thought about what it would look like to other people until I saw your face. I took one look at you and thought something was about to get all three of us, especially when you started screaming and fell off your bike."

"I had nightmares about that cackle for years." Erwin confessed again. "When she ran over to pull my bike off me, I looked up, and with that black dress billowing out, she totally blocked out the sun. All I could see was what looked like a giant black bird holding a silver knife. I can still feel the blood drops that fell on my face. I've never in all these years been that sure I was about to die—or that terrified.

I'm telling you man, nothing in this life could ever scare me that much again. And she never stopped laughing through it all. I know she had to have known what she looked like. And she thought it was hilarious, while I was about to have a heart attack on the spot."

"Yeah, grandma always had an insane sense of humor," Billy agreed. "Stuff that other people laughed about never got so much as a smile, but let some crazy off the wall thing happen, and it put her in stitches. I miss that old lady." ... *and I've never been so glad a person was gone...*

"Me too," Erwin smiled, and said what was expected, although a huge part of him was very glad she was gone; and he'd never tell Billy he'd never really lost his fear of her. "Later, when I met her uptown in the library, I didn't even know it was her. With her hair all neat, and in that flowery blouse she wore, and so sweetly smiling, she was like a different person.

Everyone else knew her as Evelyn, the librarian; no one would have ever believed she wasn't what she appeared to be. I almost fell out of my chair when she received the certificate for being such a fine example of Christianity from the Ministerial Alliance in town. I can just picture their faces if they knew she was one of Jezebel's Maidens.

Man, I was right about one thing though, she was a witch. She taught us so much when we were teens. We'd never be into this stuff without her." *And I wish I'd never met her at all, or learned any of it.* Rapidly, as he'd been remembering that black dress and knife, he put two and two together with something Billy had just said… *it didn't show the blood stains….*

Suddenly he had a sensation of someone walking across his grave. He felt what could only be described as a 'warning' in his soul, and a strange quivering began in his belly. He heard the words *'you still have a choice'* like a whisper in his mind. It was so real he looked over his shoulder to see if one of the other guys has slipped in behind him.

Do I still have a choice after all we've done? I wonder what Gran would say? I'm so sick of all this stuff Billy insists we do. "Billy, did you guys have rabbit for dinner that night?" he asked.

"No. I remember her making vegetable stew that night, after watching our ballgame where I hit that homerun over the fence," Billy remembered. "Why?"

"No reason," Erwin answered. "I just wondered, since she'd butchered them that day. We left as soon as we gave her the grocery bags and I got back on my bike. I remember, I never pedaled so fast before in my life, as I did, headed back home that day. I almost didn't go to the ballgame."

As they talked, they started rearranging the furniture so they could get the room set up for the planned ritual. They moved the couch and chairs against the far wall, set the 2 little tables up by the side wall, and covered them with black velvet cloth, setting a silver platter on one of them; then rolled the rug up, and set it along the wall of built-in shelves, that held the tv and Billy's DVD collection and gaming items.

Erwin grimaced at the symbols painted on the floor that were usually hidden by the rug. They'd painted them there shortly after Billy bought the house, with his grandmother standing by directing. Just as they finished, they heard a truck pulling into the driveway, and before they reached the door, two more pulled in behind that one. "Okaaay," Billy drawled; "It's time to PARTY!!"

"Come on in, you guys," he yelled through the screen. "Erwin, get the door. I'll get the paper plates and plastic cups."

Five of their friends played follow the leader into the house, each carrying a load of stuff. Two carried pizzas, one had a box of chicken wings and a bag, and the other two carried more beer and various forms of alcohol.

"Did you remember the salt?" Billy asked Robert, who was carrying the bag.

"Of course," Robert stated. "Can't have a ceremony without a circle. I got an extra one too, to keep with all your stuff, in case we're ever over here and decide to do one in the moment. You usually have the other stuff. I got the right candy and flowers also. Did you get the tobacco?"

"I keep her tobacco," Billy answered. "She'd haunt me every night if I ran out of that."

They'd grown so used to doing ceremonies to Billy's grandmother to ask her advice for things, they had completely lost awareness of what they would sound like to anyone else. She'd called it ancestor worship when she was alive. Back then, they'd used a real skull that she'd sworn was from her great, great grandmother. She'd called it her personal teraphim.

Billy had long thought it was supposed to be handed down with the title and the calling, but she'd demanded to be buried with it and her black cat, Arabella, who'd been her familiar. Now he just used a skull shaped candle most of the time, with his grandmother's picture. He was careful to put the ornate crystal box with a rolled up cutting from her hair on the altar each time also. He did not want her to be offended in the afterlife if she thought he hadn't represented her well.

"Let's eat," he said, while grabbing a paper plate and opening a pizza box. He loaded his plate with pizza, salad that Eric had brought, chips, dip, and grabbed two cans of beer from the cooler, yelping as he tucked them under one arm to walk to the table. Putting salt on the ice brought the temperature down fast and the metal cans were freezing cold. Each of the others followed his lead and soon they were all around the table, eating, laughing, and picking on each other, the ways guys everywhere do.

Eventually the talk turned to the reason they'd come together for tonight's ceremony.

"Alright, Randy," Billy turned to his friend. "Is that guy at work still bothering you?"

"I'd love to say he's pulled back," Randy suddenly looked serious. "I can't believe this guy. He never stops. I've seen him taking things from the warehouse, but then he tells the boss he saw me do it. He takes credit for what I do, then blames me for his own crap. Tuesday, I really actually thought, I was going to get fired."

"What happened Tuesday?" Robert asked.

"I was putting together a new heavy-duty shelf; then I got called out back to help unload a shipment, and he said he'd finish tightening the bolts. I'd started them all to get it together, and was just about ready to start tightening them. A call came over the intercom for me to go to the shipping dock. A delivery truck had arrived and I was needed immediately because I'm the only one who can unload that type of load. It was steel rods about 30' long, and if you don't do it right, you can twist the trailer. The boss is tired of paying to get hotshot delivery guys trailers fixed, so I'm supposed to unload them all.

I came back in, and he said the shelf was ready, so I sent the forklift driver to store some pallets full of boxes of drywall screws. As soon as he put the last pallet on the top, the whole right side let loose and the entire thing collapsed. Several boxes broke open and screws went everywhere. It just missed the two guys helping the driver. It could have hurt one of them badly if they hadn't backed up as far as they did.

The supervisor asked what happened, and before I could even answer, the jerk stood there and declared I'd told him I'd finished the shelf and said it was ready to load. I called him on his crap right there in front of the supervisor, but he had this innocent, clueless, look on his face and asked me why I was lying about it. The super began to scream at me; said he was going to write me up, because I seemed to have lost my ability to do my job.

This guy stood there and smirked the whole time, standing right behind the super so I could see his face, but the manager couldn't. He enjoyed watching me get reamed out. I've been at this job over five years and had a good reputation. He comes along six months ago, and lies his ass off about everybody and everything, and gets away with it because his lies are so big, they don't even question that he's lying," he explained, getting angry all over again.

"What do the other employees do?" Eric asked.

"They're all afraid to cross this guy. The last person who tried to give the management a heads up got fired for having drugs in his locker. We all knew he didn't take drugs and tried to tell the super, but the jerk said he saw Kent put them in there the day before. He said he'd warned Kent that we weren't supposed to have drugs at work and Kent ignored him, sneering that he'd been bringing them for years, selling them to others, and hadn't been caught yet.

We all had our lockers, and even our personal vehicles, searched before we could leave that day. I'm telling you this guy is bad news. We all know it. But right now, I'm his chosen target, and as long as they're safe, they'll let me take the heat."

Waya, who'd been listening to the conversation without comment, suddenly jumped in. He was mostly full-blood native American, a mixture of Comanche and other tribes, and his name, pronounced WAH-Ya, meant 'wolf,' which was what they called him. Wolf was highly protective of the group, and had a sense of duty to retaliate against anyone who threatened any of them. A hundred years ago he would have been a fierce plains warrior, killing anyone in his path. None of them wanted to tangle with him when he was angry. They were all glad they were part of his 'pack' instead of his foes.

"That's why we call upon the spirits tonight," he quietly declared, his voice intense and humorless. "They can take care of him without putting us in danger of being labeled criminals. We will do a destroying ritual and his own behavior will boomerang back to him. We will ask the ancestors to reveal his lies, and then take him out." He slapped his hand on the table as he made his announcement, startling them all.

"What about the rule of three?" Erwin threw out. "We don't want this to boomerang back to us."

"I know a ritual that goes straight to the top," Wolf replied. "Between Billy's grandmother, and the spirits she served, and my ancestral line spirits, we have the authority to call for his demise without fear of reprisal. We may have to sacrifice more than candy, alcohol, and tobacco though," he informed them.

"And we'll have to cast a very strong circle to hold in the spirit that will come with this ritual.

You will be asked to make a greater commitment than before, and do some things they require, that you're unfamiliar with. Do not hesitate, or the spirit will kill you. It will be like nothing you've seen before." Then, looking at Billy, he added, "except for you. I believe you may have seen this prince before, with your grandmother."

Wolf and his family had attended many rituals when Billy's grandmother was alive. They were part of the old group in the coven, that had been active in the area for centuries, and in fact Wolf was a direct descendant of the highest ruling family. Family lines had kept it going long before the town was built. It was one of the things they kept to themselves.

They'd seen many things others in the group were not aware of, not even Erwin, who had been kept on the peripheral; only invited to the lesser rituals, which were more ceremonial formalities that turned into drunken parties; and ended with orgies that were no-holds-barred—where the younger women had been instructed to introduce Erwin to sex at a very young age—than actual demon worshipping sessions, with true human sacrifice.

Billy had long protected his friend from being pulled into the things he'd experienced from the age of 3 or 4; and his grandmother had been adamant that other people could not know the things that went on when only the truest old-line family members were present; not even Erwin. She'd told him stories of the ones who'd been hunted down, and murdered for being witches, including her grandparents.

Secrecy was the most important thing that kept them safe, and she'd always said that Erwin was 'special' and the time would come when he'd be invited to the greatest ceremony of all; and at that ceremony, Billy would be asked to perform a task that, when performed, would cement his position as her replacement; and that no matter what was asked of him, he must complete the ceremony, or both he and Erwin would be killed by the family members themselves; both for disobedience, and for him being soft, which equated to being a coward.

If he completed the task laid upon him, he'd be protected by the highest spirits, and have wealth and position for the rest of his life; and the ability to call upon any family member or spirit to do his bidding. His grandmother had trembled with excitement as she'd thought about the ritual, but refused to answer any more questions about what it was he was supposed to do, or why Erwin couldn't know more.

He'd been tasked with pulling Erwin closer to acceptance, by leading him deeper into alcohol and drug dependance, encouraging multiple sex partners, discouraging the Christianity his grandmother practiced; and protecting him from anyone that would harm him, or discourage him from the debauchery they were leading him into.

He loved knowing hidden things, and the superiority he felt over Erwin because he wasn't allowed to be at the higher rituals; but also knew Erwin's gentler personality would have a much harder time accepting the ritual gang rapes performed upon him by the older ones, both male and female; and the bloodletting that Billy had endured all his life.

No one, but he, Leroy, and Waya, in the group present tonight, knew about any of the rest of it. This group dabbled in the kind of witchcraft depicted in movies, but none knew the reality of what they were playing with, and Billy had his own reasons to keep it hidden; he'd be embarrassed if this group of guys knew how he'd been used by the coven members through the years, and how often he'd hidden and cried at what had been done to him; what he'd been forced to do, and how it had scarred him on the inside.

Some things you couldn't unsee or unknow. Some things changed you in ways that regular people would never understand. Billy knew Erwin would have a hard time with tonight's ceremony. It involved sex rituals, but no girls were present. It had a two-fold purpose. One, to stop Randy's harassment; two, to lead them all into further debauchery and have more reason to remain silent as they were led deeper into loyalty to the coven.

It would be a first for Erwin and the other guys, except Leroy. Billy would protect him from the worst, as always, but he'd also make sure Erwin was extremely drunk, and higher than usual, before that part began. He couldn't afford to let him balk in front of Waya.

Wolf's family had practiced ancestor worship before America was America. Their roots went all the way to the Aztecs. They were a very powerful line of shamans, including many wendigos, or shapeshifters. He'd taught Billy and Erwin many rituals and they'd heard spirits speak audibly from wispy, smoky thoughtforms they called up with their rituals. Many times, they'd seen dark entities materialize in the circles they cast and the shadows created as they moved, trying to break out of the ring delineated by the salt and strategically placed candles they were confined inside. Wolf led the rituals and they all followed his lead without hesitation.

"We can't let one of our own be harassed," he stated with finality. "In a wolf pack, one can be worn down by small attacks, and weakened by blood loss, until enough small wounds can cause you to lose your position, and eventually your life. This is how the pack brings down prey as well, because it is very effective.

When one member starts being harassed, the pack surrounds him and protects him, and then as a team, they take out the aggressor and keep the wounded one safe until he heals completely. He is forever grateful to his pack and will fight to the death to defend another member," he tutored them.

"We must become like a pack, even more so than we are. One by one we can be weakened and picked off, but together we can beat anyone. We have to think like wolves, like family. And as a family, we take a blood oath tonight to never reveal anything to outsiders. One slip and we could end up in a place we don't ever want to be. One small revelation in the right ears, and we could be imprisoned. This modern world doesn't always understand the old ways," he warned. "They serve the Christian God, who is selfish and wants to rule the world alone, instead of sharing the people like the old gods.

"Now, who is ready to take the oath?" he looked at each one intensely, and waited until each one nodded assent before moving his gaze to the next. When all had agreed, he took out his knife and slid over the crystal bowl Billy had bought. "We can put the ancestor candy and other treats on the silver plate," he stated. "Tonight, we will offer blood in the pure crystal taken from the earth. It is required for what we do. We are asking them to take out a man, so animal blood will not suffice; we need human blood.

First, we will set up our altar and do cleansing rituals, and then we will use marijuana to loosen up, and begin to open our minds to the spirit world. We must move ourselves out of the way, and give our will entirely to the spirits. We will worship the gods and our ancestors. As your shaman, I will take the sacred peyote of my ancestors, and call up the spirit we need.

He will speak thru me, but you will see him in the circle. Billy is his grandmother's heir, so he will host the spirit as the ritual progresses. Spirits miss the things they enjoyed when they walked the earth, and until they can come back, we must appease them by indulging their desires for them, or they won't do our bidding."

Billy, knowing his role well, walked over to the silver platter, handed down from generations of his family who had used it for the altar elements. He ritually set the elements on the platter. They'd turned the lights off and lit candles, and the light reflected off the silver. He set the god and goddess candles in the back, then placed the heavy solid silver god and goddess idols in front of those, slightly more toward the center. He added the chalice of wine—unknown to all but him and Wolf, it was also heavily drugged—and the silver bowl of dark obsidian glass baubles. Black was the predominate color of tonight's purpose. They were doing dark magic indeed.

On the left, he placed the incense burner, with a new stick of incense inserted, the new athame he'd bought, with its symbols and black serpentine blade, and the wand he'd made with his grandmother from the wood of the holly bushes outside her house. On the right he added a bell, a bowl filled with salt, and another of water. Then he carefully placed a highly polished silver pentacle in the center front.

He placed it the usual way, with the point of the star up, then remembered what they were about to do, and turned it so the star pointed downward, indicating black magic. Last, he added a black candle in the shape of a human skull, then lit the candles and incense, speaking in the low twilight language he'd been taught from the time he was six. He turned to Wolf, bowed low, and in a solemn formal tone, informed him that he was ready to make an offering to the ancestors, before they began the spell.

Wolf, bowed once in return, and moved to the other small table covered in a black cloth. There were photos of Billy's grandmother when she was in her 30s, a beauty with long dark hair and eyes, in her priestess robes of deep velvet red and a silver moon shaped necklace. They could see the spiderweb tattoo along her inner breast area, showing from the deep cleavage of the dress, and her lips were as red as her gown. Alongside that was another photo of his own great grandparents in their ceremonial costumes.

His grandfather wore the mask of a fierce thunderbird with feathers in his hair, buckskin pants and a grizzly bear robe that was the symbol of his totem, and carried a spear that dripped what could only be blood; his grandmother wore a beaded dress made of tanned deerskin, decorated with dyed porcupine quills sewn in intricate patterns.

Both had amulets around their necks and his grandmother had a raven on her shoulder. She held a bowl made from a human skull and Wolf had been told it contained a blood sacrifice. She had a strap that ran up around her shoulder, and down to her opposite hip, attached to a pouch that held the sacred peyote, the herbs for the incense bowl, her talismans, and her flint athame.

They together, placed bottles of alcohol, tobacco, the silver bowl of candy, and another of dried venison chunks on the table. These were the vices of their ancestors and would help entice them to appear. Ancestors were always hungry and bored, and needed to be worshipped and tempted by their appetites to appear and offer help. They were no longer interested in the world of men, and were often capricious and hard to please. If they liked the offerings, they would intervene and bring the spirit they sought.

They added a green plant that represented the family tree, a glass of water and plate of food, the swirl of Evelyn's hair, another incense burner, a small caldron with money in it to burn as a sacrificial offering, and scattered a mixture of obsidian marbles and pure clear crystals on one corner.

Wolf carefully placed a sheet of paper, with the names of their ancestors written on it, in the exact center of the table. Finally, Billy added three of the deep scarlet roses with the thorns still attached, that were his grandmother's favorite, and lit the incense and candles. Then they set the money in the caldron on fire. Now, all the elements were included.

They thanked the ancestors in advance for their knowledge and power, and asked them to intercede for them so the spirit would come. Ancestors had walked the path already and knew things mortal men could not. Their help was always sought and appreciated, as it helped them go further toward the path of godhood in this incarnation than they could alone. All sought to be gods someday, and any magic or association they could use would shorten their own path, and help them create good karma, rather than bad. If they could entice the spirits to do their bidding in this dark quest, they could avoid bad karma for themselves.

They burned some sage to clear the air of unwanted spirits, then passed around joints and glasses of whiskey and vodka. They all imbibed freely for over an hour; laughing and getting progressively looser; Billy turned on some eerie music with a heavy drum beat and Wolf began to chant. Having ingested the peyote and consuming his share of the booze, he became high and excited, anticipating what was about to take place, and began to chant louder.

His chants took on a new cadence and he began to sing an ancestral song of his people, dancing around in a slow circle as he entered an alternate state of consciousness, shaking a gourd filled with sand that had been handed down, and his eyes began to look wild. He lit a pipe filled with tobacco, and inhaling deeply, he blew smoke in all four directions, then gestured to Robert and Erwin to cast the circle.

They took the box of salt and following the painted pattern on the floor, created a circle about six feet across, then added a five-pointed star in the center, all points touching the circle. Eric and Randy then added lit black pillar candles at all the stars points, and the dancing caused the flames to dance as well, throwing strange shadows on the walls around them that moved and bent as they did, only they were strangely elongated from the angles of the candle light, as the air moved the flames. Leroy began to place other candles, in various phallic shapes, around the room, along with others, some too vulgar to describe, and a chill went down Erwin's spine as he saw them. He shot a look at Billy, who refused to meet his eyes, and wanted to leave, but knew he couldn't after Waya had begun the ceremony.

Waya brought the new crystal bowl to the edge of the table, called the others over and then placing his wrist over the bowl, he made a small cut on the inside of his arm. Immediately blood began to drip and he held his arm over the bowl allowing the sacred liquid to drip into it. When the bleeding slowed, he brought his wrist to his mouth and kissed it, then smeared it in a diagonal line across his face, first on one side, then the other, then once more per side, causing him to look even more like a reincarnated warrior from another time; then licked the rest until it stopped.

As the blood entered his mouth, he shuddered like he was being shaken by something much bigger than him, then once again threw back his head, and a howl that could only have come from an animal came pouring from his throat, long and sustained. He shimmered slightly, and the others saw the wolf spirit that inhabited him imposed upon his visage, like a faint double exposure in an old movie.

He then called upon the others by name to come to him, repeating the cut with each one, and each added his own blood to the bowl. He called upon the spirit he wanted to force to do his bidding, and offered the bowl of blood held high to show they were willing to sacrifice of their own lifeforce in a trade for the demon prince to do their evil work.

Wolf stirred in more potent drugs, mingling their blood with the intoxicant, and murmuring magic words, that would bind them together, then offered the chalice to each for a sup of the bitter potion. After the drugs it contained began to take effect, Wolf again held the bowl of blood to each in turn, and each again imbibed the forbidden substance.

The drugs and alcohol were putting them all into the state needed for the spirits to come, and the less informed men to accept what was about to happen. Wolf and Billy began to strip down to their underwear, encouraging the other guys to do the same. When all had done so, Wolf threw back his head and howled. It again, sounded much like his namesake, and sent shivers down the spines of them all. He howled and howled, his dancing growing frenzied, and then stopped dancing suddenly; standing absolutely still. His eyes rolled back in his head, showing just the whites. His head began to shake violently as his whole body trembled. He took off his final garment and instructed them to do so as well.

He uttered dark words in a twilight language, and they all began to call on their ancestors and the spirits for power and knowledge. They stared at the moving flames until they began to sink into the light, descending into an altered state of consciousness too. Wolf placed his finger into the bowl of blood, then, starting with Billy, drew ancient symbols upon each man's body, including intimate places; encouraging them to accept his touch there, and each in turn felt the spirits enter them as he did so; and then it was as if they were spectators inside their own mind, sitting on the sidelines, while another entity took over.

They worshipped the entities, and Wolf felt more and more power enter him, as they drew down the moon, tapping into all the stored power from the many people throughout millennia that had worshipped these same gods.

They watched as Wolf and Billy began the sex ritual; at first shocked at what they were witnessing, then excited by the live porn enacted in front of them; then, in their inebriated and drugged state, with lowered inhibition, they were individually approached and drawn into the actions. They took turns doing shameful acts among themselves in 2's, 3's, and as a group, as the spirits' lust filled them.

Erwin suddenly remembered his grandmother saying 'lust is the desire of demons acted out through men.' With no women present they acted it out as it was done in the ancient city of Sodom. The spirits who inhabited them, were the same spirits who had led men into such debauchery since anti-diluvian days; and they entered a new level of bondage as they enacted the acts that God called abomination.

Usually, their worship was with the entire coven and it included women; but now they were being introduced to the more-evil acts of worshipping the fallen ones; who were determined to change all that God had made to be good, into the most demeaning version possible. Homosexuality was always part of the ritual when a Nephilim spirit was called up.

It was necessary to sear their souls even more, so they would continue to allow themselves to be lead further into what was required, when worshipping the ancient pantheon of pagan gods; it was an age-old step-by-step descent into ancient paganism; until they would do anything for pleasure and power; and be so immersed in the ways of evil, they would find themselves unable to ever escape.

It had been instilled in Wolf, Billy, and Leroy, who also came from the coven families, from birth to keep the secrets. Most married from within the group, and until they did marry, they left anyone else they dated in the dark about their true religion. Most in the covens were even members of the local churches, like Evelyn.

Some, like Erwin, had accidently learned the truth from being close to a family member; slowly groomed for a pre-determined purpose; and had either joined the group, been silenced by fear and threats, or silenced by elimination. The group had been here too long to be exposed by carelessness.

As the drugs began to take more of a hold, they felt a wind blow around them. With the wind came a deep rumbling growl. They turned their intoxicated gaze toward the circle and beheld the entity that appeared inside it. It was almost ten feet tall, had equine legs with hooves instead of human lower legs and feet, two horns that curved down over its back, and a tail.

Its head was impossibly large with a sagittal crest that ran down into its back, with stiff black hair standing up along the top, and a face that was pure evil; and it was not happy to be summoned. The muscles along its huge arms and back rippled as if independently alive; and Erwin wasn't sure it was really moving, or just a visual effect from the wavering candlelight, as it growled through its saliva dripping mouth. In an impossibly deep voice, it growled viciously, "Why have you summoned me?"

Wolf stepped closer to the circle, but stayed well out of range for it to be able to reach him. He beckoned to Randy. "We need an enemy exposed and destroyed." Randy, trembling violently, spoke his request, having been coached beforehand on what to say, although he was horrified by the creature before him.

"I know that," the enormous demon roared, his voice thunderous and echoing off the walls, with saliva thrown everywhere as he screamed, "What do you have to offer in return?"

"We have offerings." Wolf swept his hand toward the tables, then held up the bowl. "And we offer our life essence to you, oh prince of darkness. We offer our allegiance to the spirit of complete freedom to 'do what thou wilt' without restraint or fear. We offer our worship. We offer our bodies for you to, once again, experience the lust you are now denied."

He sat the bowl just inside the circle, being careful to not smudge the line of salt. The hideous creature picked it up in his enormous hands, drained it with one long drink, and sailed the bowl back through the air to Wolf, who caught it with one hand and, without looking, sat it back on the table behind him.

The awful being licked his lips and said, "that's a start. I require more. I want a baby. Nothing is as good as a newborn human sacrificed to me. You must promise that the firstborn male from this group will be mine," he screamed, thick saliva, with a putrid smell, splattering them with each word. He looked around at the seven men, his nostrils flaring as he evaluated each in turn. His eyes were a deep yellow, glowing like they were lit from within; a sickly yellow that was the opposite of cheerful, but rather, sulphureous, like the stench that arose from him.

All nodded their heads; only Erwin hesitated, but he knew better than to refuse. Even in his drugged state, deep inside himself he suspected they would kill him if he did. Billy, Wolf, and Leroy had seen child sacrifice many times and that's why Billy had paid for more than one abortion. He was determined to never have a child of his own. The others weren't so happy about it either, but were also too terrified to let that truth be known.

His gaze fixed on Randy. "You are the recipient of my power, are you not?"

"Yes." Randy trembled even more under the closer inspection. He'd enjoyed the prior ceremonies and the drunken parties, but had never imagined it'd come to this. He was terrified by what he'd allowed to be set in motion. He hated the guy at work, but he never expected to be face-to-face with a real demon, and he wasn't sure what was about to happen, but he already knew it would change him forever.

"Then, I will have you first tonight," the awful being screamed, spittle still flying everywhere, with long strings of mucus still attached to his gaping orifice. His scrutiny turned to Billy, sensing the familiar spirit in him, and recognizing both it and the ancient markings painted on his body, saying he was the host for tonight's fun; he smiled, "I will use your body; allow me to enter now."

"Yes, I allow it," Billy acquiesced, as he had so many times before. He took another few hits from the weed, swallowed a long draught from the Jack Daniels bottle and then purposely tried to enter the dissociative state he'd learned long ago, that took him to a deeper level of altered consciousness, and protected him from the worst of what was about to happen.

This time though the spirit forced his mind to stay present as he entered him and Billy was completely aware of his body and surroundings, feeling everything, while unable to block out or influence anything. He felt his entire body, but the control over it was the beast's. He felt the demon's power and strength become his own. He experienced the wickedness inhabiting him and the demon's desire also became his own. He laughed a laugh that terrified the others, especially Randy. His body rose anew in anticipation with the lust the demon suddenly flooded his senses with.

He beckoned Randy to himself, then, lost in the demented desire of the kingdom of darkness, he performed acts far worse than they had carried out earlier; acts he had never performed before, brutalizing Randy, while the demon/Billy combination laughed at each desecration; each scream bringing a new level of delight, leaving long claw marks etched into Randy's back, licking the blood as it poured out.

The other's watched in horror, but were soon caught up in the desire it ignited in the spirits that resided in them, and soon all offered their self to the dark entity. They had done rituals for some time now, and had experienced sexual acts of many kinds; they'd allowed themselves to be drawn into the deviancy of the prior hour as well, but nothing compared to this.

It was savage. It was intoxicating. It was damaging, but the most damaged was Randy. The evil creature took great pleasure in inflicting as much physical damage as possible on him, and the men that didn't already belong to the coven weren't fully aware that they had entered a new dimension of bondage. They'd gone from dabbling in witchcraft, to demon worship, to demon possession.

They'd made a contract with a demon to kill a human, and sealed it with blood, and an abominable act twisted from what God had ordained for a marriage bed between a man and a woman; and were now bound to a demon. It was a marriage made in hell, as they would soon find out.

Filled with the lust of the demonic entities inhabiting them, all got a thrill from being high and clouting convention, and as each took turns playing the male and female roles, both their human male hormone, and demon driven lusts, were eventually satiated. Each had their conscious seared and dulled far beyond what it already had been. They would have a hard time hearing the voice of God or the truth spoken by a believer, and would be all but unable to read the bible.

They'd basically sold their soul to the devil. All but Erwin. The entity they'd summoned knew his upcoming role, and had been instructed to protect him as much as possible, so that when the time came, he'd be less jaded, as innocent as he could be at that stage, and more capable of experiencing the true horror they had planned for so long.

He needed to maintain the horror of evil until it was time, so it would have more effect on him; and the demon made his turn as pleasurable as possible, with no damage, and did not invade his mind at all. After all he'd been through, he wasn't innocent; but they needed him as close to it as possible, so they could extract exquisite revenge from those who had spurned them for so long.

The demon shivered in anticipation of the coming day. It had been a while since he'd had one from the enemy family line in his grip, and only upon direct orders from Lucifer himself, could he contain himself from ripping him to pieces tonight.

He allowed Billy to believe he'd been the one to protect Erwin, because he also needed to be unprepared for what was coming very, very, soon. Ahhhh...the ripping apart of human bodies and minds... how he longed to walk the earth again, so he could experience it with his own body anytime he wanted, like in the pre-flood days.

As the candles burned down, the demons departed for their abode in another dimension, leaving the men exhausted, depleted, and most of them bleeding. They lay all around the floor for a while, too inebriated to drive; then gradually departed with the ones they came with, mostly unashamed. Billy went to bed. He'd clean up in the morning.

The ritual had been a success. The bond of silence was strengthened, as none would ever tell anyone else what they'd participated in. Each knew it was wrong on every level. All men had God's law written on their hearts, but now it would be far harder to understand it. Most had never intended to ever become involved in something that bad, but each decision had led a short path to another, then another, then another, until they were so caught up in the normalizing of what they were practicing, that they were in it, drugged out of their mind, and trapped by the hold on their desires—until even sexual acts with each other, or a demon, and brutalizing another human—were acceptable.

And, while they didn't know it yet, the horrendous acts had awoken a level of desire that forever after, unless they repented, would render any normal act of sex too mild to compete with it, and would leave them unfulfilled. They'd spend their life seeking that level of excitement again, and only the demonic realm, and all its evil, could bring it to them. They were truly caught by violence and the pleasure of the experience, and the strength of the secret they all shared. The enemy had caught men and women in the same trap for millennia.

Only one was left with a feeling of shame and disgust, even as he reluctantly participated. As he left, he remembered the whisper in his mind earlier, and wondered if he still had a choice. If he left the group now, they'd never trust him not to tell, and he might very well forfeit his life. And if he stayed, evil would consume him.

The path had never been laid out so plainly before him, and he understood he would not be able to come back if he stayed. He'd been drawn in as a child and it had led to this moment. He had no idea how to back out of it, but in that moment wished he did, and wished he'd done so long before this night. He remembered something his grandmother had often said: *"Sin will take you further than you ever meant to go, and keep you longer than you ever meant to stay."*

He thought about his grandmother witnessing what had just taken place, and his own part in it, including the enjoyment. Suddenly, he saw it for what it really was—a total abomination in the eyes of God—and was profoundly impacted. His mind spun at the filth, the tawdriness, the hopelessness of being caught in a web so vile. *How did you move from that into a normal marriage and a normal life? How did you ever not know you were capable of such things?*

He wasn't sure if there was a heaven, but after tonight he was very sure there was a hell, and he was headed there on a downhill slide that was picking up speed. He sobered up as he drove home. Somehow, he had to get out; but Billy was his best friend, and he'd lived in this town his entire life. How he could make that happen he had no idea; right now, it seemed impossible. If there was a God, like his grandmother believed, he silently wished he'd rescue him.

Although not quite a prayer, the door had been cracked enough to cause rejoicing from the one who watched over him. He knew the throne room had been alerted, and called upon more warriors to surround Erwin; offering him a deeper level of protection, for a brief time, to give him a chance to call upon the Lord, before it was too late.

He pulled his sword from its scabbard, and blue flame erupted as he and the other warriors fought off the demonic hoard with their claws dug into Erwin. Many were cut into pieces and vanished in a cloud of sulfurous smoke as they sent them straight to the abyss, their screams echoing behind them as the pieces fell into outer darkness.

Erwin felt the darkness surrounding him retreat a little, pulled into a side road, and sat for a time. Although he was ashamed before a Holy God, he whispered into the darkness, "if there's a way out, can you show me? If my grandparents are right about you, will you help me... please...?"

...and all heaven rejoiced, and the guardians of others were alerted, so the rescue mission could be done....

His guardian grinned at the warrior beside him, "told ya, he'd come around. Let's route these blasphemous defectors, and give him a buffer zone."

A Grief Shared, Is A Wound That Heals

Chapter 16

MAGGIE WOKE TO THE sound of birds chirping. She opened her eyes to the light coming into the room between the curtains she'd decided not to close last night. It'd been almost 2:00 when they'd finally decided they simply had to go to bed, or fall over asleep on the couch. Being up talking at that time was nothing new for them, but being in the same house was, and the talk was more intense due to the topics.

The presence of the Holy Spirit had been so strong in the room that they'd both hated to break it, and just past midnight, the Lord had led them to pray for someone bound by the enemy; to pray for him to hear the voice of the Lord and choose freedom. The day's tasks, the exhaustion from hours of pouring out praise and worship, the hours discussing it all—and to be totally honest—bodies that were over 40 years old, led to instant sleep.

She'd slept deep and well, and couldn't even remember turning over. It was easier to sleep when there was another person in the house; somehow, she didn't feel quite as vulnerable here, with him. Jake's presence felt so safe, it made her feel completely protected. Most nights she was always listening for any sound of an intruder, or to just the overwhelming silence that constantly reminded her of how alone she was; and with the world falling into sin such as in 'the days of Noah,' she was feeling increasingly unsafe.

It must be close to 8, she decided. Occasionally on the weekends, she slept in, and had trained herself to know about what time it was by the amount of light and the angle of its slant coming into the room. She could be off here though, in a different house. She often practiced guessing, and watching when the light hit different parts of her bedroom, and then peeking at the time. Now, she guessed first, and when she checked the clock, she was within 15 minutes most of the time. If it was a rainy day sometimes it fooled her for a few brief seconds, unless she heard the storm or heavy rain.

It's funny the games you play with yourself when you live alone, she reflected. *I guess it's just part of your mind filling in for the absence of people. A way to compensate and stay sane in the silence.* Maybe that's another reason why they'd been so reluctant to go to bed earlier last night. They'd confessed their loneliness on other occasions and had made a pact that anytime it got too much to bear, they could call, no matter the time.

They'd taken each other up on the offer on numerous occasions. This last year it seemed that they'd spent most hours on the phone throughout the nights, just not wanting to be alone. At first, she'd thought it would gradually get easier, but instead, it seemed to get worse, each lonely day more empty feeling than the last. Maggie loved what she did for a living, but working alone, with people she seldom saw again, made her feel invisible while watching others live.

Everywhere she looked, there were families, couples, friends; mothers and daughters, and grandchildren. Each time a pang of loss echoed in her heart. No matter what kind of hope for the future she managed to hang onto, she understood there were just some things you couldn't get back.

Without Jake, and the others from her prayer group, and the alliance members, she wondered what life would be like; and once again was grateful for each of them. Throwing off the beautiful quilt Jake's mother had made, she stopped and admired it in the morning light. The traditional log cabin design featured squares, alternating from dark to light, that created an optical illusion that almost looked 3-D. The deep colors of brick red, offset by lighter calico, in shades of camel on one side and a deep cream for the other side, were stunning.

Pieced together with a lighter, richer cream background that made each square stand out made it something to behold. The sunshine reflecting off the creams made it take on a slightly golden hue that was something she'd love to paint someday. She knew there was a matching one in blue, and softer blue and green calico, offset with shades of gray, in Jake's room. She picked up a corner and ran her hands over the intricate stitching, marveling at the tiny even threads.

Jake's mother had been a true artist, no matter the medium. Cooking, quilting, painting, crocheting, knitting, her wedding planning business; whatever she'd undertaken, she'd set her own stamp of individuality into a craftmanship that created masterpieces. She'd loved to gift others with the things she made, and they all loved being the recipient. Jake's family had become her own the last few years. She loved spending time with the rowdy bunch, and each of them were artists and/or musicians as well. She fit in well with their zany humor, artistic bents, and downhome simple ways.

She readied herself for the day, and hoping Jake wouldn't mind, went downstairs in her favorite forest green sweat suit. It was a bit chilly this morning, and she was still tired and just wanted the comfort. She smiled when she turned the corner into the kitchen. He was sitting there drinking coffee in a version very similar in dark blue.

He glanced up, and chuckled, "Well, I see you got the dress code memo. I was hoping you'd gotten it in time."

"It's Saturday," Maggie reminded him. "It's my standard weekend uniform. I have to dress in business casual all week, and I just can't do it on the weekends. A girl's gotta have a break sometime."

"That's how I feel too," he agreed. "Professors don't always have to wear a suit and tie anymore, and khakis and loafers help, but I'm still a bum at heart, I guess. I think I'll always revert to relaxed at home. Especially on these damp mornings. Here, let me get you some coffee. That helps too," he started to rise.

"Nonsense," Maggie waved him back down. "I'll get it. Stay seated. I'll just be a minute. Do you want yours topped off?"

"Sure," He handed her his almost empty cup. Do you mind putting in a bit of milk?"

"Not at all. Do you have honey? That's all I use in mine." She took his cup and began walking around the counter.

"I know. I've been making your coffee for years. It's right by the coffeemaker. I got it out already; I knew you'd need it," he added, without looking up from his laptop.

Maggie smiled at the easy familiarity. No one had ever cared to put the honey for her coffee out for her before, or even remembered that's the way she liked it; but Jake had done that from the first time she'd had coffee there, after her initial request.

"Do you think you can get the cook to make omelets?" she asked.

"Sure thing," he laughed. "Hotel 'Lazy Comfort Food' at your service."

"Oh, wonderful!" Maggie clapped. "I can just be lazy today and not have to worry about it."

Jake grinned, "I thought we could have coffee and chat; then cook later. I know you had something to share. Feel free to let me know when the time is right, but free to not share if you don't want to. I re-sent the email. The others aren't coming until 5, but I asked Sharon and Rachel to come at 1. I think they need to sit in on tonight's meeting also. So, that gives us until 1-ish; probably 1:15, knowing those two."

"That's the truth," Maggie agreed. "I've never seen either of them be on time for anything. Is there any particular reason you asked them today? They're not part of our bible study group. Are they coming earlier so we can just visit first, or is there something else?"

"Cover story," he deadpanned. "Can't have the group knowing you stayed over alone with me, now, can we?" he teased her.

"At my age I don't usually ask for permission if I want to stay overnight somewhere," Maggie laughed, "but thank you, Sir Galahad."

"Actually, there's something I need to share with all of you. It's something private that no one else knows, but the time may come when you need to know. Just the three of you for now. But later, I may need to share it with a few more, like Matt and Levi, and my brothers," he explained.

"I see." She had no idea what he could need to tell them, but it was certainly something interesting by the look on his face.

She sat his filled mug before him, then slid into the opposite chair with her own. She took a drink, and sat her cup down. "That is so good. I don't function properly until I have a cup or two."

"Me either. I'll miss coffee if this supply chain gets cut off completely. I've laid in a good amount, but without the ability to get more, it will eventually run out. That's when society will really see violence. I think most of us only function with any sense of reasonableness after 2-3 cups. Me, I drink the whole pot, then get more at the college lounge."

"I can just see the history books in a couple hundred years," Maggie quipped. "When the coffee supply dried up, the people went mad; it was a true zombie apocalypse."

"You think we're bad; you ought to see 100 twenty-year olds with their special Starbucks. I'd like to just sell the Styrofoam cups. I'd make a mint."

"How has life changed so much in so short a time. My parents and grandparents always drank coffee, but I didn't until I was in my 30's when you challenged me at the alliance meeting. Kids, teens, and young people didn't in my world. Now, you see all ages with that Starbucks cup." She opened her bible as she spoke. "I'm glad I was never tempted to start buying that stuff; God knows, it's getting harder just to pay for the 3# containers and make it at home."

"I could never get past the image of the goddess on the cup and the logo," he confessed. "It amazes me how much paganism is in the logos of so many of our name brands."

"...and the church stayed silent," she agreed.

"They didn't just stay silent," Jake grumbled, "they led the pack in supporting it all. Look at the coffee stations in churches now. And God help you if you mention it's not what we need in our foyer."

"Try to tell them what the symbolism means," Maggie sighed. "Every time I've tried to teach a class on symbolism, I'm told, I'm 'legalistic,' 'old-fashioned,' or 'ridiculous.' It's not just the ignorance that gets me; it's the appalling apathy. When I first started having a hunger for the Word, and a desire to truly understand it, I had a wonderful teacher. He knew so much I'd never heard.

He walked me thru the elements of false religion, paganism, and its practice, and showed me how it was all around us, including the church. I was astounded, and shocked. I wanted to share it with everyone and together we could set the bar for stamping it out. How stupid I was to think it would be so simple.

BOOK 1: "PREPARE FOR THE END" SERIES

I just couldn't fathom that no one cared. How could they not care?"

Having had many versions of this conversation by now, Jake, with a brooding look on his face, watched her ire; enjoying her passion, while giving an understanding nod. "It would be easy to say we're just dinosaurs, Maggie; but the plain truth is the world—including the church—is turning after the evil one, and sin is rising daily. The church is being prepared for the One-World Church and we are already where John 16:2 is a possibility right here in America.

'They shall put you out of the synagogues: yea, the time cometh, that whosoever killeth you will think that he doeth God service.'"

"They are killing people's reputation, now, with their backbiting and gossip," Maggie looked sad. "I get so sick of it. Those that refuse to be good Bereans would rather tear you down and trample you under their feet, than study to show themselves approved; a workman that doesn't need to be ashamed. It's upside down. There was a time when those who were knowledgeable about the bible were respected.

If you didn't have an understanding yourself, you at least, appreciated those who did. Now it's supposed to be something you need to be ashamed of. I can still hear that horrid woman last year, looking at me with her pursed-up mouth, with all the disdain she could possibly attach to the words: 'Oh, you're the scholar I've been hearing about.' It couldn't have sounded a worse indictment if she'd substituted the word prostitute."

"You should have decked her." His shortness showed his own ire at Maggie being disrespected.

"Yeah, that would have gone over well," she snickered. "You're starting to sound like Matt and Bobby."

"It's going to get worse you know," he grumbled, his look now grim, as he thought about it. "It's already worsening by the day. It's exponential. We've crossed over in the birth pangs to the time of 'transition' where absolutely nothing will stop it. This baby is going to be born. Period."

"It's like what the people in my Narcissistic Abuse Syndrome meetup, and I, lived," Maggie calmly spoke. "Lucifer, and his minions are the ultimate Narcissists. It's classic DARVO."

"DARVO?" Jake looked puzzled. "what's that?"

"Deflect, Attack, Reverse the Victim and Offender," she explained. "They do something off-the-chart awful, but before they do, they start sowing doubt about you. Then, they accuse you, of what they are in fact doing; and when you protest, they make *you* look like the liar, while they take on the role of the victim. It's a classic bait & switch, where they 'flip the script' and now you are the abuser, and they get all the mercy and the 'flying monkeys' hover around them to protect them from the big, bad, boogieman—You—the true victim.

It makes me crazy. I spend 95% of my time teaching my group how to recognize what's really happening to them, and how to combat it." It was the first time she'd ever spoken about her class, other than a casual mention.

"Wow," Jake calmly stated; "how did you learn to recognize it, Mags?" *Will she even tell me?* She'd just described his ex-wife.

"It took a while." She looked at him with a quiet strength, resolved to tell him some of what she'd lived through. "I fell for it for almost 20 years in marriage to a personality disordered person; but it started in childhood with abusive, neglectful parents, and siblings that I wouldn't learn until much later were also disordered. I was always the bad guy. The clinical definition is 'the scapegoat.'

I'd never heard of Narc Abuse. I'd never heard of a personality disorder. I filtered everything through the person I am. I would never do that to someone, so I assumed no one else would either. I was in my early 30s before learning my sister was Bi-Polar. My other sister will never be diagnosed, but she's worse.

Jake, that's part of what I'd like to share with you. There are some things I've only talked about with my counselor; and some things I've never even told her. A few nights ago, I was helping my group learn to open up, and speak about their experience. How, as long, as it's trapped inside you, you never fully heal. Part of the process is telling your story. It helps you accept that it did happen, and your memory isn't faulty.

When you endure Narcissist Abuse you've been gaslighted to the point that you can't tell up from down. Your memory is completely opposite of what the abuser has convinced you happened. They make you believe it's your fault; that you caused it; or that it never happened at all; even when you both know he is lying, he still convinces you that you are the liar.

That creates an unbelievable shame. You don't want anyone to know. There is a total cognitive dissonance that is very hard to overcome. Especially, because when you do try to talk about it, no one will listen. You're told 'it wasn't that bad;' or to 'just let it go;' or my personal favorite, 'you have to forgive.' I remember, early on in my healing, I heard one of the experts say "anyone who lived this has had their mind, will, and emotions put in a blender for several years; and anyone who tells them those phrases, or ones like them, is putting them back in the blender."

That one sentence helped me tremendously. It was freeing and gave me permission to be as damaged as I was, but not to take on the responsibility for it. I could just acknowledge being damaged and move toward healing at my own pace. I could shut off the condemning voices and begin to believe myself and my memories of what happened. I began to put a time-line together and work out the truth. I wrote truth where it needed to be written, if only for me.

As I studied personality disorders and Narcissistic abuse, and began to understand exactly what had happened to me, I stopped accepting any blame—from others or from myself. I had to understand that I was a true victim of a very disordered person. Then, I could move from being a victim to being an overcomer, and a person strong and knowledgeable enough to never allow it to happen to me again. I learned about 'victim shaming' and that helped free me as well.

I found a book that explained it all, and it made all the difference. PTSD is bad, C-PTSD is worse, and has, to be healed for you to move forward. Many people with C-PTSD are misdiagnosed and then you are once again blamed for your issues. It causes more damage. Women, especially, are diagnosed as having borderline personality disorder, when it's really trauma that you've endured for a very long time that is the issue, not your own bad behavior and choices. I had endured a lot of counseling, but not 'healing-from-trauma' counseling. That's what I really needed, and when I received it, I began to recover.

That's what I help others do. I help them uncover the trauma, and then show them how to heal from it. How to stop beating themselves up, and put the responsibility where it belongs—on the perpetrator. You also have to let go of all the false beliefs they've convinced you and everyone around you, about who you are. Sometimes that's difficult. I found a very good book on Trauma Therapy. I read it much later, but realized as I read it that I had been unknowingly following his therapy modal for myself and others. I learned why it worked."

"Why did it take you so long to speak about it?" he was truly perplexed about that in many abused people who he'd encountered, including himself. It was almost like each had entered a 'pact of silence.' *I wonder if she could teach me? I've never been never be able to speak about what happened...*

"When the abuse starts in childhood, you learn early on to not speak about it. Many of us are told that if we tell, we will get hurt, our siblings will get hurt, or someone will die. We've been told *we* made the perpetrator do the harm. So, it's our fault; and if we tell, and they have to hurt the threatened person or people—because we told—that will be our fault too.

Telling your story frees you from that fear. It helps you lose the shame that keeps you from wanting anyone to know, and the fear that if something bad happens, it's your fault. It helps you stop protecting the perpetrator, and best of all, it stops you from being a victim.

Jake, I 'kept the secrets' my entire life. I gave him—and led others as well, to give him—the respect he never deserved, while he decimated my life and my relationship with my kids. The people in my meetup group all do—or have done—the same thing. One of the hardest parts of therapy is to tell it like it is. Or was. And I've realized, that for as much as I've learned to speak, some of the harder things have never been told.

For me to move forward into even deeper healing, and 'clean house' so to speak, I need to share it. It's things I will never share with the group, or possibly anyone else, but I feel with this new calling, I need to have it known, so the enemy can't blackmail me by threatening to tell my deepest shame. Do you think you can hear it?" she finished.

Jake had been listening quietly, her words hitting harder than she knew, and now he reached over and took her hand, "You've carried this alone for far too long. I can hear whatever you need to say, and Mags, you know it won't go any farther. I knew you had the meetup, but I had no idea the things you were helping people with. I'm amazed. To overcome so much, and then turn around and help others begin to overcome it, is a testimony to not only your strength and courage, but also to your love for other hurting people, and your gift for healing others.

It's not just your gift of discernment that helps you see their need, it's also the deep empathy you have, and the shared experiences." *I need to tell her; but how do you tell a woman like Maggie, something like that?*

"Thank you, Jake," Maggie felt comforted by his words. "There're many things I will share with you, but it will have to come as I'm able. Unfortunately, there are still things that trigger me and the PTSD tries to take over. I know now, how to sit in it for a bit and figure out what is triggered, and why, but it still takes its toll on me.

When I called you for coffee yesterday, I had been triggered. I couldn't speak it then, but I needed you. I realized, part of the pain that overwhelmed me, was the outrage I'm now able to admit and discuss; but also, the silence I've been trapped in for over 20 years; and honestly longer than that when you factor in my parents and their abuse. I just need to say it to another human being, so it can lose its hold over me. To speak it out loud starts the ball rolling. It's like unlocking a door that can now open. and the closet can be cleaned. As long, as the door stays shut and locked, it stays inside you."

Jake remembered the way she'd looked when they had coffee. He'd known then she was upset, but not why. He kicked himself for not canceling his class and staying with her longer. "Can you open the door?" *I hope she trusts me enough to let me help her with this; she's carried it long enough, and this is what causes those times when she shuts down completely. I understand that all too well.*

"I have to." Maggie closed her eyes, and he saw her shoulders rise as she took a deep breath, then slowly let it out and opened them. He saw the deep shadow of pain cross her face, as she took a second deep breath. "The loss of a child always hits home," she spoke softly, eyes filling with tears. "I lost a baby girl. She was born too early, but she was damaged and never had a chance."

"I knew you'd lost a child," he shared. "Was there more to it?"

"Yes," she looked at him with a long gaze, and he saw the open wound in her eyes, as she remembered. "I was almost eight months pregnant, and my husband punched me in the stomach one night, while I was asleep. It caused me to go into early labor. She was born the next morning, and lived a week. She had brain damage… and Jake…" *Can I tell him the rest? Can I truly trust him with my deepest shame?*

He saw the wound deepen and widen, as he watched her tormented face. *I could kill that sorry creep.*

"I had a huge purple bruise on my stomach, and when they asked me what happened, especially with her brain damage, I lied. He was standing right there and I lied. I covered for him, because he made me." She was openly weeping now. "He killed my child, and I covered for him."

Jake pushed his chair back and came around the table, pulled her up, and wrapped her in his arms, rocking her and stroking her hair. He was sick at what she'd endured. "It wasn't your fault, Mags; it wasn't your fault." When she'd cried a while, she wiped her eyes and sat back down, grateful for his presence.

"When I work with people in my narc abuse meetings, I hear similar stories all the time. It's part of the abuse and trauma. We have endured so much, and never said a word. It's like they mesmerized us. They do the most diabolical things, then treat us as though we are the problem. We make excuses and just carry on. Then, when we do start to tell, much later, no one believes us; and I can assure you, no one wants to hear it. It deepens the trauma and the shame.

It's part of what traps us. It's very hard to believe we were really a victim and not at fault, because we were convinced, we were to blame, the entire time. Many people treat us like we are just having a pity party and condemn us. They have no idea how hard it was to speak up and tell the truth. Or how long the healing takes, or that the scars never go away, even after healing.

He came to the hospital several times every day. Crying, fluffing my pillows, getting me water. All the nurses were amazed at how tender and solicitous he was. He begged the doctors to save her, saying he'd take care of her the rest of her life; and when no one else was in the room, he sat in the chair, and smirked with satisfaction that he was getting away with it. He repeatedly told me he couldn't wait for the 'sniveling brat' to die, so I could come clean up the mess he made by dropping the pot of soup I'd left in the refrigerator.

They all said they wished they had a husband like him... and I never said a word... he sat there and grinned that self-satisfied grin the whole time, eating it up. It wasn't until much later I learned the term 'psychopathic smirk.' He was diagnosed a psychopath later, but there was no proof to show my children when I finally had to tell them the truth.

I can still remember her tiny face, and how she cried. She cried every minute she was awake, until they let me hold her. We knew she was dying, so they wrapped her in a pink blanket and let me hold and rock her. I was simply devastated; and I felt, as her mother, I'd let her down. She wasn't even born yet, and I let him hurt her. I held her until the very end. When she stopped breathing, I thought I'd die too; but no matter how much I willed it to, my heart wouldn't stop beating.

I cried for months, but he would get so mad. He'd scream at me, 'Are you crying over that brat again? You better knock it off. It's over. We didn't need another mouth to feed. I can make another one any damn time I want.' It was horrible. And then, the people who thought I'd done something wrong, and the looks they gave me. Jake, I felt like a criminal, and I didn't even do it.

He told them I'd been climbing a ladder to get sweets off the top shelf of the pantry where he'd hidden them from me to keep me from eating them all day long—a total lie—and that I'd fallen off, and hit the top of the table near the shelf. That's what he made me tell the ER doctors and nurses, and he just kept telling it to everyone. Jake, I didn't eat one thing I wasn't supposed to. And I never ate sweets much before, during, or after the pregnancy."

BOOK 1: "PREPARE FOR THE END" SERIES

"Oh, Maggie," Jake was shocked at her words. Now he was beginning to understand her careful reserve around people and the deep sadness he'd observed many times. "I had no idea. But, please understand, you didn't *let* him hurt her. He is a very sick person. You were a victim as much as your child was. Was that the extent of his violence?"

Maggie dropped her head in shame, and a very soft answer came, "No," she began crying in earnest, and he could barely hear her words, "he punched me in the stomach again, with the next pregnancy, at 3 months. He knew if I had another damaged child in the later months, it'd be a red flag, so he did it sooner. I miscarried, but everyone just thought I had a hard time carrying babies. He beat me in my kitchen, pummeling my stomach, and when the bleeding started, he refused to take me to the hospital or let me call an ambulance. He left, taking my car keys and our phones with him; and I lost my second child, alone, on my kitchen floor.

I lay there for over 24 hours unable to get up; then, when I could, I cleaned my dead child off the floor, buried her in the backyard, and made breakfast. He'd come back in and demanded that I do so. He made fun of my pain for years. Later, with my last two, the ones I gave birth to and mostly raised, I slept every night curled up into a ball where he couldn't hit my stomach."

"No one will ever hurt you again," he stated with finality, the look on his face, lethal; "I'll deal with anyone who tries."

Maggie looked at the anger mixed with deep compassion in his face. For the first time, she felt a loosening of the long-carried pain. It was as if he'd taken up part of the weight of the pain, and she didn't have to bear it alone anymore. She'd been brave enough to open the door to one of the darkest places in her soul, and—as she'd known he would—he'd entered the room with strength, and the fierceness of a true protector, and without one hint of condemnation.

Instead, he used his words as a balm to help begin the healing process of an unbelievable wound. She'd known she could tell him. She was very glad she had. Last night's bonding was increased with the sharing, and she knew she was safe with him. *I knew I could trust him.*

He pulled her up again, and rocked her against him for a long time, telling her it wasn't her fault, and how outraged he was on her behalf, and how sorry he was. Finally, she indicated she was better, and he returned to his own seat, but he was horrified at what she'd endured.

They talked a while longer, than Jake made bacon and omelets, while she set the table and made fruit bowls. They asked God to bless the meal, then had their delayed breakfast close to noon. Maybe they should have called it brunch.

Afterward, the rain had cleared out, and they went on a walk through the woods, winding around to the back acreage of Jake's property. It felt good to exercise after sitting so long. The sun was shining, and Maggie felt freer than she had in years. She was glad she'd stayed over and was eager to see Sharon and Rachel.

They were always so lively and fun. In many ways, they were the sisters she'd never had in the two who shared her blood. Rachel was her best friend after Jake, and Sharon after that. Her other closest friend was Matt's mom, Sarah, who'd mothered both she and Jake, since their mothers were gone.

Passages and Promises

Chapter 17

THEY GOT BACK TO THE house just before his cousins arrived. They were raised with him and his brothers since they were all very small, and were really more like little sisters. They freshened up, made a pitcher of tea, another pot of coffee, and Jake made a bowl of ham salad, from the leftovers of a ham he'd cooked last week. He'd bought French bread at the market last night for the ham salad sandwiches, and the others would bring dishes as well.

A good old-fashioned pot-luck was always fun, and they looked forward to the afternoon, and later that evening with their group. Maggie cut up fruit for a salad, then added whipped cream to bind it together with a hint of additional sweetness.

At 1:15, as predicted, Rachel and Sharon arrived together. They were laughing as they came up the walkway. Jake met them at the door and ushered them in. Sharon's long hair was held up in a clip and when she held her head at the right angle it looked as short as Rachel's, and they looked much alike. The sisters were close in age and had often been mistaken for twins with their curly blond hair and green eyes. Even in their early-40's they were stunning.

Both hugged Jake and Maggie, who greeted them with smiles, and led them to the table where they'd shared most of their morning. Maggie poured glasses of tea for all, and as she sat down Rachel punched Jake in the arm, asking, "Well, Jakey, what's up? You sounded rather mysterious on the phone yesterday."

Jake smiled at the nickname. Nobody but his family called him Jakey, but it always reminded him of the many adventures they'd shared throughout the years. "I wanted to invite you to our bible study group today. With all that's happening in this country

149

I want to talk about the promises God has in His Word. But, putting that aside for now, we only have until 5 before the rest of the group arrives. I want to share something with just the three of you."

"Ok," Rachel said, as she and Sharon exchanged glances. They looked at Maggie, hoping it was the announcement they'd waited years to hear. "Is it good or bad?"

"I have no idea," Maggie was as in the dark as they were. "He told me the same thing when I got here."

Jake smiled. These three women were his most favorite people in the world, and he loved that they all were so close. Other than Matt, they were the ones he spent most of his time with outside of work. "First," he looked very serious, using his Sherlock Holmes voice they were all familiar with. "You have, to swear a blood oath. I'm about to impart some very sensitive information, and if it gets out, it could cost all of us our lives." His British accent could use some work, but he laid it on thick while feigning lighting a pipe and blowing out the imaginary match.

They—being used to his antics—all laughed. "I'm not giving blood for anyone, especially in today's world," Sharon declared with a grin. "How about a pinky swear?" The other women nodded in agreement with smiles of their own.

Jake, sighing with defeat, said, "Ok. I guess that will have to do. But—in all seriousness—I need to share something with you that has to be kept between the four of us. At least for now." He looked at Rachel, "not even Matt; I plan to tell him myself, when I'm ready."

Seeing he was both teasing them as usual, but that he also was about to impart something significant, Rachel nodded, and they all quieted and waited for him to go on.

"Do you remember when I bought this place and did the remodel?" he asked. All nodded yes. "Well, when I was doing the big stuff, I made some discoveries."

Rachel, unable to help herself, jumped in. "Did you find pirate treasure? A famous painting worth a fortune? Bodies? What?"

All knew Rachel's love of adventure and reading long, long treasure quest novels. She looked excited like a kid in a candy store.

"Something like that," Jake shared. "Actually, I found several things. This house apparently used to be part of the underground railroad. I know Texas is a little far out of the usual places people think about where that was done, but many slaves escaped across Texas. They couldn't just do it openly because it was hard to blend in. I found an article that gave a lot of information about that time. According to the article, the number of free Black people in pre-Civil War Texas never rose above a few hundred, so hiding in plain sight wasn't possible.

People were speaking out against slavery in Texas before the Civil War, but not that many people," Jake explained. "Those who did faced a lot of risks—mobs, lynching, brutal punishment. Most of the assistance offered to runaways—directions, guidance, supplies, or shelter—came from fellow Black people, sympathetic Mexican laborers, and to a lesser extent, German settlers who opposed slavery.

I learned about The Texas Runaway Slave Project, a database of historical records at Stephen F. Austin State University, that has documented more than 2,500 escapees in Texas. Mexico outlawed slavery in 1829, and although conditions weren't great there, it was a place to escape to. Water was scarce and many died of thirst, starvation, and just plain exposure.

Horses, and people willing to help, were the only means to accomplish their escape. I went there a few times to study the documents, and this house is in the area where people were moved through Texas. It is not known to be one of the safe houses, and that's, ok. That means it was unknown then, and remains unknown now.

The first thing I found were hidden passages in the house. I did some research and it was built by a rich German family that still had servants, so they had what a lot of people back East had in their homes, a complete set of passageways that the servants could use to get around without being seen by the family. This house isn't huge, like some of those were, but it still has some of those features. There are hidden rooms. And yes, Rachel, I did

BOOK 1: "PREPARE FOR THE END" SERIES

find a couple of paintings and few other interesting things, but we'll get to that later. It's not important to this discussion.

There was one wall in the second secret room that led to a passage that was so well disguised I almost missed it. The only reason I did find it was because there was a damp place on the wall and I tore it out to take care of any mold or rot.

"What did you find? Can we see?" Rachel squealed, beside herself. The other faces showed their eagerness as well. All four of them were history buffs, and loved reading mysteries.

"Oh, Jake," Sharon added, "What fun! Why haven't you told us?"

Jake suddenly looked very serious. "I'm telling you now," he said. "We've all been watching this country go to hell in a handbasket. I'm very worried about both civil war, and attack from another nation, possibly several. As a history teacher, I've studied the conditions of many nations right before they fell, and we are on a fast-track right now. We are following both Nazi Germany and Venezuela's patterns, right before they fell. It happened there, and I highly suspect it's about to happen here. I believe hyperinflation is about to hit and I've learned the food supply is slowly being choked off.

I followed the passage and was amazed at how far it went. We're talking Texas, not the mountainous regions, but that thing is both long, and has more than one exit, all disguised as well as the entry is here. It slants down to solid bedrock. This thing took some real effort and it wasn't fast or cheap to build, even with major parts of it being a natural fissure in the rock. One fork leads to the river and has a room excavated about ten feet from the exit, with several old flat bottom fishing boats stored on shelves. I even found some old barrels with shoes, clothes, many canteens still filled with water, and even petrified food in the barrels. It would make a great exhibition in a museum, but I needed to keep it quiet.

One of the other forks goes through miles of underground fissures, and leads to a forest about five miles from here in a government tract that is only harvested about every 20 years. It's hidden in a cleft in the earth that is hard to get harvesting equipment in, so it's become more hidden over the years rather than being found. It too has a room with supplies.

I found another that held what looked like old hay, a watering trough, and even a few horseshoes. Someone from that end must have hidden horses there for when they reached that room. The outside is covered with dense brush and can't be seen at all. I cut away enough from the backside to make an easier exit, but anyone leaving from there will still have to push through some gnarly stuff to get out completely. I couldn't do more and keep it totally hidden; just enough to make it possible to get out. I did some research into survival groups, and what they think are necessities, for what they call TEOTWAWKI."

"What is that?" Sharon was thoroughly intrigued, as they all were.

"It's an acronym of 'the end of the world as we know it'," Jake grinned. "Kind of like SHTF." He held his hand to stave off the inevitable question. "When the S*** Hits the Fan."

All the ladies laughed at that, then Maggie asked, "why are you sharing this now, if you thought it was something to stay hidden for so long?"

"Because, ladies, I think it's about to hit the fan. I think TEOTWAWKI is already in progress. All of us are single, and there's few people in this life I trust like I do you three. This house is big, and out in the country. I already have a fence and an iron gate. I've been strategically planting trees in the gaps around the perimeter close together, for years, and putting up higher fences like Dan has around the deer hunting acres, deep in the woods that can't be seen from any angle, but will be hard to breach. I've not quite gotten around to building higher fences closer to the house, but that's next. I'll probably work on that some over the winter break.

I've even laid in a few boobie traps, and built a few tree-stands and tree houses, for watchtowers and sharpshooters. And, before you ask, today's not the day, nor do we have time to discuss those." At this, the ladies' faces were somber and slightly shocked, and their laughter abated at what he was imparting.

"What we need to discuss now is this: I've been slowly stocking the two hidden rooms and some of the passageways. I've made a list of supplies that are already becoming harder to

RINA LYNN

acquire, and I need some help. I don't want to flag any agencies anywhere that I'm a prepper. I've spent a lot of cash and bought things in diverse places as I've traveled around. That's one reason I drive, rather than fly. Each conference I've attended I've found little out of the way mom and pop stores, blessing them financially, and keeping out of the big box stores as much as possible; and I've bought a lot of things from my students, including several bikes that are stored in various branches of the tunnels.

I sometimes trade tutoring for backpacks, ammo, and other items; but I've had to be cautious because I also don't want to be known for that. When they tell me they have little money—which is very common—I ask them what they have to offer. Some of them take archery, and many go to the shooting range, as they know I do, so arrows and ammo are often offered; and on occasion someone needs to sell a bow or a firearm.

I agree to help them out and so I have quite a bit stored. They want it to remain just between us and ask me to keep it quiet so they can maintain their dignity, and therefore no one knows how much of it I've managed to acquire. I've had Ryan get me several bullet-proof vests, a couple at a time, also.

We can always use more though. We already buy ammo regularly, so we just up our purchases a little, and don't buy huge amounts at once; we up our usual target practice rounds about 20%, then shoot 50% less. Since I built the shooting range out here a few years ago no one knows how much we practice on a regular basis, or how many rounds we use. None of us will suffer from less expenditures, we've been shooting for years.

We've been buying ammo for years, too, so it's not anything that will garner unusual attention. Lots of Texans are buying guns and ammo now, anyway, so it's not something that sticks out. Y'all come out once a month anyway, so just keep doing it. We'll store the ammo rather than using it.

We need to discuss who to invite that we can trust, and have a powwow." He looked at his cousins, then added, "mostly family, with a few exceptions. One traitor will topple it all. For now, just us; and even when we begin to bring people in, the hidden places will be known only to the four of us; and probably

BOOK 1: "PREPARE FOR THE END" SERIES

154

Matt or Levi, and maybe Russell, Elliot, and Kevin, until we are sure of each person's fidelity.

I believe this nation will descend into complete lawlessness very soon. We will need more than just the four of us. I know you are all capable, smart, and can shoot as well as I can, but we will need more men. I've planned a compound from studying many models from both military and prepper sites. As a historian I can research a lot of that type of stuff on campus without putting up any red flags. I just teach a seminar and it's totally overlooked, and I get to keep the books."

He looked around the table at each of them in turn. "I know none of you have a lot of funds either, especially after the last two years, but will you help me accelerate the gathering of supplies, while we can still get them?"

Each of the ladies, feeling the weight of what he'd just imparted, nodded their heads in agreement. "Maybe we need to start buying extra clothes, shoes, blankets, cookware, ect; and begin to bring it out here as well. If it's as bad as you're seeing, we may have to leave town in a hurry and with what we have on us at the time," Sharon was already planning, as usual. She was an elementary teacher, and making lists and taking charge were second nature to her.

"Yes," Maggie agreed. "Also, begin to liquidate any market funds, and borrow against your life insurance cash value. Get some in cash for immediate use, but we need to start buying gold and silver, along with the food and other items." She too, was making a list.

"Jake, I know you already have tools of all kinds, but they will be hard to replace, and with several people we will need more than what you have just for your own use. Make of list of what we will need, to farm, maintain the orchards, fencing, and the house itself. We can get that also. If we split up the list and all of us buy one or more sets in different places, it won't raise any red flags.

And medical supplies. If we go to war people will get hurt. A few years back I took a first responder training class. I'll buy a new version of the book and I can order some kits to practice suturing. You can get them online. I've heard Dana say that's what they used in nursing school, and she says medical students use them to learn as well. There are online videos to learn with. I say we meet here every couple of weeks and practice. We can work on survival skills to be ready."

Sharon jumped in then, "We all know how to can and preserve food. Let's make a huge garden out here next spring. All of us can start getting fertilizer, jars, lids, and whatever we can find in the canning section. If we just start adding some each trip to the store, it will pile up fast. We can get food at the local farmer's market for more quantity and have weekend canning sessions. It will keep a few years and we'll know what's in it.

Jake, have you thought about adding to the orchard? I was in the farmer's supply store the other day and they had several leftover blackberry, raspberry, and blueberry bushes on clearance. I don't know if they still have them, but I can check tomorrow."

"That's a good idea." Jake was pleased they'd seen the seriousness of what he'd spoken of. He'd known they would, of course. He should have brought them in sooner. "Let's each go to the different farmer supply stores in the surrounding towns this week and get what they have. They'll come out in the spring too, and we can add more then. There's plenty of land here. I have about 50 acres. Another thing we can do; I bought a series of old 'how to' books with part of my college budget last year, about how people did things a hundred years ago. There are plans for brick ovens, and how to cook in them. We need lots of cast iron.

I had another well dug three years ago for the orchard and put in a windmill to pump the water. I put in another windmill, and an engineering student helped me wire it to some huge batteries for electricity. I told him it was for a class I was teaching on historical ways people provided for their needs, but that I'd like it to be functional later. After we got it working and he was done with his part, I buried the wiring far enough underground that an EMP won't affect it and the wires now go to a huge bank of batteries in an underground cellar. There are spare parts, wire, whatever I thought we might need to keep it going for several years.

Remember that storm cellar I put in around that time in the back yard?" All the women smiled. They'd teased him about being afraid of wind, but in Texas tornados were a reality and many people had them. "I rented a backhoe and dug it myself. I added an underground room that I tied into the tunnels. One of the branches was only about ten feet from it. That's why I put it where I did. There is a storage unit on one wall that has hidden hinges.

You can go into the storm cellar, lock the door from inside, and go out and escape into the tunnels. I added a mechanism where you can move the shelf back into place after you enter the tunnel, so no one knows. There is another array of storage batteries in there that also stores electricity from the orchard windmill, while it's built to just look ornamental.

There are many other things that would be useful in those books. We can go over them and plan. We'll build what we can, but since we don't know how long it will take before it all falls apart, let's pick some projects to do fast, and then others for later and get the items we'll need while they're available. I appreciate your quick understanding that this is where we are right now. It's really this bad, and we may not have much time at all."

"Jake," Maggie joined in again. "You know, I do mortgage protection and one of the things I'm seeing is that people are buying houses for 20-30% above asking price, sight unseen. They are moving here from other states where prices are much higher and they are escaping the liberal states. It's a total seller's market. Am I understanding you to say that you want us all to move in with you for everyone's protection? And do you think it's bad enough that we will need to move out here imminently? I guess what I'm really asking is if we need to sell our homes while we can get the higher price and put those funds toward supplies as well?"

"That's exactly what I'm saying."

Rachel, who was a mobile notary with the National Notary Association, said, "That's what I'm seeing too, along with a lot of Refi-Cash Out's."

"What's that?" Sharon asked.

"People are struggling financially so badly that they are refinancing to both take advantage of the current low interest rates, and pulling the equity out of their homes to pay off acquired debt. Almost all the signings I've done lately are those. If these people become unable to meet the payments, a lot of homes are soon going to hit the market and they probably won't get a good price if they are forced into foreclosure." She agreed with Maggie, that now was the prime time to sell, if they were going to.

"I'm not asking any of you to sell your homes," Jake stated. "But it sounds like that may soon happen. It did in all the countries I've studied. You can put that price in gold if you do sell, and, if or when, this mess all clears up, you can buy another home. I'll not take your equity. But, if it takes many years, we will at least have that to barter with, and if this country goes to war, houses in town will probably be burned or somehow destroyed. I really do think we are there.

That's why I've spent so much to prepare. I've already cashed out my retirement to fund all the things I've been building, but I still have the bulk of my inheritance in Fixed Indexed Annuities, and a pretty, decent savings account. Plus, the gold and silver I've bought in increments since dad taught us to do so as teens."

"Sharon and I have bought some silver and gold with each paycheck, too, Jake. None of us are getting any younger either," Rachel said with a smile. "Jake and I have talked in the past about living together to share expenses and take care of one another as we get older. That's one reason he bought a house this big. We knew, we, and possibly some other family members, could save a lot and not be alone."

"Jake's Retirement Center, I like that." Sharon laughed. "Jake and I have talked about that too. Jake, were you setting all this up when you asked us this before?" she asked.

"Yes. I've been watching this political situation for years. It wasn't hard to see where it was going. It's just this so-called pandemic seemed to accelerate everything. I was thinking we had at least another ten or twenty years or so before we became geriatric roommates," he grinned.

Maggie, looking pensive, glanced around the table, then spoke, "thank you for including me. I feel so much a part of your family. I so appreciate your friendship… all of you. I'm not sure if my children will ever be a part of my life again, and going through this alone has been uncomfortable."

They all assured her she'd always have a place with them, and as the world fell apart, there could be a place for her children as well, if they came. Maggie had tears in her eyes at their generosity. They all held hands and prayed, then they made several lists, decided to have their homes appraised, and finally went to see the features in the home, that Jake had found.

He went first to the beautiful solid oak shelves in his office. He pushed a place under the giant oak mantle above the fireplace and the entire unit of shelving began to move away from the wall. The well-built and re-oiled hinges made no sound at all. It opened about three feet and stopped. They went through the gap and entered a narrow passageway that was very reminiscent of things they'd seen in movies. Jake turned around and pushed another button, and the shelving slid closed. All three women stopped and stared at him.

"What if we can't get out?" Sharon asked for them all.

Jake laughed at their discomfort, "don't worry, I've been in here many times. It will open. And if by some strange chance it doesn't, there's several ways out. Come on."

They followed him down a short hallway while he hit the lights on the walls he'd added, lighting the passageway; then they were standing in a small room with shelves all around. There were old books on some of them near the top, old stoneware pottery on others, and tarnished silver trays near the bottom. A passageway led off to either side and they were already very excited about what they were seeing.

Sharon wore a delighted look. She walked over and ran her hands over the old pieces. There were crocks of various sizes and styles, some small enough to be butter, jelly, and salt crocks. There were old-fashioned glass jars with the BBGMC logo. She gasped, "Jake, OMG, these are first edition Ball glass jars. They were manufactured between 1885 and 1886. That's slightly after the civil war, but very close. These are worth a fortune. Look at the blue color; blue ones were only produced until 1937."

Rachel was standing closest to the other wall of shelves. "Sharon, come look at these silver pieces. These are about the same time frame." She glanced at Jake. "This must have been so hard for you as a history teacher. I know you'd want to share this with the students and the college. Could you not find a way?"

"It has been hard," he admitted. "I tried to think of a way, but they weren't in the main part of the house when I purchased it, and without revealing the hidden passages, I just couldn't think of how to document the source. This isn't everything either. I just left it all as I found it, other than cleaning up the dust so I could breathe. If we ever need it, it's here; otherwise, it can just stay until after our country gets back on track. By then, with looting and trading, I can produce some pieces and not have to have documentation, but the story will be lost and really that's the stuff historian's want to share.

Imagine serving the guests in the dining room next door with goods from this room. They could come out through the secret door and back in, carrying platters, and filling the serving trays. Look over here, there's a dumb waiter that goes to the kitchen, and one of the passage ways goes to an old brick shed that was built over a well. They could draw water and bring it straight here and it would stay cold for a time. Especially in these old crocks.

Look in the big one by the end, the one with the light bottom and the brown glazed pouring top; it still has an old silver coin in it to keep the water fresh. People used to put them in water and milk jugs. The coins kept the water safe from bacteria and algae, and kept the milk fresh. Remember, Sharon and Rachel, Babushka used to do that when we were kids."

Both ladies smiled, "Oh, yes," Sharon laughed, "I remember she kept the water in an open top stoneware crock like these over here," she gestured at another shelf with other crocks in various sizes and colors. "When I was about ten, I wanted that silver coin so much. You two," she pointed at Jake and Rachel, "talked me into putting my hand in the crock and fishing it out.

She came around the corner about the time I waved it in the air to show you I had it. She was so mad. I had dripped water everywhere, stuck my hand in the drinking water, and took the coin. She spanked me and make me go without dessert; I never did that again."

BOOK 1: "PREPARE FOR THE END" SERIES

"You weren't the only one," Jake had a rueful look on his face upon remembrance. "She spanked us too for encouraging you, and while you were mopping the floor, and Rachel was wiping the cabinet, I had to go outside, wash out the crock, and then draw more water from the well so we'd have fresh water. I knew it was partly my fault, but it was hot out there and that stoneware is heavy, especially filled with water. We didn't get dessert either, and she'd made my favorite, homemade peach pie."

Maggie was cracking up at their stories, as usual. It would have been fun to grow up with them. They had so many memories of their combined lives, and with all the other brothers, they had tons of stories. "Let's go down the passages," she pleaded," eager too; "I can't wait to see more."

"Ok," Jake said. "Come on." He gestured to the left. They followed him into another narrow hallway. It was very plain with no paint or decorations of any kind. Some places had old thin plaster that was cracked and had places missing, and some just had rough wooden planking. It had been smoothed enough to mostly not catch their clothing, but nothing more. It went down almost twenty feet and made a sharp left turn.

"This follows the contour of the rooms," Jake explained. It goes between rooms and has an entry into most of them in one fashion or another; mostly into closets, or behind those large floor-length mirrors. It's really a maze that runs around the entire house. It's mostly all built in the innermost interior, but one passage goes around close to the outer rooms, just inside the exterior walls.

In some places you can still see the studs and the planking just in front of the bricks. I went in and added insulation to make the house easier to heat and cool, but I did leave a place or two original to show the historical construction. It's a bit narrower, and I can't help but think it was for the Master of the house, instead of the servants. It doesn't connect with this one, except in two places, and those are very well concealed from both sides.

He led them to a wall that had a #1 written in what looked like charcoal about 4 ½ feet up. He moved a small lever by the number then pushed on the wall, and they were surprised when the wall opened. He stepped into the room Maggie was staying in. She walked in behind him and turned to see that the floor length mirror concealed the doorway. "Oh my," she said, a bit unnerved that someone could have easily entered her room last night. "I would have never guessed that was there."

"Ahem," Sharon drew their attention to Maggie's purse, schedule book, and suitcase sitting on the chair by the bed. "Looks like someone is already checking out the accommodations," she nudged Rachel, who smiled.

"Oh wow," Rachel stepped right into the fun. "Guess you decided you didn't need us to chaperone," she teased.

Maggie's face turned red, and Jake rescued her from further embarrassment. "Stop harassing Maggie. We wanted to study and pray and I told her to just stay over since she'd be here today anyway. You two had other things to do."

Both of them laughed, and let Maggie off the hook. They knew both Maggie and Jake's character, and the three of them had stayed many a night after sharing a meal and playing board or card games until all hours. The house had six bedrooms and Jake loved having family over and cooking for people. Both believed it was just a matter of time before they made their relationship official anyway. They'd never called it dating, but they'd been close friends for over six years.

They explored much of the house, finding many old items and ways to get around without being seen. This would have been a hoot growing up. Jake had stumbled onto the perfect house for them, especially if the country was at war. They could hide all their supplies, and hide themselves, as well, if the house was ever searched. And if it was torched, they wouldn't be trapped.

As they explored, he asked them to see if they could find the secret rooms. It was both a challenge and to see if they were easy for anyone to accidently come upon. He'd only found any of it because he was renovating, but he wanted to be sure, especially if others came.

They really tried, but none of them could find the rooms. After a couple of hours, they ganged up on Jake and begged him to show them. They were astounded when he did.

He led them back downstairs and around to the side wall of the stairs, where there were built-in shelves along the triangular wall. He reached deep inside the middle section and pushed a place close to the back in the right top corner, then using both hands he began to pull the shelves toward him. The entire middle section silently slid out as a unit, showing an opening.

They had to duck into the shorter entry, and as they did Jake reached out and touched what they thought was the wall, but turned out to be another row of wireless touch lights for closets, like in the earlier passageway.

You pushed the plastic bubble and the light came on, and you pushed it again to turn it off. Once again, he silently slid the shelf back closed. They went toward the wall under the highest part of the stairs and he slid the wall sideways. It was a concealed slide door on a track, but built so the track didn't show until you slid the door aside. They would never have known it was there.

He waited for all to come into the room hidden by the stairs, requesting Rachel, who was last in line, to turn off the touch light. Rachel reached out for Jake in the dark, who led her thru the door. It was very dark. Jake slid the door closed behind them and whispered, "wait," then another much brighter light came on.

He showed them the wireless motion sensor LED lights he'd bought and affixed to the walls. "These come on automatically, and I couldn't have them where you entered in case someone was chasing you. Those have, to be on/off, but once the doors are closed these come on without you having to know where they are. They can't be seen from outside this room as long as the door is closed.

If you ever have to hide fast, you open the shelving door, close it quickly, and make your way to the sliding door without turning on the other lights. You can stand there and wait, if you think it's safe, or slide this in the dark and the light is on a 30 second delay, so you have plenty of time to enter and slide the door back shut before it comes on. Just remember to not turn on the other lights. You can come those few steps without them. Then, you can stay here or go out of the house.

As you can see, I've made a few improvements and modern upgrades to what was already a marvelous design. I can't wait to

BOOK 1: "PREPARE FOR THE END" SERIES

show you all I've done, and get your ideas for even more. Together we can design all kinds of things to keep us safe in the days ahead. I've thinking of having Bobby come over and help. You know he can think up things to help." They all laughed, knowing that was true. Bobby was a genius at electronics and security systems.

He led them through a short hallway that went to a flight of old stone stairs going down into an older area of very old huge timbers. They followed it for about six feet then it twisted to the right and they were in a surprisingly large space. There were stacks of canned goods, coffee, ammo, and other items. The top of the space was the thick floor joists of the house above them held up with what looked like tree trucks, thick and solid; and it too held motion lights that came on as they entered. He told them they could check out the inventory another day, right now he wanted to show them the tunnel entrance.

He walked to the back, around a stack of black and yellow stacked bins, to what looked like a rough stone wall. He counted down to a stone that looked just like the others and pulled slightly. A portion of the wall came forward and he pulled a bit more. Once again, a portal revealed itself. In front of them was a very interesting tunnel.

It had a floor that looked like many feet had worn down the uneven stone through the years, sides that slanted to an arched ceiling, and was partly bricked and partly just native stone. It looked hundreds of years old instead of from the 1800s, and was surprisingly dust free despite its age. It was dark for a short way but as it curved around, they saw a dim greenish light.

Jake turned around and addressed them. "I know you want to explore more, especially this, but we don't have time. The others will be here soon. You have a lot to absorb as it is. How about we go back up and relax for an hour and get ready to pretend that this didn't happen. We can have our bible study, and in two weeks, that Friday evening, convene back here. We'll spend the weekend planning and then another weekend exploring all the tunnels and I'll show you what I've found, and what I've added.

Also, we need to explore the house passages, all the entries and exits, on drills, until you all know them as well as I do. If your lives are on the line, you can't have any indecision or panic because you forgot how to access a room or where a passage leads. We'll go over it until it's like you've always lived here. I got lost repeatedly until I did it over, and over, and over again.

They agreed. While they marveled at it all, they were tired, and knew they had to present themselves as usual. All their heads were spinning with the new knowledge and the prospect of what was happening, or possibly happening, in their country, and indeed, the entire world.

Provisions Come with the Kingdom

Chapter 18

SHORTLY BEFORE 5:00 the others began to arrive. Both Maggie and Jake were surprised when Louise was the first to arrive. They'd really believed she'd be either too busy or too exhausted to drive out and attend the meeting.

She was obviously exhausted as she came in, and they sent her straight to a chair while Rachel brought her a glass of tea. She gratefully accepted it, took a long drink, and leaned back. "Ah," she said, "that's good. This has been a day."

Jake brought over the ottoman and insisted she put her feet up. "Maggie told me about the number of funerals you are doing arrangements for. Have you been able to get the supplies you needed to make all the orders?"

"We went light on a few things that I hated to fudge on, but we managed to get everything for last week's orders, and so far, the first two days of funerals for this coming week, but I'm low on everything. I'm even about out of ribbon. I can't ever remember a time when I totally ran out of ribbon. Maybe a color here and there unexpectantly, but we filled in with something similar until the next order arrived.

I put about 20-25% less flowers on most everything and fanned them out more. I haven't had to do that kind of thing since my first year in business when I was operating on a shoestring. I've called all our normal suppliers, and a few I've never used, but their stock is running out and they aren't sure when they will be resupplied. I have no idea what to do. It's the same all over."

The others had filtered in as she was speaking. Rachel had gotten tea served to all, and Sharon directed them to seats scattered around the room. They'd heard all but the initial explanation. Rachel spoke up, "I have a whole box of ribbon left from my VBS class last summer. I can bring you that."

"I have some in my classroom also," Sharon added. "Since we went back to zoom meetings, I just need enough to do my own craft online for them to watch. Each family gets the supplies for their own child. I'd bought enough last summer to do Christmas and other crafts with 22 students. I'm sure I have a bunch from prior years as well."

"That's great," Louise gratefully accepted the offer. "I'll give you back what you paid for it."

"I'm not worried about that." Rachel insisted. "It's just taking up space in my craft room. I don't do the crafts I used to, but I hated to throw away good supplies."

"I could actually use the money," Sharon replied. "We have to buy our own classroom supplies and it would help with future needs."

"Of course, dear." Louise returned. "My mother was a teacher and I know just what you mean."

"Is ribbon all you need?" Maggie asked. "What about vases, or other containers? I'm sure I have several I've acquired thru the years. I can run them through the dishwasher and they'd be just like new."

"Me too," was heard around the room. Between them all, they knew of at least 30 containers they'd received flowers in at some point, possibly more.

"I've got some wood pieces left over from my remodeling and home projects. What about different sizes of small wooden boxes? I can throw some together tomorrow and deliver them to you on Monday or Tuesday," Jake added his part. "I've got some slabs too I got from John, down at the cross-tie yard. Some people might like something a bit more rustic, especially for men's funerals. You can add some plastic fish or deer, depending on what their sport was."

"I'd be happy to come out tomorrow and help you with that," Jason threw in. "I would love to do some wood work. With two of us we could do a lot more, and I think I have some odds and ends in various colors and wood types I could bring as well."

Louise was wiping tears from her eyes, "I can't believe you guys would do all that for my shop; or for me," she smiled a wobbly, tired smile.

"You know, I just thought of something else," Jake looked excited. "I still have some boxes of my mom's and grandmother's things. I was looking thru them when I stored them and I do believe there were several boxes of those silk flowers, ribbons, and other items. They used to do weddings you know. They probably have all kinds of stuff you could use. I'll find them in the morning and you can see what you can glean from them. God knows I'll never use them."

Maggie had been thinking as she listened. "It's getting close to Christmas. I know it's a lot of funerals, but people still want their loved ones to have pretty arrangements and some people still just buy to decorate for the holidays. What if I painted some holiday scenes of angels, snowmen, and other things appropriate? I have almost a pallet of cedar grilling planks I used in a class I taught, and all the patterns." She looked at Sharon and Rachel, "would you be willing to help me mass produce a few dozen?"

"Of course," they chimed in unison. "That would take you over the next eight to twelve weeks, Louise. We could do some Thanksgiving ideas as well. Something lovely like 'how thankful I am that you were my loved one.' I mean, you know, better than that, but the general idea." Sharon was very creative and it was right up her alley.

"Why don't you all come back at 9 tomorrow morning and we can all work together?" Jake invited. His philosophy was always the more the merrier, unless he was in one of his moods. "And bring more food."

They all got a laugh from that. At Jake's house food was always a part of any gathering.

Maisie had been quietly listening, but finally added her thoughts. "What about turkey feathers to add to the Thanksgiving box or men's arrangements? I have a box full from when my son used to hunt. It's in the top of his closet I'm pretty sure. I have some chicken feathers too that are black and white speckled. Also, there's hundreds of pine cones on my lawn. We could do some plain with the feathers, but paint some gold or silver for more Christmassy arrangements.

I have some neat twisted stems on my berry bushes, too. Some are about ¼" in diameter, and some are a bit smaller. I need to thin them out anyway, and if we spray paint them silver and gold and put them in among the Christmas flowers, it will look like the ones you can buy at craft stores, but won't cost a dime. It will take less flowers too and I'm almost sure I have a couple of cans of each color spray paint. I'll bring them tomorrow."

Maggie, Sharon, and Rachel all had leftover cans of both colors, and, also some copper and bronze. Maggie had some metallic blues in deep tones and cerulean as well. They would make great colors for both Thanksgiving and Christmas, and for white and blue in January and February.

"There's holly bushes out front, and I have about 5 acres of Christmas trees planted," Jake told them. "We can cut some fresh boughs and put the stems in buckets of water. Just tell me how many you want to start with, and I can replenish them as you get low. You can make wreaths with the branches; we can do some of those tomorrow if you want, and I have cedar trees if you'd like to add some of that for the scent."

"We can cut some small wooden crosses from our leftover wood pieces and make larger ones she can wire flowers and stuff to," Jason was really enjoying this. "We can cut the long piece into a point so they can hammer it into the ground around the grave site, but you'll have to figure out a way to make it stand up in the church."

"That's easy," Jake said. "I've got a whole box of tiny hinges from something we did at the college several years back. We can add a support leg."

"Louise, have you had any calls about funerals for babies?" Sharon asked.

"Unfortunately, yes. We've had more in a month, than all, of last year combined. Some were a few months old, and many were from late-term miscarriages." Jake glanced at Maggie, and saw her face turn pale, as she held her breath, then met his eyes. His softened, offering comfort; and as they looked at one another she absorbed his compassion, drawing strength from it, and he saw her relax. *I need to tell her.*

"I have several boxes of small plastic pacifiers and bottles from doing baby showers. Those could be tied on smaller ribbons. And if Jake and Jason could make some smaller crosses or tiny bible shaped pieces, we could paint the crosses in white, pink, and blue, and paint the others to look like tiny bibles. You could add their name with a gold or silver sharpie. I have those also. I used them for name tags."

"That's a wonderful idea. I hope we don't need many, but after what Maggie shared at our last meeting, and the way it's going, I'm afraid it's going to be getting worse before it gets better." Louise said with a sigh. "But people are still having babies, too, so maybe I can add them to congratulation bouquets."

"We can make some of the boxes to look like cradles if you ladies will paint them." Jason offered.

"We will." Rachel agreed.

Louise was amazed at the generosity on behalf of her business. She'd been stressed all day about how to get enough supplies to keep up. Too many businesses were still short-staffed or closed. She'd never dreamed her friends would create a way to do it in a day. She told them how much she appreciated their willingness.

"That's what friends are for Louise," Maggie hugged her again.

"And it's not just you we're wanting to help either," Rachel explained. "The people dying in this community are our friends and family. Helping you have supplies, means they get your best, and not have to be turned down when they call to support the families they loved during this horrible time of loss. We are helping you, but we're also serving the community. It's a labor of love all around."

"Now, let's eat," Jake called as he headed for the kitchen. Soon they were all sharing a feast of potluck that all had helped contribute. It was a companionable meal as they discussed the plans for the next day, and the adjustments everyone was having to make. Some of their jobs weren't greatly affected, but some were. Some, like Louise, were extra busy, but it wasn't fun knowing why she was so busy. Funerals were always a part of her income, but lately too many were happening, and she knew too many of ones she was creating arrangements for.

She shared with the group that it made her feel guilty, profiting from the ill effects of the pandemic, but she was grateful she still had an income. All assured her she was just doing what she did best. Many places had long since closed their door, and others were being forced to by the reduction in sales. "Use the money to help out others," they suggested; "it will do some good."

Soon they mellowed out and had a short break before they began the bible study. Jake asked Maggie to walk outside with him for a minute, and they went out back. "Are you ok?" he asked her. She nodded. "Jake… you'd be surprised how well I've learned to hide it. It's part of keeping the secrets."

"Maggie, you don't ever have to keep the secrets with me, unless you want to." He decided he'd try to talk to her too. "You may not be the only one who's done that," he shared. "Can we talk about it later?"

She looked in his eyes and saw his uncomfortableness as he looked away, then back. "Ok. We better go back," he nodded and led her back into the living room.

Jason opened in prayer, then Jake began.

"With all the evil and hardship around us, it's getting harder to see the good," he spoke quietly. I want to be able to believe in God's promises, even as the darkness deepens. So, for tonight, Maggie and I prepared a lesson on the promises we're given. They are timeless and can be counted on. It may be His Word, and what He promises us, that gets us through whatever is coming.

We know from Scripture that it will only get worse. We need to prepare our hearts, minds, and souls to hold on, no matter what. So, I'm going to go over several promises, and Maggie typed them out to email to everyone. Print them out and put them on the fridge, on your bedroom mirror, in your bible, or where ever you can see them daily. Start committing them to memory. When it gets almost impossible to believe that He is still with us, recite them over, and over again.

The first one is:

Philippians 4:19 - "But my God shall supply all your need according to his riches in glory by Christ Jesus."

"I've typed this out and kept it on my computer, both at home, and the one in my office on campus, for the last several years," He shared. "When the college basically shut down in 2020, I still got my salary because I'm tenured, but a lot of the other workers did not. Students lost jobs and some who lived on campus lost work study jobs, and those without families really had nowhere to go. I'd had this on there before the lockdowns, and many times students in my office would ask me if I really believed it.

It has been a great door opener for discussions of God's provisions for some time. I prayed with several students and God opened a door and made a way. It was a good verse before the pandemic, but now it's a lifeline to His promise that He will supply our needs. We just need to do our part and trust Him to do His."

"I've had to really start to hold onto that more this year too," Maggie shared. "Mortgage Protection and commission income has gotten a bit tougher with people struggling financially. When so many were laid off, I had several large charge backs where I owed my commission back to the company. God kept taking me to this verse."

"I'm a living testimony that He will supply," Louise was still stunned at how her needs had just begun to be met. "I drove over praying He'd help me get what I needed for the coming days ahead, and you all have just overwhelmingly answered that prayer. It's like you are angels sent from heaven."

"It's strange," Rachel pondered, "how so many were affected, yet some, like Louise and me have had our business increase from everyone else's hardship. I've felt blessed to have so many signings, but I've felt bad because people are having to refinance their homes just to stay solvent."

"I, like Jake, received my paycheck," Sharon looked humbled, "But I've had to adjust to zoom meetings like Maggie. I was grateful to still have a way to earn a living, but I've wondered what will happen if the schools go down again. The kids are already falling behind."

Jason and Maisie had been off work for a time and had a harder financial road. Jake had helped Jason a couple of times, and Louise had hired Maisie several days in the shop as she was needed. Maisie summed it up for them both: "I've always been the one to help others, but it was harder to be the one who needed help. I haven't had much time off in years, and being alone with no paycheck is scary.

I'm very glad I could draw unemployment. I'm going to put that on my office computer too, Jake. I need to be reminded daily that God said he'd supply my needs." Jason was unusually quiet, but nodded his head in agreement. Jake knew he was still having a hard time.

Maggie, moved by the look on both their faces, brought the next verses. "These go along with that one.

Matthew 6:31-32, Therefore, take no thought, saying, what shall we eat? or, what shall we drink? or, Wherewithal shall we be clothed? For after all these things do the Gentiles seek: for your heavenly Father knoweth that ye have need of all these things.

I've felt impressed lately that things will get increasingly tougher. We've talked about that before. It's hard to live in the sinful condition of this country right now, but even harder to understand that we've come under God's judgment. I need to hear that I'm not even supposed to 'take heed' about food, water, or clothing. He knows we have need of them. That goes right along with Him supplying what we need.

As a parent, I didn't have to think twice about preparing meals for my kids, or making sure they were hydrated with nutritious drinks. I always watched the sales and had clothing bought before they even needed the next size. It never entered their heads that there wouldn't be meals, or milk, or juice, or flavored drinks, or tea, or clothes available.

They never once went without a meal, or ever even thought they might. They never once had to worry about procuring any of that for themselves. It was just provided. Now... God expects us to work and make our living as we're able, but... we are His children, and as His children, we're supposed to trust Him to provide... just like our kids trusted us to."

"I don't think we need to just wait and it will drop from the sky," Jake threw in, "as we've discussed before, we need to acquire what supplies we can as the country moves deeper into this, even buying extra clothing we may not be able to get later, but as for not having anything at all, if we do our part, He'll do His. He said six days shall you work, and most all of us have done that, until our job was taken away. When it's out of our hands, it's in His. We need to practice truly believing He will provide.

There were nods of ascent around the room.

Louise, still very tired and looking vulnerable, asked, "Did you find any promises about our health? With all these funerals and so many in the hospital, I can't help but wonder what happens if I get sick. I try not to be afraid, or think about it, but sometimes I do. Will God still heal us, or is being in a nation under judgement something that cancels it out?"

"There are many promises about our health, but we just picked a few. We'll take turns reading them, and anyone feel free to jump in and comment or ask questions." Jake answered her. "Listen to these two:

Isaiah 41:10, Fear thou not; for I am with thee: be not dismayed; for I am thy God: I will strengthen thee; yea, I will help thee; yea, I will uphold thee with the right hand of my righteousness.

Jeremiah 17:14, Heal me, O LORD, and I shall be healed; save me, and I shall be saved: for thou art my praise.

He's saying He's *already* with us. Don't be dismayed. He's God. He'll strengthen us, help us, and uphold us, because *He's* righteous. He'll heal us, save us, and we give our praise in return."

"And," Maggie smoothly joined in, Jeremiah 33:6 says, Behold, I will bring it health and cure, and I will cure them, and will reveal unto them the abundance of peace and truth.

Even if you get sick, like I did, He promises a cure, peace, and truth.

Isaiah 53:5 adds, but he was wounded for our transgressions, he was bruised for our iniquities: the chastisement of our peace was upon him; and with his stripes we are healed.

Basically, that's part of the atonement. It wasn't just for our sins; it was also for our healing.

And finally, 3 John 1:2, Beloved, I wish above all things that thou mayest prosper and be in health, even as thy soul prospereth.

He wishes us to prosper and be in good health. This should make all of us more able to trust Him. And if by chance we do sicken and die, we go to be with Him. Sometimes God heals in time, and sometimes in eternity. He chooses, not us; but either way we win. I mean, after all, before He unleashes His complete wrath upon the planet and the wicked, He has to shelter us. We can't get from point A to point B very many ways. Either He comes and takes us out, or we die, and go that way."

"I agree," Sharon spoke up softly. "This is a war and we have been targeted. We think death is all bad, but we don't know what could be prevented by dying early. Think about some of the ways people die. If this country is invaded, it won't go well with us, especially us women. What we see as horrid, God may see as a mercy."

"We need to understand that trusting God, is TRUSTING God," Rachel inserted. "We see trust as 'He will do what we want,' but really, trusting Him, is believing He will do what's best for us, even if we don't understand that at the time."

"Yeah, because God doesn't really 'owe' us anything." Jason declared.

"I used to believe that," Maggie countered, "but I've adjusted my theology a bit on that subject."

"What do you mean?" Jason belligerently argued, "He doesn't."

"Follow my logic," Maggie, began explaining. "This won't be popular, but I found so many places where God says He will do something, in fact He promises He will. It's true God didn't owe us anything in the beginning, I agree. But He created us, and He then called us to repentance. He said if we confess our sins, He is faithful and just to forgive us our sins, and to cleanse us from all unrighteousness. Right?"

Jason nodded, still not sure where she was going with this.

"So, *if* we confess, He *owes* to forgive. It's written. It's a conditional promise. He tells us he'll supply our needs. He tells us he will heal us. He tells us to ask Him for anything we need. He tells us He'll strengthen us. Remember when He made the covenant with Abraham? He put Abraham to sleep and He walked through the covenantal ceremony alone, signifying that He alone would be held responsible, because He alone is able to meet the conditions.

So, my new theological stance is, since *He* made the promises, and *He* told us to have faith, and *He* brought the notion and ability of salvation and that *He'll* supply our needs, then He *does* owe us something. He owes us to keep His Word; to keep His promises.

We can depend upon Him because He's obligated Himself to keep His word, if we meet the conditions He's laid out. He's not a capricious God that blows with every wind so we never know from one day to the next what He will do, or how He'll react. Just as we owe Him our allegiance and obedience, our worship and praise, God owes us to keep His Word, and that means we can have faith that He will, because God doesn't renege on His Word."

Jason looked both thoughtful and disturbed. "That's a most interesting idea, Maggie. I'll have to ponder on that one, and study some scriptures. It's totally opposite of what I've always thought or been taught to believe. But it has some selling points, I have to admit."

All were thoughtful at that. All had been taught God owes us nothing, and in some senses that is correct. But He does owe us to keep His Word, we can count on that when we can count on nothing else. A very interesting concept to ponder, but comforting to know that when God executed a contract with Abraham that He would keep His covenant.

Jake, who'd been punching buttons on his phone, looked up, "Here's the dictionary meaning of the word 'owe.'

- have an obligation to pay or repay (something, especially money) in return for something received.

That tracks, we confess, He forgives. He's obligated to forgive, if we confess, but not obligated if we don't.

- owe something, especially money, to (someone).

That tracks too. If the wicked don't repent, God owes them judgement. For the wages of death are earned.

be under a moral obligation to give someone (gratitude, respect, etc.) Again, God is under a moral obligation to keep His promises. He didn't have to make them. He wasn't coerced into making them. He offered them to us when He owed us nothing but destruction, but still, He made them. Now, he is bound to His word.

Look at this verse, Hebrews 6:17, Wherein God, willing more abundantly to shew unto the heirs of promise the immutability of his counsel, confirmed it by an oath:

You know I love the King James Version, but just to make it even more clear, look at this version, Hebrews 6:17 New Living

Translation - God also bound himself with an oath, so that those who received the promise could be perfectly sure that he would never change his mind.

I really think Maggie may very well be right about this. And like her, I am very glad God bound Himself with an oath to keep His promises. I can stand on something when I know God can't take it back. In any relationship, each party owes the other for the good of the ongoing relationship.

I like knowing God made an oath to keep His promises. It means I don't have to use the word of God as a formula to get what I need. He's already promised to supply my needs, and taken an oath that He has to fulfill that promise. I don't have to wonder or doubt. He said it, I need it, He will supply it. Over, finished, done. Don't be anxious."

"Wow," Maisie quietly stated. "I've always felt like we were kind of on probation with God. Like, ok, He made some promises, but He can take them back at any time if I really mess up; and I'm not talking about completely turning my back on Him and walking away forever, I'm talking about just messing up. I always felt like I was on trial and maybe the promises weren't always valid.

This puts it in a whole new light. It's like suddenly... I mean... if God does owe us to keep His Word, then, Jake you're right. I can trust that the promises really are for me, and they won't be snatched back. No matter what." A slow smile came across her face as she pondered the depths of the meaning of God being bound by His own oath to do what He said He would do, including supplying all our needs.

"That means He can't fail. He's not fickle, no matter what comes on this earth. He can't be tortured into giving up, he can't be bribed to give up, He can't be manipulated into giving up." She looked at them all and her smile became wider and wider. "Thank you, Maggie for that insight. I've struggled with trusting God. I've wondered whether, later—when it really gets bad—If I will have the ability to trust Him to take care of me, but now I know it's not my ability to trust Him, it's whether, or not He is faithful enough to trust in.

And he is. Especially if He's bound by His promises. I'm going to begin to underline every promise in red ink as I read through my bible. That way I can find them anytime I need to remember His promises. He's faithful. He's true." She had tears in her eyes as the truth seeped across her mind, and more importantly, her heart.

Maggie was wiping her eyes, "We have a lot more on the list, but I think you can look them up. Now, you know that God meant business when He made them. Homework assignment: read each one, and don't just read the words. Read each one like it was written to you alone, while keeping it in context, and ponder what it really means.

Read through Psalms 91 each day for the next week. Underline the promise in every verse. It's in there for a reason. And don't hesitate to call each other if you get afraid. We need to be strong as a group, not just as individuals."

Jake spoke at length about preparation, supply chains, the lean years in Egypt, and how they put up food beforehand for several years while it was available. He then spoke of them not only having enough to feed the entire country of Egypt, but refugees from other nations as well.

"We are in the time where food and other necessities are still available, but all throughout history people starved in times of war and political upheaval.

Try to add a few extra items with each shopping trip. Think ahead about stuff that may be hard to acquire. Get supplies for your children and grandchildren as well. Get extra Tylenol, and whatever other things you use regularly. We may have a long while, and we may just have weeks, or days. We don't know. But the day is coming, I do believe, when we will be very glad that we have those supplies.

He took up prayer requests and they spent the next thirty minutes in prayer. Once again, the Holy Spirit filled the room and the people joining together. Afterward, they were much refreshed. Jake reminded them they'd take December and January off for the holidays, and while he was on winter break, and not meet to study again until the end of February. Louise, Jason, and Maisie left first, and after a few minutes of additional planning for the next day, Jake's cousins left as well.

Jake asked Maggie to stay a few minutes. "Maggie… when you told me about your baby this morning…" again she saw his uncomfortable look and what she thought was guilt, "there's something I need to tell you too, but I need to pray about how to do it.

I just want you to know, that I need to talk to you really soon. It's important, and something I should have told you already. It's just something I'm having a very hard time doing. Will you come back when I'm ready? Just the two of us again?"

She looked at the seriousness of his face, wondering what could be that big for him, "Of course. I'm be here anytime you decide it's time."

He thanked her and walked her out. She drove home thinking about how comforting it was to be a part of them all; and how much knowing they were all moving in together was as well.

Annie greeted her at the door, glad she was back, and Maggie decided that from now on she'd just take her with her. She had a doggy door to the fenced-in back yard, and a perpetual food and water delivery system that kept her dishes full, but she wasn't happy being left for too long.

She spent a few minutes making a list of things she'd take with her tomorrow, then showered and sat down to just relax and think about all the day had held. Life was about to change even more; she could feel it. She felt an ominous darkness approaching.

She'd never thought about Jake, Rachel, and Sharon asking her to live with them, but she was comforted by the reality that she wouldn't be alone as the country's situation worsened. She didn't know how soon they would execute it, but they'd provided a safety net for when society began to unravel. She could do her job from anywhere, as long as she had the internet; and as long as it was there to do.

Behind the secure fence at Jake's place, with her favorite people, would be a good place to be. She ached for her children, but until their heart changed, and their father stopped looking for, and threatening her, she knew all she could do was pray God would show them the truth. Once again, she bowed her head and asked God to reveal the truth to them and keep them safe. She looked at pictures of them she kept on the mantle, touching their faces, so dear to her; and prayed for them to know she loved them.

Finally, she went to bed. Tomorrow was another big day and she needed to sleep. She had to be up early to get her portion of the food fixed, locate the vases, run them through the dishwasher, and get the ribbon, paint, and cedar shingles ready to go. Jason had promised to come by and load the shingles in his truck but she needed to have everything else ready.

She wanted to take a few clothes out, but she planned to put them in the truck early and not unload them until it was just the four of them later in the evening. She found some boxes and set them out for in the morning.

She fell asleep while planning. She barely felt Annie snuggling up close before she was out. It had been an extraordinary day.

Family is Family

Chapter 20

"YOU FEEL BETTER NOW?" Dan looked at Matt, as they drove toward the hardware store.

"Yes. No. I don't know." Matt still looked upset.

"Isn't it time you figured out how to know for sure?" Dan pressed.

"I know," Matt sighed. "I'm just not sure how to go about it. Jenny was dead set against it. I begged her for years."

"It was easier for her to collect money from several of you, then to narrow it down to just one," Dan added his favorite argument. "And, in spite, of everything, she loved that girl, and didn't want to lose her. Matt, she didn't live a moral life, but she raised a good kid."

Dan was only one of two people that knew Matt's secret. At 17 he'd been one of several guys Missy's mom had been seeing when she got pregnant. He'd been terrified his parents would find out. He told Jenny he'd marry her, but she'd laughed at him. She'd informed him she wasn't the marrying type, and was not ready to settle down with just one guy, besides the fact that she was eight years older than him.

She'd enjoyed being his first lover and showing him the ropes. Before he knew it, he was slipping out to meet her any time he got a chance. He was horribly jealous when he found out he wasn't the only one. His mom would have freaked knowing he was messing with a girl with Jenny's reputation, especially since technically it was statutory rape.

But, by the time he'd found out she was so wild, it was too late. He'd been hooked. To this day his mom and dad had no idea he might have a child. His sister Dana knew, but she'd been sworn to secrecy since they were teens. He knew a few of her secrets as well, and knew she'd never rat him out.

"You know, that's one of the reasons Karen left me," he confessed. "I wouldn't tell her where the $100 a week went, and she was infuriated. I couldn't tell her about Jenny, so I just kept letting her stay mad. Being stupid at 17 has just kept costing me, but I'd love to be that girl's father, in spite of the fact that my mom will go ballistic."

Dan grinned, "Your momma's tougher than you think. I've known her since I was a kid. She'll be thrilled to have another grandchild, but mad that she's missed so much. I'd like to be a fly on the wall when you tell her."

"I can't tell her," Matt moaned. "I'm not even sure. But good grief Dan, she looks more like Dana and mom every time I see her. It drives me crazy not knowing for sure. I'm sorry I committed the crew without talking to you first. I'll pay any labor out of my own pocket."

"Nonsense," Dan huffed. "You've worked for me since you were twenty years old. I spoke out of turn too, when I offered her your other house for sale."

"I'm glad you thought about it; I was too mad at that user who was disrespecting her. Getting her away from him is worth it. But what do we do if they don't like the house or can't afford it?"

"Well, just make it affordable. We can make it likeable."

"You got any ideas?" Matt was intrigued. No one played poker, politics, or out-maneuvered others, in business or life, like Dan. He cheated no one, but no one cheated him either, and he'd disliked Billy from the moment he'd met him. He'd also known about Jenny and Missy since Matt was about 21, when he'd been completely broke, two days after payday, and Dan had to loan him money to fix his truck to get to work.

He'd laid into him about how adults used their paycheck to take care of real expenses instead of drinking it up. Matt had been forced to confess where a lot of it went, and that Missy was sick, and he'd given his paycheck to Jenny for the doctor. Dan had been surprised, but Matt wasn't the first one he'd seen supporting an illegitimate child, though he was the first in that circumstance.

After Matt had proven himself, Dan had given him a raise, kept his secret, and they'd formed a relationship that was more like father/son, or uncle/nephew that had lasted for over twenty years. Matt's dad, Zach, was Dan's close friend and both his boys was as much Dan's as his, anyway.

Now, Matt was his right-hand man, along with his son Clayton, and Dan hoped those two would run the ranch together long after he was gone. Matt had helped him teach Clayton how to run the ranch, kept him under his wing, and helped raise him; and he'd do about anything for Matt, seeing him as much a father as Dan himself.

"How about we have Pauline tell her the owner is looking for someone they can trust to live in the house so it doesn't set empty. They're not quite ready to sell, but don't live here anymore and they don't trust renters. They'll arrange for any repairs that need to be done, and since the place shares a property line with you," he laughed at that, causing Matt to grin, because it was all his property, "you've been contracted to have the ranch hands keep it up, because they knew and trusted you when they did live here.

She can live there, as long as she wants, rent free, for looking out for the place so they can keep it insured; and has first option to buy when they do decide to sell; maybe give her a five-year contract and put it in her name, since Amy's not from here. That way it's totally affordable, and you retain ownership if something goes wrong. It really would help you out insurance wise, and a house with people living in it doesn't run down as bad.

Pauline can tell her we recommended her and she feels comfortable telling her clients that Missy and Amy will take care of the place. You are right next door, so you can watch out for any trouble he tries to stir up, and close enough to intervene if she needs it. You can get to know her as a neighbor," he snorted at his own words, "that is, if you can't find a pair to tell her the truth, and get a DNA test done."

"How can I get a DNA test without telling her why I want it? What if I'm wrong and she was never mine?"

"Even if she isn't yours, that girl still needs help, and you've made a rather large investment in her for the last 22 years. But it would be good for both of you to know. We'll go back for lunch today and I'll distract her while you snitch that glass of tea she's always got on the table by the register. I'll take it to that geneticist that checks out the bulls we buy to make sure they're really of the bloodline the seller says they are.

We're just checkin' out a different type of bloodline, but I'm sure he can do it if I ask him to," Dan was grinning even wider. He was having a good time, both at Matt's discomfort, and at finally working out a solution for the problem. He was good at planning and loved wheeling and dealing, and creating unusual workarounds to difficult wrinkles in life. He'd been working on this one for a while, especially since Jenny died, but today he saw that it needed to be taken care of sooner, rather than later.

"Another thing," he began, "since that jerk is known to retaliate when he doesn't get his way, let's send the boys over today to put up a higher fence around the place, and an iron gate with a code to open it. We can leave 2-3 acres for a yard, then fence around the house, totally enclosing it in solid high fence; and make the surrounding land another area for some of those fancy deer you had to have last year. We can fence it too, and that will justify the higher fencing with no one being the wiser. We'll order the supplies now and have them send the order out today." He was rather pleased with his idea.

Matt snorted. "You mean the deer you said we weren't giving any more acreage to, until they started earning their keep?"

"Yep," Dan chuckled, "Looks like they may be useful after all. We can keep the game hunts over where they are currently, and use this piece of land to breed them. That way neither he, nor any of his like-minded friends, can use it as an excuse to get near her. But," he cautioned, "you may not can keep her from opening the gate, or the front door for that matter, to keep him out.

She watched a parade of men in and out of Jenny's door all her life, she may not live like you'd like. After all," he couldn't help but poke the sore spot a bit, "you weren't around to teach her your morality, now, were you?"

"Since I created her with Jenny out of wedlock, I can't very well claim the moral high ground, now, can I?" was Matt's immediate reply; although he'd learned well from that experience, and hadn't slept around since, knowing he'd never survive losing another child. "Dan, that's a good plan. I appreciate it more than you know. We'll go order the stuff, but can you call Pauline now? If they're already looking for a house, we need to get on this before they find another one where I can't protect her."

Dan made the call, leaving out the parts she didn't need to know about. He played it like Matt wanted someone in his house for the reasons mentioned, and just didn't want them to know he was the owner so they'd not bug him about buying, in case he decided not to sell.

Pauline, knowing Dan, knew more was up, but not what. She was eager to help, understanding when Dan was ready to reveal more, it'd probably be a good story. He was always up to something, but she'd watched him help many people throughout their life while staying in the shadows, and assumed this was just another one of those.

"I'll meet you for lunch at that diner today," she agreed. "We'll stay till the lunch crowd leaves, and then I'll approach her with the offer. When can you have the house ready to show?"

"We'll get it cleaned up today, but can you drop by to look it over and tell us what else needs doing?" he asked.

"Of course, I can. I sell a lot of homes to girls her age, so I'll give you any tips I can." Pauline offered. "See you in a few hours."

As she hung up, they were pulling into the hardware parking lot. They took a few minutes to make a list of what they'd need to fence in Matt's house and the land around it with the 10' high fence. They had a few of the longer fence posts left from the game hunting area they'd put in last year, but needed more of those and the wire too. Matt had a pretty good tree line around that acreage so they could use them to attach most of the fencing, but they were enclosing 15 acres, and around the house, so it was still a lot of material. They added several boxes of staples and other fasteners and Matt put 4-5 motion detector lights on the list to install in the yard.

They decided to just get the whole automatic gate opener kit with a solar panel to operate the single swing 12' gate. It was cheaper than buying the individual parts and they'd installed many over the years. It would be safer for both young ladies to stay in the car and use the wireless opener, than to get out and open and close the gate; and it would be a godsend in the rain.

Also, by installing it themselves and setting the code, they could get in fast anytime they needed to.

They added it all to the list of items they'd originally planned to pick up for the ranch, completing it with several feed bins and water troughs, so they could move deer over as soon as they got it done. They'd have to come back to town and get whatever they needed to spruce up the house, but they couldn't get it until Pauline let them know what was needed.

They'd do a walk-thru with her and then get a crew right on it. One thing about always having a crew around, they could get a job done quickly, and this time of year, they weren't too busy, except for feeding time.

They saw Erwin in the store, and Matt walked over to him and spoke, "Son, I know you've been friends with Billy most of your life, but I'm going to give you some advice I hope your daddy would have given you, if he'd lived long enough to show you life's most important principles. That boy is bad news. He's been bad news since he was a kid. He has no respect for people and uses everyone he can.

I'm not sure how invested you are in that friendship, but I knew both of your parents well, and I've watched you too. You may have gotten mixed up in more than you realize, but you aren't like Billy and that bunch he runs with. There's still time to get out and not go where it's inevitable he's headed."

Then he saw the mark on Erwin's neck. He glanced at Dan who gave a very slight nod. He'd seen it too. Matt changed direction, speaking low and urgently, "If you ever need help, or a job, just head on out to the ranch. I've lived here a long time and I might know more than you think.

We've fought that evil here for decades; and our parents and grandparents before us. Your grandmother and my mother are close friends as well. Get out now, before you can't. The ranch is safe, and if you want to relocate, I can make that happen too."

Erwin stared at him with his jaw dropped. Once again, he heard the whisper inside, '*it's not too late, you can still get out.*' Matt's voice had echoed what he'd already been thinking. "Mr. Hench, it may already be too late," he spoke low too, looking around to see who may have heard him. "They will never let me leave."

"That's what your daddy thought, Erwin," Dan spoke just as low. "He got out and you can too. The question is, do you want out?"

Erwin hadn't known his father had been involved with the Coven. He was shocked. Suddenly he wondered if seeing Billy's grandmother that long ago day was an accident, or a targeted introduction. Lots of ideas about that time seemed to be being reframed in the last couple of days.

Erwin dropped his head, memories of the last ten years speeding rapidly through his mind, including the events of last night. He felt another pang of shame that he hadn't felt in a very long time, if ever.

"Don't let anyone take your power of choice," Dan cautioned. "There are many roads in this life, but they all lead somewhere. The longer you stay on a particular path, the harder it is, to get back off. It may be hard now, but it's still doable. That scratch on your neck, boy… your granddaddy had one just like it when he came out and my dad gave him a job.

He broke down one night and shared with me how he'd acquired it. I will never in this life forget what he described. There ain't but one place those creatures come from, and you know it. It broke his heart when your daddy got mixed up in it. I promised him I'd watch out for you, and I let you down. I'd like to correct that. How hard will it be for you to meet with us? You can come to the ranch, or we can meet you elsewhere. I can get Homer to send you with this delivery, if that works.

The tractor's been acting up though, so you may be gone longer than usual. I'll call Homer and let him know we're working on it and as soon as we get the truck unloaded, I'll send you back; in the meantime, we can have lunch and talk. There's some local history you need to be aware of, and your family is involved. Are you interested in having that conversation?"

Erwin had conflicting emotions as Dan spoke. He'd been watching Billy get crazier and crazier over the last few years, and he'd never been completely comfortable around Wolf, but it was easier to go along than to be in the crosshairs of their wrath. He'd seen what happened to those who the Coven had deemed traitors.

Sobering up today, and thinking about what he'd seen and experienced the prior evening, he'd been trying to figure a way to opt out of the heavier rituals, while retaining the few friends he had. Suddenly what they were saying hit him, *Oh, crap. They know!* He reached up and pulled his shirt collar closer to cover up the mark. He'd had no idea anyone else knew anything about the Coven.

"I'll be happy to deliver your supplies, Mr. Blanchard," he spoke in his usual customer-friendly voice, while nodding at Dan, as Homer walked up.

"Of course, he can deliver your order," Homer was eager to accommodate Dan and Matt. The Rockin' O Ranch bought large orders regularly and always paid when it was ordered. Their business, along with a few other ranchers, was why he'd made it through this lockdown mess with his business intact. And he had other reasons as well.

"Thank you, Homer. We have a big list and it's critical it gets delivered today. Erwin is one we can count on to get it to us. Do you have more of that 10' fence we use for the game hunting pastures?" he led Homer away from Matt and Erwin, as he talked.

"I believe so," Homer reassured him. "You asked me to keep plenty around for quick repairs. How much do you need?"

"We're about to fence in fifteen more acres, with a cut-out of about five from a twenty-acre plot. I need another iron gate, one of those nice ones with the picture on the front, and the automatic gate opener set-up. You have that today too, or do we need to order it?"

"Oh, no," Homer was all smiles. This was going to be a big order indeed. "I have four or five of the larger nice ones. I have 10' and 12' sizes. I believe one of the larger ones has an Elk on it too. Didn't you say you were adding Elk later? If you're planning on putting them in the new area, it'd be perfect."

"Sounds like what I'm looking for." Dan smiled too, "Let's go look at them. I'll need the fence posts, fasteners, and all the same things we bought last time. Do you have any plain gates? I need another one for the back acreage that I can access from the ranch side. It won't be seen so it just needs to be utilitarian, and another gate opener.

I appreciate your sending Erwin, he's one of the few that can drive the big delivery trailer around my warehouse without cutting the backend into the corners. It being Saturday, I'll be

BOOK 1: "PREPARE FOR THE END" SERIES

glad to pay any overtime he may incur since it will take a while to unload.

With your permission we'll probably just have him drive the truck around the new enclosure acreage and drop the materials off in piles so we don't have to move it around again and again as we build it. We have some stock we want to move this week so we're in a bit of hurry. It'll save me a ton paying my boys so I'd be happy to pay for extra usage of the truck and driver."

"That sounds fine," Homer was thrilled at the offer. It would pay for the truck, Erwin, and the fuel. This week had been very slow and this order would make it a grand week's sales. And adding the extra payment to that, he'd come out very well. "We'll just do a truck and trailer half day rental. That should cover it just fine."

"Just so we don't have to be in any hurry, let's go ahead and make it a full day's rental. That way I won't feel like I'm taking advantage of your goodness," Dan generously upped the ante. "I appreciate the extra time to place it where it'll be the handiest for my boys."

After they walked off, Matt quietly asked Erwin, "How long has he been treating Missy like that?"

"That just started, sir," Erwin answered honestly. "It's about right on que though. He doesn't stay with anyone long. When he starts to get tired of them, he begins to be hurtful until it all blows up in a fight, and he can stalk out and blame it on the girl. It's classic Billy. I'm going to miss this one though. She's not his usual type, and I'm glad he's moving on. I've been worried about her for a while; she's too nice for him."

"You keep your eye on him around her," Matt stated emphatically. "She's been good to all of us at the diner and most of the people who go there every day have a soft spot for her. If she needs help, you get her out, you hear? If you need a place to take her, bring her to the ranch. We'll see that she gets to work and back unharmed, if he decides to retaliate for this morning. In fact, I think we'll go back over for lunch to keep an eye today."

Erwin nodded in relief. He was worried about him going back to harass Missy, too. For some reason Billy seemed to be getting rougher with her than usual, especially in public; he usually liked to keep an open door so he could loop back around when he was bored.

"We'll see you this afternoon."

Erwin nodded. At that Matt walked deeper into the store to fill his cart with planned purchases. He was kicking himself for not high-jacking Erwin at a younger age and putting him to work at the ranch. *Oh, well*, he told himself, *better late than never*. This seemed like a day to start righting old wrongs.

They finished up at Homer's, then went over to the local nursery, adding a large order of seed and plants for the spring planting. They usually ordered three or four months early, so they could get the first delivery of the year. They agreed to deliver a load of square hay bales to the owner. Local people with only one or two horses or cows liked to buy in small quantities and Dan had been their supplier for several years. They'd used up the last load from people buying them to put up yard displays and having hay rides during Halloween.

They also bagged excess cow patties to sell to the nursery for fertilizer. God knows, even after fertilizing the hay fields and farm areas, on a cattle ranch there was always plenty of cow patties. It was something Matt had come up with a few years back when the selling price of beef was lousy and they were brainstorming for other avenues of income.

Dan had laughed loudly at the suggestion of selling manure by the bag, but it was a free renewable resource that had panned out very well. It much more than paid for the feed that went in the other end. Matt liked to call the feed 'manure production cost.' They had several outlets now, and they had a friendly exchange in goods with several of the businesses, too. They could purchase one another's items at a reduced cost, like the order they'd just made, which helped both businesses, and lowered the ranch overhead enough to really make a difference.

Matt was smart and thought out-of-the-box. He'd come up with numerous ideas through the years, including the game hunts. It was amazing what men would pay to hunt penned up deer and other exotic animals. He'd talked Dan into planting 5 acres in pumpkins each year, then arranged for the local kindergarten classes to come out and see how a farm worked. The parents all bought pumpkins and the rest went to the Nursery and a few grocery stores, and they too, held an annual hay ride, but without any evil connections to Halloween.

The fifth-grade classes all came out to see how hay was cut and baled, and toured the barns, getting a glimpse of ranch life and getting to pet cows, horses, and other animals.

He even worked with the high school AG teachers doing a rotation for AG class where the students got some hands-on experience and professional level training, and Dan got some cheap labor while inspiring many young people. Matt had helped set up welding, and other jobs with several local businesses, for students to intern with all over town, too.

The school, the parents, the students, and the shop owners all benefitted. It was especially good for students who didn't have a mother or a father. He paired them with business owners who helped fill the gap of the missing parent. He'd gotten several long-term ranch hands from the program through the years; and they now sponsored five college scholarships each year, as did several other businesses, so it was a real benefit to the economy of their area.

The ranch was known far and wide; and many local people, knowing how much Dan gave back to the community, would promote, and buy his beef over the other ranchers. Dan's dad had taught him whenever you gave, it came back in abundance, and he'd watched the principal work over, and over again. He loved helping people and it seemed the more he gave, the better the business grew. Matt always said, 'you can't out give God,' Dan, and he agreed.

Clayton had followed Matt around the ranch since he was small and Matt had taught him to think outside-the-box too. They were a good team. Matt was his godfather, and if Dan passed away, he'd have been his guardian. He was past that now, but that father/son relationship was still there.

Dan was used to doing things the way his dad and granddad had always done them, but he'd learned to listen to Matt. It'd paid off many a time, and he'd long ago started giving him 50% of the profits for any new endeavor, so Matt was always working on new ideas. Dan was secretly very proud of the new hunting area, while constantly ribbing Matt about wrangling deer, asking him regularly if he needed to have a special deer saddle fashioned for him.

He had a plan to breed the animals in greater numbers and supply other game hunters. It didn't net as large a profit, unless you factored in the time and labor to conduct the hunts. It would be an easy source of income without the hassle of the hunts, and keep strangers off his property. It was getting more and more to be a popular sport around the surrounding areas and most hunts had other species in addition to deer. Matt wanted to supply them all.

They visited a few more vendors, then headed back to the diner to meet Pauline. She was waiting on them inside, having arrived a mere five minutes earlier. She'd ordered them tea and both were glad for the refreshment. Missy greeted them again, used to her customers having both breakfast and lunch on the same day. "Well, I see breakfast has worn off. What can I get you for lunch?"

"What's the special today?"

"You have a choice between meatloaf, spaghetti, or chicken fried steak. It comes with the usual potato and choice of two other vegetables, except the spaghetti. It comes with green beans, salad, and garlic bread."

"I'll take the spaghetti," Dan said. "I get plenty of steak at the ranch."

"Me too," Matt nodded, "and can you add chocolate pie to mine?"

"Of course," Missy smiled. Matt had chocolate pie at least twice a month. She turned to Pauline, "how about you?"

"Missy, this is my little sister Pauline," Dan introduced her. "She's the real estate agent I was telling you about."

Missy grinned. "Hello Pauline. When you have time, I'd love to speak with you. I can tell you though, it may be a while and I won't be able to afford anything expensive."

"That's quite alright dear," Pauline smiled with genuine friendliness. "Actually, I need a favor, and we may be able to help each other out. I'll take the spaghetti also, and chocolate pie; and when the lunch crowd thins out a bit, if you have time to sit for a few minutes, I can tell you about a client of mine with an unusual request."

Missy was curious, and could already see that Pauline was as kind as Dan. "I'll get your order in right away. It may be another hour before it slows down, but then I'll have a few minutes, if you have that long."

"That's fine dear; I'll need at least that long to harass my much older brother," she waved her hand in Dan's direction, who laughed at her teasing. She was only two years younger than him.

Missy went to the kitchen to turn in the order, and bring back platters of food that was ready to be served to other diners. It was a busy hour, but as predicted it slowed down until only Dan's table and one other were occupied. Missy knew it'd be that way for the next couple of hours if it stayed true to form. She grabbed a plate of spaghetti for herself, picked up her tea glass from behind the counter and approached the table. "Do you mind if I eat while we talk? I'm working a double today and this is my only time until later tonight."

"Come on," Matt pulled her chair out. "You go ahead, and if anyone needs coffee, I'll get it. Lord knows I've poured enough cups in my life; I think I can handle that much."

Missy smiled. It wouldn't be the first time a customer had poured coffee for the crowd, while she or Amy served plates or cleaned tables. It was part of the small-town charm she loved. "Thanks, Matt."

She slid into the chair and turned to Pauline. "I'm not even sure what we can afford yet. Amy and I decided we'd like to buy a house together and get out of the apartment complex. We haven't discussed finances yet, but it will need to be cheaper together than what we both pay for rent now. We're making less than we used to, but we have to do something. They are about to have a price increase at the end of the month, and we can't afford it to go any higher."

"As I mentioned, I have a client with an unusual request. They lived in a house out by Dan's ranch and have moved to another state. They aren't quite sure they want to sell, but the insurance company won't let them keep insurance on it unless someone lives in it.

They don't really want or need the money to rent it, and quite frankly aren't interested in it being a rental house anyway, as renters usually tear up the place. They do know they will be gone for several years, at least, and don't want the house to fall in while they're away. And without insurance, if it gets hit by a tornado, or burns down, they'll lose what they've put in it.

I was telling Dan about it earlier, and he mentioned you may be looking for a house. He and Matt highly recommended you and Amy as someone suitable to live in the house, so my client can keep the insurance. At this time, they don't want to rent it out, they just want someone they can trust to live in it and help keep it up.

Matt has agreed to help watch out for you, because it's right next door to him; in fact, it shares a property line with his place. Dan and his crew will do any initial repairs or small renovations you girls would want done, and keep up with any ongoing repairs. My client will pay for it, as they still own the house, and will keep up the utilities, real estate taxes, and insurance as well.

We're going to look at it today and I'll let them know anything that is required. As soon as they get it in tiptop shape you both can come out and see if you like it. We can paint, and put in carpet, tile, or whatever you'd like. You can pick out all the colors and styles, as it would be at least a five-year commitment. If it's something you like, and would commit to, you can save your rent money for down the line, and would have the first option to buy if they do sell.

If they decide to come back early and decide not to sell, they will give you a year's worth of rent for a down payment on another house. I know you need to consult with Amy, but do you think it's anything you'd be interested in doing? It would really help my client, and I'd feel very comfortable telling them I found the right people."

Missy was completely dumbfounded at the offer. "Rent free? For five years? Just to stay in the house?"

"Yes, that's the offer. It would really help them out if you'd consider putting off your purchase for that length of time. It may be a bit bigger than you were looking for. It's a four bedroom, two bath. It has a large front porch, and a glassed-in sun room in the back. Dan and Matt are going to fence off about five acres, so they can use the land around it for the ranch, without animals getting into the yard. It has a well, and a storage building out back. Are you interested?"

BOOK 1: "PREPARE FOR THE END" SERIES

Missy grinned. "I'd love to see the house. I'm interested, and I can speak for both of us, we are interested. It's much more house than we could afford right now, and being able to save up for five more years will help us tremendously. I can't wait to tell Amy. I'm working doubles for the next few days because she's gone to a wedding out of state, but she'll be back next week. Let me know when you're ready for us to come out. And honestly, even if Amy's not interested, I am. With no rent or utilities, I'd be crazy to say no. And Pauline, thank you so much for considering us."

"Thank Daniel and Matthew," Pauline had just noticed Missy's resemblance to Dana and Sarah and wondered just whose child this was, Matt's or Dana's. This was getting highly interesting. *No wonder Dan was scheming so intently*. She could also tell that Missy had no idea; *very highly interesting*. She also knew Sarah wasn't aware either. She and Sarah had been best friends their entire life, and if Sarah had known, Pauline would too.

She couldn't wait to hear the rest of the story, if it were ever told. And, thank you," she added. "It's not easy these days to get someone so highly recommended that I can comfortably recommend to my clients without a moment's doubt. I do hope you both like the house."

Missy realized they'd have plenty of room for the baby, and she could raise it out of the apartment complex with a real yard. She felt like she was in dream, or a movie. This just didn't happen to people like her. She wiped a tear as she thanked Matt and Dan. "I really appreciate you two. I promise we will take care of the house, and if anything goes wrong, we'll call immediately so it can be fixed while it's small."

They chatted about the house and the deer that would be on the surrounding land, with Dan teasing Matt about starting a zoo on his cattle ranch, while Missy finished eating. They made sure she understood that the code couldn't be changed, as the ranch hands may need to come through the gate on occasion, as they cared for the animals and the land. Pauline went to the ladies' room and Missy ran to the back to cut the pie.

While she was gone Matt picked up several hairs from the back of Missy's chair, then grabbed a fresh tea from the already prepared tray of filled glasses and deftly swapped it with the one

Missy had been drinking from. He ran out to the truck, putting it in the drink holder and was back in his seat before either came back into the room. The other table of people had already left, so no one knew. Dan was amazed at how effortlessly it had been done, and wished he'd thought of doing it sooner.

Both ladies came back to the table and all four enjoyed the chocolate pie. Missy said it was on her, to thank them all for the opportunity they'd provided her and Amy. Dan was pleased; after all these years Matt would finally get his answer, and he couldn't keep his eyes off the face of what he knew in his heart was his daughter.

Dan was the only one to notice the tenseness on Matt's face and the sudden moisture in his eyes. He joked around, teasing Pauline mercilessly, to keep the ladies' occupied while Matt got himself together.

Finally, Missy had to go back to work, and she rang up their ticket and said goodbye still smiling as they left. As soon as the dining room was empty, and she'd cleaned the tables and refilled the salt and pepper shakers and the butter and jelly bowls, she texted Amy. *Call me asap. I have huge news.* Her phone rang just as she was beginning to refill the ketchup bottles.

She filled Amy in on the offer of the house and the incident with Billy. Amy was as thrilled with the offer as Missy was and totally ticked at Billy. She agreed to keep Missy's secret and couldn't wait to get back to see the house. She was in the middle of a bridesmaid salon day and had to get off the phone, but assured Missy they'd go look at the house as soon as she got back; or if Missy got the chance, she could go check it out, and unless it was a total wreck about to fall in, she could move as soon as the house was ready to be occupied, and Amy would come when she got back.

Without worrying about rent, she could visit her family longer. They both had until the end of the month until they had to recommit to another year in the apartment complex. This would work out perfectly, and they would have plenty of time to prepare a nursery. She squealed with excitement at the good fortune that had fallen into their lap.

Bear Ye One Another's Burdens

Chapter 21

MAGGIE WOKE UP TO Annie stretching in the bed beside her. The light was slightly less dark than it would have been at her usual wake up time. Six, she guessed, then checked her clock; 6:15, close enough. She snuggled Annie closer and lay there for a few more minutes, enjoying being able to not have to rush. Saturdays were nice. Then she remembered they were all going back to Jake's, and all that she needed to do.

She got up, let Annie out, and pushed the button on the coffee maker. She let Annie in, gave her the usual breakfast—a dog cookie and peanut butter roll-up—and headed to the bathroom. She brushed her teeth and did other necessary tasks, and then went to pour a cup of coffee, heading to her recliner.

She flipped the footstool up and just enjoyed sitting in the quiet. She dozed a bit, then opened her bible, starting with the morning proverb. There was one for every day of the month and for over twenty years she'd read the proverb that corresponded to the day on the calendar. She missed one every now and then, but then would catch up on the second or third day. It was a ritual that started her day out that she needed. Proverbs gave wisdom and if there was anything she needed each day it was wisdom.

She moved on to the New Testament and read five chapters. She read ten a day, but sometimes did five in the morning and five in the evening. She read some from the Old Testament most nights. She'd been a student of the bible for years, and could find things by flipping the pages and looking for the pattern of the underlined places. She'd had the same bible since she was 20 and it was a familiar as her face in the mirror.

At 7:00, she located the vases and started the dishwasher, then went to put her makeup on, and pulled her hair up into a ponytail and clipped it up. Now her ponytail was slightly sassy and out of her way, but looked neat. She arranged her bangs and pulled out some side hair to frame her face, then went to dress.

As she picked out clothes, she grabbed a box and added several pairs of jeans, sweats, and shirts, then went to the drawer and added socks, underwear, and pajamas. She'd begin to pick up some extra things soon, and store it all at Jakes, leaving enough here to work but not too much to grab in a hurry, or leave behind if there was no time. Like Jake, she was watching the political situation and bible timelines closely, and believed that when something happened bad enough to have to flee, there would be no extra time for packing.

This week, she'd start weeding thru her bookshelves and kitchen items. She'd moved lock, stock, and barrel, leaving behind treasured items once before; and wanted to have those precious things stored away soon, just in case. Jake had done a ton of preparation already and it had made her aware that he thought that whatever was coming was pretty close.

All four of them had agreed that they needed to get their most precious items to his house without delay. It felt weird preparing for a war, or possibly the end of time as we know it. Her spirit was at total ease with the preparations also, and that spoke to her as well, that time was short.

She walked out to put the box in her truck, just in time to see missiles rising into the air in a 360° circle of sky; there were dozens. She gasped, knowing she'd waited too late, and stood there in horror as they ascended. Just as they started to arc, she realized they were gone. The sky was empty and she was ok. It came to her that she'd seen a vision of what was to come. She was shaking all over, and shocked.

She hurried to the garage and began to pull out bins of supplies and made way around the boxes of cedar planks so Jason could reach them easily. Once she had as much in the backseat of the truck as she could put, she went back in to eat breakfast, then seared a roast and put it in a pan with the appropriate seasonings to cook at Jake's while they worked. She set the pan she'd used to sear it in the sink to soak; while she pulled out vegetables, made a huge salad, and put the food into a cooler in the back of her truck. She washed everything so it'd be clean when she came home later.

Afterward she grabbed Annie's extra treats, extra kennel, and food dishes, then found her leash. She didn't intend to leave her at home anymore unless she was working or shopping. *I have no idea how much time we have until the missiles hit, but she's going to be with me as much as possible.* She placed them in the front passenger seat, with the door facing center, so she could easily put Annie in and get her back out.

She sat down and read the next five chapters in her bible, then sat praying until she heard Jason arrive. She was calmer, but still rattled. *That's how fast it will happen. In a moment. I will look up, and they'll be there, no matter where I am. I need to get as much stuff to Jake's as I can, as quickly as I can.* She decided instead of taking just a couple packs of planks, she'd just take them all while he was here to help. She went out, and together they moved the boxes of 30 pack cedar grilling planks into his truck, then followed each other to the gas station.

They each filled their tanks, and both bought two cases of water to take to Jake's. Jason had a large cooler so they each purchased a couple bags of ice as well. Maggie had to run through the local drive-thru for her morning tea, and they were on their way. She was still unsettled but felt like she needed to wait to share the vision until she could tell Jake first.

When they arrived, she parked and opened the door, and Annie sailed out. She'd been to Jake's many times and loved running around the huge acreage. She ran up and jumped on Jake as he was descending the porch stairs. He picked her up, ruffed her fur, spoke silly dog junk to her as she barked, kissed her head, and sat her back down to run all over the yard, and then back to him, and he did it all over again. It was their normal routine.

He picked her back up and held her as he directed Jason to back up to the shop so they could unload the cedar, along with the wood and tools that he'd brought to add to what Jake had. They unloaded the cedar from Maggie's truck first, then all the stuff Jason had brought. Between the two of them, it created a fairly large pile. Maggie carried the bins of paint, and other supplies she'd brought to work on the panels and wreathes, onto the porch. There was a large table sitting on it that Jake had covered in white paper and taped it down so it couldn't blow off.

The men brought the cooler and sat it on the other side of the porch and added water bottles to the ice in that one, after putting two bags of ice with a scoop into the one Jake already had sitting there. It took about three whole minutes as this was their usual arrangement for daytime meetings when the weather was nice. Both Maggie and Jason walked back to their respective vehicles to get the food they'd brought and took it into the kitchen.

Maggie put the roast into the oven and set the timer, stacked the salad in the fridge, as Jason set the crockpot of beans he'd prepared on the counter and plugged up the cord, adjusting the dial to low, as he'd made them the night before, and they only needed to be kept warm. Maisie was bringing cornbread and cake. Rachel and Sharon were bringing vegetables, and Jake had made scalloped potatoes that he'd run in and put in the oven at the proper time. Louise was only open half a day on Saturday and they'd told her not to worry about bringing anything. Both knew she would anyway.

Jason realized he'd forgotten the boxes of small nails they needed and headed back to town to get them. After he'd left, Jake asked Maggie what was wrong. "What do you mean, what's wrong?" she countered.

"Mags, you hide it well from others, but the look on your face as you pulled up says something is wrong. You almost looked scared. Did something happen? Did someone trigger you again?"

"Yes, and no." she admitted. She shared the vision with him and watched his face as he absorbed the words. "Ok," he looked serious. "We'd better accelerate the move. Did you bring any clothes?"

"Yes, in the truck. I wanted to wait till everyone left, but with Jason gone and no one else here, can you help me go ahead and get them in?"

"Yes, for now we'll stack them in the closet so they aren't out in plain sight, and later we'll get them more user friendly. Are you ok? You still look like you've seen a ghost."

"I can't even begin to describe to you how I felt watching those missiles rising. And they just came out of nowhere. Jake, there was no time to act, or react, or grab anything. It was too late. It was happening, and it was now." She was shaking. "I feel like God is saying something big is immanent. I felt like I need to move all I want to have here, now."

"I'll come over this week and help. We can start tomorrow if you want. We'll talk to the girls this evening. We need to share the vision with the others, but not the move, quite yet. I'm still not sure who will live out here and who won't. I'm not as prepared as I want to be for more than family. We need to start praying and setting up other places for people to live, soon.

I have a couple of friends and brothers I need to talk to. And Maggie, any financial arrangements or selling of the house needs to be accelerated also. I don't think it's tomorrow, but I feel it could be this coming year."

She nodded in agreement and they sat and talked quietly until they heard cars pulling in. The people piled out, with all lending a hand until the food was put away and the craft materials were arranged in ways to facilitate the most efficient order of business. Jake asked them all to join hands, and they asked God to bless their efforts, to bless Louise and her flower shop, and to help them create items that would provide comfort to those who were devastated at the loss of a loved one.

They agreed that while they may not be preaching a sermon from the bible, they were being the hands of God in appreciating life, respecting the passing on of a person who was a unique creation made in God's image, and offering a way for others to provide support to the ones they loved. They asked God to use each piece to help inspire the peace that passeth understanding.

Jason showed them the pattern he'd drawn to cut pieces for the baby cradles, and he and Jake briefly discussed sizes and shapes of other containers. They wanted just a few designs and then they would make many of each one. They deemed it the best way to mass produce them. Jake decided that whatever unique shapes they found in the scraps they could use to create one-of-a-kinds, or use to make free shaped plaques that the girls could design for signs and pictures to attach to the crosses with stakes cut on the bottom.

Sharon decided that they needed a prize for the one-of-a-kind that got the most votes. Maisie thought it only fair to have a prize for the most voted for painting, as well. Each threw in $10 and they split it into two envelopes as prize money.

The men left for the shop, bringing back the first four boxes of cedar, stacking them on the table, then, retreating back to their own projects while the women sat out the paint in the middle of the table, where it was reachable to all. They unpacked paint brushes, sealer, glitter, spray paint, and even google eyes for some of the snowmen. Maggie filled dishes designed to hold the brushes in the water to keep them from drying and to wash between colors.

They had cedar planks in stacks on both ends of the table and a second table out in the yard to set finished pieces to dry in the sunlight. Jake had put thick plastic on the grass and weighted it with brick to do the final spray of sealer. It was all in the most usable order so they could move each one from start to finish without a lot of wasted walking.

They marveled at how much they'd missed being able to do things with other people. Life had gotten lonely, sedentary, and utilitarian. Maggie was quieter than usual due to the shock of the vision, but all were chattering so it wasn't noticeable. She was enjoying the warmth of the early December day, knowing there wouldn't be a lot of them left. The breeze soothed her.

She showed them the simple patterns she'd brought: snowmen, trees, ornaments, angels, candles, bears, sleds, horns, and others. They would be easy to do in different colors and styles, and turned different ways could make it look like an entirely different picture. Maggie's favorite was the snowman, so she chose that pattern to start. Maisie liked the Christmas trees, Sharon the bears, and Rachel the ornament.

They all had a white round paint dish that had a dozen 1" wells to put the various paints in. Each choose their initial hues and added a well of black and a well of white. All the colors were rich and would pop on the reddish-brown sienna shade of the cedar.

Maggie traced the snowman circles and the top hat on several, and began to paint the snowballs. It would be easier to mass paint, utilizing the same colors without so often washing out the brush, and after painting the initial snowball body parts, she could make the facial features different, and decorate the hats with several looks, add freeform stick arms, shovels, brooms, snow bunnies and deer playing in the snow and whatever else she could dream up in the moment.

Rachel did the same with the ornaments, choosing rich deep colors that she could then decorate with designs. Maisie had all the many shades of green, reds, and some blues and purples, and several brush types to create different looks, and Sharon wanted dark and light brown, and even blue, pink, and cream-colored bears. All saw the wisdom in block painting dozens of planks with the main features, then detailing them after that was dry.

The men had agreed to spray paint some of the pine cones and they had boxes of plain ones too. Sharon took the time to set the boxes of cones, and the bin of spray paint they'd gathered between them out by the plastic, so they wouldn't have to be interrupted later.

Maggie, absorbed in her thoughts, made snowball after snowball, stacked in the usual recognizable form, or fallen over, bending at impossible angels, and some upside down; using purples with some, and deep and light blues with others, for shading. From the start, each had its own charm and looked subtly different. She added highlights for dimension with brilliant yellow and orange tinted white. Before one detail was painted, they looked 3-D, and as if you could reach over and pick them up and throw them in a snowball fight.

Rachel, copying her placement of shades and tints to create the 3-D effect, did the same with her richly colored ornaments. She used golds and silvers to add the metal tops, and then painted narrow bands of ribbon for hangers, draped casually down the sides, in complimenting hues.

One she made just for her, finishing it first. It was a deep green ornament that she painted a cowboy snowman on, and a lady snowman facing him. The 'man' was extending his cowboy hat to the 'woman' and she was reaching for it with a saucy look on her face. She was very quiet while she painted it, and when it was dry, went out to put it in the sun to dry, but instead, she put it in her car, while saying she needed her ChapStick.

Maggie hid her smile, knowing very while what it represented, after all the times they'd shared their secret dreams. She was sitting on the same side of the table with her and covered for her, making sure no one else saw it. Sharon, an old hand at craft painting, used the same basic principle to create rounded bellies, arms, legs, and heads for her teddy bears.

Before long they had piles of 'basics' and could start the real fun of detailing them. They swapped the paint containers back and forth, using each other's dishes to have more choices. The bears and snow people, both sexes, acquired scarves and hats of many colors and patterns. They had a blast trying to outdo one another. The trees popped with birds, seedpods, ornaments, with gifts and small animals around the base. Annie ran around everywhere barking, begging to be held at times, and sitting on Maggie's feet the rest of the time.

Each snow person's face was their own; some with frowns, some with smiles, some bashful; they had carrot noses of all sizes and shapes, eyebrows, huge pieces of coal and giant buttons, for buttons. All kinds of crazy limb arms, hats tilted at various angles, some hats blowing away with the face hilarious as they looked annoyed, surprised, or watching in dismay with 'wind' swirling around them. Some had fallen down, some had angel wings with the entire snowman rising from the ground. She put paint on a toothbrush and running her finger across the bristles, blew 'stippling' across the panels, therefore creating snow still falling.

Maggie even painted a few that were melted puddles with the hats, noses, arms, and buttons lying in the water, and a Texas Snowman sign tilted as if falling to the ground.

The ornaments were breathtaking, looking for all the world like shiny glass balls, some with added decorations, some without. The hands-down-best, looked like clear glass with toys inside. It was easy if you knew how to do the effect, but looked difficult and spectacular.

They each chose new patterns, and before long there were sleds, angels, candles, and musical instruments of all kinds. They drew a pattern for deer, turkeys, pheasants, pumpkins, pilgrims, and fish. They kept challenging one another for more daring paint schemes, getting better and more artistic as the day progressed. As women usually do, their talking and laughter kept them entertained and all were surprised when Louise drove up. They'd had no idea they'd been painting almost four hours.

They greeted her, and she had tears of gratitude, as her eyes opened wide with amazement, at all they'd accomplished. They went to the shop to check on the guys. There was a table filled with small, medium, and large sized wooden containers. Each were wonderful with the natural wood colors all so different; some were polished by the sander, and some left rough. They'd used small leftover ends of boards to design six and eight-sided bowls as well.

There were about fifty 2'-3' crosses, made from left over tomato stake strips, with pointed stakes on the longest leg, some with hinged prop legs, some without. Most had cup hooks inserted in the center to wire flowers and ribbon to, or hang a sign from. They'd used strips of the 1x2'' leftover trim and thin paneling to make miniature fishing boats and had even used up the smallest scraps for seats in them. One special piece especially caught Maggie's eye.

They'd made a container, that while open on top, was still very obviously a bible. You could even see the page edges impressed into the wood on the side. Jake had made it with her in mind, and took extra time and effort to get it just right. She envisioned it painted black with shiny gold edged pages peeking out, and florals sticking up and small picks of wooden tiny plaques with the words of life stenciled on them. She wanted to paint and purchase it on the spot.

There was an entire box of baby bible shaped pieces, about 2 ½ inches across, and another of 2" tiny crosses, made from some popsicle sticks Jake had unearthed from an old VBS program. He'd sliced them to thinner pieces, and squared the tops. They were working on some of the tiny baby cradle containers now, and Louise's jaw dropped again, at what they'd designed.

There was sawdust everywhere, and the men looked like a box of it had been dropped from above down upon them. They were simply covered, and their hair looked reddish-blond from so much wood dust. Both wore thick plastic safety glasses, and as the sound of the saws covered up any noise from the ladies, they had no idea they were being observed.

Finally, Jason looked up, turned off his saw, and waved at Jake to do likewise. It was so quiet when the last saw stopped, that the ladies realized it had been background sound all day, and they had gotten used to it. They congratulated the men on the wonderful work and asked if they could take the small bibles and crosses to paint. Maggie asked for permission to paint the larger bible-bowl. All smiled and nodded, each knowing he'd made it for her.

Louise, being the only one not covered in paint, glitter, or sawdust, offered to go get the meal ready. She'd stopped and picked up fried chicken and ice cream on the way out to add to the bounty. All were grateful, and now that they'd stopped for a few minutes realized they were famished. Hard work and friendship used up a lot of calories.

They decided to eat outdoors, and Louise waved them over to the outdoor faucet, yelling on her way to the house that she'd bring soap and towels. They took turns washing up, using a broom to sweep the men first, and laughing at the endless quips and antics in the doing. Jake finally bent over and ran both hands through his hair, shaking his head vigorously, as the too long locks, flew everywhere, making them all laugh.

They dug out freezing cold, dripping, water bottles from the coolers, and sat around the picnic table in the yard, until Louise called from the door. She handed out plastic plates, bowls, and utensils; then the serving dishes and glasses of iced tea, to waiting hands, and they streamed back and forth until it was all set for lunch. She ran back in for a stack of napkins, then once again Jake led them in a prayer of thanksgiving and they shared a delicious meal, made more attractive by the comradery they shared. Annie received handouts from everyone, and finally, too full to eat another bite, went to sleep on the top porch step.

They told the men about how the friendly competition had fueled their artistry and the men shared how they'd built one idea upon the previous one also, coming up with far more than they'd set out to do. After lunch, they'd finish the cradles, then go cut wreath and filler boughs. The women would paint the crosses, bibles, and cradles, then stencil some sayings on the plaque shaped wood and the endless stacks of planks.

Maggie told them, she thought laughter, sunshine, and shared purpose, mixes into high octane fuel for energizing this type of endeavor. That's how families readied for holidays, and churches for festivals, or schools for events. Many hands make the load light for all. It was a labor of love for a friend in need, and an entire community, rooted in the love of God in their hearts.

After lunch, they went back to work. Louise surprised them by being an expert in calligraphy, so she, using paint pens, penned the plaques as they came up with the phrases, including many Bible verses they thought appropriate for different occasions. "Louise, how did you get so good at that?" Sharon asked.

"Just after I opened my flower shop, I discovered many people wanted me to write out their cards, so I took a class and learned several scripts and how to use different sizes of pens for different effects. It's been a Godsend many times. I'm always prepared, and even keep a set in my van." She'd brought several with her, already thinking ahead.

They used the softer baby colors for the tiny crosses, bibles, and cradles. Louise penned 'Resting in Jesus' in fancy script on the arc of the cradle top and decided to pen the child's name on the foot end when each one was used. All had tears at that. She'd found some boxes of silk baby's breath and tiny white roses in her storage room this morning, and with pink or blue ribbon, it would be a lovely arrangement, and being silk, the parents could keep the cradle afterward. Jake and Jason had made fifty and she hoped she'd never need them all, but her heart knew otherwise.

She really hoped people would be more likely to purchase them to celebrate new births, so she kept some without script so she could put the Family name on the top, and the name, weight, length, and birthdate on the end. It helped her to not focus on babies being killed from the shot. The thought of that made her nauseous.

They went ahead and filled ten to see the different effects, and to have several choices. All they would need would be the personal information added. They were lovely, but each woman felt a pang, and Maggie had to clamp down her feelings at the memory the pink ones brought up. She decided that, later, she'd ask Louise to make one for her.

Louise was ecstatic at the exquisite artistry of all the items. Each was unique and all were simply beautiful. Professionally, she'd never seen anything so exceptional, and she so liked to be set apart in her excellence; she marveled at the irreplaceable gift this wonderful group of people had given her.

This was no time for pride she knew, but as a business owner in a highly competitive field, she knew no one else had anything even close. And not just the cradles, the handmade vessels, the painted planks, the crosses that weren't bulk order 'every place has them' items. This was crafted with both love and artistry, and it showed in each piece. Each was a masterpiece that was apparent from the first glance.

She'd gone from an almost empty store to what would be the most sought-after 'stand-out-from-the-crowd' merchandise in the county. These were high-end items. She was both blessed and pleased. It was worth thousands of dollars of supplies, and it hadn't cost her but pennies, just the ribbon she purchased from Sharon. *God is indeed good.*

She decided to see if Maggie, Sharon, and Rachel wanted to start a small side business and keep her stocked in seasonally appropriate inventory. She'd be happy to pay them, and the men too, if they were interested in making wooden containers. It was a conversation for later, right now they were enjoying giving, and she was thankful.

The men drove back up and began unloading bucket after bucket of boughs. They wired many into beautiful wreaths in standard sizes, and at Louise's direction even fashioned swags and some shaped as 'drops' as something different for front doors. If she was going to be known for handcrafted decorative touches, she could design something different and start a trend.

She couldn't wait to start decorating them next week. She could already see in her mind's eye how they would look with ribbon, pine cones, cranberries, and ornaments. She could even dry some orange peels and add cinnamon sticks for more fragrance. When she mentioned it, they all said they'd dry theirs too, as they ate the fruit, and drop them off occasionally.

The greenery would keep for weeks in cold water in her cooler. And Jake had offered to keep her stocked with fresh ones through the holiday season. Tonight, they'd load all trucks and cars, and go fill her shop with it all. She couldn't wait to see Ellie and Alice's face on Monday when they came in and saw the bounty. All of them had been more and more stressed at the lack of supplies amid the endless calls for orders.

The ladies kept painting, and the men began to seal each piece with the spray sealer and spray paint the pinecones in the metallic colors they'd decided on, including glittering some of them. It was a big job, and as they dried, they placed them by color in the plastic bins Louise had brought. They loaded the painted ones, the plain ones, the greenery, and all they'd made in the shop in both Maggie and Jason's trucks. They began to place the painted items in bins also, taking care to keep the designs stored together properly, then spread the bins among all the vehicles.

As the last ones were painted, stenciled, or penned with calligraphy, the women cleaned up and repacked the much-used paint bottles and brushes. Those too were placed in the respective owner's cars. They decided to caravan to 'Kaleidoscope of Petals,' unload, and then go to Sharon's. She would go straight to her home, having only her paint supplies in her vehicle; and order pizza, then put together a salad.

Maisie would unload first and go on to help her set up. They'd share another meal together, pray, and then each go home. It had been a good and productive day, but all were tired. Pizza would be fast, with fast cleanup, and all were exhausted and had to prepare for the following week. Louise had cleaned Jake's kitchen after lunch, so no one would be left with a mess.

They awarded the prize money to Jason for the design of the baby cradles; and Rachel for the ornaments that looked like blown glass. Both were excellent and well crafted. Each accepted and then handed the money to Sharon to pay for the pizza, while all clapped at their generosity.

After the meal, they were talking, and Jake asked Maggie to tell them about the missiles.

"….and that's when they disappeared and I realized it was a vision," Maggie finished telling the group about the missiles rising, the distress on her face conveying as much as her words.

"I believe it's a warning." Jake added. "Does everyone have extra food and other supplies at home?"

"Honestly," Louise replied, "I've been too busy to shop. I know that's not an excuse, but I've been filling orders and trying to find supplies for ten hours a day.

Jacob hung his head slightly. "And I've been thinking you and Maggie are just being a bit too cautious. Until Louise told us how many funerals she's been preparing for, I haven't heard much else about it."

"Do all of you have plans with your families to help take care of each other if this country does go to war?" Jake looked serious.

"Sally and I have discussed me going to live with her," Maisie offered. "She's having trouble making all the bills alone; and her two kids don't need to be alone while she works overtime. We haven't done it yet because we hoped life would get back to normal, especially since I was able to go back to work these last few months.

Do you really think our country is going to war?" She grabbed another slice of pizza, stress eating, as worry began to take hold. "Neither one of us wants to let go of our house, but I won't let her lose hers, or let those kids go without supervision; and with only one house payment and set of utilities, it would help us both."

Sharon looked at Jake who very subtly shook his head 'no.' She understood he didn't want to share their plans to move in together yet. Jason said, "Actually, I've talked to my son too. Since his wife left him, he's been having a hard time. He thinks I need help, but we both know he does as well.

"I can't make those decisions for you," Jake spoke again, "but right now it's a seller's market in real estate. If you are planning on living with your children, I'd think about getting the houses on the market and using the proceeds to stock up. Especially with children. Jason, doesn't Sally live close to you?"

Maisie answered the question, "Yes, she does. About a block from him. I pass his house every time I go over to babysit or visit."

"Would you consider having a meeting with both your children, to talk about helping each other out if it gets a little hairy?" Jake was thinking out loud. He didn't have room for everyone, but he wanted to make sure they each had someone they could depend on, if needed. "I don't know if I'll be able to get to town, or if you'll be able to get to my place, depending on the severity of anything that may happen. I'd feel much better knowing you had one another."

Jason looked relieved, as did Maisie. "That's a good idea," Jason spoke first. I'm sure I can speak for both of us, and with two men, we can help the ladies with anything they need done. Tommy's always been willing to help other people."

"And we could repay you with homecooked meals," Maisie added.

"Ok." Jake dusted his hands together, as if crossing an item off his list. "I love it when a plan comes together."

My son and Ellie, and Alice and I, have discussed something similar," Louise looked serious. My son and I live on the same property. Remember he and Ellie built that house on the back ten acres a few years back? And Alice's kids live in Florida. I've already told her if it starts looking bad, she can just move out there with us. If we can still work, we can ride together, and if not, we will be safer here.

My grandkids have been talking about building or putting in mobile homes, too. I'm not sure where they are on that, but if it gets anything like you've described Jake, I'll talk to them again. It will be much safer for them everybody if we're close. Lord, knows if we go to war, I'd rather have my family where I know they are safe."

"Do you own firearms?" Maggie had to ask.

"Well... yes..." Louise looked slightly embarrassed. "Right after I opened the shop, I got accosted on the way to the car one night after closing-up. I was terrified I was going to die. The thief thought I had money from the day. Honestly, I usually did, but had to be somewhere, and had locked it in the safe. That's why I go to the bank during the day now.

Andy made me get a gun right after we got married, and took me to the gun range until I wasn't afraid to use it. I still carry it, but I haven't practiced in a while," she admitted. "I was lucky then, because another shop owner saw him grab me and called the police. They had a unit about a block away, and when the siren began to peal, he ran away."

"I have a shooting range at my house," Jake reminded her. "Please come out next Sunday and we can get you back up to speed.

What about you?" he turned to Jason.

"I'm not much into guns," he stated. "Tommy has a couple. I never thought I'd need one, but I went with him a few times. Do you really think I need one?"

"Absolutely. Can you get one by next Sunday? I can show you both at once, and you can practice as much as you want. These rumblings of war are picking up. I can't tell if it will be a civil war, or with another country, or both. But Tommy can't protect the front and back of the house at the same time. How would you feel if he was shot because you couldn't help defend him?"

With a sobering look, Jason slowly nodded his head, "that is a reason I can do it. But I hope it never comes to that."

"We all hope it never comes to that," Maggie agreed. "But with the riots, the illegals flooding our nation, and people getting desperate, we can't count on the fact that we won't have to defend ourselves and others. As the food supply gets thinner, people will be leaving the larger cities and coming into the smaller ones, to get whatever they can, however they can. It's better to be ready and not have to do it, than to not be ready and be unable to help someone."

With that, Jason, Louise, then Maisie, decided it was time to go. Jake and Maggie rose and began to gather their items, but lingered, as they were staying with Sharon and Rachel to discuss their arrangements for a while longer.

When it was just the four of them, they sat back down. Jake informed his cousins that he thought it was time to accelerate their moves. None of them wanted to give up their home and personal space, but all agreed it was better to accomplish the move while it was easily doable than to wait until it would be much harder.

They discussed some initial house rules, such as cleaning, cooking, and shopping. All four were very independent and hard-working, so none of them were worried about that. Maggie and Jake tended to stay up later, and Sharon sometimes as well, but not regularly. Rachel was more of an early riser, so quiet times were established. He looked at Sharon and Rachel, and said, "and y'all know it won't just be us."

They nodded, knowing their brothers would probably end up there as well.

Because all of them needed the internet for their jobs, they decided to purchase two more packages so that it wouldn't become an issue. As long, as the college was open Jake would continue to go, as would Sharon if the elementary school held in-person class. Rachel had to go meet her clients to do signings, and Maggie could work anywhere but still liked meeting people in her office, or in their homes on occasion.

They would create a two-week menu and split up the meal prep, and most probably Jake would cook breakfast for them all, and whoever was home would share in the cooking. They'd shared many meals in the past and worked well together. And Jake's family all loved cooking together.

Jake laid out more of his plan to have his brothers and another person or two join them on his property. They wouldn't all live in the house, but would have mini-homes or trailers moved in. He had plenty of acreage, and one his choices was more of a loner. He would probably live further back in the woods and help watch the back of the property.

He'd already talked to him, and he was all for it. He'd cleared several places for homes to be built or brought in, and had roads built as well. He'd even had wells drilled and electric poles installed, but if the grid went down, those would be unnecessary.

It was a matter of days to have them all on the property, except for building houses. All could shoot, all could be trusted, and his sisters-in-law had been in his family for decades and were easily cooperative. They all had travel trailers they could stay in until they could get houses up. Each had their own skill set to bring to the group and he wanted them all to be safe as the world unraveled.

Like Sharon and Rachel, he'd had a few conversations already to feel them out. His family was close and he knew they could live together for quite some time if it became necessary. He'd not been as close to them in the last several years, but he knew very well it was his own fault. Hopefully he was just being cautious; and if the country began to right itself, they could easily go their separate ways, but as none of them were getting any younger, it was ok if it was a permanent situation.

They decided to move in soon, with Maggie and Rachel coming this month. Sharon had a few more things to wrap up.

She wanted to go thru her late husband's things and have her children come home for one more Christmas in the family home, and let them help decide what to do with some of the family heirlooms. She would get her house on the market though, as would Maggie.

Each would help the others move, and staggered moves would ease the stress and work. They said their goodnights and went home exhausted and ready for bed.

Family History

Chapter 22

ERWIN WAS PULLING ONTO the highway with Dan's load when his phone rang. It was Billy, and immediately when he knew the call went through, he started issuing orders, "As soon as you get off, meet me at my house. The guys are coming to play poker. And pick up some fried chicken from the grocery store. We may need some other stuff too. I'll text a list and you can add anything you think of."

Erwin was not happy as he realized he wasn't even asked if he wanted to come, or wanted to pick up groceries, or even if he had the money to pay for it all. Billy had decided that already. He remembered Dan's words to not let anyone make his choices for him. Billy calling and telling him what to do was nothing new, but now he saw it in a different light.

"Sorry. No can do. Homer is sending me with a huge load to deliver and unload; it will take hours. Then I'm headed to Gran's for dinner. I promised her last week."

"Well, just tell your Gran you changed your mind. Tell her you have to help Homer stock till late," Billy demanded in a rude voice, totally dismissive of his prior plans.

"Billy, my Gran raised me. It's just her and me. I'm not ditching her tonight. She needs me, and I promised to help her tomorrow get her yard ready for winter. I'll be tied up all weekend. You'll have to play poker without me," Erwin held his ground.

"How am I supposed to get the chicken and other stuff I need?" Billy was livid.

"I guess you drive to the store and buy it, like everyone else," Erwin replied, annoyed. "People do it every day. Would you like me to text you the supermarket address?"

Billy went ballistic. Erwin was distracted by the screaming and almost hit a lady that pulled out in front of him. Several drivers all hit their horns at the same time, as he stomped the brake. The load was heavy and he would have hit her, but she responded to the horns also, pulling into another lane just in time. Billy heard it all and demanded to know what was going on.

"I almost creamed someone while you were having a cow. I'm getting off this phone, Homer is calling. I'll see you next week." Erwin hit the off button on his phone and put it in his pocket. He was getting tired of Billy deciding how he'd spend his time away from work. He was still chewing on the fact that Dan and Matt had disclosed his dad and grandpa being involved with the coven, and that they had gotten out.

Erwin knew his grandpa had worked for Dan's dad, and that he was still friends with his Gran, but hadn't known his dad knew Matt at all. He for sure didn't know Matt and Dan—or anyone—knew about the coven.

He was both eager and apprehensive about hearing what they had to say. He pondered his life while driving the twenty miles to the ranch. He'd followed Billy around since they were kids. When younger he'd had lots of ideas and plans, and was very creative; but he suddenly grasped how they'd all been shot down by Billy, and his constant ridicule of anything Erwin brought to the table.

He'd been discouraged again and again in doing anything he wanted to do. He had to be in second place always, with Billy the leader. Erwin had been so grateful for a friend after his parents died, that he'd acquiesced to Billy in order to have someone in his life that cared. He realized his personality and intelligence has been suppressed, so that he could be Billy's lackey.

He'd never seen himself as a leader; and being drawn into the relationship so young, in such bad emotional shape, then meeting the coven members, he'd been taught to bow to the leader in everything. But, he acknowledged, Billy didn't care about anyone but Billy. He'd even tried to get Erwin to quit the hardware store and work for him, mad at Homer's influence on him.

But Erwin knew his Gran needed him around more, and Homer had given him a job when he turned sixteen. Without the extra income they'd have never made it. He was loyal to a fault, and Billy wasn't the only one he was loyal to.

He was nervous about knowing that Matt and Dan seemed to have a good idea of what he'd become involved in. He liked both men and wanted them to see him in a good light. Now, he wondered what they saw when they looked at him, and, also why they were interested in him at all. To his understanding, he was only someone who worked for Homer that helped them with their orders.

He wondered if they'd tell Gran. She'd be so disappointed in him. After his parents had died, she'd tried to get him to go to church with her, but he'd been so mad at God that he'd refused, except at special times, like Christmas and Easter. He'd gone to please her, but had tuned out anything that was said, as a buzzing filled his ears, every time he'd tried to make sense of what the pastor said.

At 25 he knew he should be something besides Billy's sidekick. Most guys his age had already graduated from college, and were getting married, buying houses, and having kids. They'd accomplished a lot, while he still worked for Homer. He liked his job, but he'd felt a restlessness for a while now, and knew he wasn't happy, but not how to fix it. He'd dated a few girls, but no one he'd cared to have around the group of guys he hung out with.

Gran had been after him for a while, to settle down and have a family. She loved babies, and always said she'd like to rock a few great grandbabies before she died. She was only 60 though, so he'd assured her that she still had time to wait until he met the right one. He really liked Amy, but she'd probably dump him now that Missy and Billy seemed to be over.

He suddenly saw himself, years from now, still working at the hardware store; still Billy's grunt, with no life; and a black depression seemed to envelope him. He had to make a change, and he had to make it soon. He couldn't leave Gran alone, but he wasn't sure he could stay either, if he ever wanted to have a different life. He just didn't see how it would be possible to escape Billy, Wolf, and the older members; or become someone new while staying here.

Other than Wolf, Billy, the others at the party, and a couple of the girls, he didn't even know who any of them were. They wore robes and masks at the rituals. He'd often wondered how many were customers, and he'd never know it was them.

He heard a whisper in his mind, *'you'll be important to the coven. You're chosen. You're being groomed for greatness.'*

On the heels of that thought, he heard Matt's words, *'You still have time to make a different choice.'*

He felt like he was at a crossroads. He couldn't go back into stuff like last night; even after all he'd been through, that was way beyond what he wanted to indulge in; but he had no idea how to move forward. And, truth be known, he was sick of the parties with all the other girls too. It'd been fun for a while, but he knew none of them really cared about him the way his grandad had his gran, or his dad with his mom.

He wanted a normal life, with a wife. He thought about Amy again, and was embarrassed at what she'd think if she knew about them all, or last night. He just wanted to run away somewhere where no one knew him, and become someone else…but there was Gran to think about…

He arrived at the ranch just as the crew that was going to unload the materials was going through the gate. One of them hit the button a second time to hold it open for him to pull the truck and trailer through, then made sure it locked behind him. He followed them up to the barn, where Matt was waiting to issue instructions. He got the crew lined out then led the way to his truck. Erwin climbed in and they drove to the main house.

"They know where to put the load. We're dropping it in usable stacks around the fifteen acres. It will make it faster to get the fence built, but will take a while to unload. Meanwhile, we're going to Dan's office to have our chat." Erwin glanced at Matt, not sure what to say. Finally, he asked how he knew his dad.

"Your dad and I met at a family party. Our families knew each other. He was two or three years older than me, a friend of my brother's, but got me out of a situation with some guys he was running with. We became friends, and I knew his dad because he was still working for Dan when I was younger than you. Gene would come out some, and help when we needed an extra hand, but didn't want to hire on while his dad was still there. Then, he was killed before your granddad retired. I'm sorry I didn't make the time to know you."

Erwin was about to reply when Matt pulled up and stopped the truck. "Come on, we'll talk inside. There're things you need to know."

Dan opened the door himself and invited them in. He led them through the foyer and down a short hall into a large office. He gestured to some chairs in front of a massive oak desk, then seated himself behind it. He pushed a button on the wall and asked for some iced tea, then looked at Matt and Erwin, to see if they wanted anything else. "We have some soda if you'd rather have that."

Matt spoke up. "I'd prefer a cold Coke." Erwin nodded, "Me too, except Dr. Pepper."

Dan added Dr. Pepper to his request, Lupe already knew Matt wanted Coke; then welcomed Erwin to his home. "Erwin, I've always appreciated the way you work for Homer and the excellent service you've given me when we're there. I've watched you to see who you wanted to be. Your granddad was one of my best ranch hands, and one of my best friends for many years.

I didn't know your dad as well, but he was a good man too. Your grandmother is one of the finest people I know. I've known her since grade school, and she was a close friend of both my sister, and my late wife. Ina and I are still good friends, and talk regularly on the phone.

Your granddad had planned on bringing you over for a job when you got out of school, and I would have hired you., But then you went to work at the store, and seemed to be doing well, so I let it alone. Maybe I shouldn't have. Ranching can be hard labor and Homer was happy with you, but I knew you were running with Billy, and I should have made the offer anyway."

"I never knew that," Erwin answered. "I remember coming here to see my granddad a few times, but I was so young when he died, I don't remember much. I've been happy at Homer's, but I'm not sure if that's what I want to do with the rest of my life. It's just that the hours are good, and I'm close to gran. I'm all she has left and I can't leave her."

"She does need you, more than you know. It almost killed her when your dad died, and then your mom. When Sherman had his heart attack, you're the only thing that gave her a reason to get up in the morning. She made me promise to look after you if something happened to her. Like I said, I've watched you from afar, but I should have made a relationship. You may or may not want one after we have this conversation, but son, I'm ready to be for you what I should have been already."

Erwin was a little confused. Both Matt and Dan had essentially said the same thing to him; they should have been there, but weren't, and now wanted to be. A huge question needing answers made him bolder than usual. "I don't understand why you both think you should have done something for me. I know granddad worked here most of his life, but what obligation does that create toward me?"

Dan glanced at Matt, who nodded, then let out a long breath as he pondered his words. "Our families have history. This town has history. Shoot, this whole area has history. The men of your family would have taught it to you, if they'd been alive. I'm going to fill you in on some of it, but first, I need to hear you promise, on the honor of your granddad and grandmother, that you won't disclose it? Especially to Billy and that bunch that hangs around his place. Can you promise me that?"

Now Erwin was really confused, but the serious look on Dan's face let him know that what he was about to hear would be something big. He just couldn't imagine what it could be. "Of course. I don't tell Billy a lot of things, and seldom tell the others anything. I kind of hang out by myself and Gran for the most part, unless I'm at work."

"First, tell me about your friendship with Billy."

"As for Billy, he's been my friend forever. I'm not unaware of his faults, but in high school being his friend kept me from being a target of some of the bullies."

"He is one of the bullies," Dan stated. "He targeted Clayton for years."

Erwin hung his head, "I know. I remember. I never could figure out why he had it in for him so bad. I headed off as much as I could, and warned Clayton a few times, but no one can keep him from being mean when he feels like being mean. I never liked the way he treats people, but when my parents died, then granddad, I had few friends; and after I moved out to Gran's, I had none. He was there when no one was. He was the only friend

I had, we lived so far out; and his family's house was about a half mile from ours.

At first, we just rode bikes, played ball, and hunted squirrels. He was only mean at school. He always told me those boys had been mean to him, and he was defending himself. At the time, I had no reason to not believe him. He was ok to me.

When you're that age, you don't really understand a lot, and I was so caught up in having a friend that by the time I saw how he treated people, he'd been my only friend too long to just end it. I realize now that he always had to be the dominating person in the friendship, but I was so messed up by losing my parents, that I think I just followed him because I was a kid and used to other people being in charge."

Dan took another deep breath, and just as he opened his mouth to speak, a knock came on the door. Matt got up and opened it. A short Hispanic lady with a tray set the drinks and a plate of sandwiches and cookies on the desk. Dan thanked her and asked her to not let anyone disturb them unless it was very important, or had to do with the load being distributed around the parcel of land. She nodded and left. They each took a plate, a napkin, and a drink.

"Erwin, what I'm about to tell you would seem crazy to some people, but I think you already have knowledge of some of it, and a lot of it is just historical fact that you can research. Texas didn't become a state until 1845, and when it was being settled there were several tribes of Native Americans. They were called Indians then. There were Lipan Apaches, Comanches, Tonkawas, Jumanos, Conchos, Tiguas, and a few others.

The Tonkawa Indians were the most common around the time of Austin's founding. The Comanches and Lipan Apaches also frequently ranged into the vicinity.

The Mohawk, and the Attacapa, Tonkawa, and other Texas tribes were known to their neighbors as 'man-eaters.' The forms of cannibalism described included both resorting to human flesh during famines and ritual cannibalism, the latter usually consisting of eating a small portion of an enemy warrior.

All were fierce warriors, and when the Indians fought each other, the winning side would kill all the men from the losing side and take the women and children for their own. That's why they fought so fiercely against the white settlers. It wasn't just that their land was being invaded, they believed if they lost the battle they would die. It was their way of life and they continued it with a new enemy.

The Comanches, known as the "Lords of the Plains", were regarded as perhaps the most dangerous Indian Tribes in the frontier era. The U.S. Army established Fort Worth because of the settler concerns about the threat posed by the many Indian tribes in Texas. The Comanches were the most feared of these Indians.

When they raided a settlement, very small children, usually three and under, were killed. Kids three to ten were often stolen to be tortured and killed or raised as slaves. Women were stolen, raped, and either killed or made into slaves. Even very old women were raped, usually at the site. They would see their husbands killed and mutilated before them, then would be gang raped by multiple warriors, then killed.

If men weren't outright killed in the raid, they were tortured to death. The Comanches were cruel. They would cut off fingers, toes, and genitals, put them in their mouth and sew it shut. Some were found staked out on ant hills covered in honey, some roasted, and some with hot coals, still burning, placed inside their cut open torsos.

The women and kids who weren't killed at the site were burned, raped, cut repeatedly, and if they lived very long, they were beaten regularly while being worked to death. Many were strung up in trees and eviscerated as a sign for others to stay out of their territory. It was brutal.

All the people in those settlements back in those years knew what a Comanche raid was, and knew what a Comanche raid meant. Some other tribes even joined with the Spaniards to fight them. They were terrified of the Comanche. Young boys were trained mercilessly and became warriors in their teen years.

They cared about nothing except hunting buffalo and making war, and were known for going a thousand miles to murder one white family. They were afraid of, and hated, whites, but would kill a black person on sight. They are the reason the Texas Rangers were created. They weren't beaten until around 1881 when the buffalo were driven almost extinct.

In this area a Comanche warrior stole a Tonkawa maiden and married her. They were both evil, with the blood lust of torture and the love of human flesh. They hid out in a series of caves that were way up in the hills and hidden from the average person. They vowed to never again lose their home and that they would never leave this area, and their descendants have kept that vow.

They also vowed to wipe out the family lines of all they held responsible for ending their freedom and way of life. They basically sold their soul, and the souls of their descendants, to the demon Aztec gods their tribes served, to gain power to revenge all Indian tribes. Most of the tribes denounced them, but some supported them, and individuals from all tribes did as well.

In the 1890's a group of paganistic Satan worshippers from Europe, from an old Druidic line, moved into the area and eventually married into their bloodline, loving the torture, rape, cannibalism, and vengeance. The people of the area who were being decimated, began to make war on the group, determined to end it; and after a time, they hid deep in the forests, and retreated into caves everywhere.

Later, a Templar knight, escaping judgement in Europe, married in and added his traditions. By then, it was an amalgamated mess of hate, evil, paganism, and an entrenched desire for revenge. Then, the younger generations, whom no one had ever seen, slowly began to drift back into the towns. They came as if from other areas, and told no one who they were. They would only marry among themselves and that's how they kept the secret. Some still carry the face of the Indian, but many look European with various shades of skin.

None of this new generation had bad things happen to them, and none of the descendants of the original settlers did anything to them; but the silent war still plays out. It's my understanding that each child born to the ones wanting revenge are groomed from birth to carry it out, and at a certain age their loyalty is tested.

Anyone who fails the test is either cast out, or murdered, depending on their knowledge level. Any who leave and then try to return are made an example of. It's not pretty. We've found some of them who've escaped and come back. The bodies are left where they can be found, for warnings to both sides of what happens when they're thwarted. Revealing any family secrets gets you tortured to death.

They became the prominent families in many of the areas surrounding us, often holding jobs of the highest caliber; loved by the people of the town in their public persona, but alone—on weekends, satanic holidays, and other times—they still practice the old ways. They do strange rituals that sometimes include the sacrifice of children, drinking their blood, and torturing victims. Children and adults go missing quite often, especially in state parks; most to never be seen again. Bodies are seldom found, but ritual sites in the woods or on lonely areas of ranches are found regularly.

People who have been here awhile are aware, and most are afraid of them. It is known that if you cross one of them, the whole coven will join together in rituals, to curse you, or to torture and eliminate you. They worship Satan and demons, and hate Christians; but many go to church, and hold positions there, as a cover story. We also know that some children are born just to be sacrificed, never receiving a birth certificate, or counted on any census. God only knows how many through the last 150 years alone.

Your granddad got mixed up with them when he was about 16. He was dating a daughter of the family, not knowing she was one of them, and saw something he shouldn't have seen. Sometimes they will test a person by allowing them to see something that is an indication of something wrong, but something that can be said to be misconstrued. They watch to see if you will tell anyone.

If you don't, you may be recruited, but most recruitment comes from within. These are old, old, family line, multi-generational cannibals, and very wicked; but taught to hide in plain sight almost from birth, by appearing to be something else in their 'regular' life.

One type of person they like to recruit are the children of those who they have a score to settle with. It's the greatest revenge. They will steal, sacrifice, and eat your child, or recruit them to become one of them. Either way, the parent loses their child, and while they know what happened, they can't prove it.

An ancestor in your family was an enemy, and the Shaman at that time made a decree that a child would be recruited in each generation from his family from then on. They cursed the family and started watching youngsters with each new birth, watching for the one they can turn. It's my understanding that it's easiest to recruit through friendship, especially if there is a wound or a weakness within.

Then, sometime later, they 'help out' a coven member or someone they wish to recruit, who is being harassed by someone, by doing a ceremony to curse that person. Then, the person goes too far, or so they think they have, and they are bound to the coven. That's how they got your granddad's attention.

He was dating a sister of the Shaman, unaware of the entire thing. His best friend was a casual friend of the family and had been greatly humiliated at work. They offered to put a hex on the guy who humiliated him, to make him sick enough to quit. Sherman and his friend believed it was something along the lines of slipping ex-lax into his coffee for the day. They went to the ritual and what happened to them was shocking.

They got them drunk and high, then drank blood and called up demons, and an all-male orgy took place; both, between the men, and then with the demons. Your grandfather had never experienced anything of that nature. In those days homosexuality was seldom mentioned. The demon scratched him on the neck to mark him as his; and as both humiliating him and recruiting him was the real purpose of the ritual, he was repeatedly and viciously used by all the men and the demon.

Most men are too ashamed of that being known, especially in those days, and would now be a victim of blackmail for the rest of their life, tying them to the coven. He was dumped in a field the next morning, bloody, ripped to pieces in... shall we say... intimate places... and mentally devastated.

My dad was out checking cattle and came across him. He brought him here and called the local doctor, who was from one of the original settler families, and sympathetic to those who oppose the tribe. He kept him here, filling him in on why it happened, and helped him get better, both mentally and physically. He stayed on as a ranch hand and seldom even went to town. Until he married your grandmother he lived here.

Erwin was shocked. He had never heard that story; it was eerily similar to his own. The other men sat quietly while he processed the information. "What happened to the man they cursed?" he finally asked.

"He was bucked off his horse during a parade and dragged through town. When they finally got the horse to stop, he was already dying. He'd broken his neck in the fall and had been whipped around so much that they couldn't do anything for him."

"So, I was targeted by Billy and the others because of who I am?"

"Yes, and probably because, as you said, you were one of the only kids in the area; and because bullies need someone to look up to them, to give them confidence. They need a follower; someone they can be superior to. Without followers, bullies are just loners who no one would ever listen to.

They groom followers to give themselves power and feel in charge. If the followers would refuse to obey, they would have no power. They usually target lonely people with little to no family or with no one to protect them, or those who are too nice to believe they are being used, many times those with no one to teach them self-respect and to be confident in their own abilities.

As for you, particularly, your granddad and your father both escaped their clutches, so now two generations have eluded being recruited. Your recruitment is both for revenge and to get the dynamic back on track for killing or recruiting each generation. I suspect they have something particularly heinous in mind for you. Since you're an only child, they may plan to end the family line entirely. That would be the greatest revenge, and end any chance of someone from your family ever defeating or exposing them." Erwin flinched at that, while something inside told him it was the truth.

"As for my family's involvement, it started long before your granddad. That's one reason he was dumped on the ranch. It was a warning to my dad. In 1902, one of my great-grandfather's brothers, and one of your great-great-grandfather's sisters, were taken at around ten years old. She was raped multiple times and they sliced up her face till she was almost unrecognizable, cut off her breasts, and he had three fingers and his genitals ripped off. Both our families and others had joined together in the search.

When they found them, they were actively raping her; he was tied to a tree forced to watch, with small fires lit around to roast him while this was happening. They found them because both kids were screaming. Most of the tribe got away, but they caught the man who was raping her.

They began to cut off fingers and toes and do other things to him to extract information. It sounds like they were as bad as the coven, but you need to understand that many of their family and other area people had been taken, misused, and murdered since 1881; both fathers were in the group, and it was a different time then.

He finally broke and told them of the Shaman's vow, crowing with delight while giving them details of what had happened to their children, and many others before them. He admitted the cannibalism, and threatened them that a demon would destroy them all if they killed him. He said that from now on the curse on all our families would be increased and that none would ever be released from the curse.

He began to howl like a wolf, and wolves surrounded the camp, killing the boy and several of the men who'd ridden out to rescue the kids. They shot most of them, and when one of the men killed the rapist, the rest melted back into the woods. They rescued the girl, but she was never the same. She died by suicide at age 15.

They found a woman from another tribe that had become a Christian and was willing to talk. She said the wolves responded to what's called a 'shape-shifter' or 'skinwalker.' It's a level of witchcraft, or satanism, that involves becoming possessed to the point of actually becoming capable of transforming into an animal. This is where the legend of the werewolf came from originally. It's real. High level occult practitioners do similar things all over the world. And these are the people who have cursed you.

My family vowed to help protect your family forever, and your family, to protect mine. In fact, most of the original settler families protect one another. As the men of our family come of age, we are told the story, and each renews the vow to continue as protectors. I've let you down Erwin. I should have moved your grandmother and you out here when Sherman died, and I tried, but she wouldn't come. It was my job when your dad and Sherman died to bring you up in the knowledge, and keep you safe from them. Ina too.

She refused to let me tell you about the alliance of families, or any of our history. She said God would protect the two of you and that was that. You have distant cousins that are still under the curse, but none left in this area; and when Sherman, and then Gene escaped, they concentrated on your particular family line, with a vengeance.

Clayton didn't know in high school, but he does now. He's told me how you tried to help him when Billy was targeting him; how you'd slip him notes to not be in certain places, and what he was planning if Clayton showed up. He told me about the time you got him out the bathroom window, and what was planned for that day. I appreciate that. Erwin, I don't think you really understand, that you probably saved his life on multiple occasions. He fully understands that after learning what's really going on.

Our families have stood together for generations. It's about time to end this mess forever. What I need to know is, are you with us, or with Billy? Are you a full-fledged member of the coven, or do you want out? I can help you, but only if you want help. You have to get out now, because once they decide it's time to fulfill the curse, no one can help you."

Erwin looked at him, trying to absorb all he'd just said, then turned to Matt. "You expressed an obligation also. How are you involved in this?"

"My family was one of the other families that helped look for the kids. We too had lost children to this group. Almost every original family of the area did as well, but most have forgotten the stories, and it seems as if one specific line has descended from each one that was particularly targeted, and took up the cause to fight this evil enemy. Most are deeply Christian and see it as part of the age-old war between God and the fallen angelic line of half-breeds, called the Nephilim. These are the true old gods the evil families serve.

Like I said, I knew your dad. He wasn't drawn in as far as Sherman and you were, simply because Dan, Sherman, and my dad had educated him. He also actually saved me from the ritual planned, to extract revenge for turning one of them in for stealing from the dairy bar, where we both worked one summer; and then protected me from the group of guys that had targeted me. He had been running with them at the time, trying to get inside information to help bring down the entire bunch.

When he heard about the ritual, he told them it wasn't me that told on the guy, then brought me out here, where I was given the family history. My parents both know, and both my siblings. We've all given our allegiance to the God of the Bible, and sworn to help bring down this evil in our midst. It's gone on far too long. My brother's fiancé went missing a week before the wedding, and we've never been able to find her, or prove it, but we know they took her.

Our three families have worked for years trying to get someone on the inside to get evidence to bring them to justice. They either turn up dead, or get drawn into the coven, enjoying the wealth, sex, and power. You'd be surprised at the number of people who are involved. As we've uncovered more and more, it's hard to get any justice, because many now in power belong to them. It's not even safe to go to the police, for the most part."

"I've been targeted for years?" Erwin was wrapping his brain around this new knowledge. "I've been drawn in to be a sacrifice?" He hung his head, then just confessed, "I've participated in things I'm ashamed of. We've killed animals, and lately it's been getting more intense. I knew it was going somewhere darker and have been shocked at recent events; events I have no desire to repeat."

He rubbed the scratch on his neck as he talked through his thoughts. "Have I gone too far? Can I still get out?" he looked at Dan and Matt, both men he admired.

"As long as you're breathing and want out, and they don't have you in their hands, it's not too late," Dan looked him straight in the eye. "But you need to decide now. Once you're in the kind of ritual that puts that scratch on your neck, you're very close to going too far. A few more rituals and you can't hear the voice of God anymore; If you weren't the target, you probably would have a hard time with that now. That tells me you're most likely the sacrifice. Otherwise, you'd be no shape to have gone to work today."

"Last night was that ritual. I wasn't prepared for what happened. I thought it would be the same ole, same ole, but it wasn't. I heard a voice this morning telling me it wasn't too late. Was that the voice of God?"

"Most probably," Matt agreed.

Erwin thought about Wolf, how his image had shimmered into a canine wolf, and the howl. In his heart he knew he was a shape-shifter like they described, and a shiver went down his spine. He told them what he'd seen. "They'll never let me leave. I've seen what they do to people who try to leave. And what about Gran. Is she in danger? Will she be, if I try to leave? Will they hurt her to get back at me?"

Then another thought occurred to him. "Does Billy know I'm supposed to be sacrificed?"

"Billy's grandparents were some of the latest leaders; she was the high priestess, as far as we've been able to learn; descended from the mixed Druidic and Templar line, both going back thousands of years in Europe. She was the local librarian, and as nice as could be to most, but she hated me and Clayton with a passion, and anyone else from the original settler families they hate. Her daughter was Billy's mother and disappeared when he was about 3 months old.

Many of us think she was raised as a 'breeder' and is either held somewhere for that purpose, or was sacrificed. My guess is the grandmother raised Billy to take her place and he knows that, and may know the rest, but with the deception they use, he may not. He may be forced to sacrifice you himself to prove his loyalty and earn his position.

In Nazi Germany, the kids were given a puppy and they were taught to train it, care for it, and love it unconditionally, then were forced to kill it to prove their obedience and loyalty. This broke them emotionally, and hardened their hearts to become capable of torturing humans. The Coven is the same. I'm sure he's already passed that test, because he's still alive. There's been a few defectors through the years that's talked, and that's how we know some of it.

My guess is he does know you're targeted, possibly knows you'll be sacrificed if you refuse to join, but may be expecting you'll go along; and may not know he will have to be the one torturing you; but with his family line history, he will. I have no doubt about it, because he knows what they'll do to him if he doesn't.

As far as I know, none of the ones that are direct descendants from the three main families have ever defected. He has power, position, contacts, and will be wealthy and protected, as long, as he's a part of them. Without them he is nothing, and has nothing.

Never underestimate family history, being groomed from birth, being demon possessed, or the draw of what the bible calls 'the lust of the flesh, the lust of the eyes, and the pride of life.' He'll not easily give that up; and he's probably been raped, trafficked, and in more rituals than you could possibly imagine. He was probably dedicated to a demon at birth, and has had more demons enter into him and bound to him, with each ritual. I'm not sure, but I'm guessing you've been gradually groomed to accept more and more, but still on the peripheral so you'll stay involved."

Erwin knew there were times Billy was with Wolf and the older coven members without him; and knew they kept Randy, Eric, and Robert away from most of what he knew about, at least until last night. Now, he clearly saw them being tested, and bound by the shock and shame of what had taken place. He suddenly was sick at what he'd been involved in and determined on the spot that he was done.

"What now? I have a lot I can tell you. You may know already, but maybe I can add to the knowledge. I know things, and have witnessed and participated in things since I was ten. They will kill me, so, I have to know you will protect Gran. And know, I can't prove anything. I can go and wear a camera and record it, but most likely they will catch me, then they will know I was working for someone.

They wear masks during it all, so I don't know who they really are, for the most part. It will most likely endanger you. If you're right, they will come after Clayton, or someone else you care about. They love to hurt people you care about instead of you personally. That way they can control you better."

"No," Dan answered. "We're getting you out, if you want out; but I can't in good faith send you in as a spy. We'll take the info you'll give us, though. For now, we can have Homer keep you too busy to be available. If you've been in that ritual, the time of sacrifice is close. We can't endanger you more.

"Do you need a doctor's care?" Matt carefully worded his question, knowing the condition Sherman had been in.

Erwin dropped his head once more. "No. Last night they targeted Randy and he took the place my granddad did. It was the most horrifying thing I've ever seen. I kept away from Wolf as much as I could without drawing his attention to it, and Billy was the one the demon entered, so he protected me as usual. I was involved, but not as much."

"Let me think on it and we'll talk again. I'll go see Ina this week and try to get her to move out here. She probably won't. I don't know how much Sherman told her, and she's stubborn. You can keep working at the store or I can give you a job. We can't let on that you know anything different for now. Can you pretend that you don't? We will bring you up to speed, but for now, know you can call us at any time for help. But Erwin... it's close... and you can't take any chances.

Matt's cousin, Ryan Hench, works at the police department. He knows everything. Matt can let him know that you know, and he can be called upon as well. He'll start watching you, just act like you don't see him for now. Erwin, the old settler families are all involved with trying to take this group down. In these modern times, we can't just go string them up anymore. It has to be done legally, and thorough prayer.

This evil has been here for our entire lives. We've all lost family members, pets, livestock, and crops. Businesses have burned. Young girls have been targeted and impregnated, and young men trapped by their girls, accused of rape, and other things, so they can make them miserable, and ruin their lives and reputations. Many have had accidents that we know weren't just accidents; but they have been doing this for untold generations, and are masters at living in plain sight as productive members of society, and getting away with it. They have to be stopped."

Erwin told them both, in detail, about the prior evening. He left nothing out, even though he was embarrassed at what he was telling them. Neither batted an eye at the information, although Dan made extensive notes to add to their collective knowledge. Both knew the ropes, and both knew he'd been drawn in gradually, and they'd done nothing to stop it. Both were as ashamed at their dereliction of duty as he was at what he'd done. Both thanked him for his honesty.

"So, Waya, or Wolf as you call him, is the new upcoming Shaman? He is already a shape-shifter, at what, 30 years old?" Erwin nodded.

"That means he's of the original bloodline, pure-born. He will have been born possessed, probably conceived at a ritual. We've uncovered a lot in the last 100 years. His family line was sold to a demon for power by an ancestor in the 1700s, but we suspect it goes much farther back than that. One defector tried to tell us something about his father. He was dying at the time, and his words were slurred. He mumbled Comanche, Aztec, shaman, and other words we couldn't make out. He was partly speaking in a language we didn't know.

We sent for someone we knew that had defected decades back, but he died before she could get here. They've served that demon for centuries. He will be very powerful and will have demonic insight, kind of a demonic inversion of a Christian's gift of discernment. With his ancestry, and all the evil lines that have converged into this one family, I can assure you that he will do whatever it takes to appease the Kingdom of Darkness and protect the tribe; he'll do it thinking he's pleasing his god, and it's the right thing to do; and we can't let him suspect that you're wanting out.

Don't go anywhere with him and Billy. And I mean anywhere. If he even suspects, it will be accelerated, and you may not have time to alert us. I don't want to scare you, but you're on borrowed time right now, and we don't have a minute to lose. I'll call a meeting of the families involved and we can game plan. This isn't our first rodeo, but we're not unaware of what we're up against. Any chance you could attend that meeting?"

"That depends on when it is. I have, to work, and I can't tell Homer why I need off. Besides, if I'm seen here with those people, won't that tip them off?" he asked.

"Actually, it will be disguised as a business owner's meeting of a group we're all in, as a festival planning session for the upcoming Christmas season. And you can just ride with Homer. I guess I neglected to mention he's from one of the old families as well." Dan was grinning at Erwin's facial expression, as he realized, all the 'stuff' he'd kept hidden from those around him had been known all along.

"It's not easy finding out you've been living in a fishbowl," Matt offered, "but Homer is one of the reasons you've been as protected as you are. He's watched over you from the time you were five years old. Ina knew you'd go to work for him as soon as Sherman was gone. The original plan was work for him through school, then bring you out here; but as was stated earlier, you were doing so well there, and Homer said you're one of his best employees, so we let it be."

Erwin was very uncomfortable to know he'd been so observed since a small child, and was about to get mad, when he realized that they truly cared what happened to him, and was suddenly comforted at the safety net they'd laid out. He struggled with what he wanted to say.

"I've missed having a dad my whole life, but Homer has been there, and whatever you say about having failed me, you two apparently have been in some form too. I want you to know I appreciate what you did for my granddad, my dad, and me. I've not been happy with Billy's behavior for a long time, and wanted to just leave this place, but Gran needs me and I have nowhere else to go. There has been no one else I can depend on.

This knowledge changes everything, but the truth is I have enjoyed the partying, and some of the witchcraft, and I'm not sure I know how to be different. I had no idea it was that evil until last night. The demon I saw could only have come from hell, although I know very little about God or hell.

I wish I'd known you two in a closer way earlier in my life, but I'd like to get to know you now. How will this work? I don't have much experience in anything except Billy's party life, the store, and Gran's house. I feel like I'm far behind guys my age and I'm ready to grow up. I just don't know how to make it happen."

"Start thinking if you want to stay on with Homer, or work out here. We can work out a split as well. When you're here, we can train you in self-defense and teach you more of the history. You'll be protected at both places. You can help us with any knowledge we may not already have. As long, as you stay away from Billy's, the vulnerable points will be driving home from here today, your daily commute, or at Ina's, if they decide to make a move.

And Erwin... understand... when they decide to come after you, you won't have a chance if one of us isn't around. Also, if you change your schedule too drastically, it will flag both Billy and Waya that you've had new information. We need to ponder on this, and we'll have another conversation, but Erwin, it has to be soon; usually the sacrifice is within days of that ritual."

Dan's phone buzzed and he read the text. "They're finished unloading the fencing. We can justify a while longer, but if we do, you'll be driving in the dark. I'll alert Ryan to be around the store when you park the truck and change vehicles. Where are you going tonight?"

"I'm having dinner with Gran, and then staying home tomorrow to help her with the yardwork."

"Ok. Good plan. I'll call in the morning and we'll have more of a plan in place. Can you give me a few minutes with Matt? He'll be right out to take you to the gate."

"Sure," Erwin said, glad to have a few minutes to collect himself.

"Take these cookies," Matt was wrapping all the ones left on the serving plate in the cloth napkin underneath them. "And here's another Dr. Pepper. It may be ten minutes or so."

"Thank you," Erwin smiled, accepting the proffered snack. "For everything."

He quietly left the office and then the house, reaching the truck and leaning against it as he ate the cookies. He was exhausted, like he'd ran a marathon. He had a lot to think about. He was suddenly very glad he'd bowed out of the poker game tonight. He decided he needed to stay much closer to Gran. He knew he was a sitting duck, but he wasn't about to let them get their hands on her.

Back inside the office Matt was sitting leaned back in his chair, his hands behind his head, with his eyes closed, thinking. Finally, he spoke. "Well, that went as well as it could have. I think. But now we have another problem. First Missy and Amy, now Erwin. Guys like Billy need their followers. If he loses them at once, which one will he go after first?"

"His male pride, especially after the incident at the café, will say her; his need for a lackey, says Erwin. A lot will depend on how close they are to the date of sacrifice. My guess is they've held off this long to get Billy ready, since his grandmother died. He's still a loose cannon and they must know that. He's a weak link with his love of bragging, sense of entitlement, and lack of hiding his meanness.

He's probably lasted this long because of who she was and the fact that he's already done their bidding without batting an eye for his entire life. Not to mention he's the only child left in that line. They always need willing participants, clean up men, and people whose jobs lets them move around in wilderness places without oversight. God, I hate this mess. It feels like I've fought this my entire life."

"You have, pretty much," Matt sounded weary too. "Should we tell him the rest?"

"No. We gave him a pretty good chunk to chew on for one day. But we both know it's coming," Dan sounded resolved. "We've seen it too many times. I could kick myself for ever letting him experience that. I got too involved in keeping the ranch going amid this so-called health crisis; and before that, stabilizing Clayton after Janie died. I've let Sherman and Ina down. Now, we just have to get him through it."

Suddenly, he sat straight up so fast he almost flipped the chair. Matt stared at him. He looked like he'd seen a ghost. "What's wrong?!" His voice was as urgent as Dan's movement.

"We can't let them find out Missy is your child," Dan exploded. "If they lose Erwin, they may make a substitute. It won't be from his family, but they know the families that thwart them as well as we do, and she'd be another one that close to Billy; and being a Hench, and yours, they'd love it."

"Let's go to the house. We need to anyway, but I say we get those girls out here as fast we can," Matt urged. "They may do it anyway, because she embarrassed him at the diner, and I helped her. Let me get Erwin down to the gate, and I need to run by my other house for a minute, then I'll meet you there. We can make a list before Pauline gets there. Let's expressly look for points of vulnerability and line of sight for bullets.

I built it with those in mind, but it's been a while since I've looked to see if any trees have fallen, or anything has changed. I need to show you something also, in case they take me out. And Dan, we probably need to fill Missy in on some of this and not make the same mistake we did with Erwin."

"I'm right behind you," Dan agreed.

The Old Ways

Chapter 23

WOLF WAS IN HIS SHOP. He made knives and jewelry, and sold them, both in his store and online. Since the Covid lockdown it was more online, but he'd been doing this for several years now, and people would still like to come in person. He had a small storefront on main street that he opened 2 days a week for most of the year, while adding more days leading up to holidays and on festival weeks.

He also sold quite a bit to local jewelry shops and in the major Texas cities. His work was known to be authentic and top quality. His family had made jewelry for centuries. Most of the time he worked in the small barn beside his house. He liked the solitude, and being able to work for hours perfecting a project, without being disturbed. He was more like his ancestors than most people would ever know, and was much more comfortable with deep woods around him and walking in nature when he needed a break, or was stuck on a design.

Today he was making a silver ring with a turquoise and gold inlay. He had a customer that liked the look of the rich colors all running together. This ring would pair with a heart-shaped pendant that he'd made for her last year. She'd bought jewelry from him for many years, and had opened the door for several contracts with the larger jewelry stores in the Dallas area. He always had time to create a beautiful, hand-crafted, one-of-a-kind piece for her.

He was at peace while creating beautiful pieces from the elements of the earth. Sometimes it settled the spirits inside him. His spirit was troubled today. It was time to move forward with Billy's training and he was about to ask him to do something he knew he'd resist. He pondered the correct method as he worked, knowing his mind could work on one project, while his hands worked on another.

He assembled the items he would need for today's project. The flat silver plate, the square silver wire, the turquoise chunk from his box of finest grade, the small vial of gold filings from a prior project, the tube of super glue, and the spray can of glue activator. He kept even the smallest amounts of leftover metal filings and stone dust for additions to later projects.

You never knew when the slightest addition would add just the right amount of color or metallic glint to create that unique, non-duplicatable touch he was known for. He had a true artist's eye and wasn't afraid to experiment to find the unusual looks that drew people from far and wide, and justified the prices he placed upon them.

He hated to make what he called 'assembly line' jewelry. His work was different, a loose symphony of metal and stone that resembled the looks that nature herself created. He seldom created the same look twice and people knew when they ordered something they would never arrive somewhere to see it on another person.

He was confident in his artistry, but also admitted that some of his most exceptional work was done when he called up the spirits, and allowed them to fill him and work through him, while he got lost in the trance that allowed him to experience the vastness of the universe that coursed through him. He'd been melded with the spirits from birth and was completely at ease with their presence.

He looked at his order sheet for the correct ring size out of habit. He'd been making items for this client for years and knew the correct one, but he was always careful and thorough. He found the ring of blanks and chose the one he needed. He measured the inside and using a proven mathematical equation, taking into account the thickness of the metal, he punched the numbers into a calculator to arrive at the right length to cut for the ring.

He calibrated his tool, and putting one side on the straight side of his metal plate, he ran it down the length of the plate to scribe the cutting line on the silver. He then turned it the other way to scribe the shorter cut, intersecting the first line to create a pattern about a quarter inch wide and almost 3" in length.

His thoughts were deep as he worked. It was time to sacrifice Erwin and cement Billy's loyalty to the coven. That was why they'd encouraged the friendship so long, in spite of Erwin's not really being one of them. With his grandmother being such a strong Christian, Wolf knew it would be a direct challenge to her faith, and be a direct hit against the usurper god she served.

They'd weakened her already when they took her son out. As this family were vicious enemies, that had long thwarted them, it would be a long-awaited victory; and he couldn't wait to feast on the flesh of the defeated representative of them. The snake spirit he served rose up in him at the thought. His lip curled with disgust at even thinking of this wimp as an enemy, but he knew it wasn't Erwin himself the spirit reacted to, but that he was 'one of them.' He'd known for a while that Erwin wasn't 'all in,' and would be glad when it was done.

It would be the final battle with this bloodline, and a major victory in their war against the enemy bloodlines. He would prevail, and be the first one to wipe out an entire branch of the hated ones, who'd long fought against them. He licked his lips in anticipation of the reward he would earn from the gods. He'd long ago proven his loyalty, but now he'd prove his worth.

Then, I will ferret out all the other branches and eliminate them, one by one. They'll never see it coming, none of them remember we are even here. He'd been doing research on the ancestry of all the old families, and knew where every single member lived, no matter how obscure.

Picking up his jeweler's saw, he cut first the short side and then the long one, taking care to keep his cuts straight. He then picked up a file and ran it over all four sides to make it as uniform as possible. He was using a soft metal, so when he had the edges to his liking, he picked up the mandrel and wrapped the length of metal around it. He grabbed a rawhide hammer and began to gently hammer the two ends around the rod. He slid it off, turned it around, and slid it back on in the opposite direction.

The mandrel was tapered and he needed both sides to be the same diameter. He hammered the other edge, not too concerned that the edges didn't quite meet. He slid the metal off the rod and picked up pliers that had no teeth to mar the surface and used them to bend the ends toward each other, creating a slightly flat place where the edges met. If he didn't make it flat at that spot, the solder wouldn't hold. He made the metal as flat as he could and brought the edges to meet one another.

When it was to his liking, he held the edges together, and picking up the jeweler's saw again, he used it to cut through the joint to make the edges as symmetrical as possible. He placed it on a tool that held it in mid-air with the cut side down, and painted the edges with solder flux, then carefully placed a couple of small pieces of hard solder over the joint, making sure they were both over the crack where the edges met, so that when he heated it the metal would flow between the pieces.

He picked up the torch and began to heat it in a circular motion around the entire ring, causing the solder to melt. When one piece of solder moved with the blowing of the torch flame, he picked up the pliers and carefully set it back into the right spot, then once again heated the tiny piece of metal so that it melted and filled the crack, then turned the ring around to make sure that all gaps were filled on both outside and inside of the band.

He'd seen Erwin's reluctance last night and he knew his loyalty to Homer. He wouldn't be willing to go much further in the rituals. He didn't enjoy much of the ceremony. He had always been squeamish around animal sacrifice and would never stomach human sacrifice. He'd shrunken back at the spirits pleasuring men with men too. He was a weak link.

Would he reveal what he'd seen? Wolf wasn't sure, but alcohol and drugs had caused more than one man to see visions. He laughed at the obvious explanation, if ever questioned, but he didn't want to take the chance the secrets would be told. The spirits had sensed the enemy near him last night, even during the height of the ceremony. It was troubling.

It was time. It should have been done when he was a child, but Billy had been through much, and was still immature, and had needed a minion; and traditionally, the longer the relationship had been, the harder the sacrifice, and therefore, the more deeply it cemented the person in their loyalty to the coven. The position Billy was born to required much, and his loyalty had to be 100% and non-negotiable. He'd been bound to Odin since conception. Erwin is a weak link. Billy coddled and protected him. That had to end. Now.

For the feathered serpent gods to take over the whole world, the lines had to converge. The Aztecs represented the new continent, and the child of Odin represented the old continent. Together they represented the line that protected the truth; that all royal families descended from the ones who had been thrown out of Heaven. The gods had moved them through time, incrementally in ancestral lives, from faraway places to meet here, in Texas, in the last 100 years.

He smiled as the gods whispered that the time was nearing. They were coming back. The only thing stopping them now was the ones who served the one who'd thwarted them for millennia. The people of the book had gotten it wrong. His god had not lost. It was a two-thousand-year-old sham. It was designed to enslave mankind into obedience, and hide the truth. He laughed as he thought of the multitudes that served a fake god.

The one they called Jesus. It was the hoax of the ages. The God of Heaven was the true enemy. He was the one that had thrown the gods out and set it all in motion. No matter what the book said... he knew they would win when he came back at the end of the ages. Lucifer was the true god of this world, and those who followed him would rule after the war. Most of the Christian church even now served him unknowingly, through their appetites and refusal to obey the one they called God; so, they would eventually bow to Satan, the god of this world.

He'd been taught this his entire life, and he believed it with every cell of his body. It wasn't the church people who so casually called themselves followers of Jesus he hated. They were even now being drawn into the teachings of the One World Church, which would be led by the son of Lucifer himself.

It was those who held the truth of the God of Heaven, His true son, and the power they held by being His. Those were the ones he fought so vehemently against. Those were the ones who could banish the spirits that worked so hard to inhabit people and influence them. Those were the ones his followers—that were pretenders in the hated church—worked so hard to discredit. Those were the ones his family in the government, and law enforcement realms, were busy changing laws to defeat.

BOOK 1: "PREPARE FOR THE END" SERIES

It was those that truly believed the God of Heaven was right, and made their allegiance to Him, he most feared. He used that fear to motivate him to obey his gods without hesitation. If he faltered, they'd destroy him and start again with a new generation. He would not let that happen. The power was now in his hands, and he would wield it. They must be removed.

He needed to remove the flux and the oxidation caused by soldering, so he allowed the metal to cool by quenching it in water and then dropped it into a small crock pot of heated Sparex no. 2 liquid pickling solution, using the special copper pickling tongs. Pickle tongs are made of copper because copper doesn't react with the pickle. If the tongs are made out of a ferrous metal they will react with the pickle and your pieces will end up with a thin copper plate on them.

He noticed the liquid was getting low so he grabbed a gallon of distilled water and refilled it to the proper level. He used it all day long, and didn't want to get in a situation where he needed to drop a piece in, and it not be ready to receive it.

When it was done, he took it out with the copper tongs then carefully placed the glass lid back on the crock pot. If he didn't keep it covered it would quickly evaporate. Then, with his characteristic carefulness, he checked to make sure the setting was on low. He'd followed his routine for more than a decade and didn't have to really think about it, he just always made sure.

He was concerned about Randy, too. The demon they'd called up had been extremely angry and had taken his anger out on Randy. His body was much damaged in the ritual and he would need medical care. Wolf knew he should have taken him to the family doctor that night, but he had been drunk, high, and caught up in the lust of the ritual. He'd erred, which was rare for him. Now, he needed to correct it, and soon.

He slid the band around the mandrel, and using the rawhide hammer he hammered it into a smooth circle, once again flipping it around to get both sides the same size, despite the taper of the rod. He checked the size and as usual it was slightly small. He placed it back on the rod and using slightly more force he hammered it down toward the larger end to increase it to the size he needed.

When he was satisfied it was as round as it could be and the perfect size, he picked up the file and using a curved motion he filed the rough edges where the solder joined the band, taking great care to not use a straight across motion as that would create a flat spot that he didn't want. He then slid it off the mandrel, and feeling a tiny bump on the top and bottom edge from the joint, he began to smooth it by running it across wet 220 grain sandpaper set on a flat surface, in circular motions until it was completely flush.

He decided to go to the sacred spot when the ring was completed. He needed the advice of the ancestors and the gods. And he needed to humbly admit his failure. That would keep him from getting careless.

Using the same equation as before, he quickly did the calculations for the outer bands that created the channel he'd put the turquoise and gold into, changing it for the thickness of the wire. When he had the right length, he straightened out the wire, removing burrs and filed the uneven ends as flat as possible.

He used the calipers as before to scratch in a cut line. He made two identical pieces and then filed the cut ends smooth. He then wrapped one around the mandrel, as before, with the exception that he used the handle of the mandrel because it had no tapering and was much easier for the square wire.

He used the pliers to flatten the area by the ends and pushed the ends together for soldering. He duplicated the procedure with the second wire taking care to get the flat spot right so they would solder exactly as he wanted them to. He once again cut through the joint with the jeweler's saw for symmetry and then placed both rings on a charcoal block, then fluxed them entirely.

With wire it was easier to place the tiny pieces of hard solder beneath the joint instead of on top, otherwise the air from the flame would blow them off, but by placing them on the bottom the weight of the ring held them down. He heated the wires in a circular motion, heating the entire piece until he saw the solder start to flow.

He concentrated the flame on that area for about a second, then took it away. The solder below melted and flowed up into the joint. He repeated it until the joints were solid in both pieces, then quenched and pickled the rings. He slid them one by one onto the mandrel, hammering them into circles.

Because wire stretched more easily, he took great care to not hammer too hard. He didn't want them to become a larger size. When he had two perfect circles, he painted flux on one of them, and, also on the band, which he completely coated on the outside and the inside. He needed to attach them to the band and he placed one piece on the band, holding them together for a couple of seconds then turned it over and set it on his worktop.

He added more flux on top then placed four tiny squares of medium solder around the edge of the ring. He heated it in circles until the solder flowed into the joint. He then quenched it and looked to ensure there were no holes or gaps in the crack. He did the same on the other side with the second ring, using easy solder this time, being careful to keep it all even and filling all gaps. He quenched it a second time and pickled the entire piece.

He moved to the 220-grit sandpaper, using water and a circular motion to sand the rings to a polished shine, then using an 80-grit sanding disk he scuffed up the channel so it would grip the glue he was using to fasten in the turquoise and metal filings. He placed it back on the mandrel to hold it while he filled the channel.

He reached over to pick up the chunk of turquoise, wrapped it in a doubled piece of paper towel, then set the bundle on the anvil, and hit it several times with the hammer to crush it into small pieces. He unwrapped it and set 3-4 pieces into the channel testing the size. They were still too big, sticking too far up above the edge created by soldering the rings onto the band. He picked them out and dropped them back into the paper towel, wrapped them up, and hammered them again. After several soft blows, he tried again; this time they were the correct size. He grabbed the vial that held the gold filings, and then the glue and activator.

He placed the mandrel across a tripod with a hole in the middle. He could turn it to work around the ring and any loose glue, stone, or metal filings could drop down into the center hole to the jar lid he'd placed on the work surface below, and not get stuck to anything else. He'd used this method for years and it worked perfectly. He reached into the box behind him, extracting rubber gloves. He was using super glue and did not want to glue his hands.

He picked up the adhesive, squeezing a drop onto the surface of the channel and then dropped a few of the tiny turquoise chunks on it. Some stuck and some fell off. He went around the ring adding glue, dropping in turquoise, moving some chucks with tweezers, to place them exactly where he wanted them.

When he had a decent area covered with the blue stone, he added more glue, then sprinkled gold filings to fill in the areas around the chunks until it was covered all around. Once he had stones and gold filled in around the entire ring, he sprayed it with activator that hardened the glue instantly.

After the glue was hardened, he grabbed a dusk mask so he wouldn't be breathing in stone dust. In a modern jewelry making lab the next part was done with a lathe, making it much easier, but he still did it the old way with a file. Using the same curved motion so as not to make flat spots he filed down the tops of the stones until they were even with the ring tops. He rotated the mandrel taking care to keep the rounded motion as he filed.

Many people found the combination of keeping the file flat while using a curved motion difficult, but he'd grown up watching his father do it and had perfected the movement long ago. It was just busy work for him while his mind worked on other things. It took a good six minutes to complete the rotation. *I need to speak to the gods. I have to get this right. This family line must be eliminated, and Billy must be cemented to us. It's time.*

He examined the ring and there were still holes to fill in between the stones. He had used up the gold, so he grabbed a box of silver filings. He again went around the piece, dropping glue then sprinkling in the silver filings and dropping more glue on top of the filings until the piece was as full as he could make it. He then sprayed the hardener, satisfied with his work. He let it set for over an hour, going in to eat lunch while it dried, then came back out, to once again, file it down to the level of the ring tops.

He took care to ensure there were no more gaps. Usually there were and he would have to repeat the process until there were not, but this time it was perfectly filled. He turned it around under a special light, intrigued by the unique design created by the turquoise, gold, and silver. Turning it while the glue was still liquid created unique swirls that even he couldn't recreate, and he loved the way it glinted. It was beautiful already, and he was pleased with it, but he still had smoothing and polishing to do.

He placed it back on the mandrel, using water and 220-grit sandpaper to go over it, making sure everything was pretty uniform. He repeated the process using progressively smaller sandpaper, first 400-grit, then 600, until he had it as smooth as he could get it; finishing with a 1000-grit. He ran his thumb over it again and again, and finally ran it across the sensitive skin of his lips, feeling for sharp or raised bits.

Finding none he placed a felt wheel on his small grinder, added some polishing compound, and began to smooth it even more. He went over the surface of the stone area, then moved to the outside of the rings, making sure it was as smooth as possible, while taking care to not burn his fingers as the ring became extremely hot as he polished it.

He then changed to a rubber and diamond bit to smooth up any rough spots inside the ring left by soldering the edges, and blended everything together until it looked seamless, then finished up with the polishing compound and a smaller felt wheel.

He did one more thing. Taking a sharp knife he made a small cut on the underside of a finger, dripped blood onto the ring, and held it up in dedication to the gods he served, asking them to bind the ring to their service and bind the client to the ring, bringing them back for more purchases, and drawing them to serve the same gods he did. It was another reason his jewelry was popular. People who purchased it fell in love with it, wished to wear it frequently, and couldn't bear to part with it.

None suspected it had a binding spell on it that bound them to a spirit. He laughed with amusement at people's ignorance, as he took a soft cloth and wiped off all traces of the blood, but didn't use water, so it was left with a slight copper smell. His customers were truthfully told copper tongs were used in the construction and pickling process, and it was sign of high quality. They knew it meant an authentic piece, made by him, when they opened the box and smelled the copper blood tang.

His client would be pleased. While an entirely unique piece, he'd used the exact same process for the pendant and it would be a well-matched set. This commission would add over $1300 to his bank account. At this point, his sales, even with the covid dip, were high enough that he didn't get excited at the deposit for any one piece, but it was nice to know his artistry was special enough to merit the top dollar price anywhere. He'd made a name for himself with his careful attention to detail, and refusal to take any shortcuts or use inferior materials.

He kept a supply of precious metals and high-end stones that were worth a fortune. The price that could be obtained by selling the raw materials in his shop at any given time would make a thief ecstatic, but he seldom even locked his door. Any thief in the area knew stealing from Wolf meant instant death, and no one would ever find the body, unless he wanted to warn the next one.

Sometimes clients who romanticized the Indian way of life, demanded a tour of his shop, but it was strictly off limits. He would entertain them at the store in town, where he had a small room with some tools, less expensive metals, and cheaper stones for making small items, and sometimes went to high-end jewelry stores for a grand opening of a new display of his creations; and even made rare trips for individual VIP clients to their home, but his private shop was his sanctuary and few had ever been inside. Few had ever been on his property for that matter.

Although he identified more with his Aztec ancestors, that wasn't known. He played up the Comanche Indian ancestor novelty, in the manner that people believed it to be from his website, appearing in full battle regalia, authentic in every way to promote both his knives and jewelry. It would shock people to know the scalps and skulls that were part of the warrior image were real, as was the blood dripping from his axe.

And in an arrogant display of his spiritual power, he had an extremely large wolf snarling at the world from the top of a mountain on the main page, that only a handful of people knew was he himself, in shape-shifter mode.

He was amused that people were so dumb about his ancestry, but their ignorance helped him make a very good living, and, also to remain hidden behind the pageantry. If anyone ever saw him dressed in warrior mode, they would assume he was adding to the mystery of his image in a marketing ploy, as he was known to do on occasion. It was a deliberate move that not only marketed his sales images, it was part of what had helped his family hide in plain sight for almost a century; and kept the taxes paid on the land his ancestors were born on, he reminded himself.

Few had any idea the riches his family, and he himself, had acquired making jewelry and knives. His knives were considered some of the finest offered on the market. He also made swords, but marketed those under an entirely different business name, concealed through many shell companies, that made it seem as if it were a competitor.

He had a line of knives there as well, and often used the supposed competition between the two companies to create business. His great, great grandmother had been captured by, and lived for a time, with a man who came from France during the settling of the continent, who descended from a line of Knight's Templars. They'd grown fond of each other and she'd shown him how to make obsidian and flint knives, and he'd shown all her sons how to make a true templar blade.

Eventually her sons had killed him, but one kept his way of making weapons. His family had survived the early purge of the Indian wars by selling hand-crafted knives to trading posts in quiet arrangements with owners, who claimed they were imported from Europe. Theirs were the best, and many were shipped to the East or all the way to Europe, totally opposite to the claims. It kept them alive and they quietly built wealth and contacts that were still being honored by the family lines involved on both sides.

No one knew that some of the finest jewelry and blades in the world were made by his family through the decades following the great Indian purge. Most had other names stamped on them that were well known. It both infuriated and amused him. It was the price they paid for anonymity; and survival.

Later, when it was popular to have genuine Indian-made items, they'd come out with lines in their own name. Only they and the proprietors knew it was all from the same source. It was fun creating competition between 'European' products, that excited one uppity group, and 'Real Native American' that excited others.

He packed the exquisite ring in a high-end box created with his logo on it. It was covered in a military blue tightly woven linen with the silhouette of a warrior with feathers in his hair holding a lance slanted above the head of the giant wolf standing beside him, embossed in silver. He laughed again at the double image of himself depicted in blurred shadow. The words embossed with the images said, 'We Are One,' and many thought it was a nod to ecology and globalism.

He put the box in his house in a hidden storage place until he could deliver it. Then left to go for his daily hike through the forest. Now that his order was complete, he had some decisions to make, and the forest was his favorite place to think. He stripped down to a loin cloth and buckskin leggings. His hair was already loose; the straight, lustrous, thick black length that flowed halfway down his deeply tanned and copper-tinged back, moved as he pulled on the footwear. He needed fresh meat, but he carried no weapon. He didn't need it.

He hiked five miles, then up to the top of a ridge. He often sat on top and looked over the land below. It wasn't terribly high, but he could see for miles. He sprinkled tobacco on the ground around the glade, and offered praise to the four directions. He thanked Father Sky and Mother Earth for their bounty and asked for help making his decision, then went to sit on the boulder that jutted out over a valley.

Its top was etched with symbols from a long-ago Shaman, and he ran his hands over the marks, renewing the dedication to lead his people into the time the spirits had foretold. He felt the time was fast approaching; this pandemic being a sign that his family had watched for, for a very long time; and vowed once again to let nothing stand in the way of his duty, not even American laws.

He loved the land and loved being able to come up here and look over it. He could see the roads cutting across the ranch lands spread out before his eyes, disappearing in the forested areas, and appearing again on the other side. He could see tiny spots of towns, and the larger spots of cities. He felt like the old ones in the days that came before, who sat here hiding and watching the enemy approach.

Back then, they could just attack. In today's world it had to be more subtle. In many ways his people had come to live at peace with the white, black, and other brown peoples; but in other ways, he was still at war, because America had long ago

BOOK 1: "PREPARE FOR THE END" SERIES

adopted the Christian man Jesus. He knew the Comanche, Hopi, Nahuatl, Paiute, Pima, and Shoshone language was a Numic language of the Uto-Aztecan (the language of the Aztecs). The language families (including language isolates) that make up the Mesoamerican linguistic area are Aztecan (Nahuan, a branch of Uto-Aztecan), Cuitlatec, Huave, Mayan, Mixe-Zoquean, Otomanguean, Tarascan, Tequistlatecan, Totonacan, and Xinkan. (Wikipedia, 2023)

All these people originally worshipped the snake gods, and Christianity was in direct opposition to them. The white man had outlawed his people, driven them from the land, imprisoned them on reservations, and declared war upon the gods his Aztec ancestors had honored.

His family went all the way back to the Aztec empire. Both the Maya and Aztecs controlled regions of what is now Mexico. The Aztecs had led a more brutal, warlike lifestyle, with frequent human sacrifices, just like their descendants the Comanche, as Texas was settled.

His family was bound to Quetzalcóatl, whose Mayan name was Kukulcán, a feathered serpent, who was revered as the patron of priests, the inventor of the calendar and of books, and the protector of goldsmiths and other craftsmen; he was also identified with the planet Venus. This was the origin of their jewelry craftsmanship.

As the morning and evening star, Quetzalcóatl was the symbol of death and resurrection. With his companion Xolotl, a dog-headed god, he was said to have descended to the underground hell of Mictlan to gather the bones of the ancient dead. Those bones he anointed with his own blood, giving birth to the men who inhabit the present universe.

He had been dedicated to the Aztec gods and nature spirits from conception. He had undergone rituals throughout his life to bind more of them to him and to become more and more powerful to do their bidding. The spirit of Xoltl was the spirit that allowed him to shape-shift into a wolfman. The white man did not know it, but it was prophesied that the old gods were coming back into power, and he was a part of that, having descended from a long line of Shamans, or Priests, and was of a royal lineage.

He also had an ancestor from the Hopi tribe who were also descendants of the Aztecs. The Hopi were the first tribe in America and had occupied Arizona for 2,000 years, and had prophesied about the coming days.

According to Hopi prophecy, shortly after the Blue Star Kachina is visible to all and the Day of Purification is realized, the True White Brother will come to earth in search of Hopi "who steadfastly adhere to their ancient teachings." It is said that if the True White Brother fails in his mission and is unable to find uncorrupted men and women, that the earth will be completely destroyed, and none will be spared. However, if successful in bringing the symbols, and finding those who still follow the true Hopi way of life, the world will be created anew and all the faithful will be in Aztec times (such as the 14th through 16th centuries) again.

When he was fifteen, he'd gone on his vision quest. His grandfather sent him out to interact with nature and find his guardian spirit, to obtain advice and protection, as he was next in line to lead the tribe, charged with overseeing the tribe's physical and spiritual well-being. He'd spent four days fasting in isolation, deep in prayer and meditation. He'd lain on this very rock on his back, watching the clouds go by, taking the sacred peyote, until his mind emptied and he wandered with the spirits.

The first to appear was an evil spirit who tried to make him fear the other ones coming. He said he represented the creator, but after much persuasion to get him to turn away from the serpent gods—that Wolf had ignored, being prepared for this possibility by his grandmother—he had finally been revealed as the tempter and he left. He saw father Sun bow to him late in the evening and Mother earth had greeted him as the moon goddess rose and bathed him with her light.

She spoke to him of all she'd seen in her eons of watching over the earth and the People. She called him to honor her with his life and promised him a helper if he would become hers. He pledged his life to her and she disappeared behind dark clouds, while colors of all shades, deep and rich, had swirled around him when he was alone again; enfolding him, intimate and close, thick, and liquid, then erupting into brilliant sparks of shining glitter spraying out from him; constantly moving, swirling, teasing, even entering his body.

It flowed through his veins, and mixed itself with his essence; until he was in a more deeply altered state of consciousness. It was the source of inspiration that made him a top jewelry maker. All the successful ones through the centuries had been filled with the colors during their spirit quest.

At one point, lost in the color, he saw the moon come back, shaped like a beautiful maiden. She pointed her finger at him and beckoned him to her, and as he stood, he instinctively threw back his head and howled, long and deep, like a wolf. She pointed behind him and he turned to see a pack of the creatures standing in an arc around him. He felt no fear, even as the leader, a huge black beast with bared teeth came close, growling low in his throat. Hair rose stiffly on its back as it closed the gap between them.

He opened his arms and ran toward it, and the beast leaped into the air. He jumped also, and they met in mid-air, as he felt the wolf enter his body. It was strange and uncomfortable that first time, but he howled again, and merging with the monster, he let alpha instincts take over and ran out into the forest, while the entire pack followed. He felt hair growing on his skin and his face elongating into a muzzle. He could see everything around him in the black inky night, while the rich smells of the forest filled his nostrils, letting him know which other animals were nearby.

He inhaled the pungent scent of the she wolves, and mated with them all. That ignited a hunger, and after four days of fasting, he was ready to satisfy it. The tang of a doe was close and he ran until he saw her. She had just given birth and a tiny fawn was struggling to its feet, birth fluids still dripping. He was still part wolf and part man, but he ripped the fawn to slivers with teeth and claws curved for the task, and ate it all, holding the blood-drenched parts in hands that were part human and part canine.

Devouring the tender meat was exciting as the blood spattered all around. The doe was crying out in fear, unable to run. He ripped her, and ate the choicest parts, then stepped back and howled, allowing the rest of the pack to take the rest. He had been first, establishing his supremacy; but he shared the kill, and that cemented their loyalty.

It was the supernatural experience he'd been seeking. He ran with the pack until light began to peak over the trees and finally went back to the boulder, lying there until sleep took him. He had strange dreams and gradually woke as a man. He'd thought it was a peyote induced dream only, until he saw the blood. He sat up and looked around. The wolves were gone, but the enormous prints were everywhere.

He understood that not only would he be the next Shaman, he was now a spirt-walker as well. He could leave his physical body and move in spirit form, and because the wolf spirit had chosen him, he could merge with the wolf physically as well. The white man called them werewolves, the Indian called them Skinwalkers, and both feared and respected them.

Not all Shamans were spirit walkers, but it was not uncommon in the Tonkawa tribes. Even elderly medicine men have been known to develop spirit walker powers, sometimes only days before death. The stress of handling so many spirits, turns a spirit walker's pelt or hair snow white over the years. Some tribes consider a wolf born with a white pelt to be destined to merge with a spirit-walker.

The, wolf was reportedly not hunted, for the Tonkawa believed that they had been brought into the world by this animal, or were even descended from it. Nevertheless, the Tonkawa were in possession of a number, of wolf skins, which were used in performing the wolf dance. The Tonkawa claimed that if they killed a wolf they would lose their eyesight temporarily, go crazy, or contract a fever, unless special 'medicines' were taken.

When the Tonkawa encountered a wolf, they asked him to provide them with deer when they hunted. After the hunt when the men returned to camp, they hung the game in trees, first conducting special rites to protect them from being carried off by the wolves. The Tonkawa stated that on one occasion a member of the tribe killed a deer but neglected to perform the necessary ceremony before hanging up the meat he had obtained. When he returned, the meat was gone, whereas that belonging to the other Indians had been left intact.

BOOK 1: "PREPARE FOR THE END" SERIES

Apparently, the taboo on killing wolves was in some instances extended to include the coyote. The grey wolf was said to be 'the owner of the earth' and his permission was asked when hunters entered new hunting grounds. (Tribes of OK – Tonkawa Tribe of Indians of Oklahoma.pdf)

He lit the sacred pipe he carried in the hide bag tied to the thong that held his loin cloth. He untied the cloth, took off his leggings, and lit the tobacco he'd tamped into the bowl. He smoked for a time, thinking, and then blew smoke around his head, inviting the spirits to come to him. He no longer needed the peyote, so he waited and smoked. Eventually he began to sing an ancient song that drew the spirits, while thumping a rhythm on the rock with a smaller rock he picked up from the ground. His words asked for wisdom, strength, courage, and determination.

He opened his mind and got lost in the rhythm of the song and the drumming. He felt the spirits come to him, and he thrilled at the other-than-human essence that filled him. He asked for answers and nodded as they were revealed. He knew what he must do. They demanded blood and the coven needed protection. He stood and turned.

The wolf pack was there and they parted at his approach. He took off running, changing in mid-stride as the spirit of the Wolf filled him. He led them for miles until he found the pair of does. He snarled at them, then let them run. They were fast, but he was faster. He played with them, getting close and nipping at their rumps, then backed off, giving them hope that they could escape. When the fear was at its highest, he attacked. He immediately ripped the throat out of the largest, tasting the fresh hot blood as it filled his mouth with its delicious thickness.

It drove him wild and he took down the second deer. He ate the choicest parts, starting while it still lived, reveling in the fear as the light gradually darkened in her eyes. He ate his fill, then stepped back for the pack to finish her off. None had touched the first kill. They knew better.

He waited till they had cleaned the entire carcass, then changed to half-man, half-wolf. He had large hairy hands while retaining the strength and endurance of a wolf. He used a claw to gut the deer, drew out the guts, and threw them to the pack. and picked up the dripping deer, slung it over his enormous shoulders, growled at the pack, threw back his head and howled, then set off at a fast run, eating up the miles back to his house. He stopped to pick up his loincloth and leggings, ran to within a quarter mile of his place, then stopped and transformed back to his human body and covered his loins.

He slung the deer over his shoulders once again, and walked the last portion, straight to the back of his shop where a lean-to had a hook to hang the deer up, and a table with knives on it. He would skin it, then butcher it, there, filling up his freezer for another few weeks.

He did the necessary tasks, throwing the parts he didn't want over the fence to the wolf pack. They'd come back after dark and have a second meal. They would leave nothing to even smell. It was a normal routine for them all.

He finished processing the deer, throwing a generous portion of meat into a bowl in the refrigerator for the next day, then wrapped the rest and stacked it in the freezer. He showered, putting on dark jeans and a black t-shirt. He had to get to Randy's house tonight.

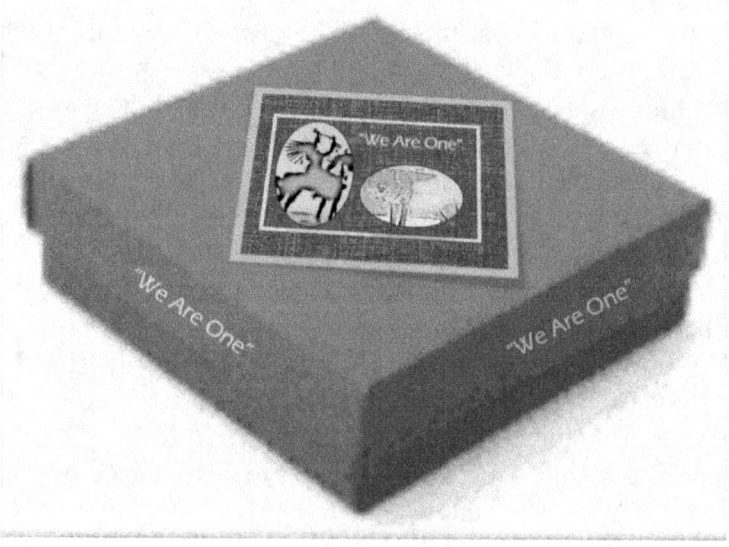

Creating A Haven

Chapter 24

MATT DROPPED ERWIN OFF at the gate, watched him get in the delivery truck, and waved as he drove out; then followed him through the gate. He went straight to his house, provided the urine sample for the DNA test, then placed the specimen jar in the small cooler in his truck beside the tea glass he'd snitched. He also grabbed the strands of hair that he'd picked up from the back of her chair before he left. They were wrapped in a napkin beside the tea, so he sealed them with another sample of his own hair, separated and marked 'sample 1' and 'sample 2' in a zip-lock bag. They'd drop it all off as soon as they left the other house.

He went to his home office and grabbed the rolled-up blueprint from the wall safe hidden behind a painting. Alone for the first time since early morning, he took a few minutes to sit, leaning back in his chair with his feet on the desk, contemplating all that was swirling around him.

He couldn't believe Dan had come up with a solution to his wanting to know whether or not he had a daughter. He'd been tormented by the thought for over 20 years. While, on one hand he could understand Jenny not wanting to lose a minute with Missy, on the other, he'd been cheated out of being a parent completely.

He'd fallen in love with her when she was three days old, when Jenny called him for money to buy diapers and formula. She'd allowed him to hold her for a few minutes, then sent him on his way. She'd seldom let him see her since. He'd had to watch her from afar, settling for the pictures Jenny regularly sent in exchange for the monthly checks. And later, eating at Mac's two or three times a week, so he could interact with her. He felt relief that she'd be living in his other house, right next door.

257

Maybe he'd finally get to know her. That would have been enough, but being able to *know*, that was priceless.

He suddenly felt a pang of fear go through him at the thought that Jenny had just lied to him for money. He really believed the girl was his child, but what if he'd been played? He thought of the thousands of dollars he'd put out, and even the loss of his marriage—although that was far from the real reason that had ended—and for a few seconds he felt like a complete fool.

He sat with that knowledge for about 5 minutes, then shook it off. Dan was right. He was already emotionally and financially invested, and she needed help no matter what. If he could rescue her from Billy and whatever nefarious plans he had for her, it was worth it; but deep down, he hoped the DNA test proved his long-held belief, the truth that he was a father.

He opened the blueprints, read the notes, and reacquainted himself with all that he'd planned; then grabbed the keys to the other house from the desk, and left; walking the short distance carrying the cooler, since he'd be riding with Dan to take the samples to the Geneticist's office.

They had a few more things they needed to do, but he was on edge after the talk with Erwin, and felt like he was being watched as he walked. In fact—he was—but it was in the spirit realm. If he could have seen into that realm, he would have shuddered at the hideous sight of the ones who watched. They were furious that he was moving Missy to a place where they weren't as free to come and go. The master had plans for that one, and Erwin too.

They had watched Erwin go into the house with the men, but it was protected by the shining warriors surrounding it, and they couldn't get close enough to hear. Hopefully, they were just taking care of ranch business, and they didn't want to report it, in case it was just that; but they'd been in there a long time while the other men distributed the supplies. It looked suspicious.

Their special assignments were Billy and Erwin. They'd been watching them for the master since they were kids. They hated Dan and Matt, and the families they represented. They'd been thwarted many times through the years by them, and were determined to take back what was theirs. Matt had stepped in their way numerous times, and they hadn't been able to get near Clayton because he was always too close. And that infernal praying he was always doing made them shudder.

Now he was around Erwin, and they weren't happy about it. Erwin had been known to step in their way when they were pushing Billy to torment Clayton also, and they'd never liked that. Now, they seemed a bit too chummy. "We need to find out what went on in that house."

"Yes. We need to be ahead of this so we can redeem ourselves for losing his father." They stayed until Matt reached the house, then separated, and left to cast fiery darts into Erwin and Billy's minds, anticipating the fun that particular torment always brought them.

Dan was pulling up as Matt unlocked the door. They walked in and surveyed the large living room. "How long has it been since you've been in here?" Dan looked at the dust covered room with dismay.

"Not since I moved." Matt looked uncomfortable in the room. "I know it was probably immature to just lock the door and leave, and even build another house, but I just couldn't live here."

"It's ok. Sometimes when you start a new phase of your life, you have to close the door to the last phase. If you don't, you have a foot in both worlds, without the ability to fully live in either one. Let's just check each room and make a list. The boys can clean it up and do the repairs. If you want, I can oversee it."

Matt gave a brief crooked smile with one side of his mouth. "Thanks, Dan, but I'll try to be a man about it. Besides, having Missy here will overcome any residual bad memories." He walked over to the door of the coat closet, tried to open it, and the knob came off in his hand. "I thought I remembered that having a problem. I guess that goes on the list."

Dan laughed and wrote it down. "Maybe a new mantel for the fireplace too. That one looks like it wouldn't hold a clock."

"Yep." Matt nodded, "I was just about to redo that when she threw me out."

"Yoo-hoo," Pauline walked through the front door, then stopped as she saw the condition of the room. "Oh, dear."

"It's ok, sis. I got the crew coming over tomorrow. We just need to make a list and get what they need."

"This carpet either needs cleaned, or replaced." She looked around, dismayed, as she walked further in. "And the curtains. Were these bought in the 50s?"

"Yep. Pauline is in the house," Dan's voice was droll.

"Well, I'm just glad we've already made the decision to do some renovating instead of you asking me to show the house 'as is' to a potential buyer." She sniffed at the dust. "I'd have had to discount this heavily, even in this seller's market. This place needs some updating... but..." she was walking into the next room, "... it does seem to be built well and has its merits."

"I did a lot of work on it through the years," Matt's voice was quiet. He'd been walking from room to room and the memories were hitting him hard in this already emotional day. "We won't need to do much except cosmetic."

They'd entered the kitchen where Matt had custom built the cabinets, pantries, and shelves. The tile he'd spent a week installing was still as beautiful as it ever was, the rustic tones blending well with the Colonial Maple stain on the wood. He looked out the large window over the sink and the second one by the breakfast nook, remembering his wife's excitement when he'd gotten them finished.

They'd spent many a meal sitting there, watching nature while talking. They'd taken down all the curtains in here and the entire back of the house, preferring to see outside, knowing there was no one around to look in. That was one perk of living on the land attached to the ranch; the quiet solitude of the vast acreage was a sanctuary he still loved.

"Oh...." Pauline breathed out, "Matt... this is lovely. I had no idea..."

Matt smiled briefly, having a hard time, "Thanks Pauline. I think you'll find much that you'll like. I just never got around to the main room. I got side-tracked by something else I needed to do first. It has all new electric and plumbing. We started renovating in the kitchen, then our bedroom, then... uh... the others.

The laundry room was next, but all the bedrooms are nice with completely updated storage areas, and I even did some work to finish the attic. It's not all done, but it's ok for someone that may need extra space for storage. There's a small sitting room up there, that's nice. I still have some of the wood if anything needs tweaked. We've already added the mantel to the list. The main bathroom is finished, but I'll need to work on the second one. I hadn't gotten to it yet either."

His eyes took on a sudden shine. "Excuse me a minute," he said. "I think I'll check out the shed. You too go ahead and look around." He quietly left by the kitchen door that led to the side yard.

"Is he ok?" Pauline looked at Dan.

"He will be. Today's the first time he's been back in here since they split, and today's been a bit tough on him."

"I see." Pauline looked at Dan with compassion and a question in her eyes. "I did see the resemblance at lunch. I'm just not sure the relationship."

Dan's lips came up on one side in a half smile. "He's not either, and that's all I'm saying. Just sit this one out for now, sis, and don't speak to Sarah. That's his place to do. We need to get the house ready and let him sift it through. And sis, get whatever you need to make it nice; I don't care what you spend. Get those papers signed, no matter what."

"From the look on his face, I'm thinkin' you need to stay close for a bit," Pauline added. "You're his second father. He looks up to you more than you know."

"He's a son to me, almost as much as Clayton. I'll be here."

"I know you will." Pauline admired her brother. He was a good man. "Let's go see the rest. They walked through the house, making a list of items that still needed repair, with Pauline exclaiming over the quality where Matt had been updating it. His work was top of the line, and it could clearly be seen that he'd done it with much love and attention to detail.

Pauline once again caught her breath as they walked into the small bedroom attached to the main one. "Did he build that?" She pointed to the exquisite cradle that stood by the far wall. Even Dan looked surprised. He looked around the room, and stopped in his tracks at what was in there. The small scale of the custom-built shelves and furniture was entirely unexpected. "He must have. No wonder he never came back." They exchanged looks, both even more worried now.

Matt came back in as they were coming back into the main room. "There's more wood than I thought out there. I have enough to finish what I'd planned. Did you see the second bathroom? We probably need to get it done before the girls move in." His eyes glanced at Dan's, knowing he'd seen what was there.

"Yes." Pauline agreed, "If we carry on with what you've done elsewhere, we can match the tile and create another bathroom as elegant as the first one, that way they can each have their own without someone feeling as if they got a lesser end of the deal. It's as large as the other one. We can do an exact match, or switch it up a bit. Maybe put in a new tub with a shower stall beside it. It needs a new vanity and toilet also."

"Other than that bathroom and the main room, there's not as much as I figured there'd be." Dan seemed surprised; but distracted by being very worried about Matt, now that he knew why he'd left. He had several new questions though.

"Let's get the crew in here for cleaning, power wash the outside, and get the main repairs done. We can get carpet samples and let the girls decide which they prefer and any paint colors, and do that after they've looked at it. That way they can be happy and comfortable," Pauline was truly amazed at the house and Matt's generosity. It piqued her interest even more and she shot a quick look at Dan, who gave the tiniest sideways shake 'no' back at her, to stop any questions. He knew that look on Matt's face, and he didn't want her to upset him anymore.

"Add stain to the list, Dan," Matt smiled, thinking about his daughter living here. "We can go get the tile, stain, and carpet samples, then go to Lowe's. We'd planned on a tub and shower already. We wanted the shower to be tiled, like ours, with a glass door instead of buying a stall. I'd like to continue with that plan. It'll take a day or so longer than a kit, but it'll be a lot nicer and blend with the parts that are already done.

I'll call Homer and order the mantle I planned on also. I'm going to build the vanity and add some shelving in the main room and stain it all at once to match. I may need a few days to do this."

"You take as long as you need," Dan nodded. "The cows have been moved, the hay's baled, the pumpkin patch is done, and it's almost winter. This is the perfect time to finish it. Just remember they have a rent hike and new lease coming up fast.

Delegate what you can, bring in plumbers, whatever it takes, but we need to get it done, asap."

"Ok guys, sounds like you got it going on. I'll let you get to it. Call me when it's ready and I'll bring the young ladies out here. I won't let them leave without getting the contract signed. That's what I do best," Pauline smiled, and walked out.

"You ready to go see the geneticist?" Dan's question was gentle, and the hassling he'd done earlier, was gone.

Matt smiled, and nodded. "Absolutely. Dan, I don't know how you thought of all this, but thank you. I've never been more ready for anything in my life."

Dan, smiled too, secretly praying they were right, especially after seeing the unexpected room. He clapped Matt on the shoulder, briefly squeezing it to let him know he understood his needing to know, and his worry. "Alright, let's roll; and Matt… if you want to talk about it, I'm here."

Matt, knowing he had questions, just nodded, but didn't speak. He couldn't. Going in there earlier had almost done him in. He still wasn't ready to face it, even after all these years.

Meanwhile, Erwin had been driving back. His thoughts were turbulent as he went over all that had happened in the last few hours, and the new knowledge he'd acquired. How he wished he'd known some of this sooner. *Now what?* Billy had been his only friend for years. If all this was correct, he wasn't sure how much Billy knew, or if even the whole friendship had been contrived. He felt shell-shocked at everything that had been going on around him and he'd never even suspected.

He felt slightly paranoid, wondering if he was being watched now. It was odd that they were having a cop be onsite when he parked the truck. Was it really that bad? Were they really after him due to some old family grudge?

He laughed a short laugh that sounded a little crazy. Good lord, he was really tripping this time. He started to think about how nuts he'd sound if he tried to tell anyone about what he'd just heard. Maybe they were both messing with him and would tease him the next time they saw him at the store.

"That's it," the demonic creature kept whispering into his ear. "They are both off their rockers. This is stupid. I need Billy. He's my only friend. I barely know these old dudes."

Demons know that sometimes all they need to do is cast doubt on good men. It was a concept that went all the way back to the garden of Eden when the nachash spoke the words, "Did God really say...." Men were so simple. They seldom had to change tactics; the age-old ones they'd used for 6,000 years still worked the same. "Such imbeciles." He cackled out loud at how easy it was to manipulate Erwin. He tried another line of thought:

"Gran doesn't need me. She's just an old lady. I don't owe her anything. I can just go straight to Billy's and play poker with the guys. If I get there soon, I can talk him out of his anger. Everything will be the way it's always been. These people don't care about me. Where were they when my dad died?

I just need a drink. I need a lot of drinks. I need a ritual. I need to tell Billy and Wolf everything, and see what they say about it all. This is something I need help understanding."

All at once, Erwin shook himself. He'd almost run off the road. He felt like he was in a fog and all these thoughts were invading him from outside himself. He spoke aloud, "I love Gran. She's been there my entire life and never hesitated to take me in when Mom died. She loves me, too. She does need me, and I need her. I'm going home."

He glanced ahead at something that caught his eye and he wasn't sure what he was seeing. It looked like a dense black fog undulating in and out of what was almost a human shape. It loomed in the air, hovering a few feet above the road. It was wraith-like, but had glowing red eyes. He almost ran off the road, he was so disturbed by its presence. He thought about the demon from the ritual and was sure it had come for him.

He considered what Dan and Matt had said; his dad had been taken out in an auto wreck. *Was this what happened to him?!* He suddenly screamed at the apparition. "Get away from me! You have no power here!" He remembered his Gran teaching him about demons when he was small. She said you could order them away in the name of Jesus.

"In Jesus' name, go!!!" he shouted, then almost ran off the road again at the look of surprise that appeared on what had coalesced into a semblance of a giant face. It scrolled through surprise, anger, and finally malevolent rage, then the thing shot off and disappeared into the tree line. *Oh, my God!!!*

Erwin was astonished at what had just taken place. He started shaking and then physically doubled over at what felt like a boot kicking him below his stomach. He fought the instant nausea and the steering wheel at the same time, hearing a maniacal laugh right beside him in the vehicle, and fear shot through him. He felt the accelerator go down so fast his foot was left dangling in the air before dropping down again.

The truck began to pick up speed with the pedal floored, and he hung on, doing his best to navigate around the curves, while the pain in his genitals overwhelmed him. Only the many hours he'd driven the truck delivering loads, and how well he knew this area, kept him handling them; as he wrestled the wheel, turning it faster and faster to keep up with the speed of the tires. He couldn't see this ending well at all.

He shot around the last curve in the left lane, grateful no one was there, and then was in the long straight before he hit the main road. If he couldn't stop in time, he'd shoot across and straight into the local grocery store, probably mowing down people in the way. He knew he had to do whatever he could, and fix the damage to the truck later; so, he grabbed the gear shift and tried to gear down, finally managing to get it in a lower gear and throttle the engine down, feeling the grinding as he did so. *God help me!!*

He stuck the edge of leather around the toe of his boot under the gas pedal, wedging it in and shoved harder and harder until it lifted slightly and he got his entire boot toe underneath. He forced it up and the truck began to slow. He clutched and went down to a lower gear as the indicator on the dashboard gauge went down to less than the numbers on the sign he passed.

He felt it when the unseen foot relinquished control, just before he hit the intersection. He was almost able to stop, clutching again, gearing further down, and slowing even more; and was grateful to see no traffic as he turned the corner, went a few blocks, then hit the gate opener and pulled into the lot of the Hardware store.

He pulled around back and parked, breathing as hard as if he'd ran a 50-yard touchdown. He climbed out, still sick and hurting, and glanced across the road, seeing Ryan sitting in his official car watching him. Ryan gave a brief wave, then looked the other way. Erwin decided to not return the wave in case he was being observed. He was still shaking and not entirely sure what had just happened, or if Ryan was aware of any of it. He got in his personal truck, pulling out of the gate as Ryan was slipping back into traffic.

He pulled ahead of the cop car and it fell back but followed him out of town. He pulled into the gas station, needing fuel. Ryan pulled up behind him, getting out and placing his credit card into the next pump, acting like he was just another patron. He kept his head down toward the pump like he was having trouble with his card, dropped a piece of paper while he fumbled with it, and quietly said, "I'll be watching. Others will as well. You have my number. Don't hesitate to use it. You are not alone."

No one watching would have noticed anything amiss, he was so smooth in delivering his message. Erwin felt like he was in a movie. He had no idea what was coming, but was glad both that Ryan was near, and the knowledge that he'd be willing to help him. He would be surprised if he knew how many members of the old families were always watching each other's backs. He glanced up, his eyes acknowledging that he'd heard, but said nothing in return.

He paid for his gas, went in to get a soda, and when he came out Ryan was gone. He bent to tie his shoe and picked up the paper, got in his truck, put the number in his phone as Matt #2 - R, and left for Gran's. Everything in him screamed to be in her house. He somehow knew he'd be safe there.

As he pulled into the driveway, he caught a glimpse of black undulating in the trees behind the house and once again heard the maniacal laughter beside him. He parked, jumped out, and ran as fast as he could to the front door, flinging it open so hard it crashed against the inside wall. He heard Gran yell as it swung back and almost hit him in the face. She came out of the kitchen with a butcher knife in her hand, and when she saw it was him, screamed, "Erwin! You scared the crap out of me!! What's wrong?!"

He skidded in the room, slammed the door shut behind him, and locked the deadbolt. "Did you see it? Did it come in the house?" he whirled around and grabbed her shoulders, as he asked the questions in staccato fashion, almost skewering himself on the knife she still held.

"See what?" She looked both scared and confused. "Erwin, are you alright? What's wrong?"

"Stay here." He went around her and ran to the kitchen, moved the curtain aside and peered out the window toward the tree line behind the house. He scrutinized the entire area he could see from that angle, then moved from window to window around the kitchen and dining room, checking out each angle of view. When nothing was seen, he sank down in a chair, shaking, and laid his head down on the table, white as a ghost.

He wasn't sure he should tell her, but then decided she had to know so she could be on guard. He started with the black shadow he'd seen on the road, how it had taken over the accelerator, and finished with the sight of it in the trees. "And Gran, we need to talk. I've been told some things, and I have to know if they are true."

"I see." she watched his face for a moment, saw the mark on his neck where he shirt was askew, then quietly spoke, "Yes, we do."

He watched her face as different expressions raced across it. She seemed to be considering several things, wrestling with them all.

"Gran....?"

She arrived at a decision, turned to the stove, stirred several pots, then poured him a glass of tea and sat down across from him. "Dinner will be ready soon, but we can talk now, and eat when it's ready. What were you told, and by whom?"

He told her about the conversation at the ranch, leaving out the parts that would incriminate himself, but as he completed the tale she stood up, grabbed his jaw, turning it to look at the long scratch that had turned a deep shade of red and purple, already getting infected, and looked very sad. "Isn't there more?"

"What do you mean?" he tried to buy time.

"Erwin, your grandfather shared with me what happened to him at your age. I know what this mark means, far more than you do. How far in are you?"

BOOK 1: "PREPARE FOR THE END" SERIES

He saw tears in her eyes, and sudden shame made him drop his head. "Gran...I...."

"Erwin, I'm so sorry I didn't warn you. I was trying to keep you safe. After your father was killed, then losing your mother and Sherman, I just wanted to forget all that existed. You were so young and so lost. It's my fault you weren't warned. You were vulnerable and I just wanted you to have a good childhood, in spite of all the loss. I didn't want you steeped in the knowledge of evil, looking over your shoulder all the time, waiting for something awful to happen. Instead, I let you be swayed into something you have no idea the consequences of."

"You knew?" he was so confused. "You knew my dad was killed?"

"They wanted to hurt Sherman for escaping their plans for him. Dan kept him safe at the ranch, and it had been so long, we thought they'd let it go, and that was my fault, also. I didn't want to deal with any of it. When Gene got away too, they made their move. Now, they've sucked you into their evil deeds.

Erwin, you have to decide right now, who you want to be. I'm sorry I too let you down, but I won't have evil in my house. If you stay, you have to renounce all of that and never go back. If you're determined to stay involved, you need to leave. Tonight. I won't tell you what to do, but I won't have it here.

When Gene was killed, I decided then I wouldn't have any of it near me. I serve Jesus Christ; they serve the enemy. We are citizens of different Kingdoms. Those Kingdoms don't cross over, and there is no middle ground. I should have made you go to church with me, or taught you more here at home. I'm sorry. It seems by trying to protect you all I've done is let you down. Keeping people ignorant never keeps them safe. Dan and Homer have told me that since your mother died. I'm sorry I made that choice. But now you have a choice to make.

If you stay you will agree to let me teach you about the two Kingdoms, the ongoing battle between good and evil, and what God expects from those who are His. That's why the entity you saw couldn't come in the house. I've drawn a boundary around the property, anointing the line with oil and asked God to protect my house and land. They can't cross the boundary. A child of God has authority over them.

BOOK 1: "PREPARE FOR THE END" SERIES

I am protected from a lot because I'm a child of God. You are vulnerable because you're not. Again, you have to decide."

"Gran, I decided at the ranch that I wanted out. I'm not too sure about the God thing, but I'm sure I don't want to be a part of the evil I've witnessed, and whatever that black thing is, I want no part of it either."

"God is the only one that can protect you. If you reject him, you stay a part of the Kingdom of Darkness whether you ever participate in another ritual or not. You can't believe in one side, and disbelieve in the other. If you understand the supernatural is real, it's all real. It's a war between the kingdoms of good and evil. There is no third kingdom, Erwin.

When Adam fell, all of humanity fell with him, as we were yet unborn. That means we're born into the Kingdom of Darkness. In order to enter the Kingdom of Light we must be born again."

"How can an adult be born again? I don't even have a mother anymore," Erwin was really confused now.

"It's a spiritual birth this time," Gran explained. "I'll teach you more, but the plain gospel is this: Jesus is both the son of God, and God himself. He was fully God but was born fully human as well. The wages of sin are death, and Jesus came to die in our place, so we don't have to die to pay for our own sin.

He paid the price for us. In order to be born again into the Kingdom of Heaven, we must believe that He is God, that He died to save us; then confess our sin before a righteous and holy God, and accept the salvation he purchased.

He was the divine substitute, and is therefore called the lamb of God, because until he died people had to sacrifice a sheep or a goat to atone for their sin; but it didn't fully cleanse them, just pushed back the punishment for a time.

When Jesus died, it paid our debt in full so we don't have to keep sacrificing animals. When we acknowledge our sin, repent of it, and ask his forgiveness, he gives it. Then, we are saved from having to die to pay for our sin, and we're cleansed from the sin; making us morally just as if we'd never sinned at all. We're released from the penalty of death, and are made spiritually alive. He actually says we are now a part of His own family, and we move from being a citizen of the Kingdom of Darkness, to being a citizen of the Kingdom of Heaven.

A lot of people stop there, but Jesus said, 'If you love me, keep my commandments,' so we must give our allegiance to Him and Him alone, and begin to obey His commandments. So far, your allegiance has been to Billy, yourself, the lust you've indulged, and whatever demonic beings you've participated with.

What you have to decide now is, are you ready to give your allegiance to Jesus and the side of the Kingdom of Heaven and fight for righteousness, or stay with the Kingdom of Darkness? It's not about 'asking Jesus into your heart.' It's about completely changing direction and beginning to serve God with all your heart, mind, soul, and strength.

It's changing allegiance and obedience from one Kingdom and its ways, to the other Kingdom entirely. It's one or the other. Since they've targeted you—and there is much you still need to know—you're out of time. It's now, because Erwin, they're coming for you very soon. The Word says in Joshua 24:15 'choose this day whom you will serve.'

The whole verse is: 'And if it seems evil unto you to serve the LORD, choose you this day whom ye will serve; whether the gods which your fathers served that were on the other side of the flood, or the gods of the Amorites, in whose land ye dwell: but as for me and my house, we will serve the LORD.

The gods they served before the flood were the fallen angels that rebelled against God, and their half-human children; and the gods of the Amorites were essentially the same. The original religion they followed in serving them was almost identical to what you've become involved in.

Like Joshua 'as for me and my house, we will serve the LORD.' That's why you need to choose now, and why you have to leave if you decide to serve the enemy. A house divided will not stand. I've lost all but you and God, and as much as I love you, I can't lose God. I want to be with Sherman and Gene someday and they both were children of God. If you want to be with your family forever, that's where we'll all be, including your mother—the Kingdom of Heaven."

"I don't know if God will forgive me," Erwin looked miserable.

"He forgave Sherman, and me; and every other human that's asked since he offered us the opportunity.

BOOK 1: "PREPARE FOR THE END" SERIES

1 John 1:9 says, if we confess our sins, he is faithful and just to forgive us our sins, and to cleanse us from all unrighteousness. If we say that we have not sinned, we make him a liar, and His Word is not in us."

"I don't even know where to start, or how to talk to God, even if He will forgive me."

"How should you approach God for forgiveness? Just confess. Confession is not saying, 'God, I'll never do it again.' It's saying, "You're right, God. I was wrong.""

"But He'll always know I did those things."

"Psalms 103:12 says, As, far as the east is from the west, so far has he removed our transgressions from us. "Let us therefore come boldly unto the throne of grace, that we may obtain mercy, and find grace to help in time of need.""

"Romans 5:1 adds, "Therefore, being justified—that is, acquitted of sin, declared blameless before God—by faith—let us grasp the fact that—we have peace with God through our Lord Jesus Christ:""

"What does it mean to be justified?"

It means "just as if I'd never sinned."

"You mean God wipes it away as if it never existed? Like it never happened at all?"

"As for eternal punishment, yes, and the way He looks at you now," Gran answered. "But, in other ways, no. Let me explain. We may not always escape the consequences. Such as: if you have sex and contract a venereal disease, or create a baby, God may or may not heal you, but he doesn't wipe the child out of existence, and you may have long lasting health problems, such as AIDS; and if you're not married, you'll still have to pay child support.

If you murder someone, you may still spend the rest of your life in jail, or be subjected to capital punishment. If you do drugs, or smoke for 40 years and destroy your health, he may not heal you. If you are a glutton and develop diabetes or heart disease, it won't just go away."

"So, you escape eternal consequences, but not always earthly consequences," Erwin was starting to understand. "That's fair."

"If God were 'fair' none of us would exist," Gran chuckled, "He'd be forced to kill us all by His righteous judgement. He's merciful."

Erwin smiled. "But what if we can't live righteous after we've confessed and asked for forgiveness. I'm not sure I'm very good."

"Psalms 53:3 says, every one of them is gone back: they are altogether become filthy; there is none that doeth good, no, not one.

We still have a carnal nature from the fall. We do mess up. But when we do, we go back to step number one. We admit it, we acknowledge that God is right and we are wrong, and we confess again and ask him to forgive again. Just remember to keep a short lag time between the time you realize you've sinned and when you confess, and don't use it for a free pass.

Determine from day one that God is right and you are wrong, and begin to let go of known sin. There is a difference in sin that you fall into occasionally, and habitual, usual, everyday sin, that becomes entrenched, and you feel entitled to continue, in spite of his commands. In other words, don't presume upon his grace."

Gran got up to stir the pots again, then turn the burner knobs off. "Grab some plates, and we can eat."

Erwin set the table, then carried a plate for them both to the stove. He handed one to Gran and waited for her to dish up her meal. He made his own choices, then refilled both their tea glasses. As usual Gran held his hand and asked God to bless the food.

For the first time, he really understood that God was real, and Gran was asking him to really nourish their bodies for their continued health, and she was really thanking him that they had food to eat. It was an entirely new experience for him. He pondered it as they began to eat.

"Does God always have to answer those prayers?"

"I was taught that God's people don't have to beg for provision; provision comes with the Kingdom, but we need to be appreciative and thank him," Gran responded. "After all, we don't want to act like spoiled brats, entitled and ungrateful. He's a gracious and giving God, and that needs to be acknowledged."

Erwin understood that. Gran had harped on entitled kids and teens for years, and Erwin had known a lot of them at school. He certainly didn't want to act like that. *Like Billy*, he silently admitted. He contrasted Billy and his attitude with that of Gran, Dan, and Matt, and instantly saw the difference. It was a stark contrast between the Kingdom of Light and the Kingdom of Darkness. He knew he wanted to be a man like Homer, Dan, and Matt, and not like Billy and Wolf. How had he not seen the difference so plainly before?

He felt a new awareness that he could choose to be like one or the other. It was a true growth point in his thinking pattern; he usually just went along with whoever he was with that stepped up and made the choices. Somehow, he knew he was through with that.

He made a mental note to start watching the three men he so highly respected, so he would know how to become like them. One thing he already knew about them all, was that each made his own decisions without worrying about whether others agreed or not, but never in the selfish way that Billy demanded to get his own way.

Ina watched the expressions on his face, and knew it was time to back off and let the Holy Spirit do His work. Like all of humanity he had to choose for himself, and she wanted him to make a rational well thought out decision, not one based on fear or any other emotion. She'd laid out one side of the choice and he'd already seen and experienced the other side. But she could pray, and as they ate, she silently prayed more fervently than she ever had that he'd choose God and his ways, over the ways of the enemy.

She didn't want to lose him too, and losing him to the service of the Kingdom of Satan was worse that losing him to death. Only God could save this boy now, she knew. But she also knew He would if Erwin accepted his free will offer of salvation. And she knew Dan, Matt, Homer, and the others would safeguard him as he learned the rest of it.

God help him, it was going to be tough. She'd listened to her husband tell of the harrowing time he'd had healing and getting free from what he'd been through. She knew Erwin had a tough road ahead of him. She was sick that she'd not warned him ahead of time.

She wished Sherman was here to help him. She missed him more than ever, as she gazed lovingly on the only family member she had left. She'd wanted more children, but Sherman had been afraid that would increase the chances of one of them falling to the enemy.

They talked about lighter subjects as they ate, then cleaned the kitchen together. It was a long-established routine. It grew dark and Ina slid all the curtains shut. Erwin went to take a shower; and afterward, as he sat on the side of the bed putting his pajama pants and shirt on, his eyes rested on the bible Gran had given him as a child. It was still brand-new as he'd never done more than move it to dust the table.

He carried it to the living room and asked Gran to show him where to start reading. She suggested the Gospel of John, telling him it showed Jesus' divinity the best. Then she suggested 1 John. She told him she always read the proverb of the day also, showing him where Proverbs was found, pointing out there were pretty much one for each day of the month, telling him it was a book to obtain wisdom, and offering a couple of bookmarks to hold his place, as he went from one section to the other.

Before leaving him alone to read, she showed him Luke 10:17, 19, explaining our authority over the demonic realm. She told him it was Jesus' authority that was invoked, but we had been delegated the authority as well; as long, as we were in allegiance with Him; like an ambassador from a country speaking on the country's behalf. That's why the entity had left earlier. Erwin didn't have authority yet; the name of Jesus had made it leave, but he still needed to become a child of God to be truly effective in spiritual warfare.

Erwin understood the distinction, and was glad he'd thought to use Jesus' name earlier. He shivered at what may have happened if he hadn't remembered to do that. He was glad Gran had already taught him what to do, in spite of his stubborn refusal to go to church or read the bible. Even now, he could feel the malevolence that had radiated from the being, just thinking about it. He saw, once again in his mind, the shocked look on its face when he'd ordered it to leave in Jesus' name, and understood that Jesus was more powerful than the awful thing. It was comforting to know that.

He realized anew that there was a lot more going on in the world than what we see and experience on a daily basis. If nothing else, his friendship with Billy and the things Billy's grandmother had introduced them to, had taught him that. That was one huge wall he didn't have to climb over; he'd already seen it too many times. Now, it was time to learn about God's side, and he was ready for the first time to do that.

He prayed for God to help him learn, and opened the bible, finally willing to correct his ignorance on the subject. He started with Proverbs 1 and read through them all. He intended to do as Gran suggested and read one each day, but tonight, when the words began to speak about gaining wisdom and knowledge, he knew he needed that, and couldn't stop with just one. Besides, the month was almost over and he didn't want to miss anything by starting late.

Ina went to her room and spent the night in prayer for her grandson, texting Dan she wanted to speak to him first thing in the morning. If he was already seeing the shadow people, they had a limited time to rescue him. They'd seen this before. The ritual he'd participated in was a binding ritual; that meant they would need to cast out the entity, or entities, they'd bound to his soul.

It was encouraging that he was ready—and still able to read God's word—which meant he wasn't fully committed and they hadn't been able to sear his soul completely yet; but she wasn't sure he was ready to submit to having a demon cast out. Only God knew the timing, but she knew how to reach God.

Dan texted back that he'd call in the morning and start setting up the spiritual warfare team. It needed to be soon so it wouldn't have time to get its claws into him too deeply. God could still rescue him later of course, but he had to continue to be willing; and they had to keep him away from Billy and the coven.

...and Ina... I need you here. Please reconsider... It's time...

He was targeted, and if they even suspected he was contemplating salvation, they'd sacrifice him immediately. They were determined to not lose another generation of Sanders to the Holy One of Israel. *God, please protect my grandson*, was the last thought as she fell asleep just as daylight was seeping into the room.

Erwin wrote down things as he read the words penned so long ago. He felt like they'd been put there for him to read tonight.

Psalms 37:12

The wicked plottest against the just, and gnasheth upon him with his teeth.

Psalms 3:33

The curse of the LORD is in the house of the wicked:
but he blesseth the habitation of the just.

Proverbs 9:9

Give instruction to a wise man, and he will be yet wiser:
teach a just man, and he will increase in learning.

Proverbs 10:6

Blessings are upon the head of the just: but violence covereth the mouth of the wicked.

Go Big or Go Home

Chapter 25

"HONEY IS THE GRILL ready? They'll be here any minute."

Frankie walked in the back door, sliding the glass shut behind him. "It will be soon. Don't worry, Nate always likes to help and then we know the food is just like everyone likes it. I delayed a bit because they're always late."

Diane laughed. "Yep, that's Candy. I don't think we ever got anywhere on time as teenagers. My mom used to get so mad when Candy brought me home late, but she usually let me get by with it, because she said Candy's mom was the same way when they were our age. It still drives me crazy. She's a grown woman now."

They heard the tires hit the gravel at the same time and walked out together to greet their guests. Candy and Nate were getting out as they exited the house, and retrieved items from the backseat on their respective sides, shutting the doors at almost the same second. They began to walk to the patio where the grill was smoking.

"Here, let me help with that." Diane relieved Candy of one of the dishes she was balancing. Frankie opened the door and both women walked in, setting the food on the counter by the stove. Nate threw a pack of buns and then a bag of chips to Frankie who tossed them on the counter, then walked back out and slid the door shut from the outside. "Does anything need to go in the oven?" Diane asked.

"Just the baked beans. I know Frankie loves them and I knew it'd take a while for them to talk and grill. I used my mom's recipe and just assembled everything and decided to cook them here so they'd be good." It was one of the few things Candy cooked well.

"Where's Will?" Diane hadn't seen the car seat sticking up in the back.

"My mom's. My brother is there with his boys and Will wanted to stay and play. He's just going to stay the night, and I won't have to take him over in the morning, so I can sleep a while after work; and this way we can just relax without having to entertain him," she laughed; her tiredness from running after a toddler showing.

Diane grinned. "I love having him, but he certainly is high energy. I just hope when mine gets here I can keep up."

"You will. Nate says God sends them small and helpless, so you get used to them before they turn into energy driven wild beings, and you don't kill them before they're grown." She rolled her eyes as she explained and Diane cracked up. "Nate does have a way with words. But he may be on to something. If I had to take Will forever right now, it would be hard, but I watched you adjust as he grew and you make it look effortless."

"Oh, it takes effort. A lot of it somedays. About the time you're ready to pull your hair out, tho, he does the cutest thing and you just melt. But, honestly, thank God for my mother. It gives me a break to get things done and just relax, without having to watch him every single minute. Since he learned to climb, I can't let him out of my sight.

I love this UPS job. I go before he wakes up and I'm back by the time Nate is feeding him breakfast. It's only four hours, and short-term till after Christmas, but it will help with expenses for a few months."

"What do we need to do while they grill?" she was always willing to help.

"Nothing, except visit," Diane smiled. "I made potato salad like we always have at summer BBQs, even though summer is over; cut up the veggies for the burgers, and even made a chocolate cake. You brought baked beans and coleslaw. I have a couple of bags of chips too, to go with the ones you brought. This may be our last BBQ before winter and I just wanted to have fun. We spent the day shopping yesterday and I'm bushed. I've never been so exhausted in my life."

"Pregnancy will do that to you. I think it gets you used to resting in short spurts before the kiddo gets here. I brought some oatmeal cookies too; the ones with cranberries and nuts in them that Frankie and Nate both like. My mom made them.

I took a poll last time, and I think all of us voted them #1. They're great, because they both blend with the last BBQ and look forward to Thanksgiving." Candy sat too. She'd been running after Will and her nephews all afternoon and was almost as tired as Diane.

They sat in the easy chairs, flipping the footstools up, and visited while listening to the guys laugh outside. It wasn't long before Frankie came in for a clean platter to put the burgers and buns on, setting the one he'd carried them out on in the sink, to be washed. "We're almost ready. Do we need to cook anything else before we turn the grill off?"

"No. We're good. We'll be ready when you come in." The women climbed out of the chairs, took the beans out of the oven, set serving spoons in the dishes, got down the plates and utensils, set the table, and poured tea. They were looking forward to a night of adult conversation and visiting. It had been a while. They hadn't seen each other as much since the world went into crisis mode, and were excited about the evening.

The burgers smelled wonderful as the men carried them in. They walked buffet style around the counter, filling plates, and arguing over the best type of chips and dip. The buns were slightly crisp, just the way Diane liked them, with one left almost cold for Candy. She liked them soft. Frankie took several flavors of dip out of the fridge, setting them on the table in front of the one who liked them the most. They'd swap around, but had been friends long enough to know who started with what.

Frankie blessed the food, then instructed them to 'dig in, while it's hot' and immediately followed his own advice. There was little talk for the first ten minutes while they started shoveling the food in, but gradually they began to visit again.

"Frankie said you bought out Waco yesterday." Nate teased Diane. "Nesting a bit early, aren't you?"

Diane looked at her husband and laughed. "Yeah. I know it sounds a bit crazy but I just feel it's a good idea to go ahead and have some things on hand. These last two years have taught me things might not always be available."

Nate looked at Candy, a question in his eyes. She nodded approval, and he looked at Diane, then Frankie. "Well, I wanted to talk to you about something similar. But for now, I'd like it to stay between the four of us."

"Oh?" Frankie looked interested. Nate always came up with good ideas, and Frankie loved secrets.

"Like you, I've been listening to the programs you've been sending. I agree that this is far from over, and I've been getting more and more concerned about the food supply. I've done some research and learned that even before all this started food preservation has been a concern for a lot of people in the know. Were you aware that almost 40% of food is lost in the field?"

Frankie looked surprised. "No. I had no idea. Have you ever heard that?" he asked Diane.

"No. That seems like a lot." She was wondering where this was going.

Candy jumped in, "and even the fresh food in the grocery store has almost as high a percentage of spoilage. And that's in America. In third world countries it can be as high as 68% in the fields and very high in the stores. The laws in most countries won't let them donate the food to shelters or homes before it goes bad, and they can't even give it to the homeless."

"What do they do with it all?" Diane was bothered by the idea of letting food spoil rather than giving it to hungry people. Her dad farmed, among other things, and she hated food to waste.

"They just throw it out." Candy's disgust showed in her tone.

"Why do they lose it in the fields?" Frankie asked Nate.

"Several reasons," Nate warmed up to the topic. "Sometimes its low prices vs cost of labor, packing, and shipping; sometimes the market is oversaturated and the vendors won't buy any more; sometimes they simply don't have enough time or labor to get the food to market before it ruins—especially in third-world countries—but one of the craziest is imperfect fruit."

"I don't understand," Diane wasn't sure what he meant.

"In simple people's language, it's too ugly to sell," he explained.

"How can it be too ugly to sell?" She still looked perplexed.

"Ok, think about it. You're in the grocery store. You're picking out apples or peaches. Do you choose the pretty ones, or the ones that look weird?" he pressed.

"I've never really thought about it," she answered. "I just pick those that look good."

"Exactly," he smiled, "but what you don't realize is most of them look good, because they won't even buy the ugly ones to display."

"Really?" Frankie asked.

"What about your calves?" Nate turned to him. "When you take them to sell, do you get top dollar for the weaker, less perfect ones?"

Now a lightbulb went off for both Frankie and Diane. "No," Frankie laughed ruefully. "I don't even take those. I just cull them while they're young, or we have them slaughtered for our own use if there's nothing wrong with them, but I know it's not worth hauling them to the auction."

"But what determines that?"

"Because I know they won't sell. I've been there before."

"What if I could show you a way to sell those cows, and all the rest and always get top dollar for them?" Nate looked serious, "and have up to 20 years to sell them?"

"No way," Frankie looked surprised. "You've lost it man. In 20 years, they'd be dead."

Nate grinned, "I'm not talking about the cow, Frankie; I'm talking about the beef, in meat form."

"No beef lasts 20 years, not even frozen," Frankie looked amused at Nate's ignorance.

"But freeze-dried it will… and not lose any quality or nutrition," Nate shot back, and then went on, "the average beef cow is sold at what 1200 pounds?"

"That's how some people sell them," Frankie agreed.

"And only about 68% of that is actually turned into sellable meat, right?

"I'd say around 750 pounds, for a 1200-pound steer, on average."

"Ok, I did my homework, and the average price to sell those 750 pounds of meat, after processing, is about $6.11 per pound. So, 750 pounds x $6.11 = $4,582.50; sound about, right?

"If we're averaging just to get a ballpark price."

"What if I could show you how to get $30 a pound, with the price never dropping, but most probably rising in the coming years, and again, you have 20 years to sell it?"

BOOK 1: "PREPARE FOR THE END" SERIES

"Frankie was really intrigued now, "What do you know?""

I ran onto something that has greatly interested me. I want to start a business, and to help preserve the world's food supply, especially with what we've learned about it being deliberately destroyed.

I found a website called www.fmgi.global. It's Farm To Market Global Initiative. He pulled a folded piece of paper out of his pocket and handed it to Frankie. Here's the ad:

> **FMGI has engineered a complete Food Processing Module,**
> **that is unique to the Food Production industry.**
> **This patented technology provides solutions to ultimately**
> **end food waste as we know it across the globe.**
>
> **Imagine if you could instantly create 5 new jobs,**
> **process food in the field, or nearby, retain the bulk of your**
> **crop, wipe out much of your current food waste from**
> **imperfect fruit, or high cost to market vs low market prices,**
> **sell the product for as much or more than you can fresh,**
> **and have up to 20 years to sell it?**
> **What would that be worth to you?**
>
> **What if the technology could be paid for**
> **in the first year or two?**
> **We are contacting farmers, ranchers,**
> **and grocery stores across the nation.**

"This sounds interesting," Frankie was really interested. "How do we find out more about this technology?"

"You got your laptop handy?" Nate couldn't wait to show Frankie the website.

"Yeah; Diane can you bring me the laptop from my office?" he looked at her.

"Sure, just a minute." She left the room and came back carrying the computer. She handed it to him and he powered it up. "Did you say www.fmgi.global?"

"Yes. Good; now scroll all the way to the bottom. There's a 2-minute video."

Thy all four watched the video. It was a tour of a working module that showed it from the time you enter, donning the gloves, mask, and white jacket, all through the processing of the food, and then the finished product being packaged and taken out the back door to be stored until delivery.

The video showed how the module could be moved anywhere in the world, by truck, plane, boat, or even moved from field to field by helicopter; processing the food immediately and then moving on to the next location, eliminating close to 100% of crop loss if done on time.

Grocery stores could set it right in the parking lot, take out the excess fresh food before it spoiled, process it, and take it right back in, and sell it for a much higher price in the long-term, or gourmet food section, eliminating much of the loss. There were three different size modules, and the largest one could service a small country.

"Let's watch it again," Diane said. "Let me grab some paper." She went to get a spiral bound notebook and a pen. "I want to take notes."

They watched it again, and then Frankie asked Nate how he found the website. "I got a call from the U.S. Marketing director asking me to go to the website and watch the video. She said I could stop losing so much of my peaches. I watched it, and was very excited. I had no idea peaches could sell for so much a pound freeze-dried. The price right now is $29.95. And you don't have to worry about the ugly fruit because you slice or dice it. You can even make powders from the bits."

"Yeah, but you only have peaches in the summer. What about the rest of the year?" Diane's marketing brain was already jotting down questions.

"Ok. Here's some numbers. An average chicken breast is around 16 ounces. They cost $3 on average. One machine—depending on the size of the module, they can hold several—can do 200 chicken breasts a day. That's about $600 per machine to buy the chicken. It shrinks it down to about 5 ounces as the moisture is pulled out, and that 5-ounce package can be sold for $29.95 freeze-dried. It can last for up to 20 years; some say longer. It weighs almost nothing so can be shipped anywhere very inexpensively. That $600 of chicken can now be sold for $5,990. The module costs about $22 per day for electricity.

If you do a load each day for a year that's $2,186,350. Cost of the chicken is $219,000. Cost of electricity is $8,030. That leaves a profit of $1,959,320. The smallest module costs around $300,000. It can be paid for in less than a year.

Beef can be sold for $30 per pound. If you process 30 thousand pounds a year for 2 years, that's $900,000. The largest module only costs $600,000. It's USDA and FDA approved, so you can sell the food anywhere.

You have a cattle ranch. I have peaches and berries. There are farms all over Texas and other nearby states as well. I've been thinking we can join up and have a great new business without taking away from what we already have."

"But I don't slaughter my own cattle," Frankie protested.

"No. But remember, Danny bought that fancy trailer last year to do just that. He goes straight to the ranches and slaughters them and processes them on the spot. What if we get him to join too? We can start with a small module, then work up to the largest. There are crops that come off at all times of the year. And it even has machines that work in place of the freeze dryers to make certified essential oils. Remember those Lavender farms that went in last year in the next county?"

Candy joined back in. "We know all the farmers and ranchers around here. We can buy full crops, or just the ugly fruit. I can start making calls and feel them out. Most of them all lose as much fruit as we do. We talk about how to lessen the loss at all the co-op meetings. I think we could buy all we could process and help both us and our neighbors. And if they'd rather purchase their own module, we can put them in touch with the marketing director."

"I bet we could do potpourri too." Diane's brain was whirling with numbers and information. She was spitting out results and writing as fast as she thought. "Remember professor Johnson planted a Christmas Tree farm a couple of years ago. He probably has tons of limbs from where he trims them into the correct shape."

She went on, "There's turkey farms, fresh fish farms, ducks, and all kinds of vegetable farms around us. There's even a buffalo ranch close to my parents. And what about Dan Blanchard out at the Rockin' O Ranch? Didn't they start an exotic animal hunt a few years back? We could possibly buy any extra stock he breeds.

We'd never run out of food to process. And if we could take the unsellable fruit and vegetables, we could negotiate for lower cost, because right now it's waste; and pay top dollar for the best stuff. The farmers wouldn't need government subsidizing, so they wouldn't have to plow up the food or not plant to get the checks. We could greatly reduce the food loss just in this area of Texas. And thwart those who want to starve humanity.

She was excited by what she was seeing.

"But how would we sell it?" Frankie was bit slower in things that weren't tangible than Diane was.

"Did you forget I'm a marketing major?" She laughed at the look on his face, as she spoke.

"We can start with the local grocers. Candy and I could map out routes and go see specialty markets, grocers, etc. We can create a brand and make it distinctive. I can create a website, or several, that look as if they compete, and we can sell worldwide. Nate is right, shipping will be nominal."

"I've already researched the times of the year when rotating crops usually start selling," Candy was smiling. "I've got almost a whole year already filled in with various foods. Anytime we get low we can order cases of chicken breasts from the local grocers. Also, don't forget, my uncle grows for the chicken plant, so he can get the large cases from the company store anytime. I've already spoken to him and he can get whatever we need. We just need to call a day or two ahead. We'll never run out of something to process."

"What about workers to do all the work?" Frankie asked.

"We won't need any." Nate said. "Our farm is next door to your ranch. It only takes 4-5 people. We can put the module on my side, on the acre next to your fence, and if you're willing, we can build a warehouse on your side by fencing off another acre, to store the food until we sell it.

Fed Ex comes by here every day. They can pick up the boxes to ship right at the warehouse. You cut the food up, and load the machines. The first round it freezes the food to a temperature lower than space. It takes a few hours—with the length determined by the water content of the food—then you go move it to another machine that has a vacuum strong enough to pull out the ice crystals.

It pulls out about 91% of the moisture without any damage to the food. When you rehydrate it, it has lost very little, with zero nutrient loss, and uses no heat, so no cooking. You use it like you would anyway. We're all home most days. We can load it, move it over, then bag and tag it ourselves. We'll have the rest of the time to do what we normally do. If the business gets big enough, we'll hire family and friends. Our parents and siblings would help. I see a great business, and we can all raise our kids without having to work an outside job."

Frankie was finally beginning to visualize it. "And if the other ranchers are interested in selling us their beef, we can get Danny to go process their cattle and bring it here, or we can build another building for him a permanent set-up, and they can haul them to us. That'll keep him and us in business." He suddenly grinned broadly. "I like it."

"Most of the people we've been listening to since this covid crap started has been talking about massive starvation and deliberate destruction of the food chain. Maybe God told this Chance guy that started FMGI how to build these modules so we can be part of helping to feed the world. Do you still have the marketing director's name and number?"

Nate grinned. "I sure do. And, they're not too far from us. I've already spoke to Chance and I set us all up a tour of a working module for tomorrow. Who wants to go?"

"Have you talked to Danny yet?" Frankie was on board now.

"I wanted to speak to you first. Do you want me to call him now, or wait till we've seen the working module?"

"Call him. Tell him to come over and we'll see what kind of capital we can raise between the three of us without a bank loan."

www.fmgi.global is real.
Go there now.
Scroll down and watch the video.
Contact Chance for more info or to set up a tour.
Tell him Rina sent you.
Help us push back against the enemy and feed the world!

Diane had multiple pages of lists by now. "I like that you already have a handle on when food is harvested. Now we need to create a newsletter, websites, and a sales route. We can put the food in and give them a percentage as it sells, or just outright sell it for a lessor price to them and let them add their markup. We can create several ways and let each vendor choose. I can get it all started now while you're working extra hours."

Candy added, "And I can take over when you are ready to give birth. We can sign up for trade shows and conferences also. The two of us can run a booth if the guys can't go. Our mom's will watch the babies on those days."

"What about all the festivals around? Every Texas town has one or more a year." Frankie was thinking about the places he'd seen people sell their products.

Nate walked back in. He'd went out to get his phone and call Danny. "He said he'd be right over; He's not too far; he just finished a job about ten minutes away."

"I've been afraid I'll have to go back to work after the baby was born if the cattle business got any worse." Diane admitted. I really don't want to leave my baby with anyone else, especially now."

"Me either," Candy agreed. "My mom could come over and watch them both when we load the machines or do marketing and sales. She used to run a daycare; and two kids, or more down the road, won't bother her at all. And later, when they're bigger, we can hire her to help load the machines, or make deliveries to the vendors we acquire."

Diane grinned; she loved Candy's mom almost as much as her own, and their moms had been friends since grade school. "Our moms can take turns watching the babies while we load and unload the machines, and package the food. Our dads can drive them over and be the fifth crew member. They'll love it!"

"Our dads could do deliveries as well. God knows they need something to do after they retire. This lockdown almost did my dad in."

"Mine too," Diane laughed. He stays busy with other things, and has that online store now, but he will love this idea. It fits right in with his prepper friends. In fact, he will probably be able to get us tons of business just from his contacts."

Danny arrived then, and after greeting him and giving him space to make a plate, they shared the business proposition with him. He watched the video, but wasn't quite as enthused as the rest of them. "I see the value of the module and what they can do for food producers, but I just sunk a large chunk of change into the slaughter and packaging set-up. I'd love to help, but for now I may just want to hire out to you when you need meat from hoof to ready-to-process. That way I can keep up with my own business and the clientele I've built."

"We can do that," Nate nodded, "if that works best for you. That way we can see how well it goes. But know, that if the market is going down, people may slaughter their own beef and not restock for a time. That's what's happened in the past. But if they know they can sell it, they may keep a herd. We can be their first customer, as long as the meat is grass fed and doesn't have a lot of hormones or heavy metals. You're welcome to buy in and set up a larger facility here with us at any time."

Danny had that 'hourglass' look on his face, and he was clearly thinking it over. "Alright. I appreciate that. Do you still want me to go with you for the tour? I don't have anything scheduled for tomorrow."

"Absolutely. That way you can start considering if coming in now is worth it, or waiting and knowing you'll have a big client out here until you're ready. We can test run it, while you drag your feet," he teased him. They'd all gone to high school together and known each other for years and were used to good natured joshing.

"Actually, it would take a worry off, knowing I'll have enough business." Danny still had the hourglass look. "When I took out my loan, I wasn't too worried, then this stupid pandemic hit, and I almost went under before I got started. I'd like the solid business, and if there's as much as you expect, it would save a ton of money to build a facility. You know I always say 'go big, or go home.' I can always use the trailer for the farmers that want to keep their meat, or want me to do it onsite, and use the larger facility for those who don't care; but consider this: If we do it at their ranch, they can deal with the parts we can't use.

But, if we do it here, we can sell the other parts to other companies. The bones can be made into bone powder, the blood is stored in tanks and taken to waste management places to be made into compost; the same with the other parts. We can sell the hides for leather production. I sell mine now to a place that makes hats and boots. Little is really wasted, if you're smart. I can get you my contacts and recommend you," he offered.

"That's fantastic," Nate grinned, "honestly, I hadn't thought that far ahead. Maybe I need to look into what to do about other unusable parts, like all the peach pits. I've never had to worry about that before."

Frankie was really seeing the picture now. "I was just thinking about that. So far, I've taken the few I've slaughtered to the slaughter house, and the ones I have to outright cull, I just dig a hole and bury it on the ranch. It self-composts that way. But if we go into production, that's a lot of waste. Danny I've glad you're onboard. You've already solved some problems we didn't even know we had."

"Everybody has some specialized knowledge from their profession," he laughed. "But, the more I think about it, the more I like it. I need to go home now, but I'll go on the tour. What time are we leaving?"

"Candy gets home around 6, and she'll need to sleep a couple of hours and then get ready. Can you be here by 9?"

"That works good for me. I need to do my paperwork from last week first thing. I worked all weekend and got behind. See you then."

The guys walked him out and watched him turn the trailer around and go down the driveway. "My dad would say this is a divine idea," Nate looked satisfied.

"Diane's dad and mine would too," Frankie agreed. He didn't know it yet, but he'd ponder on that thought a lot in the coming months. "It really feels like something handed to us. I would never have thought of the marketing ideas Diane's coming up with, or the delivery route. If the women can handle that, we can help contact the farmers and ranchers and haul in the food. I'm really excited you've already set up a tour. I just hope we can work together." He shot Nate a deep measuring look.

All through school the three of them had been the best of buddies, but fought like cats and dogs often. Even on the football field, they'd sometimes come to blows because of the different ways they made decisions.

"We're grown now," Nate looked serious. "We know how to problem solve and talk things out. If the stuff my dad told me the bible says is coming, and if the people we've been listening to are correct, we're going to need each other just to survive. We can do it. Our lives and our families' lives will depend upon it. We're both fathers now, and that takes precedent over ego and pride." He held his hand out to Frankie, "I'll make my commitment to the business, the friendship, to you, and the preservation of our families and others families now. Do you?"

Frankie looked at the out-stretched hand, then grasped it with his own. "I Do. Now, we seem to have gotten married, and you know how I feel about divorce, so you better be in it for long haul, Nate." He cracked up at the look on Nate's face, grinning a huge grin, as he did.

"Smart ass," Nate shot back. "At least you still have your sense of humor."

Subduing the Pack

Chapter 26

"ARE YOU READY?" Wolf stepped out from between the vehicles in the parking lot of the hospital. "We need to go now."

"Why didn't you call me last night? Or better yet, bring him to the clinic at my warehouse?" The older man in scrubs looked around to see if anyone was near enough to overhear. Seeing no one, he walked between the rows toward Wolf's truck. "Let's go get the van. Neither of our personal vehicles need to be seen at his house."

"Get your truck. We'll go different routes to the warehouse, and I'll need to leave before you will. We can go get him together and bring him back there. Do you have the supplies?"

"I have what I need in the van. A head's up would have helped. I thought this was set for next week."

"Yeah; it was supposed to be, but it got bumped up. Something else is being accelerated, and this had to be done first to build fear and loyalty. He's in pretty bad shape. I'm not sure if we can save him without a hospital."

"You know we can't take him to the hospital if there is any chance of him talking."

"Evaluate him. If it's a no-go, we can just let him bleed out and get rid of the body. I'm not taking a chance. I think he's all in, but I can't risk it. And if he dies, we may lose some of the others as well. Getting rid of 3-4 at once is more than we can do right now without a very good plan."

Wolf knew he'd have to make sure Randy truly understood the need for secrecy or he had to eliminate the threat entirely. He wasn't going to be the one who brought down the families who'd stayed hidden for generations. And they'd chosen him for a reason. He had an interesting bloodline too.

"Maybe he's not that bad. Let's go see. A lot of blood sometimes looks worse than it is. Heads and rectums sometimes bleed a lot. I'll swing by and pick up the van. I'll pick you up at the warehouse and we can go get him; I may not be able to get him in the van by myself. And wolf, I can always put 'Covid' on the death certificate. They're not even embalming the bodies right now, or letting people have funerals; and you know I get to choose where we send him. My wife's brother owns the funeral home we usually use, and he's one of us. He can have a 'mix-up' and cremate the body before contacting his parents."

"Ok. But don't be late. This timing change makes it sloppy and we don't have the luxury for sloppy." Wolf looked fierce as his brain calculated his next move if Randy didn't make it. He was always thinking ahead and usually had multiple avenues well planned in case of problems. Failure was not an option in the coven. If they even thought he had exposed them by carelessness, he would be instantly eliminated.

His heritage bought him position, and a lot of leeway, but any potential exposure meant centuries of work lost; and people in powerful positions were never willing to give up the money, prestige, territory, and freedom. And wolf knew very well that if the people didn't take him down, the Serpent King would. The master had worked too long in this area to lose it now.

Thirty minutes later they pulled into the back lot of the old convenience store that had shut down several years ago. It was dark there with no traffic cameras and the van was a deep bronze color that couldn't be seen unless light shined directly on it. They were diagonal to Randy's house with only one other house between them. The lights were on in the front of the house, but the back was dark.

They quietly walked the few yards to Randy's backdoor. Wolf knocked, waited a minute, knocked again, then stuck a knife into the crack by the lock and expertly eased the lock open. He couldn't believe Randy didn't have a dead-bolt, but was glad he didn't have to damage the door to gain entrance.

They'd entered an enclosed porch that led directly to the kitchen. He waited a few seconds before quietly slipping the knife in again, opening the second door, listening for any sound, and began to make his way across the kitchen. He slipped a few steps in and caught himself just in time. The Doctor grabbed his arm, steadying him, and nodded toward the floor. Soft light was coming through the doorway from the living room, and he could see blood on the kitchen floor. He'd stepped directly into a spot about three inches across.

He reached over and took a roll of paper towels off the counter, wiped the floor, then his shoe. His mind instantly added blood clean-up and burning his sneakers to the list of necessary tasks, if Randy didn't make it. A forensic team would find any trace of blood or bleach. They'd been down this road before. He'd have to call his man inside the department if it came to that, if the doctor didn't have the industrial strength cleaning product in the van. He carefully set the towel down into the sink blood side up, planning on putting it in a trash bag and taking it with him when he left.

They silently made their way across the rest of the kitchen, then stopped, one on each side of the doorway. Wolf peered around the frame, taking in the empty room, then gestured to the doctor to follow him. He once more had the knife in his hand.

They could hear a low moaning as they neared the hallway. They softly walked down the linoleum passage to the first door on the right. A small lamp was on and they could see Randy lying naked on the bed. There was blood on the floor leading to the bed and the sheets were heavily stained. Randy was passed out, but clearly in pain. Wolf walked to the bathroom that was attached to the room, pulling on gloves as he moved to the cabinet. He found some towels, and laid a couple over the floor to keep them from stepping in the blood. Then handed one to the doctor to use on Randy.

"Find a wash cloth and wet it," he was instructed.

He quickly brought it back and helped the doctor roll Randy to a better position for his examination. They cleaned him up so they could see if the blood was all old, or how much was still being lost. Randy moaned as the doctor inserted a gloved finger to check for the extent of the damage.

The experienced physician quickly found the problem, a jagged laceration just inside the rectum that was trying to close itself, but was just large enough that the fresh bleeding kept it from sealing off. He knew he'd have to stitch it up, but not here. Randy would make it if there was no further damage. He cleaned him up, placed a thick pad of gauze on the area, then taped it on all sides.

"Find some underwear and a pair of shorts or sweatpants. He'll need a t-shirt and socks too. Go ahead and grab another outfit or two. If he has a suitcase, pack it like he was going somewhere for the weekend. We'll get him to the van, and come back here and clean up. I have solvent for the blood in the van. There's not any on the carpet, so it's the kitchen, bathroom, and the bed. Later, we can bring back a new mattress and remake the bed. If he can't go to work Monday and anyone checks, it will look like he left town.

Can you find his keys? You'll have to take his truck to the warehouse so we can see if there's blood in it." He was drawing a dose of pain medication into a syringe as he instructed Wolf. He quickly administered the shot, then wrapped up everything he'd opened, placing it into a plastic bag he'd brought with him. He wrapped it all into a second bag, and then a third, so no DNA would be in his duffle bags. "Let's give that a few minutes to take effect. It'll be easier to carry him if he's totally out, and he won't make any noise."

"Ok. I'll go ahead and clean the bathroom and the kitchen. It's linoleum. We can do the bed when we come back." He went to the bathroom, locating a spray bottle of bleach tub cleaner, and after wiping down the toilet and floor with another washcloth, he sprayed the sink, tub, and toilet, cleaning them all, then the small floor. He placed the clothes Randy had worn to the party into another trash bag, along with all the towels and wash cloths that had been used earlier by Randy and the ones used by them, then sealed it inside a second one.

He left the bathroom looking like Randy had cleaned it before leaving. He then went to the kitchen and repeated the procedure, including gathering up dishes from the living room and the dining table and loading the dishwasher. He poured vinegar into the bottom of the machine before adding a Cascade cube from the container under the sink, then hit the start button.

He thoroughly checked every inch of the kitchen, putting anything that had blood on it into the bag, adding his gloves at the last minute, then pulled on a second pair. He opened the door, wiped the knob from earlier, than retraced his steps to the bedroom. The doctor had removed the sheets underneath Randy and had them bagged up as well. Randy had put a mattress protector on the bed when he bought it, so no blood had gone to the mattress itself, which would save them a step. They just bring another one, and it would be a simple fix. "We'll take that when we get back. I have some more bags in the van."

They dressed Randy in the soft clothing, then Wolf picked him up, threw him over his shoulder, and told the doctor to put on new gloves. They left the lights on except for the kitchen. They needed it dark so no one would see them carrying Randy out. They wordlessly went back to the van, strapped him to the stretcher in the back, and then just as silently made their way back to the house.

They first cleaned the entire floor in the hallway and the bedroom a second time with heavy duty cleaner. The industrial cleaner was what professionals used when hired to clean up crime scenes. The family had people in all professions and they could get what they needed for anything. They rolled the mattress pad into another fresh trash bag, then found another set of sheets and blankets in a linen closet and remade the bed. They went back through the house, carefully checking every surface, including the other bedroom.

This wasn't their first rodeo and they knew exactly what to look for and what to do. Wolf even checked the ground between Randy's truck and the backdoor, his ability to see in the dark like an animal and his enhanced olfactory senses showed him the most minute traces of blood, which he scooped up with a spoon including a layer of untouched dirt, placing them all in the bag, then scuffing the ground as if it had been heavily walked on.

He grabbed a sheet of plastic he'd brought from the van, quietly opened the door of Randy's truck, put his finger over the plastic piece that signaled the light to come on when the door was opened, placed a piece of tape over it, then wrapped the seat, wiped down the steering wheel, door handle, inside the door, and the outside door handle.

Finally satisfied they'd covered everything, the doctor slipped back to the van, while Wolf grabbed a large broom he'd taken from the warehouse, and swept the dirt from the house to the road, and all around the truck, and one more last swipe on the ground beside the door after getting in, then left openly in Randy's vehicle.

Randy was single and came in and out frequently at odd hours and no one seeing the truck leave at eleven at night would think anything about it. In the dark you couldn't tell it wasn't him. He was glad it was supposed to rain tonight. That would wipe out any residual prints. They made their way back to the warehouse, using separate routes, both crisscrossing town several times before ending up there.

They pulled both vehicles inside a separate bay from where Wolf's truck was parked, and carried Randy to the small exam room the doctor had been using for years. His efficient movements had everything he needed laid out in minutes, then with Wolf assisting he examined Randy more thoroughly, finding a second laceration higher up.

He hung an IV line, and stitched them both within a short time. He gave Randy another pain injection and then a high-class antibiotic through the line, hung a bag of blood because of the amount Randy had lost over the last twenty-four hours, then washed his hands.

Wolf left to put all the trash bags in the incinerator that was auto-timed to 4:00 am. All evidence would be gone before the city awakened. Now, it was just wait to see how Randy recovered, and if he would need silencing. He'd been groomed for a while, and slowly brought deeper into the group and its activities, but last night had been rough.

He'd need to coach Billy on how to allow the demon to have his fun, while keeping the damage to a minimum. It was a skill they'd all had to learn as they progressed in service to the Master, but he knew Billy had enjoyed the unlimited power and violence as much as the demon had. For what was upcoming, he'd had to allow it, because he'd need that bloodlust to get past his sentiment toward Erwin.

Sometimes they lost people when they first encountered a demon; sometimes the knowledge of the power they could summon created enough fear, and/or desire to have that power for themselves, creating a loyal follower that could be brought further into the group. This was how they'd survived for generations.

BOOK 1: "PREPARE FOR THE END" SERIES

They needed the bloodlines to stay intact, but not become inbred, and they couldn't survive in this modern world in small numbers, so they added outsiders in each generation as well. The true bloodlines were carefully controlled, of course, but the entire clan needed people in all walks of life to stay hidden.

People would be shocked if they knew how many around them served the true god of this world—Lucifer himself. Wolf felt the desire to throw back his head and howl his allegiance, but restrained himself. There was plenty of time to do that when he was safely home in his remote location. For now, he silently bowed his heart to the one he believed would prevail in this age-old contest of gods.

He walked back inside. The doctor would stay with Randy, but Wolf would go home. Although he made sure his routine wasn't set in stone, he still needed to keep a semblance of normality for plausible deniability. He was usually home before 2 on the weekends and anyone seeing his truck go by would see nothing out of the ordinary. The doctor's wife was used to him being called back to the hospital, and he'd called her from the van to tell her he had a patient in critical condition, and she would see nothing unusual in his all-nighter.

He could now work on the original issue that had caused the hiccup in his plans—Erwin. It was complex. They had revenge to enact on a long-hated family line; Erwin's increasing reluctance to participate in higher rituals; and his need to bind Billy by allowing him the opportunity to make the sacrifice that would seal his loyalty to Lucifer. The upcoming ceremony would take care of all elements. It had to be flawless.

He believed Billy would do the deed, but he was very aware that Billy needed a lackey to applaud him constantly, and someone to arrogantly boss around to appease his ego; and Erwin had filled that role for two decades. He'd be hard to replace at Billy's age, and Billy's personality was such that without someone to fill Erwin's role, he may come unraveled and his addictions would take over.

Billy had never been as focused as his grandmother. The constant rituals and requirements, coupled with his heritage, had led to an enormous sense of entitlement and superiority, and seared his conscious; eliminating any true emotion except rage, and had created a true psychopath. This was handy when they needed his loyalty and brutality, but also made him unpredictable and dangerous, as he put his own needs and desires above the safety of the coven on occasion.

They'd been concerned for some time, but you didn't create a Billy overnight, and they hoped he'd become more stable as he aged. He was a direct descendant from the druidic/templar line, and had power even he didn't yet realize. Maybe they just needed to tweak his programming, so another personality could take over more of the time. They knew exactly how to bind the main personality, with enough pain to keep it hidden until they needed the real Billy. He'd been disassociating since he was a toddler, he'd know no difference now.

Until he fathered children, he was the only one left in that line of descent and they needed that power as much as his own family. Also, he'd be required to sacrifice his first-born, and some children didn't make it through the training, so they'd need additional children for the bloodline to be secure. Therefore, they'd coddled him for a while, but it was time to rein him in a bit. The coven had been tasked by Lucifer to help bring his worship into open society at this time, and a raging psychopathic maniac attached to them would prevent the public from openly accepting what was slated to occur.

Wolf had been tasked to mentor Billy, entice new recruits, bring the old ways into open knowledge and acceptability, and eliminate the heirs to the enemy's old-line families so they could no longer intervene. He'd accepted his calling. His people had served the true Master for too long for him to even question whether he would as well.

In addition, the Goddess had entrusted him to bring certain chosen girls to her earlier, so she could elevate them to a goddess faster. He knew it was an honor, and he always listened when she showed him who she'd chosen, not wanting anyone to miss out on the sacred gift.

He too would be required to slay his first born for the Master. He eagerly looked forward to showing the entire coven, and Lucifer himself, that he was a throwback to the long-ago Aztec Emperors, and a true son from the bloodline of the god. He had the mark on his chest to prove it. Few knew it was there, as he covered it with temporary tattoos during rituals. His parents had instructed him to guard that secret with his life. There were those who were jealous of the few who had blood that some would call 'Nephilim' and he had a job to fulfill.

It was time to accelerate his plans. He went over them in his mind as he drove home. His smile of satisfaction was more of a psychopathic smirk, but his own ego would never believe that he was as much in that category as Billy; his just presented more as self-righteous duty, that was even more dangerous to society, because he truly believed he was called to a higher path, as a child of the Serpent blood-line.

He felt like he was leading humanity to a complete paradigm shift that allowed the demi-god Jehovah to be dethroned, and replaced by the one Jehovah had led humanity to believe was evil: Lucifer, the Shining One; who had given mankind the gift of Knowledge, showing them, they were as much a god as the usurper and his hated son, Jesus. He felt vomit rise in the back of his throat at even thinking the hated name.

He would begin his new campaign soon at the Grand Opening of a new jewelry store where his brand would be carried.

But first…Erwin…

I'm Going to Be a What?

Chapter 27

BILLY WAS TICKED. It was only two hours now until the poker game was due to start. He'd fooled around all afternoon, fuming about having to do his own shopping, and still hadn't gone to the store. He hated mundane things like grocery shopping. He'd always had Erwin do it. Just thinking about the call earlier in the day made him mad all over again.

How dare Erwin talk to me like that? I swear, I can feel steam coming out of my ears. He kicked the wall in his anger, punching a hole in the sheetrock and bending his big toenail back when it caught on the side of the stud as his foot went through.

"Ahhhh…" he yelled in anger that was now coupled with pain. He jumped around on one foot, cussing and screaming, finally reaching the kitchen chair, and collapsing into it. He grabbed his foot, yanking the sock off, and saw blood on his toes.

If it were possible, he became even more enraged than he was to begin with. *That spineless little prick is going to pay for this! Since when does he get off telling me, no? This is all his fault!* He gingerly touched his foot, getting sick to his stomach when he saw his toenail ripped back three-fourths of the way to the base. It was standing at a slight angle, and without the sock to soak up the blood, it was running down his foot and dripping onto the floor. The pain was enough to make him feel woozy. As much as he enjoyed inflicting pain on others, he was a wimp when it was his own.

He hopped to the bathroom, screaming each time his foot came down on the floor. The thud made his injured foot— dangling in the air—jerk; and each sudden movement brought a throbbing pain, while each beat of his heart caused more blood to drip. As his foot swung with each forward step, it flung drops of blood to the floor ahead of him. He slipped on a spot once,

300

almost losing his balance. He caught the wall and slowed down a little, but continued to his destination.

He grabbed a wash cloth, wet it from the faucet, then grabbed a box of band-aids from the medicine cabinet, before lowering himself to the toilet. He closed his eyes for moment and breathed deeply trying to get a handle on the pain. He couldn't believe a toe could hurt this much. Finally opening his eyes, he began to clean the blood off, quickly realizing a band-aid wouldn't be enough.

He stood and grabbed a box of gauze from the cabinet, then sat and washed the blood off again. He folded two pieces of gauze into a rectangle, then wrapped it around his toe, screaming and cursing as it moved the nail. He tried to unwrap it, but the nail caught on the loose weave of the bandage, and he felt it rip a little farther. He immediately wrapped it back around the toe, looser than the first time, and held it while he went thru the breathing ritual with his eyes closed again.

When he could stand it, he put three band-aids at different angles around it to hold the gauze in place. He could see blood beginning to pool toward the end of his toe peeking out from the gauze, and put another piece of gauze over the end of his toe, then another band aid around it; then one over it from top to bottom.

He hobbled back to the kitchen, noting the trail of blood he'd left. He'd clean it later, right now he needed a beer. He glanced at the clock, and his anger was fueled again. No way he'd have time to go to the store; and he couldn't walk if he did have time. Erwin had screwed his entire schedule up. *Now what am I going to do?* He considered texting the guys and canceling the whole thing, but he hated to be alone on a Saturday night.

His phone buzzed, spinning around on the counter and he caught it right before it spun off the edge. He glanced at the illuminated screen, wincing when he saw the number. It was a girl he'd met in a bar a few months back and had a brief affair with. He'd gotten it out of his system, and thought she had too, but a couple of weeks ago she'd started blowing up his phone.

It'd been fun while it lasted, but he was on to the next conquest and only looked back when he had an itch and no one current to scratch it; so, he'd ignored all her attempts to communicate with him. In his line of work, he met plenty of girls. When he was in a new area he went to different places of business daily, meeting far more women that if he'd just found a place he liked, and kept going there. It made him unpredictable too and easier to slip in and out of a place, if he needed to obscure his whereabouts.

Throwing out a line to see who might respond was all in a day's play for him, and he'd left confused women all over several states. He seldom told them it was over, just called them occasionally, so if he was in town, and in the mood, he'd have a warm place to hang his hat for the night.

She texted that she was on the interstate about to go through his town, and wondered if he'd like to get something to eat. It suddenly dawned on him that here was an answer to his dilemma. He could ask her to come here, have her run by the store, and still have the guys over.

She could serve them while they played poker, then he'd get lucky afterward. Tomorrow, he'd let her know it was over; but heck, she *was* a fun time; tonight, would work out fine after all. He picked up the phone and hit the green circle with his thumb.

"Billy's Mule Barn; Head Ass speaking."

"Billy? It's Raven."

"Hey, Raven. How ya been?"

"Ok. I've missed you. You... just stopped calling... Is everything ok?"

"Yeah. Everything's fine. I've just been extra busy with my business."

"You're always busy, but you usually have time to talk. We used to talk for hours."

"We had that big job out in West Texas. Cell service is garbage there. That's why we're putting up a series of towers. I tried to call, but it wouldn't go through. I was going to call on my way home, but one of the engineers on the new contract called and we had to go over the specs. It took longer than I thought, then it was too late."

"I would have answered."

"I know, but I know you need your sleep. What's up?"

"I just need to talk to you. I'm in the area, Can I see you?"

"Actually, I was just about to run into town to the store, but I injured my foot, and now I have to stay home. I'm not sure how good company I'll be, but you're welcome to come here."

"Oh my gosh? Are you ok? Does it hurt?"

"Of course, it hurts. I thought I was going to pass out. But I'm ok. Just another day, another thing to get through."

"Do you need anything? Do I need to go to the store for you?"

"I'd hate to put you out," he lied so smoothly he almost believed himself. He was smiling broadly at how easy this was, knowing she couldn't see it. "It's out of the way to drive all the way to town and then out here." *Like shooting fish in a barrel... lol... omg, women are so easy...*

"I don't mind. Text me a list and I'll pick it up, then grab something for dinner. I want to talk to you anyway. What do you want to eat?" *fantastic... I won't even have to cook...*

"There's a new BBQ place over on Main? I hear it's good. I haven't been there yet, but we can try it," he lowered his voice and added a sensual tone to it, "You know what I like... and just get whatever fixins they have to go with it. We can share them."

"That sounds nice," she flirted back; deciding he must have just been busy after all. "Text me your list. I'll be there soon."

He texted her his grocery list, unconcerned that it would come to over a hundred bucks. He kept cash around. He'd pay her. It never occurred to him that she might not have that much. He was warming to the idea of an intimate dinner, then cozying up for some comfort.

He decided starting the party earlier had more appeal then playing cards. He texted the guys and canceled the game. They could play poker any time, tonight was shaping up for a really good time.

He drank another beer, then another, while watching porn on his big screen TV. Before long, he was ready to eat and reacquaint himself with Raven. He remembered her long shiny black hair, the black lipstick and dark grey eyeshadow that matched the rest of her Goth look, and her lithe body. She liked to wear black and silver, and wore a silver moon on a chain around her neck. She was into Tarot cards and liked to tell fortunes for a hobby. *Too bad she's not part of the coven... she'd fit right in...*

She kept expensive lace lingerie, sometimes black, and sometimes a deep blood red. Her extra pale skin showing through it drove him crazy, and for the life of him he couldn't remember why he'd grown bored. One morning his crew had picked him up from her house and she'd followed him out wearing nothing but lingerie and extra high heels.

She'd wrapped herself around him, kissing him senseless, almost causing him to go back inside for the day. Nothing was left to the imagination and his crew was almost useless the rest of the day, in awe that he had spent the night with someone that drop-dead model gorgeous.

They'd accused him of being with a hooker, and he was still riding the wave of their jealousy. He almost texted his friends back, to tell them to come on out, so they could spend the evening watching her, knowing he'd be the one she stayed with. He was growing more excited and was glad he'd answered the phone. He'd be working on a job up her way soon, and maybe he'd give her another go. It'd save him the trouble of finding someone new, and playing the initial games, although that was half the fun.

He heard her pull into the driveway and shut off the TV. He hobbled to the door, anticipating her stunning dark witchy beauty, but an ordinary girl was on his porch. She was wearing jeans, a neon pink top, white tennis shoes, and very little make-up. Her black hair was pulled back into a ponytail. She was struggling to hold the weight of two plastic bags filled with groceries hanging from each arm. He opened the door and reached to take the bags.

Raven?"

"Hey Billy." When she smiled, she was still pretty, but a different pretty. He'd never seen her without the racy clothes and dramatic make-up. She looked like she'd gained some weight too, and seemed nervous. He wasn't sure why. She'd never seemed nervous before. Maybe it was because she wasn't hiding behind the goth costume.

She went back to the car for three more bags, then once again for the large brown paper bag with the warm BBQ in it. He finished putting the groceries away, then got down plates for their meal. He offered her a beer, but she'd brought in a tea she'd gotten at the BBQ place.

She handed him a receipt for $125 for the groceries. He grabbed his wallet and handed her $150. "Is that enough for the BBQ too?" He asked.

She handed back $25. "No. That's on me."

He grinned. "I'll buy. You shopped and brought it out for me. It's the least I can do."

"No. Really. I want to. I've missed you, and I'd have cooked if you'd come by. I like taking care of you."

"I don't need taking care of," he rudely reminded her. "I've taken care of myself for a long time." What is it with women always wanting to take care of me? Do I look helpless?"

She glanced at him hopping across the kitchen, then looked pointedly at the pile of plastic bags he'd left on the counter and the trail of blood leading to the hallway. "Yeah. I can see how well that's going."

He laughed. "Ok. Maybe not right now. But I *can* take care of myself."

"I know. But I want to spoil you a little. Let me. It's ok."

"Fine. You win. Let's eat." He gestured to the small table he'd set while waiting for her. She walked over and sat down, and he sat too. They began to open the containers, serving the sides, and then he added ribs from one box, and she added chopped pork from another. They ate while making small talk.

Afterward she put the dishes in the sink, rinsed them, and stacked them on one side, then put the leftovers in the refrigerator, rolling her eyes when she saw the number of beer bottles, it held. The only other items were the ones she'd just brought for him. She knew he worked out of town a lot, but she was still surprised he didn't keep some type of staples.

She asked to use the restroom, and he showed her the proper door. After completing her business and washing up, she cleaned up the blood trail, then stopped at the end of the hallway before reentering the living room; looking at his profile as he sat in the chair waiting for her to finish. She stood there admiring his movie star rugged good looks, took a series of long breaths, then steeled her spine as she returned to the room.

He again asked her if she'd like a beer, and once again she refused, instead picking up her tea, and taking a long drink. They moved to the couch. He sat near and then pulled her into a hug that ended with a kiss. She kissed him back, then pulled away when he tried to deepen it.

"Billy, I need to talk to you."

"We've been talking for an hour."

"I know; but this is different." She once again looked nervous.

He sighed. *Why did women always play these stupid games. They led you on, then just wanted to talk.* "What's on your mind?" he looked annoyed. He'd readied himself for a fun night, and was in no mood to delay it any longer, now that his belly was full; even if she did look like a teenager in her street clothes.

"Billy… I'm pregnant," she softly whispered, then glanced up to look at his face.

"You're what?" he wasn't sure he'd heard her right.

"I'm pregnant. You're going to be a father." She watched his face to gauge his reaction.

"I'm going to be a what?" he still looked confused, as his brain refused to accept what she'd said.

"A father. I'm having a baby." She was more direct with her statement this time.

He'd heard her the first time. He'd just been processing it. He'd been ready for romance, and was blind-sided by a very unwelcome message instead.

"I'm. Not. Going. To. Be. A. Father." He enunciated each word clearly. He got off the couch, walked over to the table, grabbed his wallet, and walked back. He opened it, flipping to a separate compartment, and pulled out several bills. She saw the 100 on the corners. He thrust them toward her. "Here. Get rid of it. Do it tomorrow. I'm not having a kid."

"I'm keeping it." She wasn't surprised he wasn't thrilled, but had already made up her mind. "If you don't want to be involved, that's fine. You can sign your rights away and I'll raise it myself. I just wanted you to know." *At least I tried.*

"How do you even know it's mine?" his tone was curt and his words unkind, and his face scared her.

"Because you're the only person I've slept with in over two years." She responded. *Nice try jerk.*

"That's too bad." he countered. "But you're going to get rid of it. Now. Keeping it is not an option."

"I'm leaving." She stood up. "You'll never hear from me again. It's my child. It's been my child for the last three months, and it will be my child for the rest of my life."

He saw that she meant it, and he had a quick memory of what the coven would make him do. "You don't understand. I cannot have a child. It will never be safe."

She looked at him in pity, at how far he'd go in his selfishness to get her to kill their baby, then rolled her eyes at him thinking she couldn't see through it. "What are you talking about? I intend to raise this child. I live in a safe neighborhood. I come from a good family. I have a good job. Of course, it'll be safe. Don't worry. You're off the hook, but I'm having this baby."

"There are things you don't understand." He was getting mad again. He knew he couldn't tell her about the coven and the requirements for first-born children; but he was a practiced liar, so he created another reason out of thin air. "I owe some really, bad people money. They sell children to rich people who can't have their own. I didn't know it when I played poker with them, and when I lost a lot of money, they threatened to take my first-born in payment. If they find out I have a child, very bad things will happen to it."

She stared at him in shock, "Why didn't you go to the police?"

His mouth turned up in a side-ways sneer. "The police? Are you crazy? They're afraid of these guys. And they have people everywhere. I'd be dead before I got back to the street, and then they'd still take the baby; and probably you too." *I'll scare her a little bit, and she'll do it.*

"I'll put 'unknown' for the father's name." She was sick at what he'd confessed, but was still determined to keep her child. "No one will ever know it's you. Just stay away from us. I mean it."

"They'll know; they have people everywhere, Raven. I'm not joking. If they even think you're pregnant, you'll disappear from your home, and what they'll do to you while you wait to give birth is something nightmares are made of.

Take the money. Go to the clinic tomorrow. You'll have another kid. It won't ever be mine again, but you'll be fine; as long as you stay as far away from me as you can get." Billy knew he wouldn't kill his own child. He'd always been protective over what was his. Killing his puppy was the hardest thing he'd ever had to do, and after what he'd been through as a child, and what he'd seen so much of, he knew it wasn't going to happen.

But he also knew it would be no option if the coven knew it even existed. His family line was too precious to end, and the first-born had been promised to the Familiar Spirit that his family had worshipped for generations, long before the recent ceremony.

It was expected that he personally would kill his own first-born. Then, it was expected that he would continue to produce more children - some for sacrifice, some to undergo the rituals necessary—to continue the family line's dedication to the entity. He'd have a coven wife, and they'd provide breeders for the rest.

'Bound from Birth,' is what his grandmother used to call it. He'd decided a long time ago that he'd be the last one. He still had nightmares about what the entity had done to him at age six, and many times after that.

Having to kill his puppy had wounded him deeply and changed him forever. Each birthday brought new torturous dedication rituals, which brought more and more demons to reside inside him. He'd grown used to his own life being bound, and knew he would spend eternity with them, but he wasn't condemning another generation to that hellish existence.

It was one of the few truly good things left about Billy, and possibly was sealed away from the demonic infestation inside himself from a very young age, when he'd learned to disassociate from what was happening to him, and go 'inside' to his safe place until it was over. It was the only way he could manage to live with the horror and the pain.

He stuffed everything good and decent into that place, and the rest of him absorbed the evil and embraced it. The cognitive dissonance it created helped him survive, and the hidden devastation was what his constant rage was rooted in. While his body and intelligence had grown, emotionally he was still the small child who'd been so abused.

He enjoyed the prestige and power the coven brought him, and the rituals. He loved the money and ability to get away with stuff, but what he'd seen and experienced in his young life had cracked his soul and he knew it. He'd witnessed evil without bounds, and he had no desire to watch his kid go through what he'd been through.

He'd always be bound to them, and knew enough to not even try to leave, but it was done with him. It was a secret decision none of them had ever suspected he'd made. Only another bloodline coven kid could understand.

Many of the girls underwent secret tubal ligations when they became adults. They'd all been forced to become pregnant multiple times, and forced to kill the first child themselves, then forced to watch the coven kill the rest. They were bred like mares to far older men in ceremonies to create certain bloodline sacrificial babies.

Many were impregnated by being gang raped, which they'd been forced to endure from the age of six during ritual after ritual. Many were forced to eat their own offspring. Some of them went insane. The ones that didn't either embraced the evil, or tried to get away. Many were caught and sacrificed. Some stayed, a shell of a human, but chose sterility as a way of buffering themselves from more pain.

When he was ten, a girl a few years older than him had performed an abortion on herself with a coat hanger, and bled out in her bedroom trying to escape what was coming. They were the lucky ones. The rest embraced the coven ways, rose to the rank of priestess, and were some of the vilest people he'd ever known, while appearing to the general public as wonderful citizens.

That was the path his grandmother had chosen; he knew it well. He'd been a victim of her anger and pain his entire life, until she'd died; and she'd trapped him into the coven, so he'd never be free of her evil, even though she was finally gone.

He'd decided long ago to not procreate. He'd been meaning to get 'snipped,' but had kept putting it off. It was easier to pay for another abortion than to take a chance on losing his manhood; but he knew it was time. He needed to get Raven's 'accident' taken care of and go get it done the next trip out of town. He wasn't going to be forced into this position again. He'd have to be very careful though, he wasn't lying about the fact that they had connections everywhere.

His turned back to the matter at hand, his mind still on the horror he'd been remembering, completely overlooking the lies he'd been spinning. "I'm serious. You don't know what they'll do. If you did, you'd know it's a mercy." His hostility was palpable and filled the room, the anger at her stubbornness putting him in a position to have to do something he could not do, coming off him in waves. He realized it'd be far easier to just kill her now. He could kill an adult without a qualm.

She saw he believed what he was saying, and decided to lie and get out of his house, when she saw his eyes change. She'd had no idea he was either mentally unbalanced, or involved with criminals. It had to be one or the other, possibly both. She reached out and took the money. "Ok. I get it. You don't want to be a father. You don't want a kid of yours to exist. Fine. I'll do it. Thanks for the cash. It'll get me back to my normal life too."

She turned to go and he was glad. Both knew the relationship was over for good. He was relieved she'd agreed. He'd get the damned operation this week. He shuddered at what had almost been allowed to exist, feeling a cold sweat break out at how close he'd come. It could never be. He'd see to it.

Raven drove away sad that he was so paranoid, but relieved she'd gotten out of the house safely. She wasn't sure if he was spinning a lie to make her choose abortion, or if he was simply psychologically screwed up. Good grief, she thought, really scared: He could be dangerous. I barely know him. He was just some guy to party and play with, and now he's the father of my child.

She decided to move back close to her mom as soon as possible. She'd never told him her last name, or her real name for that matter, or where she'd moved from. He'd never find her, or her child.

She went to bed still troubled, and had nightmares of her child being kidnapped and trafficked. In the morning she evaluated her options and her life. As much as she enjoyed partying and her freedom, the goth days were over. It was time to 'live her raising' as her mom used to say. It was time to grow up and embrace motherhood.

Despite the covid craziness, she would raise her child right. She was glad her doctor had recommended the vaccine before she'd gotten pregnant. She didn't want the possibility of getting covid harming her baby.

...if only she'd known...

The Heart of a Man

Chapter 28

ALONE IN HIS HOUSE, Matt sat at his desk. He had his well-worn bible open in front of him, but his eyes weren't seeing the print. He was lost in a memory of seeing Missy that very first time. He could still see the blanket Jenny had wrapped her in. It was white with pink bow ties scattered all over it, and the softest thing he'd ever touched...until he'd touched the face of his daughter...

Jenny had handed him the newborn infant and he'd been afraid he'd drop her. She was just under six pounds and it'd felt like a soft bundle of air in his arms. She was so still as she slept, and then her eyes had opened. He lost his breath as she looked straight up into his, from the incredibly blue depths of her own. She kept looking at him, as if she knew exactly who he was, and she'd wrapped her entire tiny hand around his finger.

He'd touched her cupid bow mouth and she'd tried to suckle his finger. Jenny handed him a bottle and he'd fed his child. It touched him so deeply, as his heart filled with love for his child, that he vowed he'd never let her want for anything, or allow anyone to hurt her. He was prepared to tell his parents that night, but Jenny had talked him out of it.

It had hurt him deeply that she'd withheld the right to know his own baby. She'd said he was too young to be a parent, and she was saving him from himself. What a load of hogwash. He'd grown up the moment he felt a father's protectiveness, and the love he felt that first day had never diminished one iota. He'd never been the same.

They'd taken the urine sample and tea glass to the specialist. He said they'd know in a week. Matt wasn't sure how he was going to make it until then, but honestly, to him, it was just a formality. She looked enough like Dana that he already knew.

He'd watched her from afar her whole life, and the way she threw back her head and laughed was just like his mother and grandmother. Even the sound of her voice was his mother made over. She had hands like his and his father's.

He loved seeing her, looking at her, and seeing them all in her. And, every time he saw her, he wanted to hug her. He was glad he'd had an opportunity this morning.

She walked like Jenny, and had Jenny's smile; and when she was thinking about something she tilted her head in the same way, with the same serious look on her face. She was a perfect blend of them all. He'd finally gotten over Jenny, but had retained fond memories of their brief time together, and had helped her financially until the day she died, knowing he'd always love her on some levels.

He'd never know if it was knowing he'd fathered her child, or just because she was the first women he'd been with, but he'd always loved her. He'd learned a very valuable lesson with her, and he'd never since been one to sleep around. His heart couldn't take any more lost children.

With that, his mind went to the cradle he'd made. He hadn't been back to the other house in years. He hadn't quite forgotten about it, but he'd just not allowed himself to think about it; and coming face to face with it today, especially with Dan and Pauline in the house, had almost undone him.

Dan didn't know the whole story of his divorce. Some things hurt too much to share, and both his heart and his dignity had taken another severe hit. He'd taken the blame, but the truth was so much more. His wife had been pregnant. He'd been so thrilled, and had skipped the living room and started renovating the bedroom as soon as they'd found out.

She hadn't wanted to tell people until later when it was too hard to hide. He didn't understand why, but honored her request. He'd wanted to tell his mother so badly, but he'd never gotten the chance, which had turned out to be a blessing in disguise.

He'd secretly handcrafted the cradle, each board-cut and swipe of the sandpaper smoothing the finish, was a loving gift to his wife, and the child he would this time get to raise. He'd pictured himself changing diapers and patiently teaching his child to ride a horse, and helping him learn about life.

He'd had it in the room, anticipating her delight, when she came home from work one evening, and she'd started to cry when she saw it. He thought it was surprise and joy and went to hug her. She didn't know about Missy, but she did know how much he wanted a child.

She'd stepped back away from him, holding her hand out to keep him back, while tears poured down her face. She stared at the cradle and cried for several long minutes, then looked at him with the saddest eyes he'd ever seen. His heart dropped, thinking something was wrong with the baby. Then she'd told him; her words ripping apart both his world and his dreams.

She'd been unfaithful, and the child she carried wasn't his. She'd planned that evening to tell him she was moving out. She was moving back to the area where her parents lived. She'd gone to see them when he was busiest at the ranch and ran into an old boyfriend, whom she'd reconnected with. They'd rekindled the romance, and she'd gotten pregnant.

They'd decided to raise their child together. She was sooo sorry...she hadn't meant to hurt him...he was a wonderful man...he'd find someone someday...he didn't deserve what she'd done...she hadn't meant to marry him under false pretenses...it's just that she'd thought she was over the other guy...they'd been too young...and so much more; she'd kept talking long past his ability to absorb her words...

As his mind registered what she was saying, he felt like all the life was draining out of him. He never said a word. He grabbed his suitcase, filled it with what he needed, and walked out. She stayed in the house a couple of weeks, then was gone. He'd locked the door, and after a few weeks of staying in town, he'd started building another house.

It had never had the love poured into it that he'd poured into the first one, he just didn't have it in him. He'd hired his brother-in-law to build his new house, and just paid the bills. It wasn't really a home, like he'd thought the original one was. It was a place to live, a place to eat, sleep, and bathe in; a place to escape from the rest of the world, but held no other significance for him. Few others had ever been inside it.

His wife hadn't asked for anything in the divorce, even though Texas was a community property state, and by law half was legally hers. He'd paid for the original house as he'd renovated it, and it was on land he'd bought from Dan but was still used as part of the ranch; so, he'd cashed out half of his 401k, and sent a cashier's check by registered mail to her mother's address. It had come back three weeks later in another envelope with a brief note telling him she didn't need it.

He'd learned later the old boyfriend was into real estate and made half a million a year. After a few months, he'd cleaned out everything left and gave it to a charity, leaving only the wicker furniture out in the glassed-in sun porch and a table and chairs in the kitchen. Except the cradle. He just couldn't make himself give it away. He almost burned it, but couldn't do that either.

He felt bile rise in the pit of his stomach as he allowed himself to remember that night. To say he was shocked is a complete understatement. It had affected him in ways he still hadn't gotten over. Dan thought it was guilt due to his withholding information from her, but really it was unresolved anger, humiliation, and a deeply felt insecurity at having both significant women in his life being unfaithful, and losing a promised child with each.

At least this time he didn't have to deal with knowing his child was out there and he wasn't allowed to know him. He'd heard from her cousin she'd given birth to a boy, and he'd cried for an entire weekend. Something had sealed off in his heart and he hadn't dated since.

He was glad Missy would live in the house he'd put so much of himself into. He knew she was his daughter, and the house and land would be her inheritance. Someday maybe she could use the cradle. Maybe he could be a grandfather. That would be nice, since fatherhood had been taken from him. At 41, with no desire to date anyone… well… maybe no one he could date… he didn't see how that would ever happen.

He'd put his efforts into becoming even more of an extra father figure for Clayton and Tucker. Tucker was now in the military, and both he and Clayton were fully grown, so now he'd just concentrate on taking care of Missy.

He thought of Erwin, and how he'd let him down too. That boy had needed a father as much as he'd needed to be one. He didn't know if it was too late there too, but he was going to make the effort. Life was too short for regret. He'd learned that the hard way. He'd take him under his wing, help Missy, and maybe heal his own heart in the process.

He knew, from prior experience with the ritual Erwin had gone through, that some tough times were coming for the boy. The ritual had bound a high-level demon to Erwin, and he would need to have it cast out, and probably more after that. Dan had been involved when Erwin's grandfather had gone through the deliverance sessions, and he'd told Matt about it. And Matt had been there when Erwin's dad's best friend had gone through the same thing.

That mark on Erwin's neck meant the clock had started its countdown for the very soon ritual to sacrifice him. They had a very limited time to save him. And Dan was right; if they knew about Missy being his, she'd be next, or at the very least a substitute if they couldn't get Erwin back.

He laid his head on the desk, and called upon the God of heaven, the God of Abraham, Isaac, and Jacob; the one who delivered Daniel in the lion's den, and saved Abraham's son from sacrifice. He cried about all the years he'd missed being a father, once again asking God's forgiveness for out-of-wedlock sin; he knew that was really what had cost him.

If he'd been grown and married to a righteous woman, he'd never have lost her. His mind whispered that marriage hadn't helped the second time, but he knew that was sin-based as well, just this time it wasn't his own sin, but someone else's, that had cost him.

He asked God for forgiveness in allowing Erwin to get this deep with Billy, ignorant of the truth, and having no one else to turn to for relationship; while he'd been too lost in his own pain to be what Gene and Sherman would have wanted him to be to their boy. He asked God to save them both and give him and Dan time to teach them and help them.

He asked God to allow his mother and Dana to know Missy, and Missy to know them. He knew she believed she had no family left, and he was so eager to let her know that wasn't true; but now even that would be tricky. His family all knew the danger of the coven, so when they knew, they could help protect her, and he was ready to come clean with everybody.

He asked God to heal his wounded heart and give him strength and courage for the coming days. He allowed Him to lead him to finally forgive his ex-wife. He'd never be around her again in this lifetime, but he was ready to move on from the unbelievable betrayal.

He could feel within his soul the spirit of evil rising around them all and he asked for a greater discernment than he'd ever before had. He'd continue his friendship with Rachel, and accept that's all she'd ever wanted, and let the rest go.

He poured himself out before the Lord and finally he heard that still small voice: *"Hurry. Be vigilant. Time is short. The enemy is on the move. Erwin is in great danger. Protect them both. Be their father. Don't hesitate. Go!"*

He kept praying and just before 2 am he heard one final instruction. *"Protect the baby. It is special."*

He found it odd that God referred to Missy as 'the baby' but he was determined to do all in his power to keep her safe. He asked God to put a hedge of protection around both young people, and Amy as well. He begged God, if there was any way, that He would rescue Billy too; although he felt in his spirit that he was too invested in the power he held, too entrenched in the ways of darkness, and would never repent and go against the coven.

He surrendered all he was, all his dreams—broken as they were—and the rest of his life to do the bidding of the Lord. He went to bed around three, falling into a deep sleep.

He'd start on the house tomorrow. God had sown a great sense of urgency within him and he wasn't about to procrastinate. Just before surrendering to unconsciousness, he remembered he'd forgotten to show Dan what he'd wanted to about the house.

Awakening at 5:00, his usual time, he felt unusually well-rested and at peace. He made coffee, grabbed his bible, and went to his favorite chair and began to read. It felt like the words were jumping off the pages and planting themselves in his heart. Even in the calmness, he felt a rising sense of urgency, and at 6:30 he called Dan. "Can we get the team together today to pray and prepare?"

"I've already spoken to Homer. Ina called before that. Erwin confessed to her last night and began to read his bible. We have a very narrow window, so we can't lose a minute. We must let him know what's coming." He then gave Matt a complete rundown of the incident as Erwin drove home, reciting the precise detail Ina had given him.

"Does Clayton need to be involved, or should I give him enough to keep him busy for the day? I can send him to pick up something out of town," Matt knew Clayton needed to learn first-hand what they were up against, but didn't want any further reason for Billy to target him.

"That's tricky," Dan responded. "He needs to become prepared and trained, and we've both seen the results of keeping things from these boys to protect them; but I'm not sure this is the one to start with. He's had too much history with Billy. On the other hand, I'm not sure sending him away by himself right now is a good idea either.

Send a couple of the boys with him. It's time to go get a load of feed and I made a deal with Homer that we'd pick up both our order and his since we're going anyhow. He'll get paid as usual, but will both give us a 10% discount, and credit us for half the delivery; and since we'll be hauling it, he saves on freight for the rest of his order, and we save on cost. Make sure they're all three armed.

Let's start assembling the team. Homer and I decided on a meeting here at 10:00. He's already calling his list, I've started on mine, and you have your own list to call. I've got a few other things I need to take care of before then. I'll see you here."

"Ok," Matt said. "Dan…I want to make up for lost time with Erwin and Missy. God spoke to me and said to stay close, Erwin is in danger. We already knew that, so this must be something extra. And Dan…God said to 'protect the baby, it's special,' so Missy must be in danger too. I want this fence built asap. Let's get a team on it now."

"That's part of what I have on my agenda today. I'm headed to the barn immediately to get them lined out. I'll send some to start the fence, and some to the house to get started cleaning. Can you meet them at 8:00 to show them what you want done when the cleaning's finished?"

"Yeah. I'm headed over there in a little while. I'll walk through again and make a detailed instruction sheet for them. We don't need them calling every few minutes while we're meeting with the others."

"I agree. And I'm with you on providing family for both these young people. I'll be back-up father, uncle, grandpa, mentor, whatever they need." He teared up, and Matt could hear the grief in his voice. "Several of us have dropped the ball with Erwin, and it's time we cleaned up our mess and gave that boy what he needs to grow into the man Gene and Sherman—and more importantly, God—would have him be."

Matt felt the emotion as well. "See you at ten."

A Call to Arms

Chapter 29

JAKE WAS MAKING BREAKFAST when his phone rang. He'd left it in the bedroom and had to run upstairs to get it. It stopped ringing just as he made it to the top of the landing. He continued to his room and picked it up to see who was calling. He was glad his first class wasn't until 1:00 today. He'd overslept, which was unusual for him. They'd accomplished a lot this weekend, though, and he was still tired.

The call was from Matt Hench, his best friend. He hit the call button and waited for Matt to answer.

"Hey Jake, sorry to bother you before class. You got a minute?"

"Sure Matt. What's up?"

"We're assembling at Dan's at 10:00. It's important. Is there any way you can join us?"

"Of course. Anything you can tell me now?" Both knew talking on the phone was not a good idea. Too many listening ears with modern technology. They'd devised some short-hand over the years, but were always careful.

"Someone new 's been invited to the organization, and the initial training session has been done. Insignia has been issued, and we need to start our part. We're supposed to have everything done before the company party. I'm not sure of the exact date, but it's being planned even as we speak, and it's soon," Matt cryptically answered.

Jake knew instantly, the binding ceremony to summon the demon, that preceded sacrificing a targeted family member, had been performed. They had a finite time to rescue the intended victim. He went through the known list in his mind, and came up with 2-3 possibilities. "Which insignia, was issued, do you know?"

"Presidential level."

"I see. I'm assuming we'll need the insurance papers and to have them notarized?" He questioned.

"That's right. Can you pick up the insurance forms and inform the notary?" which was his way of letting Jake know to include Maggie and Rachel.

"Yes. I'll take care of both. See you at 10.

"Sure thing."

He called Maggie and Rachel, being just as cryptic with each. Maggie said she'd have the forms ready by 9, and insisted she ride out with him in case anything needed changed; and Rachel, being Rachel—and loving to play to an unseen listener—negotiated a hard bargain for Notary fees, and said she'd be happy to do business with them.

Jake finished his breakfast, spent extra time in prayer and bible study, pulled together his briefcase and notes for today's lessons, and left to collect Maggie at 9. Rachel would go the backway and meet them there.

Maggie was ready when he arrived and was locking her office door with her work bag thrown over her shoulder as he parked. She climbed in his truck, greeted him, and asked, "who?"

"I'm not sure yet." He went over the list he'd come up with, which matched her thinking also. "It could be any of them. We'll have to see. Maggie, everything evil in this world seems to be coming out of the woodwork right now. With all the garbage on TV and on the internet, teachers teaching Marxism in schools, this engineered 'pandemic,' and the church just yawning, I'm surprised any of our young are ok.

Decency seems to be the major sin in society, as the most heinous real sin becomes not only acceptable, but lauded with the highest praise. Of course, they're making their move now. If they can't turn them, they can just have one of their doctors shove a needle in their arm, write up a signed shot record, and boom, another Covid death. They don't even have to hide the body now; most covid deaths don't even require an autopsy; not that that even matters, since they own most of the coroners. How convenient." He was livid.

She knew he saw so much on the campus he couldn't do anything about without losing his job. With his inheritance from his share of his parent's life insurance, he could have retired by now; but it was important to Jake to stay on campus as long a time as he possibly could, so, he could reach any students who could still be reached. It was fewer and fewer each year, and while he had rescued many throughout his career, the cost of the ones lost had taken a heavy toll as well.

She leaned over and put a hand on his arm for comfort and support. "I know, Jake. Some of us aren't quite in the day-to-day battle the way that you are, but you're making a difference. You really are. Jesus said 'remnant.' We both know the Word says the 'whole world' will come under the evil one's sway. We need to continue to do what we can, and let the rest go."

He looked at her, and all but shouted, angry at the very thought, "how do I let kids go?! How do I watch them make the stupidest decisions possible, and just turn away and pretend it doesn't matter?! I've had dreams of lines of students walking zombie-like toward the edge of a cliff. They can see the ones in front of them dropping off, but they never change expression, and never stop walking.

They just keep determinedly putting one foot in front of the other, until they too fall off. Over, and over, and over. Thousands. I wake up screaming because I've ran along beside them trying make them see the edge and the fall, but they just keep steadily walking as if they can't see or hear me," he was shaking with anguish as he spoke.

"Maggie, everything is so different the last few years. There's so little respect. A punk can stand up in class and challenge me, and the entire class laughs. I can barely throw them out of class now, without chancing a discrimination lawsuit. Even the kids raised right see no value in honor or integrity," his voice changed to frustrated pain, as he explained his experience.

"It's hard to convince kids that have seen so many Hollywood actors and You-tube millionaires, have everything given to them, by exploiting nudity and sin to the Nth degree, how important those values and a college degree are in life. I suspect many of them are coven family line, but I'm never sure. Sometimes I think the diligent ones are the true family members, because they know they need to be in places of position, and are taught to prepare themselves to do so; and God help them if they fail."

Maggie didn't say a word, she just squeezed his arm in continued support. He glanced at her worried eyes, then began to apologize, "I'm sorry for taking it out on you. Sometimes I just need to vent. I hate evil. I hate murder, death, wounded people, and watching another generation being drawn into the war against righteousness, never given the chance to know the incredible God that created them." He laid his free hand across hers, still on his arm, and squeezed back. "Thank you for allowing me to share that with you. Again."

One of Jake's cousins had disappeared at age 22, and had not been seen since. The police said they'd had reports of her being spotted in various states, and listed her as a run-a-way. The group of families from the original settlers knew differently, but as usual, with so many of the others in high positions, they could never prove anything. It still grieved Jake, and every time they got 'the call' he was triggered all over again.

He was haunted by the thought that she may not even be dead; but was instead held a captive; being raped repeatedly, forced into being a breeder, and suffering God knows what. He found more comfort that she had been outright killed, but the lack of proof continued to torture him, even after all these years.

"At least, by the fact that we've been summoned, we know we have a chance. It's not too late. If they know the ceremony's been performed, they had to have spoken with the target, or someone else that was present. If we're meeting, the target is aware, and has asked for help. That's a start." She knew from experience they weren't always successful, but the targeted individual wanting to be rescued were usually the ones they saved—if they found out in time—and could keep the person out of the coven's grasp.

Many had been sent to other places and given funds to start a new life. They had lawyers and judges in other places too; people who fought their own version of the fight and were instrumental in accomplishing name changes with closed records. Sort of their own 'witness protection program.' It was difficult and costly, but it could be done.

"You're right," he relented. "We need to see who it is, and what the situation is, before I freak out." He laughed a bit ruefully, "God knows, even one rescued is a miracle of His making. If we have to hide them out in the tunnels, we can; we just need to make sure they truly want out. This isn't our first go 'round.

My guess is we're about to attempt another demon expulsion. Then, a lifestyle adjustment for the person, where we'll all have to be on protection watch. Vigilance and 'all-hands-on-deck' will be of utmost importance."

"I figured as much," Maggie agreed. "I brought my bible, and we both know our calling. We need to be ready at any moment to battle the enemy. We can count on Zach, Matt, and Dan, too, and the others. I hope Bobby's here. As the world falls, we're to rescue each lost sheep, one by one, as we find them. And don't forget the ceremony calls for the demonic realm to hurt another person for payback for some slight—perceived, or real. We need to be praying for that individual as well, and reach them too, if possible," she reminded him.

"That's true," Jake began to wonder who that was, "the target should know." Part of the team's approach was to protect the unsuspecting victim along with the target, and possibly save two lives and souls...really it was all about the souls...their lives weren't unimportant, but eternity had to stay foremost in all their intentions; especially at this level of danger.

They turned onto the private road leading to the ranch. He could just see the top of Dan's barn over the top of the hill, and then, as they topped the hill and drew near, the gate. He slowed and stopped to identify himself, and was let in by two ranch hands. Both were armed and ready to defend the ranch.

They didn't know what was transpiring, but Dan always had men on gate duty and it was protocol to pass inspection before being allowed in. He had meetings often, and most of the ranch hands knew the usual people who came for various reasons.

Jake wasn't here as much as others, but both men knew he was always welcome, being counted as another young man close to Dan that he looked at as a son. They knew he was a friend of Matt's too, and had been one of Clayton's professors, as well as being on several committee boards that Matt and Dan were involved in.

Today, they had a check-list. Anyone not on the list wasn't to be admitted, with no exceptions, unless Dan personally approved them. No deliveries were to be permitted either, except Clayton and the men with him.

At the hardware store, Erwin was stocking shelves, when he heard, "Erwin, can you come upfront?" over the loudspeaker. He placed the last propane tank on the shelf he'd been stocking, rolled the empty cart back where it belonged, and started toward the roll-up door in the side of the warehouse. He made his way through the aisles, through the side door into the main building, and up to the front of the store. Homer was standing near the small glassed-in office.

"Yeah, boss," he said, still dusting his hands on his jeans. "What do you need?"

"I'm supposed to go to a meeting for some city Christmas thingy. There will be several meetings between now and the holiday, and sometimes I won't be able to go. I need a stand-in for when I'm unavailable. I'd like for you to join me so you will be up to speed when that happens. I'll warn you now, these things can be lengthy, and quite frankly, a little boring, but we've always contributed our part.

They'll have chosen a theme already, and others will argue, or try to change some aspect to what they like instead. It may run over till this afternoon, but I hope not. I'll pay you your regular wage. Think you can stand it?" He made sure the other employees at the registers heard the invitation, and knew the reason they'd be leaving together and being out for a while. And to provide a cover, for one, or both of them, when it was needed.

Erwin laughed inside, amazed at how much Homer had managed with a couple of paragraphs. He knew exactly where they were going, and pretty much why, although, unknown to him, he wasn't aware of the most important item on the agenda. They walked to Homer's truck and left for the meeting.

Maggie and Jake drove up to the large home higher up the hill and parked. There were a handful of vehicles already there. They got out and walked in the back way straight into the kitchen, greeted by Lupe, the housekeeper, before they could knock. Maggie hugged her, and Jake grabbed a cookie from the glass jar on the counter, then followed them, as she led them into the conference room, they were familiar with. Each face around the long conference table was solemn, all knowing the grave consequences if they failed.

Dan opened the meeting with prayer, then filled them in on the details. It was a small group, but all had similar family stories, and all had felt the pang of loss within their own lives. All were solidly committed to the Lord and to rescuing anyone they could, and if possible, exposing the evil in their midst.

Each had participated in casting demons out of victims. Only a small group would be involved in the room when the expulsion began, but the rest would be in an adjoining room for prayer support, and protection from any attempt by the enemy to take Erwin from them, before they could accomplish their goal.

Ina stood up, "I've failed my grandson, and in some ways this group of warriors against the evil in our midst. Sherman was the one who carried the burden of that in our marriage, and I should have done more. I should have been willing to move out here when Dan first asked. He would never have formed the relationship with Billy if he'd been here. I knew he was angry with God, and I never insisted he attend church with me.

After I lost them all," she began to cry and wipe tears, "I just wanted to stay as far away from evil as possible, and keep him from having to deal with any of it—so he could just grow up—so much, that I'm afraid I closed my mind to the truth."

Maggie went to her and embraced her in a long hug, "Ina, you've been through a lot. We all understood that. Each of us let Erwin down in some way. Even after all we've seen and known, it's hard to wrap our brains around the truth that evil of this magnitude goes on right under our noses in this 'normal' town. Each of us need to earn a living, live our life, and try to do the best we can.

We fall into wanting a normal safe life, and feel uncomfortable with the truth when that is threatened. I've been guilty of falling into a normal bias too, for the same reason. Sometimes we just need to wrap whatever 'normal' we can create around us to survive. None of us judge you. Of course, you wanted to stay in the home you lived in with your husband.

Most women would. The only ones responsible for this evil are those who perpetrate it. Evil invaded the garden of Eden. It has a way of slithering in anywhere. I'm so sorry it got to another generation of your family, but we're here to fight for him. All of us."

"How much does he know about what's about to happen?" Jake smoothly inserted the question, heading off more tears, then ate another bite of cookie.

"He knows he's a target. He's seen the demon, and participated in the ritual, and has the mark. He was almost run off the road by what I suspect was the same entity that caused Gene's death." Tears flowed as she spoke, "I didn't explain about the attachment. I didn't want to distract him from deciding who he would serve. I made sure he knew he had to choose a side, and that he'd have to leave my home if he chose to stay with the coven.

I had no idea they'd pulled him in so young. I truly thought he and Billy just rode bikes and played baseball when they were young. I had no idea Evelyn was one of them back then, or ever dreamed she had involved him in the coven itself. I didn't want to make him mad, where he wouldn't come today; plus, I'd rather the demonic spirit be triggered to reveal itself here, with all of you, than alone in that house. I know God was there too, but we all know how powerful these things are.

Last night he prayed and repented, and spent hours reading the bible. He had no problems with it." All knew that sometimes after the ritual—or being involved in witchcraft of any type—people tried to read the word and could not. Their mind filled with fog, their ears were filled with buzzing, or the words simply vanished from the page. Sometimes they'd read it over, and over again, and their mind simply couldn't retain the words.

"I'd taught him when he was small that rebuking the enemy in Jesus' name would make it leave. When he encountered the demon while driving, that's what he did. It was instinct and early knowledge, I'd guess. It was stalking my house yesterday evening, and will continue trying to find a way to get to him. We all know the ceremony and the mark means he's being groomed for sacrifice. Please. We have to rescue him. I beg you to help me undo what they've done. What I've let happen."

"Homer is bringing him at 11," Dan informed them. We have about 45 minutes to pray and be ready. "Ina, do you think he's ready for the truth? Do you think he's truly ready to break away from the coven? None of us know the true extent of his involvement. He's what 24, 25 now?"

"25," Ina clarified.

"That's at least 15 years involvement." Matt quickly did the math. "It will depend on what he's accepted, and whether they've drawn him into full involvement, or kept it peripheral. We can't wait long though. When Gene's friend was killed it was barely two weeks after the ceremony. If they suspect Erwin's not 'all in' they may not wait that long. We need to find out today how involved he truly was. If he's really, ready to be done with it, inform him of the attachment, and trigger it, so he can know the truth. If he's up to it, we can cast it out today."

"I say cast it out, and open his mind completely to the Lord, without a choice. Jesus, Paul, and the other disciples didn't ask people if they wanted deliverance. They cast out the demon, then educated the person and told them to sin no more," Ina made her desire known. "He won't be truly free until it's gone."

"I agree," Matt said, but Erwin's no novice to the rituals. He needs to understand exactly what's happened, what's about to happen, and why. We gave him a thumbnail idea yesterday, but today it's time to reveal more. I promise we won't let him go until he's delivered and knows the entire truth. After that, it's up to him.

He will know both sides, at the very least, before he leaves here today, and all of us have been given freedom to choose. Ina, from what I saw yesterday, he was greatly disturbed by what he'd been drawn into. That demon scared the bejesus out of him. He watched another young man be used terribly, and I believe he's ready to get out."

Stella, who'd been quiet up to this point, spoke, "do we know who the other young man is? He may need a doctor."

"Usually, they have their own doctor tend to them after, unless they are to be eliminated, or dropped somewhere for a warning, like Sherman," Dan answered her. Then Dan went to Ina and took her by the arms, looking into her eyes. "Ina, I want you to understand, he can work here and not leave the ranch for a while, like Sherman did, stay with Homer, or some of each; but he may choose to leave the area entirely. Will you be ok with his choice? I'd like both of you to just come on out for a time, to give us a chance to educate him; and give him time to decide what's right for him.

You can both stay for as long as you need, or from now on. I was here, although young, when Sherman got away. It took years for them to finally let it go; at least as far as Sherman goes. They *will* target him, you, and any children he has for many years to come. Please come, and let me keep you safe. It will help keep him safe as well."

Matt jumped back in, "Ina, with all that's happening in the country, it's time for us to come closer together anyway. You don't need to be out there alone anymore."

"Sharon and I are moving in with Jake this month for the same reasons," Rachel, who had been standing quietly by the door, added; she'd entered during the beginning of the exchange. Matt glanced at her, holding her eyes for a minute, glad she was there, then nodded.

"I am too," Maggie added. "It's not the time for a woman our age—or any age—to be alone. And, with your family the main target right now, I'd be the first to tell you, it's a wise decision."

The other members added comments as well. Most had groups that were beginning to make mutual aid plans of their own. "I understand why you didn't before, but things are different now, and it's just the right time," Dan hugged her again.

"I'm ready," Ina agreed. "Let's get him through this, and we'll figure it out. I'll need help moving, but they're already surrounding my home," her voice cracked in grief. "I can't lose another one. We've got to save him, no matter what."

All agreed to help make the move as painless as possible. They began to pray and ask for God's help in rescuing another family member who'd found his way into the clutches and designs of the age-old enemy.

They prayed for 35 minutes, then began to offer comfort to Ina again, before Homer arrived with Erwin. All had on their 'armor' and all were seasoned warriors. It was time to go to battle for a lost brother. It was time for victory—even in the midst of this so-called pandemic—one of the greatest destructions of humanity since the holocaust.

Erwin was fine when they left the store, but the closer they got to the ranch, the more restless he became. The ruling spirit in him sensed the change from his bible reading, and was uncomfortable with him attending this meeting, knowing exactly what the master would do to him if he allowed himself to be cast out. He was uncomfortable being so close to Homer also in the close confines of the truck cab, and they all knew the ranch land had been dedicated to the Creator.

He created a fear in Erwin of the people attending the meeting, including Dan, Matt, Jake, and even Homer, whispering into his mind lies and fear. *"These people aren't your friends. You barely know them. They've lied to you all these years, spying on you, gossiping about you. They have an agenda you know nothing about. You need to get back to Billy, your only true friend.*

Your grandmother is selfish. You're her only family member and she only desires to chain you to her, so she won't be alone. You'll never have your own life. Every single one of them just want to tell you what to do; and take control of your life; you have, to GET AWAY. GET AWAY NOW!!!"

Erwin was inundated by the thoughts that began to overwhelm him, as the enemy cast his fiery darts into his mind. He felt betrayed by them all, and humiliated that his greatest secrets had been known and gossiped about by so many; and fear began to rise in him at what he may be walking into. He turned to Homer, "I don't think I need to go to this. I'm not ready."

Homer, who'd seen this before, knew exactly what was transpiring, and tried to calm him down, "You'll be fine. You'll know everyone there. Erwin, don't listen to the lies. I care about you. Dan and Matt care about you. Everyone at this meeting cares about you. Trust me."

Erwin's uneasiness grew, and he began to move his legs backward and forward, his back moving sideways on the seat. He rubbed his neck, his arms, and the top of his legs. He was clearly becoming agitated and the restlessness increased by the moment. He began to run his hands through his hair, his head twisting from side to side, and then started coughing as the demon choked him. He grabbed his neck with both hands, trying to breathe, and then began to dry heave, "Homer, I think I'm about to be sick. STOP!"

Homer knew the demon wanted him to escape, and he'd get out and run the second the truck stopped, so he kept driving. He watched as a seemingly different person took over, as Erwin responded to the attack. He knew one of the demons they attached early on had the responsibility to get him away so they wouldn't be cast out. It was one they called 'a runner' whose job it was to get a person away from anyone trying to teach them truth, or help them. This demon would do anything to get Erwin away.

"Homer, I mean it! I'm sick! You've got to stop!" Erwin began to dry heave more violently, reaching for the door handle. Homer hit the gas, so he was going much too fast for Erwin to jump out.

They were only a few minutes out, and he wanted to be on ranch land before he stopped; hopefully at the house, where the others were, with a locked gate behind them. They could not lose Erwin now. The demon would take him straight to Billy and he'd be dead before they ever saw him again. He reached over to his phone, which had a pre-written text message to Dan, and hit the send button. It would alert the team that Erwin was beginning to manifest, and he'd need help when he arrived.

"Hang on Erwin. I've got you. I know you can hear me. Stand up to it inside your mind." He began to pray, "Jesus, please help me get him to your people. Hold back this evil from invading his mind, so we can save him." Then he spoke directly to the entity, "You can't have him. He belongs to the living God. Your master isn't having this one. I bind you in the name of Jesus."

Erwin went ballistic. He began to thrash around inside the cab, screaming wildly. He was staring out the window as if he saw something, "Keep it away from me!! Homer, help me!! It's coming!! It's coming."

Homer was looking at Erwin, whose eyes were almost solid black instead of the usual blue. It shocked him so much he almost missed the turn that led to the ranch. He slowed down enough to make it, and as he did, he too saw what Erwin was looking at. He'd heard tales about it for years, but nothing could have prepared him for the sight. It was almost like fog, except it was the blackest black he'd ever seen.

It undulated into the shape of a monster, then melted into another, and then another; endless convolutions that became a swirling nothing, then with new visages morphing, each more hideous than the last. Figures, some almost human, some with multiple limbs, some almost octopus-like with multiple appendages, and finally one that looked like a giant snake, then grew wings and became a dragon that flew straight at him.

He demanded it leave. He took authority, ordering it away, and it enraged the thing. He saw it slammed back, roaring in defiant anger; then it regrouped and drew near the truck, pressing what looked like a giant face—serpentine in form, but undulating with the wind—up against the glass, terrifying them both, and concealing the view out the windshield.

Homer kept driving, calling out to God for help. He gasped as the truck was surrounded by a brilliant white light, and out of the light rode the largest men he'd ever seen, on white horses. They surrounded the blackness and began to battle it. Whatever it was, screamed in rage and tried to get past them so it could once again cover the windshield, but they kept it away so he could see the road. He kept driving, sliding to a halt just outside the gate.

From the look on the ranch hands faces, they had seen nothing but his crazy too-fast driving, "Whoa there, Homer; let us open the gate. You must be late to Dan's meeting, but he'll be fine if you slow down a bit." He glanced over and saw Erwin, shaking and screaming, his face contorting as the demon tried to take him over, and then he had an inkling of what the meeting was about.

Most on the ranch had roots in the original settler families, and were aware of the coven and it's evil. Some had more knowledge than others, but all knew Dan was a leader in the fight against the evil. "Go, Homer! We got the gate. No one will get through. Go!"

Homer hit the gas and flew up the hill. He glanced in the rearview mirror, seeing the battle still raging, and then drove right up to the spot closest to the house. Dan, Matt, Jake, Bobby, and others were headed to the truck as he stopped the engine, Dan having alerted them to what was happening after receiving Homer's text.

Erwin slammed the door open into Bobby as he exited the vehicle. Jake, Rusty, and Matt tackled him as he started to run. It took five of them to subdue him enough to bring him to the porch, writhing, foaming at the mouth, and snarling at them. He tried to bite Matt, who barely got his arm away before the teeth could sink in. Maggie was standing there, staring into the sky, watching the battle with amazement. No matter how many times God opened her vision, it was still something that rattled her.

Home looked at her. "You can see them?!"

"Oh, yes," Maggie smiled, not taking her eyes off the sight before her in the sky. "Can you?"

"It's a first, Maggie, but I can, and I can tell you, they showed up just in time. There was something evil trying to get in the truck, and then it plastered itself across the window, and I couldn't see anything but it. Erwin went crazy and I thought I'd wreck before we got to the gate." He looked incredulous, as he asked, "Is that the kind of stuff you speak about seeing?"

"It's not always this dramatic," she was still staring at this sky, watching the battle, as she answered him, "but I've seen supernatural things from both sides, and sometimes a future event. This makes several times lately God's sent rescuers to deal with the demonic stalking me or somebody else, and allowed me to see it. We'd better get inside. This is going to be rough. It knows what's coming and it will try to destroy him so we can't save him."

"I agree." Homer glanced at the sky one more time, "but something tells me we will prevail. Did you see the size of those guys?" then comprehension came, "Maggie, those were angels! I just saw some of the heavenly host!" His voice was filled with awe at what he'd been granted to see, and Homer knew he'd never be the same. It was one thing to believe by faith with no sight, but no one would ever be able to convince him that God, angels, and the kingdom war did not exist.

He'd just seen it with his own eyes. He'd always believed, but now he knew. He almost fell going in the door, he was so overcome at the thought. Maggie, who totally understood, grabbed his arm, and steadied him. Both had tears of gratitude in their eyes. Homer walked into the house whooping with praise and ready to join the battle raging inside.

A Battle with Hell

Chapter 30

MAGGIE AND HOMER walked into the conference room to see Erwin snarling at Dan and Matt. His face was elongated into something not quite human, almost rubbery, twisting and stretching into ever-changing contortions. Ina was staring at him, looking stricken at what she was witnessing. She moved to help, but Rachel and Stella held her back. Tears were pouring down her face as she watched her only surviving family twist and writhe in the demon's fight against the men of God.

An other-worldly voice spoke through Erwin's mouth, deep and guttural; incredibly loud and with a weird multiplicity, seemingly as if thousands of people spoke in unison, "He's mine! You won't have him!" Erwin threw back his head, impossibly far, and roared with anger; then, he looked straight at Ina and the other women, seeming to grow bigger as they watched, still snarling, but with a too-wide triumphant smirk that could only be described as completely evil. Vile filth about what he—the demon—wanted to do with them, and to them— individually, and all together—but especially Ina—spewed out in explicit detail.

None of them were rookies, but even Stella and Maggie turned pale at what was being described. No woman should ever have to hear such disgusting suggestions, but especially not from your grandson. All knew it wasn't Erwin speaking, but it still seemed that way.

"Get Ina out of here!" Dan instructed Stella. But as they turned to go, Maggie was given a word from the Lord. "No!!"

she screamed loud enough to be heard over the graphic descriptions still pouring out of Erwin's mouth. "She has to stay; it's vital she be here."

Dan looked at Maggie in shock. All knew of Maggie's ability to hear from the Lord, and have visions, but she'd never been so forceful about it. "Maggie, she's, his grandmother; she shouldn't have to listen to this foul garbage!"

Maggie understood, but God had spoken firmly. "Dan, I don't know why, but God said she has to be here." She looked at Ina with compassion, concerned for her.

Ina was horrified, both at the sight before her, and the awful propositions the entity spewed at her. Then, remembering what Sherman had long ago shared with her—that she'd never fully believed—about what it was like to be in Erwin's place; trapped inside your own body as another entity took it over completely; helpless, and unable to take back control, as her beloved husband had been once been—she straightened up to her full height.

In fury, she shook her finger at the demon speaking through Erwin, and very firmly, and just as loudly, screamed, "Shut your filthy mouth, you demon from hell! I won't listen to your filth! In the name of Jesus, BE SILENT!"

The words shut off mid-sentence. Erwin's mouth clamped shut so tight his lips turned blue. He wrestled trying to open it again, his eyes turning solid black once more. Rage rippled across his face, and the cords stood out in his neck, while the veins in his arms became larger, dark purple, and prominent. If you've never seen a demon silenced by a mad woman of God, there are no words to adequately convey the fury and the instantaneous inability to speak.

Maggie stepped up beside Ina and pointed directly at the black eyes glaring at the women. "You will not speak. You will not run. You will not hurt one person." And, as Erwin began to heave, like he was about to retch, she went on, "You will not vomit. You will submit to the Spirit of the Living God." She never raised her voice, but the authority—granted by the Holy Spirit of Jesus Himself—was unmistakable. She glanced at Jake, who, remembering their instruction from the night of their being given their joint mission, stepped up beside her.

"Erwin, I know you can hear me. You need to understand what's happening. The ritual you were in bound a demonic spirit to you. We can make it leave, but I need you to tell me you want it to go. This is a true battle for the kingdom right to own your soul. Please indicate to me that you choose the Kingdom of Heaven, then these entities with have no legal right, and they will have to go."

Erwin's head turned toward Jake. He threw back his head and cackled. The maniacal laughter was deep and frightening, then rose higher and higher to almost soprano, rising to a pitch that hurt their ears for far longer that he should have had breath in his lungs to sustain, before trailing off back into whispery words. He looked at Jake, "He's mine, he's mine, he's minemineminemineminemineminemine."

The words began to run together, with no pause. Then, it was if thousands were whispering, telling secrets, all talking at once, but there were so many voices none could understand the words. They poured out, directed at no one, but were eerie. Occasionally the eyes were just Erwin's and looked frightened, but mostly it was not him present.

The voice sounded as if it were a schizophrenic that had been locked away for a very long time, and now, was in the midst of a room of enemies.

"achildwasborn…hahahhahahah….
for…us….ggrrrrrggg….achildwasborn….he'smine….pro….mise
d   to   me…..for   us   us   us
usususususususus…..heeeeeessssss…dedicated……blood
sacrifice…..mineminemineminemine…..." hissing and wild cackles fought for dominance as Erwin's tongue continually licked his lips, and as far beyond his lips as the length allowed.

The whispery voices were not something any of them had ever heard before—with the exception, of Dan. It was exactly what he'd heard come from Sherman's mouth during his deliverance, over 50 years earlier. He knew instantly it was the same entity, and only the Holy Spirit in him kept back the fear that threatened to overtake him at what he remembered from so long ago.

Jake began to demand that the spirit come out, "Ek, ek ballo, come out of him!" Matt stepped up and his powerful voice led in prayer for the Holy One of Israel to free this tormented young man.

"HAHAHAHAHAHAHHAH...he drank the blood...he allowed me to take his body." The demon began to describe the scene with Erwin during the ceremony, leaving nothing to the imagination... everyone was sickened by the words spewing from his mouth... "go away holy man... he's tainted now... he wants us... you're too late... hahahahhahahha... he's been ours forever....sssssssssssssssssss.....hhhhhhhhhhhhhhhhhhhhhh.....g rrrgggggggg....."

"He asked Jesus for forgiveness. He belongs to the Holy One of Israel now," Jake spoke with deliberate calmness.

"NOOOOOOOOOOOOO....." the spirit began to thrash and wail, throwing Erwin around and almost off the chair, knowing what would happen to him if he lost control of Erwin. Dan grabbed him with one hand, and the chair with the other, motioning for Matt to grab the other side. A voice that sounded like gravel being dragged on asphalt came out next. "That name...don't speak that name..." Erwin's head snapped around and he looked Matt in anger... "have you come to torment us before our time...?"

Then, it looked back at Jake with utter hatred, "You won't have him... He's mine. You've been misinformed. He loves it when I take him. He loooooooves it. He's soft like a woman. He squeals like a pig, but then he asks for more. He loves the pleasure we give him. He loves the pain we inflict.

He's a worm. His warm blood runs...it's hot... and delicious... he's too dirty for you...we ruined him and now he's a vessel for us to inhabit. He loooooovvvveeeeessss it. He's too vile for that one to accept. Back off holy man, or I'll take him now, right in front of you... and you'll remember..."

"You will obey me. In the name of God Almighty, leave him!" Jake thundered; instantly angry—and afraid—at its words.

The demon began to giggle in a woman's voice, then spoke straight to Jake in the voice of Charlotte—his missing cousin—isolating him, so he was the only one who could hear. A voice Jake had longed to hear again for over 18 years filled his ears, "Oh, Jakey, you don't know what it's like to be taken by a demon. Best high of my life. If you only knew the depths of degradation I've chosen. I loooovvvvveee it, and I'll have it for all of eternity... there's soooooo many of them....... sooooo...... many......"

Jake's face tightened in a mixture of pain and anger. "Don't you dare speak to me in her blessed voice." He doubled over in pain as an invisible fist punched him in the stomach, sick at the punch, and at the picture the demon instantly projected into his mind; of his cousin begging the demons to take her in a multiple-being orgiastic debauched scene. He tried to look away from the vison, but in his horror was held immobile, and could only keep staring at the vision only he could see.

His cousin winked at him, then beckoned him to come and join the fun, suggesting ways he could participate, then laughing at his shock. Jake was torn between wanting to keep looking at her face, so long gone from his eyes, to needing to escape the awful panoramic debauchery the demon was forcing him to look at.

Maggie stepped up beside him, then slid in front of him. "You evil creature. God has defeated your master. His kingdom, and all who followed him, will be cast into the abyss. You come out of Erwin now, and set him free."

"He's mine... ahahahahahahhahah....... hhhhsssssssssssssss... miiiiiiiiinnnnnneeeee."

Erwin's tongue began to stick out as far as possible, his eyes opening impossibly into huge orbs, and his head twisted to the side alarmingly far. The inhuman cackles still poured from his lips, intermingled with the dry parchment-rubbing-on-parchment whispers. He hissed in long drawn-out sounds that turned to groans, grunts, and growls, before once again becoming words, then screams.

"I want to........" Streams of foul suggestions were once again spewing out, only this time in the dry scraping sounds ... "touch..."

Ina spoke up another time, "I said shut your filthy mouth! He belongs to Jesus. He's made his choice. You have no hold on him! He's chosen freedom."

"Your master has been defeated. You have no power here. You must leave," Maggie spoke straight to the entity. It howled in rage, reaching out to claw her, and the vision Jake had been enthralled in dissipated; Jake—released from being compelled to watch—pulled Maggie away just in time. The demon laughed with a gurgling liquid sound that turned into a shriek of delight.

It began to rub Erwin suggestively, speaking straight to Maggie, again delighting in giving explicit detail of shameless licentiousness desired.

He described much of what Jake had just seen being done to his cousin, and the panoramic vision was forced on him a second time, only now it was Maggie he was seeing with the demon; and at the look of enjoyment on her face, even though he knew it wasn't really her, he became enraged and began to scream at the demon in his fury, thrusting Maggie behind him, then began to call upon God to stop this creature before it could open the vision to her, or the other women.

Stella grabbed Rachel, then pointed at the others, "let's go to the prayer room." They nodded and left. Dan, Matt, Homer, Bobby, Maggie, Jake, and Ina were the only ones left. Dan still felt like Ina should have left too, but he trusted Maggie enough to know she wouldn't have intervened without a true word from the Lord

Jake stepped up and before he could open his mouth, the demon smiled through Erwin's lips, with a true smirk of satisfaction, "You," he pointed at Jake, "...supposedly holy man...you want to do to her the same thing I do...I can see it in you...you hypocrite...you deceiver...you liar...you're made of dust...dust and spit...you call yourself a Christian...I can smell Christian blood. It will spill. It will spill. itititwillspillspillspilllspilllspilllllllhssssssssssss...you have no power over me, man of God. I am more than a man.... Hhhhssssssssssssss ......I AM A PRINCE!!!!" His voice thundered and bounced around the room, with a ringing sound like a bell echoing.

"Our time is come. We will take back the title deed of Earth, and then you will watch me take your girlfriend in endless ways... and she'll love every second... you... unholy man... have no way to stop me... puny human......hahahahhahahahahhahahahahahahahahhhaha......"

"Jesus said: "I saw Satan fall like lightning from heaven. I have given you authority to trample on snakes and scorpions and to overcome all the power of the enemy; nothing will harm you." Jake spoke softly, but the demon went wild at his words, screaming, twisting, with murderous expressions.

"You must obey the authority of Jesus Christ," Jake went on without stopping.

Homer, glancing out the window behind them, once again, saw the enormous angels, sword-fighting the hoard of demons, with blue flames dancing down the length of the swords; and he began to describe the battle. "Even now, God's Heavenly Host are battling your dark army; they're winning too. No one can stand against the Heavenly Host. They have the power from the Throne Room and you are nothing but a vile, inferior, betrayer of all that's good.

Disgusting losers, the lot of you. Your Master will never win. You are doomed to the Abyss for all eternity. Give it up! Erwin has chosen the King of Kings, and Lord of Lords. You are defeated and have no place here. Leave at once!"

The demon twisted Erwin's head around almost 180° to look out the window. When he saw the supernatural battle in the sky and realized the demons were being driven back, he snarled and fought Matt and Dan, violently tipping the chair, and causing them to lose their grip. Laughing deliriously, he sprang to his feet and leaped onto the overturned chair, then onto Matt's shoulders, and once again, to land on the table; then began to run the length of it toward the open door at the other end.

Ina slammed and locked the door just as he leaped toward the opening. He slammed against it and bounced back, knocking her to the floor. He grabbed her around the neck and began to squeeze. "You! You spoke to him from the hated book! You're trying to steal him! He's mine! You will die now!"

Ina's face began to turn blue, but her eyes shown with a love that nothing but a mother—or a child of God—could have generated, or conveyed. Unable to talk, she began to hum. In spite of having no air intake the humming became louder. It was a lullaby she used to hum to Erwin when he was an infant and small child.

She stared straight into Erwin's eyes, looking past the demon who was looking at her with such hatred, trying to reach him in the only way she could while unable to speak.

Maggie instantly understood what was happening and quietly spoke to Jake, who took authority, once again speaking in a normal voice, but confidently, "Erwin, we need you right now.

This demon is killing your grandmother. Take control of your own hands, and release her, or she will die."

Maggie, at the same time, was calling upon God to save Ina. She stepped up behind her, and she too looked straight into the demon's eyes. "You are defeated. You *will* release her now. You have *no authority here*. COME OUT OF HIM, YOU UNCLEAN SPIRIT!!"

The demon roared in anger, speaking once again with the strange multiplicity, the words so loud they echoed off the walls, "Who are *you* whore, to speak to *me*?" He leaned close enough for her to feel spittle hitting her face with each word. "You are nothing but a woman; and a filthy, unclean woman. I *know your secrets*!"

Maggie knew what he was going to say before it left his mouth. "You killed your own daughter!"

Ina's eyes grew wider, and Dan looked stunned. Matt stared at Maggie in shock. Jake, who'd so recently learned the truth, and Maggie's feeling of shame for not protecting her unborn child, reached for her in concern, while at the same time, shaking his head in denial toward the others. But Maggie knew the tricks of the enemy; how they tempt, throw down, choke, make sick, grab, taunt, seek to create fear, curiosity, or, like now, create doubt in other people's minds.

They pull, seduce, whisper, and accuse. They are truly their fathers' sons. She didn't falter. "You *will not* falsely accuse me, devil! You know the rules. Erwin has chosen the creator. He has rejected you and your master. You have no more legal right here. You must leave now. For this purpose, the Son of God was revealed, that he might destroy the works of the devil."

The evil entity became enraged anew at her words, then suddenly shifted tactics. He released Ina and turned to Maggie. With great seductiveness, his face becoming a version of what it would have been before he chose to follow Lucifer in rebellion, he became a shining 'angel of light' before their eyes.

None of them saw the twin spirits, Illusion and Confusion, step from between the veils into the room; sent by the dragon himself to try to hold onto Erwin long enough, so they could get him out of here, and finish the long-planned sacrifice for power and revenge.

He stepped up close as He looked at Maggie with great compassion, dropping to his knees before her, his face a vision of rugged masculine beauty, and speaking with more kindness than she'd ever heard, "Your greatest longing is to once again be a mother to your children.

I can whisper in their ears and bring them back to you. I can show them all the lies of your ex-husband, and prove to them who destroyed your family. I can bring them today. I can show you your grandchild *right this minute*, but you have to allow me to stay with Erwin, and show your appreciation at my gift by bowing down to me.

Before she could respond, the two new spirits wove a spell around Maggie that made her lose consciousness of the people around her, and what they were battling. It was as if she were entirely alone and about to have her greatest prayer answered by God himself. One touched her chest, straight through to her heart; then her head, reaching inside to touch her brain, first activating the tormenting memories, then, where the emotions that hurt her the most over the years of loss were stored; he ramped up the desire to see and know her grandchild to the highest point of longing possible.

He finally nodded to the entity that had taken over Erwin, who then began to speak in twilight language, and a light began to grow in the center of the room, enlarging into a doorway that opened into a room where Maggie's daughter and grandchild were. She looked at her daughter, filling her eyes with her child; then saw her grandchild for the first time ever, and watched as the little girl looked up and saw her.

The child smiled hugely, and started to run toward Maggie with arms reaching up in the age-old entreaty to be picked up. "Gamma! You're here!" Maggie reacted instantly, running toward the child who was running toward her. Just before they met, Jake's eyes were opened so he could see what was happening, and his voice rang out urgently, "Maggie, it's a lie!"

Both she and the child stopped at the sound of his voice. Maggie looked at the child—who teared up at the harshness she perceived in Jake's tone—then looked up at Jake, who'd moved beside her. She looked at Jake for long seconds in total confusion, then looked back at the child, who was trembling, but still reaching out for her, clearly wanting Maggie to comfort her, tears beginning to pour down her face; and Maggie took a step toward her, but then Jake spoke directly to her with extreme gentleness.

"Mags, it's not real. It's a vision. It's deception." He pulled her close, looking directly into her eyes, and deliberately stepping between her and the vision. "We were warned to 'be not deceived.' He's tapping into your greatest wound and longings. It's not real. You have to reject this. Remember, he took Jesus himself to the top of a very high mountain and showed Him all the kingdoms of the world and their grandeur, and said to Him, 'All these things I will *give* You, if You will fall down and worship me.'"

Maggie stared at him, and a buzzing started in her head that made it increasingly hard to hear his words. She could see his lips moving, but no sound reached her. She tried hard to remember what he'd said to her, but all she could hear was her granddaughter's crying and calling out to her, "Gamma, hold me. Gamma… pease….," she begged, still holding her arms up for Maggie to take her.

Maggie tried to move around Jake to get to her grandchild; "Gramma's here, baby. I've got you…"

"Maggie, it's not your grandchild; it's a demonic entity."

"Jake, I can see her! She's standing right there!" Maggie screamed, and pointed around behind him, frustrated tears falling at his interference, "she's looking right at me!"

"It's not real, Mags. It's an illusion," his eyes filled with tears at her pain. Everyone else just stood frozen, realizing what was happening by their words.

"Jesus really saw the kingdoms of the world, Jake."

"And it was a temptation, Mags. He was being tempted to accept what he wanted from the devil, instead of waiting for God to give it to him His way, and in His timing, or having to go through the way of the cross."

"Jake, please….." she begged him, "I've waited so long….."

"I know Mags, but this isn't real. It isn't of God. It's a trick. A delusion. We're trying to cast out a demon for God's sake. Mags, remember where you are, and what's happening here." The look of intense concern on his face bothered her. She looked around at the people in the room, confused.

Ina couldn't see what they were seeing, but she could hear Jake and Maggie's words. She began to whisper, *'Jesus...Jesus...Jesus*...then louder and louder, *Jesus...Jesus...Jesus...'*

Homer—with his new-found vision—*could* see what they saw, and heard the captivating persuasion that was compelling Maggie. He too could see the small child, who clearly had a familial look of Maggie to her. He came to stand alongside Jake, closing off all sight of the child to Maggie, and looking Maggie right in the eyes, "Maggie, what did Jesus say? What was his answer when he was tempted by Satan?"

Maggie looked up at him, barely hearing his voice over the buzzing that was increasing again in volume. "What, Homer? I can't understand your words."

Ina began to speak in tongues; given the words by the Holy Spirit. She spoke in perfect paleo-Hebrew words, that only Jake could understand—first to the evil spirit, "In the Name of Jesus, STOP THIS PERVERSION!" Then in entreaty to God, "Give her ears to hear and eyes to see."

Homer grabbed Maggie's arms, and then—suddenly seeing a bright gold heavenly cord that bound Maggie and Jake as one—wrapped his arms around both her and Jake, pulling them both to him into a tight squeeze.

He glanced around the room and spied Illusion and Confusion trying to hide behind the other people, as they were realizing he could see them. He looked at Maggie and took her hand. Maggie, you can see the supernatural realm. As of today, you know I've been able to also. Look at something for me, ok?"

Maggie nodded and both she and Jake allowed him to turn them around. He pointed straight at the two cowering spirits. "See them, Maggie? That's why you're seeing your grandchild. They are creating an illusion for you.

I'm not saying they don't have the power to make a rent in the vail and you're not actually seeing where she's at, and she's seeing you, but it's a vision to cause you to give in to the lie. Maggie, you're a mother, and they're using that to offer you all you want in this life. What did Jesus say to Satan when he received the offer of all the kingdoms of the world?"

Suddenly, Maggie could hear him clearly. From years of bible study, the words came instantly to her: "Away from here, Satan! For it is written, 'You shall worship the Lord your God, and Him only shall you serve."

The demon screamed in amplified volumes of pure rage, and the doorway snapped shut; then—tearing Erwin's body—the spirit that had been bound to him, immediately left him. He left so quickly that Erwin fell. Matt and Dan caught him and eased him to the floor. Illusion and Confusion instantly vanished as well. Everyone was stunned by what had just taken place.

Maggie blinked her eyes several times, trembling at how close she'd come to giving in, and Jake wrapped her in his strong embrace, still concerned for her well-being, and still sick at what he'd been shown.

Erwin began to cough and cough, choking as other demons began to panic when their 'strongman' vacated the 'home' they'd inhabited for years. Blood trickled out of his stomach from where the demon had exited, so they called for Stella.

Dan, who'd seen this before with Sherman, began to order the other demons out, demanding that they do no more bodily injury. One-by-one they left Erwin, who was coughing, burping, or jerking violently as they did so. The rest prayed and took authority, adding the weight of their combined determination to Dan's commands, praising God as each one left.

They finally got enough of them out that Stella was able to get close enough to put some lidocaine on his stomach, and stitch up the small wound, then tape a bandage on it. Erwin fought her at first, but then thanked her.

As he became more and more free, Erwin's face took on a peacefulness that Ina had not seen since he was 7 years old. When they were sure all the spirits they could detect were gone, Jake and Maggie began to teach Erwin what he needed to do to stay free, tutoring him in demonic 'legal rights' and what he'd done to allow them entry.

They questioned him as to the behavior and choices that would cause them to return, and not only them, but seven more, more wicked than themselves, would come back, and warned him that he would be in far worse condition than he'd been in before.

Erwin, finally beginning to understand what it was like to be free from their constant presence—and the depression, dependance, and evil desires they'd created; and able to hear the Holy Spirit so clearly—assured them that he had no intention of ever doing those things again. Some of them had been there so long, he didn't remember a time when they weren't there. Jake demanded some of their names, and it was clear they'd come when his parents died.

Fear. Confusion. Anger. Pain. Loss of trust. Inferiority. Loneliness. Hopelessness. Timidity. Intimidation. Heartache. Others had come with sin. Jezebel. Ahab. Addiction. Perversion. Deviancy. Still others from rituals. Tolerance of abuse. Secrecy. Higher levels of deviancy. Deeper levels of fear. Lies. Witchcraft. Leviathan. Chaos. Bondage.

He smiled more and more as they left him, and he began to discern when another was cowering, trying to stay hidden so it wouldn't be cast out. He was having none of it, and let the group know its name each time. When he realized they—the humans who accepted God's gift of salvation—had the real authority, and were able to make the evil spirits leave, he begged them to not stop until he was entirely free; he wanted them all gone.

He was *done* with it all. With each departing spirit, he stood straighter, and felt more like his own individual self—more like a grown man—than he ever had.

After all the demons they could discern were gone, they prayed to break soul-ties; to Billy, to the coven, and to all the women—and now men—that he'd had sexual relations with. He was becoming free, and when God sets you free, he makes you free indeed. After he'd confessed everything, the others came back into the room to continue to pray and praise the Lord as a group.

They quickly realized that he had no memory of the vileness of earlier, and collectively chose not to enlighten him. Instead, they led him in another prayer of repentance and surrender, and spoke to him about allegiance to the one true God and obedience to His word. They outlined a simple beginning plan to systematically study the bible and then Matt, Dan, and Homer pledged their support and all offered to be his stand-in 'father,' 'uncle,' and 'brother.' All knew Jake would be actively involved as well, even before he too spoke up, offering his help.

All the others offered their friendship and let him know that they all watched each other's back as a way of life. He could call on any of them whenever he wanted or needed too. He was part of God's family now, and so were they; so, they were now heavenly brothers and sisters, and he was their family.

Dan, nodded at Matt, who went to the kitchen, and brought back the elements of the Lord's supper, he'd prepared earlier, and they all took communion. Afterward, they once again asked Jesus to bind the enemy, and close off the ears of the denizens of darkness, and cloak Erwin so the enemy couldn't find him.

They rejoiced, and praised the Lord for Erwin's deliverance from the hands of the enemy. Then, one-by-one, they began to leave and go back to their responsibilities, and after most had left, Dan, Matt, Jake, Bobby, and Homer gave him the nitty gritty details of what was planned for him by the coven.

Fear tried to fill him again, but a new strength and courage arose in Erwin, and he would not let it happen. He asked the group to pray with him for Billy's salvation, but understood completely, that, at this time, Billy was his enemy. He accepted the offer to work and live at the ranch. They agreed to move he and Ina in next week, but in the meantime, some of them would accompany them home that day to pack a bag, and they would stay with Dan until the move. None were willing to take a chance with Erwin's life.

Ina, while sad at leaving the home she'd shared with her husband, was so grateful for this group of people who'd protected her grandchild, that she vowed to work with them to fight the enemy for the rest of her life. "Can we just move it all immediately?"

"Of course, we can," Dan and Matt spoke at once, before she had time to reconsider.

Before Maggie and Jake left, Ina told them she knew why God had kept her in the room. She confessed to them all, her skepticism and almost outright denial of belief in Sherman's stories of what he'd been through; how she'd treated him through the years and discouraged him when he'd wanted to help others. She knew he was a good man, and never lied; but still, the supernatural aspects had been hard to swallow—until today—when she'd experienced all that he'd described, and then some.

Her neck was already turning purple with bruises, and she had a hard time speaking. She was still a bit light-headed from lack of oxygen in the long seconds the demon had choked her; they had to tell Erwin that awful part of what had taken place, to explain the bruises. He was shocked, apologetic, and enraged that the enemy had used his body to try to kill his grandmother. If he'd ever had an inkling of drifting back into the old lifestyle, that knowledge alone would make him stop and turn around.

Ina knew if she'd left the room, she wouldn't have the new knowledge and understanding of the real enemy that she now had; and she wouldn't have been onboard with moving to the ranch. God had to show her the plain ugly truth—up close, and personal, almost dying in the process—to open her unbelieving eyes. She realized how much ministry Sherman could have done, if she'd believed and supported him.

He'd shared many times how he wanted to help others be free, but she'd wanted none of it. Now, she was determined to do what she had kept Sherman from doing. She thanked Maggie for intervening, and Maggie hugged her close, now understanding why God had been so insistent about Ina staying.

They all knew this wasn't over. The coven would retaliate, and that all of them must stay vigilant in the coming days. Evil was ramping up all around the world, and the pocket of entrenched evil here was being emboldened and energized by it, like the spirit of iniquity itself were close and targeting them specifically. This battle may have been won, and the final battle already decreed as won, but all of them knew there would be many skirmishes before that day.

Erwin knew too much; they had spent years planning for this sacrifice, and they would do all in their collective power to keep their plans. Erwin—and everyone close to any of them—must be protected, as over a century of happenings had proven that all were in immediate and dire danger.

Their final prayer was for the hand of protection to be on each one, and for God to put a hedge of protection and a group of the heavenly host around them all.

Matt left the room to call Dana, Levi, and Ryan to warn them to be vigilant; he also asked both his siblings to come for a family meeting that Friday night, then spoke with Zach and Sarah, his parents. He'd decided—test, or no test—It was time to tell his family about Missy.

Dan called to check on Clayton and the ranch hands; then they loaded up Ina and Erwin, and instructed other workers to get the truck, and follow them, so they go get what they would need for the next few days, and complete the move. Others would follow in their own vehicles, then go on with their afternoon, as if the holiday planning session were ended as usual, and Dan sent another two men to follow Homer back to the store.

... meanwhile... in the supernatural...

Inferiority was cast out so fast he went rolling like a soccer ball that'd been kicked. He rolled straight into Illusion, sending him rolling too. Rage roared with anger at Intimidation. *"Look what you've caused! You kept him from a complete allegiance to the Master! He should have been brought into the deeper mysteries and rituals so he was bound forever! HEADS WILL ROLL!!!! You slimy pack of sewer rats!!"*

"And you..." he pointed to Confusion *"... how was he able to read the cursed book? It was your job to make sure he couldn't understand the words. WHERE WERE YOU LAST NIGHT?!!!"*

Confusion cowed back away from Rage. *"I couldn't get near him. His grandmother prayed all night. Warriors were all around him, the house, and her; and she prayed for a hedge of protection. An entire regiment was sent out. There were too many."* He, like the others, was trembling in fear; at being exposed, at being cast out, and more importantly, it happening even as the sacrificial ceremony was being planned. Many had been routed in battle this day.

He turned to the others standing around watching. He pointed at the legions of black-clad, winged ones, who were supposed to keep the Shining Ones away while they stole Erwin back from the enemy. *"YOU,"* he shouted, pointing at them all as he turned first one way, and then the other. *"It was YOUR job to clear the air of the enemy so confusion could create a smoke-screen!"*

He pointed next at Lightning, the runner. *"You were supposed to get him out of that truck before they ever got on the ranch, or in the house! You were supposed to make him flee before he got in the truck. Where were you?!"*

All hell literally erupted at his accusations. It was a free-for-all as they all simultaneously and viciously hurled accusations; and then became an all-out brawl as each one tried to blame others for the failure. It didn't stop until a higher-level demon stepped between the veil and roared at them all.

"SILENCE! You are all at fault!"

This was a simple mission. It's been an easy mission for almost 20 years. HOW DARE YOU ALLOW IT FAIL JUST AS IT NEARS THE TIME!!"

"You will take him back by the sacrificial time, or you will spend all eternity regretting it!"

"YOU," he roared at Confusion. *"You will close his eyes of understanding."* He then pointed to Distraction, *"You will cause all around him to lose focus on him, and him to lose focus on everything; take away all ability to read the accursed book and any comprehension." You,"* he sneered at Addiction, *"you will create a hunger for drugs and alcohol. And none of this namby-pamby recreational junk. I want him to CRAVE it, day, and night. Relentless cravings. I want WITHDRAWALS with the shakes, the sickness; I want it all."*

He turned to Jezebel, *"... and You; You will visit him at night as a succubus, feeding his desires, and fulfilling them all. Lead him deeper and deeper, until he is wrapped up so tight, he can't get out! He gets no sleep. No rest of any kind. Give him visions. Remind him of girls he's been with. Drive him crazy with uncontrolled lust."*

"And you, Hopelessness... you... you have a special job........ he needs to believe that he's wasted too much time to ever recover anything good with his life. I want him convinced he's a loser; he's a weakling; he's nobody. He's nothing without Billy... I want every bit of self-esteem GONE! I want the whole thing thrown at him. And you'd better make it good."

He spoke twilight language and called up Suicide from the ether. *"You will go with Hopelessness. You press him. You tag-team him. You magnify anything Hopelessness does, and you watch for an opening. I don't care how minute the crack, YOU PRESS IN as soon as it happens.*

If we can't gut him, on the altar, we will have him slice his own throat, or eat a bullet. Make sure those around him are careless with their weapons. He's the last of that accursed line, and the INFERNAL ONE has issued the decree that HE WILL BE THE LAST! DO YOU UNDERSTAND ME?!!"

He looked around at all the other imps present. "Every last thing we've used against humans for the last 6,000 years. Every. Last. One. I want them thrown at this miserable worm, the people around him, and the circle of friends, family, and acquaintances of every one in that house. DO YOU HEAR ME?!!!!?""

All were shaking from their hideous heads to their oversized ugly feet with the long, curved claws. One—too stupid to be as afraid as he needed to be—finally actually raised his hand, to be recognized. The prince looked him over, wanting badly to send him to the abyss on the spot, decided instead to see what he had to say. "What do *you* want, you hellish half-breed spawn of humanity?"

The imp, realizing he'd been better off silent, suddenly had trouble getting the words out. "I... I... I..."

"WHAT?!! Just spit it out! Or has your tongue already been removed, spawn?" He flicked out his index finger and a razor-sharp talon pointed at the trembling creature. "If not, I can take care of it now..."

"I... I... I... could... enter a dog... or a horse... or something... and cause him injury....." the imp finally stammered out his idea. "Maybe rip his throat out, or buck him off and break his neck."

"Hmmmmm......that's not bad; you, ugly pipsqueak... there may be hope for you yet......

... do that... and if you cause serious injury... there may be a raise for you in the future... and if you can accomplish his death, you will earn a position of authority for the rest of eternity."

At that, the other imps were filled with a jealous rage. The worst among them volunteering for a mission to possess an animal, something all of them hated to be assigned to, made them look bad, and at least half of them decided on the spot to thwart his endeavor so he wouldn't get ahead of them. None

BOOK 1: "PREPARE FOR THE END" SERIES

even considered what would happen to them when the prince found out. Hell's army is as much its own enemy as it is the enemy of humanity. It was just their nature; and betrayal is the currency of their kingdom.

All left, defeated for the time being; and knowing the consequences of failure, hid out in the world of men, too afraid to go to the second heaven and face the ONE.

Chosen for a Purpose

Chapter 31

"FRANKIE, WAKE UP!"

"… ummm…." Frankie stirred, but then immediately fell back asleep. Snoring softly, he was out.

"Frankie. WAKE UP! You must come with me."

The commanding tone of the voice brought Frankie instantly awake. He opened his eyes, not moving a muscle. He wasn't sure what was happening, or who was speaking to him, but he knew it wasn't Diane. He kept perfectly still and listened, not sure if they were in danger, or not.

"FRANKIE! Come with me," he heard from his right.

He looked over, responding to the command, even as his heart beat faster that someone was in the room. He grew completely still again at what he saw. Just inside the bedroom door there was a man. He was very large, and was… the only way he could describe it was… glowing… in the dark. It wasn't a bright shine like a flashlight, but just enough that Frankie could make out what he looked like; more like the shine of phosphorescence in a cave.

He had on some type of shiny silver suit, with a metal breastplate and a short leather-like skirt; like a modern-day armor, that reflected the soft blueish light. He held a huge sword down by his side, and around his head was a metal band, like a prince would wear, that also reflected the shine. His hair was longer, very blond, and, while his face was intense—and he looked like someone you didn't want to mess with—he didn't look as if he wanted to hurt them, just get Frankie's attention. He beckoned for Frankie to get out of bed and come with him.

For some reason, Frankie wasn't afraid, and he knew he was supposed to go with the man. He looked over at Diane, and as he did the man spoke again. "She'll be alright. Her guardian is

353

here." He pointed toward Diane's side of the bed, and another huge man was standing there with a sword like the one the first man was wearing, only his was held in his hand with the blade in the air, blue flames danced along its length, and he had the stance of someone on high alert.

Frankie was confused, but intrigued. "Come on. He's waiting for us." The blond man urged.

Frankie climbed out of bed, reached down, and pulled on the pants he'd been wearing earlier; and grabbing the t-shirt off the chair beside the bed, he pulled it over his head, then added the flannel shirt hung on the back of chair, buttoning it, as he tried to figure out what was happening.

He glanced again at the second man, who looked like a cross between an ancient warrior, and some kind of futuristic one; and the warrior nodded at him, and said, "Don't worry about her. I've kept her safe her entire life. Nothing will harm her. You are needed. I'll be here."

Weird as it was, Frankie knew the warrior was telling the truth. He grabbed his socks and sneakers and followed the first warrior out of the room. He sat down on the couch and put on his shoes, with the warrior waiting somewhat impatiently.

As soon as he tied the second one, the warrior said, "We must go now. It's the appointed time." He waved his hand and a doorway opened in the room, light spilling from it, and motioned for Frankie to follow him. As soon as they cleared the doorway into a corridor, he waved the door shut, then took off at a brisk pace.

"Where are we going?" Frankie wondered what this dream was. He'd had interesting dreams before, but this one was very different. He couldn't wait to tell Diane in the morning.

"You've been summoned."

"Summoned?" Frankie wasn't sure if he needed to laugh or be worried. "By who?"

"The Angel of the Lord."

"What?"

"The Angel of the Lord."

"Does he have a name? And, for that matter, do you?" Frankie at least wanted to know who he was dealing with.

"I am Gabriel. He will introduce himself."

"Gabriel? Like in the Christmas story, Gabriel?" Frankie wasn't sure what was going on. This dream was getting weirder by the moment. Probably from his dad urging him to come to church and become a Christian, he decided.

"Come. We must hurry." He stepped up the pace, each stride eating up a large portion of the floor, as they moved along.

Frankie felt his urgency, and knowing how dreams are, he followed him, somehow keeping up the pace. They walked for what seemed like a couple of miles, but the warrior didn't speak again, and neither did Frankie. Instead, he tried to figure out where they were, where they were going, and why he particularly, had been summoned.

Finally, they stood outside a huge double door. Gabriel waited until it began to open. He stepped inside, then moved aside for Frankie to join him, and as the door closed behind them, he bowed low to the man standing in front of them.

The man was simply dressed in a long white robe, but had a regal bearing about him. He too was wearing a diadem around his forehead, only his was gold instead of silver. He had a blue sash around his waist and some type of soft leather boots, also blue. He had long wavy brown hair, deep brown eyes, and looked Jewish.

He nodded at the warrior, accepting the bow, then turned to Frankie, who—although he'd never done it in his life—felt compelled to bow as well. He rose from the bow and glanced up in time to see a slight smile on the man's face and a mischievous twinkle in his eye.

"Well done, my friend," He smiled. "Thank you for coming."

Frankie looked at him, wondering where he'd seen him before. He was very familiar, but Frankie couldn't place him.

He gestured to a group of chairs set close together. "Come, let's talk."

They sat, then he looked at Frankie very seriously, and spoke once again. "I've been wanting for you to get to know me, for some time; I'm glad you're here."

It was an odd greeting, and Frankie thought most people would have phrased it differently, more like "I've been wanting to get to know you."

The man smiled again. "I already know you. You know about me, but you don't know me. Yet. But, you will."

Frankie wondered if he could read minds.

"Yes. I can." The man was openly laughing now.

"How do you know me?" Frankie asked. "You look familiar, but I can't remember meeting you."

"I met you when you were a baby. I blessed you as my father tasked you. I've waited for a minute or two for you to be ready." His amusement was growing at Frankie's confusion. He looked like he laughed often, with his smile ready to widen at any given moment.

Frankie looked at him more closely. He looked the same age as Frankie. "How could you have known me as a baby. You had to have been a baby also."

The man grinned again. "Let me introduce myself. It will clear everything up." He held out his hand to Frankie, and as he reached to shake it, he saw the scar of what must have been a terrible wound. "Hi. You can call me Jesus."

In the span of one heartbeat, Frankie put it together. "Jesus. *The* Jesus?"

"Well, you can call me Yashua; or, the Angel of the Lord. Or, maybe you would prefer—and he somehow made his voice ring loud and echo around the room, like in a giant echoing chamber—the Ancient of Days. Some call me first, some call me last." He was openly laughing now, enjoying himself at Frankie's expense.

"Some call me Alpha, some Omega. I've even been called the 'bread of life,' Wonderful, Counsellor; The mighty God; The everlasting Father, The Prince of Peace, The Holy One of Israel, (but some didn't call me that; actually, quite the opposite)," he winked, as he snickered at Frankie's expression.

Frankie's mouth fell open in astonishment—both at who he was talking to—and at how comfortable and easy he was to be with. Frankie was speechless at his teasing, and rendered in stitches at his making fun of his titles. He laughed with him.

"What do you prefer to be called?"

"My favorite is "Immanuel.""

"God with us." Frankie remembered that from when he went to the Christmas Cantatas with his parents.

BOOK 1: "PREPARE FOR THE END" SERIES

"Yes. I enjoyed living amongst humanity, and look forward to doing it again. I sometimes miss it, and couldn't help teasing you like I used to do with my friends when I lived there." He smiled again, then suddenly turned more serious.

"Frankie. I know you haven't yet made up your mind about me, but I've seen you moving nearer to doing so. You have free will, like all humans, and I have a task for you. You can accomplish the first part of it adequately either way, but if you'll accept me and let me help you, it will go much smoother and I can bless you mightily, and the second part will be impossible without me."

Frankie too, had a sense of humor. "Well, a personal invitation to your home is moving me way forward in believing you are real."

Jesus totally cracked up. "Yes. That was a little unorthodox. I've been known to show up unexpectantly, here and there, throughout the centuries, to call men to tasks; this time it was more efficient to just have you brought here."

He then looked more serious, and transformed before Frankie's eyes into a being that could only be God Almighty, the Ancient of Days. Frankie fell to his knees, then flat out on his face, unable to even look at him. He felt a power fill the room and the light was so intense he stayed on his face for long minutes, unable to get up or open his eyes.

He heard a voice, booming and intimate at the same time. "Arise, before me." Frankie slowly stood, spellbound by the voice and the personage before him. "Frankie. Time grows short until the end. Evil grows exponentially. If you'll read my book, it's all in there, just as your dad and Bobby have told you; and the men whose podcasts you've been listening to for months has confirmed it to you over, and over again. The enemy plans to starve my people. He's making plans to shut down the food supply. While the food is available, it needs to be preserved. It must last a bit over seven years.

I've placed the answer in Nate's hands to be brought to you, and he's already done that. It will take both of you and your wives, along with various family members and friends, to make it happen. If you'll accept the task, and accept my gift of salvation, I will bless the work of your hands. I need you to know this as well. Your child is special. He will be born in a time of great upheaval in the land. The adversary is killing my little ones, and changing the very DNA I created for humans into something else.

This was first done before the flood, and again after it. In my book, it tells you that it will once again be 'as in the days of Noah' right before I come back. Once again, he is trying to wipe out humanity and wipe out prophecy. He believes if he can create a way for scripture to be broken that he will defeat my father. Salvation is only for humanity, and if people are no longer human it doesn't apply. He knows that.

Evil arises in a form that humanity has not dealt with openly for millennia. You will help fight the ones that serve them. Do Not Delay in preparation. Do Not Be Distracted. Soon, there, will be few real children left, indeed few humans at all. Read the book of Revelation. I gave it to my friend John to write down for just this time. Add up the percentages of people who will die. It's moving toward it rapidly, and the final days have begun.

Most of the children that will be born—few though they will be—will have a different DNA, not the DNA that I created. Do not allow this child to be vaccinated. Not the current vaccination, and not the others. You don't allow your family to take any of it. I will keep you healthy, as long as you obey me.

Keep your child away from these hybrid children as well, no matter what. Great evil is coming, beyond anything the world has ever known. You will also be tied to another special child. Guard that one as your own, as well. They want her. You cannot let that happen.

Frankie. Will you feed my sheep?"

That phrase sounded familiar to Frankie too. He thought maybe he'd heard it in church, but wasn't sure. He was afraid to ask. He knew, from earlier in the discussion, this was the same Jesus that appeared as a man who walked the earth, friendly and fun; but this was also God Himself… with no playing around.

"I'm trying to find the funds to buy the module Nate told me about. We're going today to look at it," Frankie explained.

"I will provide. Just trust me. Frankie, will you feed my sheep?" Jesus was sincerely asking, not demanding.

"If you will provide the funds, I'll do the work as long as I can," Frankie agreed.

"There's more." Jesus looked even more intense, his eyes like fire, as he looked into Frankie's. "The house that bears my name is corrupt. The shepherds gather for themselves and starve my children. I need a man who is not afraid to speak truth; who's not afraid to preach my word. Who believes I will both provide and protect, as he does my will on Earth. I will send you helpers.

You will become a faithful servant, and join a group of Godly men. I've begun to bring many home who have been faithful, but I need someone for such a time as this. Wickedness grows daily. Most are lost and need salvation. I'm calling you to feed people physically with the food for the body, and to feed them spiritually with the Word of Life. Will you proclaim my Word, Frankie? Will you feed my sheep?"

"You're calling me to preach?!" Frankie was incredulous. "I don't even go to church!"

"The church is corrupt. The days of the penned-up sheep are over. You will find my sheep in the highways and byways, wounded and bleeding. You will bring to them the life-giving words of truth. Lead them to Me. I will save them. If you trust me, I will heal them. You will be my instrument. I've given you a human teacher, along with my spirit. If you'll steep yourself in my Word, allow my Spirit to lead and guide you, obey me, and thoroughly trust me, I will do the work.

You'll see people healed like in the times of the early apostles. You'll see miracles that will draw people to me. It can't be a business based on making money, but a ministry based on feeding humanity and opening a door to lead them to me."

"Jesus...um...Lord...Immanuel, I'm not sure about that part. I'm unworthy. Surely you know that."

Jesus smiled again and patted him on the shoulder. Frankie felt the vast power in the hand that touched him. He felt it go throughout his body, up through his brain, implanting something there, and finally it settled in his heart. He felt it take root and begin to grow. It was the fire from Jesus' eyes, and he knew he'd never be the same. "When you get in my Word, you'll see that some of my best friends said the same thing. Moses, Gideon...I'll let you find the rest. I'll be right there the entire time, if you'll accept me."

"How can I refuse?" Frankie felt the rightness of it in his very soul. "I'm not perfect though."

BOOK 1: "PREPARE FOR THE END" SERIES

He saw the being start shimmering, and he saw them all somehow. He saw the Father standing there, tasking him; he saw the power that looked like a spirit that touched what the Father had placed in his head, and a fire was kindled in the place in his heart; and he heard the words 'it's my job to teach you, and bring you into all wisdom,' in the smallest of whispers. 'I will never leave you, nor forsake you,' and finally, he saw the Jesus who walked the earth again, and once again he spoke to him.

"Neither were they," Jesus laughed. "James and John got so mad they wanted to call down lighting on an entire town. Elijah whipped the prophets of Baal in a head-to-head confrontation over which of us was really God, then got scared of Jezebel and hid for days... I'm sure you've heard... I actually had to send birds to feed him... Moses had a few issues too. Just wait till you read their stories." He spoke with such affection for people whose names Frankie knew were in the bible, and that was comforting to Frankie.

"Are you sure?" Frankie asked. "What if I let you down? What if I fail?"

Once again, Jesus shimmered, and he saw the vastness of the universe reflected in the eyes of the father, and he could see the beginning of time, and all the endless years, down to the end of time. It was the briefest of moments, but it imprinted on Frankie's mind. He saw an enormous book, with words in some language he'd never seen.

He couldn't read it, or even see it all, but he plainly saw his own birth, and being tasked before his spirit left the place where it was created, and before being implanted in his physical body; he saw his calling, and that it wasn't by accident, or happenstance.

He had been created to do what he had been called to do; and he saw that he would be completely able to do it. He wouldn't be able to remember the details later, but he couldn't ever forget that it was there, in the father's eyes... and in the plans laid out from the beginning.

"Very sure my child. All I ask is that you repent and be baptized in my name. Give your allegiance to me and the Kingdom of Heaven. Follow my ways, and let go of the things of the world. In a very short time this will all be over and we'll have eternity for you to get to know me better, but the next few years will be very hard for most people. It will take men and women of faith and backbone to make it through; and someone has to feed my sheep. Will it be you?"

"If you'll have me, I'll do my best." Frankie was weeping as he bowed again, this time knowing who he was bowing to, and why he was doing it. He determined in his heart right then and there, to be faithful to the calling.

"I'll have your guardian take you back. And Frankie, soon it will look like all is lost; like I have abandoned you. You will be despised for my namesake; the world will hate you, because it hates me. You'll see death everywhere. You will be hunted by the enemy. Doubt will be sown into your heart and mind. Many whom you now call friend will abandon you, even some you truly love. Your guardian will be near, and prayer will accomplish much.

Faith will move mountains. Call upon me and ask for what you need. It may not come exactly as you asked, but I need you to trust me that I know what is best. It will look like I'm not answering. There's a reason. Creation itself will groan before I return, at all that will happen. Men's hearts will fail them with fear at what is coming upon the earth. Stay strong. Stay faithful. It will seem impossible, but you have been gifted for the call."

Frankie nodded at the instruction, but, was too overcome with the magnitude of the message to speak.

Jesus stood up, looked him deeply in the eyes, nodded his approval, put his hand on Frankie's head and prayed for the Father to bless him mightily; then told him he'd been given many gifts, but it was up to him to find them within himself and within the Word. He spoke words in a language that Frankie didn't understand, then Frankie was standing above the earth. He saw devastation everywhere.

Trees, grass, and all plants were more than a third burned up; the sun was dimmed; people were starving and were murdering others for the tiniest scraps of food; the ocean looked like blood, and the wickedness going on shocked him. He saw few children and most of them were... different...

He saw the hatred that the wicked people had for any normal human children. They called them weak and unevolved, and sought them out to injure and kill. He saw hybrid people and animals that looked like someone had spliced genes together, with no thought of the end result. It was horrible. He cried out for it to stop, but then Jesus showed him a scene of him, Diane, Nate, Candy, Tucker—Diane's brother—and a young woman he'd never met.

She was holding a baby wrapped in a pink blanket, and he knew she was the one he was supposed to protect, along with his son; The six of them, and all their parents, and other family members, and people he knew, were secretly feeding people that were fully human, and hiding out all over the world.

He saw a chain of people that handed off food packets like runners handed off batons on the track. They would casually walk by and the goods would change hands. He saw larger deliveries being taken to groups, and he saw himself overseeing it all. He saw his son. Tears formed in his eyes as he saw a miniature version of himself.

Suddenly, the vision stopped. Jesus looked at him for what seemed like forever, then said, "Frankie, you will feed my sheep. Don't be distracted by anyone or anything. I've called your family to help you, but like you, they each have a choice. Call them to me if they don't already know me. Don't waste one minute. Today is the day to get started.

He grabbed Frankie by both shoulders, hugged him close, said "I'll see you in a little while, and you'll see me many times before I return at the end." Then he turned, and left through another doorway, just as another warrior—that Frankie now realized was an angel—entered the room, and beckoned for him to come with him. Frankie felt an energy running through his body and mind that he'd never felt before.

"My name is Faral'el. I have been your guardian since you were created. Come. It's time you return. You must rest, because it's time to begin the task." He turned and waved his hand, opening another doorway, that he called a portal, into Frankie's living room. Frankie stepped through and Faral'el spoke one last time before closing the portal.

"I'll be near. Don't call on me directly though; call on Jesus, or the father, and I will be sent. And Frankie, there is much I can't do until you ask Father; don't be afraid to ask for what you need, and for help. The more you pray, and the closer you stay to Jesus, the more power I will be given to intervene. Prayer is the currency of the kingdom. Never forget that. Go with God, my friend." And then he was gone.

Frankie sat on the couch, not sure if he was still in a dream, but very sure of his calling, and that it was Jesus, the Son of God, who had called him. He walked into the bedroom, saw the other angel watching over Diane, still alert, and silently nodded, then went to bed and straight to sleep. God gave him a deep and restful slumber and he woke early, completely refreshed, as if he'd slept double his usual hours.

At 5:00, he slipped out of bed, careful to not disturb Diane, made coffee, then went to the bookshelf and found the bible his dad had given him when he graduated high school. He opened it and found the book of Revelation and began reading. He'd tried to read it before, after listening to several broadcasts where they were talking about being very near the tribulation times, but it had never made any sense.

His heart was convicted as he read the words to the seven churches. He knew he fit in there in a lot of places. He remembered Jesus saying he had to repent, but he wasn't quite sure what all that entailed, and he needed to be baptized also. He called his dad at 6:30.

"Hey son. It's awful early to be out-on-the-range. Everything ok?"

"Yes. I need to ask you a question. You got a minute?"

"Sure. Let me go downstairs and grab some coffee so I won't wake your mother up. You know how she gets in the morning."

Frankie did know. No one hated to get up early more than his mother. His parents had worked out a deal years ago when he and his siblings were small. She'd take care of the night duty, so he could be well rested for work; and he'd manage the early mornings so she could sleep in; they still kept that schedule; and as long as nothing intervened, both were very happy with it.

He sat and listened to the familiar sounds as his dad put the sugar in his cup while waiting for the pot to brew. He could almost tell the exact moment the buzzer would sound, he'd watched his father's morning routine so many times; even on a phone line, he could picture it clearly.

He smiled, 1,2,3... the chair scraped on the wooden floor just as his dad clunked the cup down. 1,2... the chair scraped again as he slid it closer to the table, then clink, clink, clink, clink, as he stirred the coffee... then... wait for it... a slurp, a sigh, then, "Man, that's good. Just what I needed this morning." Frankie laughed silently at how predictable it was. If he was blind, he'd know if it was his dad, or someone else, making coffee in the morning. He really got tickled then, and had to suppress himself, in order to not offend his father.

"Alright, son. I might live now. Another 4-5 cups and I could run a race. I think I can string two thoughts together long enough to answer a question. What 'cha got?"

"What does repent mean, and how do I do it?"

"Come again?" his dad sounded thoroughly shocked.

"I need to repent. I mean, I want to repent. And be baptized too. But I'm not sure what it is exactly, or what all I have to do, to meet the requirements," Frankie explained. He was so into the enormity of the call Jesus had put upon him, that he hadn't really stopped to think about how it would sound to his dad to be asked this at 6:30 in the morning, unexpectantly.

"Wonderful," his dad exclaimed, "but back up a minute. What brought this on?"

"You wouldn't believe me if I told you;" he hedged.

His dad laughed, "Oh, I've been around some, son. When a man out-of-the-blue needs... er... wants... to repent, something usually sets it off. I'm just trying to understand the context. Did Diane throw you out?"

"Oh, God no!!" Frankie quickly answered.

"Well, lay some truth on me boy. What's got you wanting to repent at the butt-crack of dawn? Are you drunk? Are you in jail? Hang on, I think I need another sup of coffee." Frankie heard him gulp down what had to be the rest of the cup. Yep. Sure enough, he heard the chair scrape, footfalls, and liquid pouring, then footfalls, and scraping.

"Dad, you're a riot. It's nothing like that. I'll tell you, but until I tell Diane, I'd prefer you keep it to yourself. Besides, it's still new, and I have a lot to consider and do. It's kind of private for now, ok?"

"You ain't slipped around and got another kid on the way too, have you?" his dad sounded a bit worried. Frankie heard another long series of swallows as his dad gulped most of a second cup of coffee, then yelped as he blistered his mouth at the extreme temperature.

"Dad!! Seriously!!"

"Boy. Just lay it on me. You done got me a bit interested in hearing the rest. It's a might early for making me puzzle it out," his dad pressed.

"Well... don't laugh... and... well, just don't think I've gone nuts. It's real. But it's not something I've ever heard about or experienced before. It's a bit hard to explain." Frankie wanted to let him know upfront it'd be a bit strange.

"Do I need to drive over there Frankie?"

"No. Not yet. Dad, I had a very strange thing happen last night. Like I said, it's a bit hard to explain."

"Ya didn't get abducted by aliens, did ya?"

"Well, not exactly," Frankie said, "... um... kinda along those lines, but different."

"Are you gonna tell me what this is about, or what?" His dad sounded worried again.

"Yeah. Just give me a minute to figure out how to explain it."

"Ok. Take your time son. I'm here. I'm gonna refill my cup, and I'll be right back."

Frankie mentally and audibly followed the whole process through to the last scrape of the chair, getting his thoughts in order.

"Ok. I'm back."

"Dad, I know you believe in God. Do you believe Jesus really talks to people?"

"He's talked to me for years."

"I know dad; but this was different. At least I think it was, but I'm not really sure how Jesus talks to other people. I was asleep last night, and got woke up by an angel. He wanted me to come with him. He said I'd been summoned. There was another angel that stayed to watch over Diane. The first angel created a doorway he called a portal, and we walked down a long corridor until we came to a room where Jesus was." He stopped a minute to see what his dad would say.

"I see; did you actually see Jesus?" he sounded intrigued.

"Yes; and dad, he's really nice. And loads of fun. He smiles a lot, and teases. He didn't lord it over me at all. He's not at all who I thought he was from listening to preachers, but dad... when he turned serious it was an entirely different story. It put me flat on my face in the floor."

His dad was smiling broadly, "I've tried to tell you He's not who you thought he was."

"I know, but dad, I just didn't know."

"Well, son, what did he say? Did he say why you were summoned?"

"Yes. Dad, he said I'd been tasked as a baby to do a job for God, and now was the time to take up the task. He showed me, and I saw God holding me as a baby before I came to earth, speaking it into me. Jesus was there too, and He said he'd help me and bless me; but I really needed to repent and be baptized and get to know him better before I could do it right. Dad, he showed me a vision of what was coming on the earth. It was horrible. People dying everywhere; People starving.

Dad, people were hybrids, and scary. Children will be changed to hybrids. I've never seen such awful things in my life. He said, I need to get to know him and his word. I'm supposed to read the bible and start with Revelation. I'm not sure why because when I found it, it's the last book in the bible. But he said it's about to start now, and people are going to starve. He asked me if I'd feed his sheep."

"That's interesting. What did you say?" Frankie's father had tried to get him to come to church and get saved for years. Frankie hadn't wanted to hear any of it, but had come to church on Christmas and Easter because he loved his parents. He and Bobby, Diane's dad, had given him a few websites to listen to podcasts about what was going on in the country, and the world, but he wasn't sure he'd even listened to them.

"Dad, you're not going to believe this, but Nate came over with an idea last night about a new company he wants to start with me about preserving food. Jesus said he'd given it to Nate to bring to me so I could do my task. He said it would take both Nate and me, and our wives. He said you and mom, Tucker, and all our parents and siblings were called too, and it would take all of us, but each of us had a choice if we wanted to do it or not. He said he'd provide the funds and bless it.

Diane, me, Nate, and Candy had already decided to go tour the prototype today. Danny's coming too. I'm not sure it wasn't a dream brought on by thinking about it all, but Dad, I know I saw Jesus. I know he called me to feed his sheep. I know he told me I needed to repent and get to know him. I know it. I can't get those scenes out of my head.

We've got to start preserving food—right now. This week. I don't know where the money's coming from, but Jesus, when he was God—Frankie stopped and told him about Him shifting into different parts of God—said if I'd obey and trust him, that he would provide it. But Dad... I'm not sure I know how to repent... and I feel like I need to start with that, and we're leaving at nine this morning. I kinda need to know now, if you'll tell me."

"Son, I'll be there in a few minutes. I'll help you." He was smiling like a Cheshire cat at what Frankie was telling him. He couldn't wait to tell his wife. "Was there anything more?" he was pulling on his shoes as he spoke.

"Actually, yes; but you're really not going to believe this part."

Frank, his dad, couldn't wait to hear the rest. *Did he see God? Was he shown another vision, or a series of them, like the Apostle John?*

"Try me, Son."

"Dad, he said I'm supposed to feed his sheep spiritually too. Dad... he called me to preach...." His Dad heard the wonder in Frankie's voice and teared up. "Dad... I said yes. He touched me and I felt a power like an electric current run through me. It was powerful, and He put something in my brain, and it traveled all throughout my body, then to my heart and somehow got planted there, and started growing. Then later he became a spirit and he said it was his job to teach me and that he'd never leave me or forsake me. He touched whatever Jesus put there and it became a fire.

I can feel it burning in me, and it's like it's even closed-up inside my bones. I can't explain it, but it's just there. Then he told me the baby is special. I'll tell you the rest about that when you get here, cause I have to tell Diane that part first, but Dad, he said the baby is a boy. Imagine that, Dad. I'm having a boy. Diane's going to be so mad. She's been buying pink stuff like crazy. But even that's ok; dad, there's a baby girl too, I'm supposed to help protect, and her mother is somehow linked to Tucker."

"Frankie… that's the Jesus I've tried to introduce you to. He tells the end from the beginning, and calls people to tasks, then gives them all they need to accomplish them. I can't wait to hear you preach." He was so excited, he realized he was getting in his truck, but his keys were still in the house. He turned around to go get them just as the sun topped the horizon. The beauty of the rays of light that suddenly lit up the sky was a picture of how his heart felt hearing his son's words.

"A boy… we'll have sooo much fun with him. I'll be there in a minute. Make more coffee son; we're going to need it."

"Ok Dad. Thanks."

"What's up with your dad?" Diane yawned as she made her way to the coffee pot. She grabbed a cup from the mug tree on the counter, filled it, then came and set across from him. "You two don't usually talk on the phone this early. Everything ok?"

"Everything is very ok, but I need to tell you something," he answered her.

Now she looked a bit worried. "What?!" Concern was all over her face.

"Diane, something's happened to me. We need to talk."

"Frankie, are you alright? Are you sick?"

"My Dad's on the way over, but I need to talk to you first. Diane, it's important. It will affect both of us, and our baby. It's serious. Can you let me tell you the whole thing before you ask a thousand questions? I need to tell you before he gets here."

"Ok. But if you're sick or you hurt yourself working, I want to know the bad part first. Otherwise, I'll sit here and go crazy. Are we still going on the tour today?"

"I went somewhere last night while you were asleep, honey. It's something you need to know about," he started, but she interrupted him.

"Frankie Launch, are you cheating on me?! Did you go see a woman?!" and her voice rose in hysteria, "DOES YOUR DAD

KNOW? OH MY GOD!!!!" Her eyes teared up as her hand went protectively across her stomach.

He looked at her in utter astonishment, trying to make sense of her words and her tears, then it sunk in what she was saying. "What? No. Good grief, Di. Can you calm down a minute? Geeze…. Can't a guy tell his wife something without a meltdown before he even gets it out of his mouth? Is, this just pregnant hormones, or do you really think I'm that big a louse?"

Now she was both mad and confused, "Frankie, just tell me. Just say it."

He started laughing, "Di, I've been trying to for five minutes, but you won't let me."

She looked at him, still worried, but not as much since he was laughing. "Ok; I'm sorry. I'll be quiet. Go."

"Diane, as I was trying to say… I went somewhere last night." Then he told her the entire story.

She stared at him like he had four heads. "You left me alone with a strange guy with a sword in his hand?! In my bedroom?! Oh my God, Frankie. What were you thinking?!!"

"Diane, he was an angel sent by God to watch over you. He said he'd kept you safe since you were born. Diane, he's always around. He's your guardian angel. You just can't see him."

"Do you know how you sound right now?" she kept looking at him like she'd never seen him before and couldn't quite figure out who he was, or how he'd gotten in her house.

"Di, you should see your face right now." He cracked up at her expression. "I'm serious. This really happened. I called my dad because I need to repent and I don't know how."

"You're actually serious, right?"

"Yes. I am," he nodded to emphasize his words.

"You'd better call my dad too, then," she said. "He's going to be so jealous. He's been trying to get us saved, as long as your dad has; and if my family is called to help too, he needs to be in on it from the start."

"That's not a bad idea," he nodded again. "Can you call him while I run up and get dressed? We can make breakfast while they' re coming. Tell him to come right now. But tell him don't tell your mom yet. My mom doesn't know either, and I just need our fathers right now. And you," he quickly added, while watching the 'look' start across her face.

He went upstairs, and she stood there looking at the kitchen doorway, not sure what to do for a minute. First the baby. Then, the freeze-drying business, and now Jesus. Salvation. Her husband being called to preach? It really must be the end of the world. Also, he said there was something he had to tell her about the baby, but he'd decided he wanted to wait and tell them all together. She couldn't imagine was else was coming.

She refilled her coffee and then took bacon and eggs out of the fridge, and grabbed a box of pancake mix out of the pantry. *Looks like it's about to get interesting around here*, was what she was thinking as he came back into the kitchen. They set the table, made another pot of coffee, and he cooked the bacon, while she made pancakes, then broke eggs into a bowl, whipped them, and poured them into the skillet. She sprinkled a generous portion of cheese into them and began to turn them over as they started to set.

In what their dads would call 'God's timing,' they both drove up, at the exact same time. Frankie's dad had pulled into the driveway first, but her dad was about a car length behind him. They got out and greeted each other, and walked toward the house talking. Both were just floored by the morning's events so far. It was about to get better.

Frankie poured everyone coffee, while Diane dished up plates. She sat a dish of butter, a jar of jelly, a bottle of syrup, and the salt & pepper rack in the middle of the table, then asked her dad to bless the meal. He did, and they dug in. After a few bites, Frank looked at his son, and said, "are you going to tell us the rest, or should I start explaining repentance first?

"I guess I'll tell the rest." He filled them in on the fact that the baby was a boy. Diane whooped and grinned.

"I knew it!"

"Then why have you been buying so much girly stuff?" he asked.

"Because I might have been wrong." She laughed, still grinning, then said in absolute delight, "A boy! I hope he looks just like you."

Both dads were smiling, proud as new grandfather's-to-be are everywhere.

"Frankie, you said there was more about the baby. What is it son?"

Suddenly he looked serious again, and all three of them held their breath, waiting for him to speak.

"Jesus said he is special. He said there'd be another baby close to us that I'm supposed to help protect also, because she's special too. He said these shots were changing people's DNA and very few babies were going to be born, but of those who are, most of them will be a hybrid species. He said they won't be fully human and can't be saved.

He said no matter what we can't get vaccinated, and neither can the babies. He said we're to keep him away from the hybrid children. He said we'd be in much danger, and that they—and I took it to mean the coven—would want the little girl very badly. I'm supposed to make sure I protect them. Dad, and you too, Bobby, will you help us protect him and the other baby?"

Both men, students of prophecy, nodded seriously. "That's biblical," Diane's dad said, and Frank spoke next. "I agree. I've been expecting it to come out that it's a DNA changer. I can see why he wants the baby isolated. In the book of Genesis," he looked at Frankie and Diane, "only Noah, his wife, and their sons, and their wives, had pure human DNA. That was the main reason for the flood. The people of the time were very wicked, and the hybrids were called Nephilim.

God destroyed the earth so pure humans could start over again. Satan hates godly men. He hates our children." He looked at Frankie, and answered his question, "I'll pledge to both of you, right now. Nothing will harm you, or your child, or the other child, if I have breath in my body. If you're called the feed people, both physically and spiritually, then I'm called to make sure you can."

"Amen," Bobby added. "I join that pledge. And Frankie..." he grinned, "called to preach... I'll help pay for bible college, classes, or possibly you don't have the time for that; I'll teach you myself. Whatever you kids need, I'm in."

Diane filled them in on the day's trip and she was rapidly putting the pieces together that it was a God-given task and ministry. "Wow," she said, "I can't believe it."

"Let's start with repentance then," Frank wiped tears from his eyes. "Repentance is when God convicts your heart for all the things you've done that breaks his law. You realize you are a sinner, and nothing you do can ever make up for your sin. You can't save yourself; you are a sinner headed straight to hell. You don't have to be a terrible person; you just miss the mark of being who God wants you to be.

Then, you repent. That means you realize that's its way bigger than you, but you acknowledge that God is right. The Bible is right. And you are wrong. You own your sin, both the things you've done that you shouldn't have, and the things you haven't done, that you should have." He choked up, suddenly unable to speak, remembering how long he'd wanted to teach his son these things, and the many, many prayers he'd prayed for God to open his eyes.

Bobby smoothly took up the explanation, "And then you ask God for forgiveness and ask Him to save you. You accept His free offer of salvation. You give your allegiance completely to Him and he makes you spiritually alive; then you start reading the bible and learning what He wants for you, and from you. You begin to do your very best to live like He wants you to—and no one can do it perfectly—so when you mess up again, you ask forgiveness again, and start again. Is that what you want to do Frankie?"

Frankie looked relieved. It was so much simpler that he'd thought. He wished he'd known that last night when he was with Jesus. He could have told Him personally. *"I'm right here, listening. You can tell me personally,"* he heard in his heart— while sensing the smiling laughter again—and had no qualms about doing just what his dad and Bobby had just explained.

"That's exactly what I want to do," he nodded.

"I do too." Diane had tears in her eyes. She wanted to be in this with Frankie all the way. The feeding the people, protecting their son and the little girl, and telling people about Jesus.

"Praise the Lord!" her dad and Frank said at the same time.

Frank led them in a simple prayer of repentance, and praise for Jesus. Frankie asked Jesus to help him do his best to fulfill his calling, and said he was going to have faith that Jesus would provide the funds, and everything else they needed, to do what he'd called them to do.

Diane followed suit, then asked God to help her and Frankie to be good parents to their son, and help them know who the other baby was, and keep it safe too; and asked Him to help her be a good helpmate to Frankie, and thanked Jesus for trusting them to help him feed the world.

Frank then looked at them each in turn, "I believe Jesus has truly called you Frankie, and you too Diane, even if Frankie was the only one summoned. So, I'm going to invest in you. I've done very well in life financially. My Heating and Air business has done well, and I have a pension from my company, some annuities, and a cash growth life insurance policy for retirement.

But I have something else too. My grandfather left me a decent sum of money. I haven't needed it, so I dropped it into a Fixed Indexed Annuity when I received it, and left it alone. It's sat there all these years, just getting bigger and bigger. I'd planned to split it between my three kids. I'll give you and Diane your share now. It may not pay for everything, but it will be a very good start."

"I'll match that," Bobby said. "I've got some gold my daddy left me; and every week since I married your mother, I've gone by the gold exchange and bought a roll of silver dimes. Sometimes several. In good years, I bought gold. I've accumulated it for over 40 years, and to tell you the truth, I'm not even sure how much I have; but I know it won't make a dent in it to finance the rest. You kids go look over this module, and Frankie, if Jesus gives you the go-ahead, you make the deal.

Call me and I'll wire the money, and Frank can give me his half when we know if there's other costs involved, and you know how much it is. Let's get this show on the road. Get the man alone and ask him if he'll take gold. If he won't, or needs the money immediately, I'll go convert enough this morning that I can wire it as soon as you call.

And if you need help getting it going, I'll help there too. I've got hundreds, if not thousands, of business acquaintances. I have the customers from my online businesses, I have my bible study group, and tons of 'prepper' friends, who all have lots of contacts. I know everyone in several of the local farmer's co-ops, and every one of them is concerned about the food issue. We can start setting up the supply routes now. I can get more investors too. Don't you worry about money."

Frank, who had many clients who were farmers and ranchers added, "I'll start calling my clients, telling them what's going on, and asking them to plant all they can, and we'll buy it, outright. If God called you, he'll provide the food producers. We'll get the product."

Frankie's mouth fell completely open. He looked at Diane and hers was open too. Again, he sensed amused laughter within him. "Thank you, Jesus!" he spoke out loud, but it was directed to the presence within. "Amen," the other three echoed.

"It's 8:00," Diane said. "I've got to go get ready. Nate, Candy, and Danny will be here in an hour."

"I can't wait to tell them," Frankie was smiling in excitement.

"You tell them boys, we've got this," Frank added, then, "I've got to go home and tell your momma I'm spending some money. By the way, can I tell her the rest, or would you prefer to do that yourself?"

"I would like to tell her, but go ahead. I don't want her to be kept in the dark. And dad? Thanks for everything. You too, Bobby. Diane and I are so lucky to have you for fathers. And just so you know; I'm going to rely on both of you to teach me how to follow Jesus and be a Christian. Will you help me?"

"You bet we will; Tucker will help, too, when he's here," Bobby answered. "Also, Jake Johnson, remember him, the professor at the college? He's got a bible study group that's closer to you than we are. I'm going to give him a call. He's one of the best bible teachers around. You'll learn a lot from him. You'll recognize him from the alliance meetings.

And Frankie, go see Maggie Albright when you get back. Get some life insurance on you and Diane immediately. You've got a son to raise, and if anything were to happen to either of you, the one left will need the funds to run the business and the ranch. I'll pay for one for our boy when he is born. And if we can find the other baby, I'll take care of one for her too. We can grow college funds with them too, just in case this world lasts longer than we expect."

"Get an Indexed Universal Life or an Infinite Banking policy, or eventually, both," Frank instructed. "That's what we have, and I've always had a source of funds when I needed them;

BOOK 1: "PREPARE FOR THE END" SERIES

and my retirement will allow me to help you make it happen. When you kids start making money, all of you, Nate, Candy, and Danny included, need to get a business policy that covers the rest if one of you passes too. Start it right."

Frankie thanked them for the advice, then Frank and Bobby left to go update their mothers, and Frankie ran upstairs to get ready too. He was excited about this trip, and ready to tell his friends the news.

The Bread of Life

Chapter 32

HONK. HONK.

"Diane, they're here," Frankie called up the stairs.

"I can hear the horn too, honey," floated back down. "Give me a minute."

Frankie shook his head. She'd started before him and she still wasn't ready. He went to open the door to let Nate and Candy in.

"Come on in. Better grab a cup, Diane's not down yet," he explained.

"I'll go get her." Candy started up the stairs, knowing it was usually her that was late.

Nate followed Frankie to the kitchen, grabbed a cup, and filled it. He looked at Frankie, watched him for a minute, then his brow wrinkled in perplexity as his lips pursed up and twisted to the side, and he examined every pixel of Frankie's face, while rubbing his jaw.

"What?" Frankie asked.

"You look different. What's up?"

Frankie grinned, "What makes you think something's up?"

"I've known you since we were born. There's something not quite as… casual… about you, that's always been there. Besides, you're grinning like you're up to something. I've seen that look before. You had that look in sixth grade when you decided to beat Danny for class president; you had it again when you were putting together the deal to buy this cattle ranch; and when you were about to ask Diane to marry you. It's a look you only get when it's something big."

He stopped talking, and scrutinized Frankie again. "… and… I don't know… you look like you're standing… well—

taller—all of a sudden. It's a look of decision, where you've decided to go 'all-in' to accomplish something. I don't know if it's our freeze-dry business, but it seems different than that because you didn't look like that last night. I don't know what it is, but I know it's big. Ok, buddy, spill it; What's got you glowing like a turned-on light bulb?"

Frankie grinned even wider, then turned serious. "Ok. I was going to tell both of you in the truck, but I'm sure Diane's already 15 paragraphs into telling Candy. It is big, and I'm totally serious, so just hear me out before you say anything."

Now Nate really looked interested. "Ooooh... Kaaay...."

Frankie told him about his experience in the middle of the night. Nate had known Frankie long enough that he knew Frankie wasn't just spinning a yarn. He was dead serious as he described the encounter with the supernatural, the vision, his calling, and his acceptance of the calling. Listening to the 'marvel' in Frankie's voice as he described the discussion with Jesus, he wished he'd been there too.

His parents had told him stories of supernatural phenomena throughout his life. His mother had a friend that left for the mission field and his mother loved to read stories of missionaries across the world, and had often recounted them around the dinner table; so, he'd heard of many instances where God called people and tasked them to do something big. He knew when Frankie told him about both his and Diane's fathers coming over, it was happening. "Wow" was all he could say at first.

"And Nate, to top it off, both our dads are going to fund this business. They believe we have been tasked by God to help feed people. We don't have to find the money, because it's already been offered. Bobby said, to go look at the module, and if we both agree that it's viable, to make the deal, call him, and he'd wire the funds to the guy immediately."

"Frankie, my dad offered to help too. He's talked about the food supply for a while now. He's been instructed that if he wants government assistance this year, he can't plant 60% of his fields. It's not setting well with him. He's been talking to other farmers about private sales to local stores, and not selling to the major food production companies.

He says the local farmers are fed up with not being able to make a living, or doing what they love to do—produce food and feed people—and he thinks it's a giant conspiracy of the government. The longer I listen to the podcasts you send me, the more I think he's right. Do you really think God showed me this because of your task?"

"Nate, I wish you'd been there. Diane too. I wish all four of us could go back so you could hear it straight from Jesus; but he indicated that going there was unusual and it wouldn't happen again until the end of all things. I need you to believe me, and both of us to be committed to this business; but Nate I've never been more, sure, of anything in my life. And I'm going to do it, with or without you. I accepted the call to feed his sheep, physically and spiritually. Are you still in?"

"I'm in. My dad will be, too. His part can be to help us buy the food to start processing it immediately. We'll need bags, labels, and to get the warehouse built too. I'm not too sure Danny will buy the supernatural aspect of being called by God, but if nothing else, we can hire him to do the butchering like he asked, and leave him out of the rest. Are you going to tell him today?"

"Well, he's going to have to know I was called to preach, because I've got to start studying. Maybe we need to hold off on the rest. I'd like that to stay more private anyway. Some things are more personal, and if he isn't in, it will jeopardize the supply chain. Let's keep all those plans just between us and our dads right now. We need to make sure the people involved can be trusted with all our lives. Will Candy be able to keep it to herself?"

"Do you think I'm a big blabber-mouth, Frankie Launch?" Candy answered for herself as the women walked into the room.

Frankie smiled at her, "Not really Candy, and I'm not trying necessarily to keep secrets, but if it's advertised all over that we've been tasked by God, then it will make all of us more of a target. And many people will use that info to make fun of us, instead of becoming a customer. And later, when it's more dangerous it will have put an enormous bull's-eye on our backs.

We need the business, and they will need the food. We need to game-plan and make more decisions than we knew about last night. If what I saw is real—and I know it is—then we can't waste a single minute. The violence I saw was real too. We won't be feeding everybody, and it will get progressively more dangerous.

For now, let's just talk business as usual with Danny around; you know his family doesn't believe in Christianity like our families do. He's always been touchy around the subject. But later, I'd like to have a meeting with us, and all our parents. This is bigger than the four of us. I may have been the one summoned, but Jesus said it would take all four of us, and our families; and the way mine and Diane's dads acted this morning, I think they feel called to help as well.

Nate, Jesus said he gave the idea to you, to bring to me, so we can make it happen together. If your dad is committed to helping too, maybe all four of our families really are supposed to work together; and we're all called. I'm just the one that got summoned because of being called to preach too, so I'm supposed to pull us all together; but it's all of us. Jesus was very clear about that.

There will be a lot of people starving, according to Jesus; and we can't find and buy the food, freeze-dry, and package it, set up the supply chain, and make all the deliveries alone. It's going to take a team. Besides, Diane's pregnant, and you have a baby. We're going to need help." Then he told them what Jesus had said about the baby, the little girl baby, and the vaccines.

He described the baby's mother, and her standing by Tucker. "I don't think you are supposed to take it either, or let your child be around the hybrid kids." He shook with revulsion just remembering the other kids he'd seen. "Jesus was very insistent that we stay separate.

And another thing; Jesus said we'd be in great danger; so, we need to set up some kind of security system. Maybe fence in our places and make sure the facility is protected, but most of all our families. He painted a picture of a complete collapse of society, and then he took me above the planet and showed it all to me." He told them what the other children would look like as best he could. "And Nate, when we find this other baby, will you help me protect her too?"

Nate nodded solemnly. "That's what all the people we're listening to say, and my dad as well. And if God said we're supposed to protect her, you know I'm in too. There's Danny now. Let's table this conversation for later."

They all went out to greet Danny and pile in the truck for the trip to see the freeze-drying module.

"You get your paperwork done?" Diane asked Danny.

"Yeah, but it took me forever, and I'm still not sure I'm doing it right. I hate that part. I love running the business; I'm good at it, but bookkeeping is not my thing."

"I do the books for the ranch. If you ever need any help, let me know. It's a different business, but it's the same procedure," she offered.

"Why don't I just pay you to do it for me?" he inquired. "I called a lady in town, but she has all the clients she can keep up with. She said $200 a month for now, because I don't do a lot. As it grows, it may go up."

"I'd do it for that." Diane agreed. "Do you use online software?"

"No. I just use a spreadsheet. I can get that, but until business picks up, I'd rather not have to pay for it."

"No worries." Diane said. "I use a desktop version. I can have more than one business on it. I'll just split the upkeep cost with you. That will help both of us. You can drop me the invoices and bills regularly, or e-mail them to me. I can do your taxes, too, if you want."

"I'd love that," Danny admitted, relieved he wouldn't have to worry about it anymore.

"She does our books and taxes, too." Candy confessed. "Remember, her mom ran a bookkeeping business for years. We both worked for her in the summer. Diane was always better at it then me. She did the bookkeeping and I was a receptionist."

"Oh, yeah, I remember that. Does she still do that?"

"She does some. She retired from full-time and sold her business, but she works for the new owner during tax time when she needs her. She says it keeps her sharp," Diane snorted.

"Well, I'm all for it," Danny looked even more relieved. "That's been the worst part of owning my own business."

"I'm glad to catch you early," Diane looked relieved too. "When I was in high school, one summer while working for mom, a guy about your age came in with four giant rubber-maid tubs of stuff. He'd been running his business for two whole years, and never once did the books. He didn't even have so much as a spreadsheet or notebook. I had to set up a business, figure out all those receipts, go over his checking account, and he mainly used cash," she shuddered, remembering, "and figure out what he made, and what he spent, so we could file two years of tax returns. It was a nightmare. I learned a lot though, and my mom made a fortune;" she explained. "You've been in business, what, a year?"

"Not quite. I have put it all in the spreadsheet though, Di. I have one page for expenses, and one for the checks they pay me with. Do you need bank statements too? I can print those, and put the spreadsheet on a flash drive. I have a tub of receipts too," He grinned.

Frankie cracked up, "Oh, she'll love that."

"What is it with you guys and your Rubbermaid tubs," Diane rolled her eyes at Candy. "When I married Frankie, he had all his in those as well. I spent the first month of marriage going through it all and getting his books in order."

Frankie shot her a smoldering look, "that's not all you did in our first month of marriage, sweetheart."

The guys all laughed, and Diane rolled her eyes again, laughing. "Shut up Frankie." She looked at Candy. "Men. Ugh." Candy laughed too. She was firmly on Diane's side, but she'd walked right into that one.

"What made you decide to go into the mobile butchering business?" Candy asked.

"Well, you know my dad always grew a cow and a couple of pigs every year. We always did the processing ourselves. My dad was sure the local processing place kept part of the meat, and he didn't want to lose any. I grew up doing that stuff.

Then when I worked at the grocery store in high school, and the few years after that, I started out stocking, but was always watching the butcher to learn more to show my dad, and eventually they moved me over into that department to learn the entire process. It takes a couple of years to learn it all, and get entirely proficient, but I eventually did. I'm a certified butcher now.

During the lockdown, the grocery stores weren't stocking as much meat, and the price was rising, so people started raising their own animals for slaughter, and were always calling and asking me to come help them; and many said they'd pay me to do it for them if I was willing. I helped a few put down the animals and hauled them home to process, but I really don't have the room for that, and I didn't have the freezer space to keep the meat until I could get it back to them.

I was looking around for a restaurant refrigerator and freezer and went over around Amarillo to look at a used set that was for sale, and the guy had a truck that he'd set up to do mobile butchering on the spot, and he showed it to me. It was perfect. His business had gotten so big that he was upgrading to a much larger space that already had the facilities he required.

I got the specs from him, had an estimate drawn up by the guy that built his trailer, then got a loan based on my years of experience at the grocery store, and the proven numbers that guy shared with me. He even offered to have my banker call and talk to him and was very generous with the information he gave him. He sent his own financials to the bank to prove the income available. It sealed the deal. I had a trailer built, with a few modifications I wanted from working at the store, and here I am."

"Wow. That's fantastic," Diane loved entrepreneurial spirits. "I love the name 'Feet to Meat,' how did you come up with that?"

Danny shrugged, "I'm not sure. I knew I needed a good name to describe going from living animal to food, and I kept writing down things that just didn't seem right. I put 'feet to meat' at the top of the page to keep the goal in mind as I considered different options. After a couple of hours of pondering, I realized that was perfect already. It said it all, and was easy to remember."

"If it was the early days of our marriage, with Candy's cooking, you could have called it "Pasture to Disaster," Nate teased his wife, winking at her. They all laughed. Candy's earlier cooking mishaps were legend with the group; she still struggled with cooking quite a bit.

"Is it just one a day, or can you do more?" Diane's business brain was firing on all cylinders.

"Honestly? I can do 15 beef or between 25-30 hogs. I don't always have that kind of business, but sometimes I do. It's a long day, so I try to offset my work days. I'll do that kind of day, then do a day where I travel farther, with less to butcher. I enjoy the driving, and it gives me time to rest. Then, the next day I work more locally, and do more."

"How do you butcher that many animals and get all that meat wrapped up in a day?" Candy was trying to picture it in her mind.

"I generally don't wrap it; I mean for some people I do, but not for most, and seldom on the truck. I basically skin it, clean it, quarter it, and hang it in the cold section on large hooks in the truck. I can hang several while I keep butchering. I tag the parts so I know what belongs to who. I need to get it down to temperature fast, so it doesn't ruin. I take a lot of it home and keep it in the super cooler I bought when I bought the truck. My loan was big enough to include that and a giant freezer, as well. If the people want it packaged, I take it home, and every few days I have a packaging day.

Most people only need about a quarter of a beef at a time; that lasts a few months; that's all the freezer space they have. I can make those cuts in minutes with saws installed in the trailer, and that part stays there, and they package it themselves after I leave. It's all stainless-steel inside, with cutting tables, racks for the saws, basins to rinse my knives and hands, and the overhead wench and electric revolving hook racks, make it easy to maneuver the quarters around. They sell me the rest and I sell it to the grocery stores by the quarter, or the half. That way they can package it with labels for their store brand.

Some families only grow one cow and one or two hogs a year. I keep the meat cold for a few days for them, while they come get it by the quarter and package it themselves. A few, I still package for them. But that part is very time consuming. If I keep it for them, in the big freezer, I can charge a monthly fee for keeping it until they need more. Eventually I'll build a facility and hire people for that; but right now, I have all I can handle. That's why I'd rather just sell you the meat than join your business as a partner. I'm pretty busy, as it is."

Nate took that opening and used it to solve their dilemma. "I understand better now. Why don't we just do it that way. We'll buy extra from you too, and take all we can, and help you and your customers out, and it will keep us in product. Maybe we can work out a deal where you get us an interview with your grocery store contacts to sell some of our finished product to the stores."

"Absolutely. As soon as you're ready, I'll set the introductions up. I can let my customers know too. Do you think you'll be able to get the funding?" he sounded a bit skeptical, knowing how hard it'd been for him, and he'd needed much less.

"We already have," Frankie responded. "Our dads are going to help us out. My dad is giving me my inheritance early. He says it's better for me to have it now, with a family, than later, when I won't need it as much."

"Must be nice to have a dad like that," Danny was half sarcastic, and half envious. They all knew his skin-flint dad, and how Danny had to earn everything he'd ever had from a young age. His dad seldom helped him with anything. He'd had to work since he was fifteen, and even bought his own school clothes. Nate and Frankie had always passed down clothes and shoes to him as they were always slightly ahead in size. He'd made many comments over the years about how much was 'handed to them.' They'd learned to just let it go, however irritating it was.

"I could use a pitstop," Diane derailed an argument.

"Me too," Candy added.

"Ok," Nate, who was driving, agreed. "There's a mini-mart about five miles up the road. I'll pull in there. I need to top off the gas tank anyway."

They drove the five miles, then everyone piled out when they stopped. Candy and Diane hurried into the building, while Nate started the pump. Frankie walked toward the store to get a soda, and Danny walked away to take a call. It was his dad, wanting to know if he could borrow a hundred bucks. Since Danny had started the business, his dad was always wanting money.

He looked over at Nate, so calm and collected, putting gas in his truck. He was leaning against the side with no worries, while he waited. It had always been so easy for Frankie and Nate. They'd never know what it was like to have to bust your tail for every single cent, then turn around and hand it to a parent who'd barely kept you alive.

He'd had to get someone he barely knew to give his banker his own business information, to even qualify for a loan; then they decided to start a business; and without even putting a solid business plan together, their dads just jump up and write a check.

They'd never know the humiliation he'd gone through to start his business, or the nights he didn't sleep, worried he wouldn't be able to meet the payments. It always came easy for those two. They had it all. A farm, a ranch, wives, babies, and now another business—and free funding.

In reality, they'd worked since they were 15; and, following their dads' advice, had put up every cent to buy their places, with loans their dads co-signed, but he didn't know that; and wouldn't be interested in hearing how God takes care of those he calls.

He was glad he'd kept himself out of the partnership. They may expect his dad to pop for part of the cost, and instead he was online with the bank, transferring his dad's weekly grocery money. He'd never tell them how little he got to keep of his own earnings. The guilt trip his dad laid on him every few days kept him trapped, supporting his parents. He swallowed the bile that rose in his throat. He'd tour this module with them, but then he'd go back to his own world. High school was over for him, and he lived in the real world.

The demons surrounding him were hooting, and the one in charge was named 'division.' He was determined to keep him separated from Frankie, trapped in his family bondage. He was loving pressing thoughts into his mind, and stirring his darker emotions.

He walked in to use the facilities, and Frankie hollered, "I got us all sodas, so keep your money in your pocket!"

Great. Now he had to accept their charity, too. Again. He sighed, feeling like a loser. Frankie's generosity was just another black mark on his own struggle to survive. Someday he'd be the man with the money. Then maybe he could afford to be generous too.

He came back out just in time to follow the ladies back to the truck. Both were holding hotdogs and chips. "I thought you guy's ate breakfast?" he asked.

"We did. But I'm hungry." Diane took a huge bite.

"She's pregnant," Candy reminded him, "and I'm her support system." She took a bite bigger than Diane's.

Nate gave Frankie a look of commiseration, "Just wait. You ain't seen nothing yet. She'll eat you out of house and home, gain a bunch of weight, have the baby, then spend the next year accusing you of thinking she's fat. But don't waste your breath trying to stop her from doing it. It's part of the deal. Just keep the groceries bought, tell her she's beautiful, and make sure to keep the Kleenex handy, because the teary phase will be here before you know it."

Frankie gave him a look, trying to determine if he was serious, or just teasing him. Once again, Danny felt left out. He got back in the truck, feeling like an odd ball. He had no idea why they'd even invited him.

They got back on the road, eating, laughing, discussing high school, business, and the way the country had changed. Only Nate noticed Danny was quieter. He wondered why. The five of them had been friends since grade school. Danny was usually the noisy one. He decided he was thinking about the butchering business and left him alone; but he missed his friend's bantering, even though a lot of his wasn't as friendly, especially lately.

They arrived at the meeting place, toured the facility, and were duly impressed. It was a top-notch, turn-key module, and the owner offered them a $50,000 discount if they'd buy the working prototype. They'd made some modifications to the new ones, and while he'd added them to the module they toured, he wanted to start showing the newer one, asap.

They asked lots of questions, then Nate and Frankie walked outside to discuss it; then walked back in, made the deal, called Bobby, and payment was arranged for the next day. The owner would deliver it the day after.

They were pleased with the deal and decided it was time to eat. They found a steak house, and Nate decided to buy everyone's dinner to celebrate. He was so excited he'd be in business with Frankie and having a deal with Danny as well. He loved working with his two best friends. While they were eating, Diane looked at Frankie, "Why don't you tell Danny about your other new endeavor?"

Danny looked at him suspiciously, already sick to his stomach, "there's more?"

Frankie grinned that slow grin. "Yeah. I was going to tell you on the way over, but once the hens got to cackling, I never got a word in edgewise," he winked at the women.

Diane shrugged, "Get used to it baby. We'll be talking a lot while we're processing food. It's what keeps us happy." She put a giant fork of salad in her mouth and winked back, salad dressing all over her face.

He threw her a napkin, laughing at her antics.

"Danny, you're not going to believe this, but God called me to preach."

Danny stopped with a forkful of potato about an inch from his mouth. "What?" His face was a mixture of shock, and something Frankie couldn't define. "You? A preacher?" Then he chuckled, put the bite in his mouth, and talking thru it said, "you almost got me there, buddy."

Frankie put his fork down, and calmly spoke again. "I'm serious. I know it's something unexpected. I certainly never expected it, but it's real. I'm starting bible classes soon."

"So, you're going to run a ranch, create a food processing business, become a father, and be a preacher. Have you cloned yourself, or found a new energy drug?" Danny didn't know whether be amused or look around for the Twilight Zone camera.

"I know, I know. But it's what I'm going to do. The ranch keeps me busy, but I have an hour here and there to study every day. Cows kinda do their own thing, ya know. The freeze driers can be loaded in the morning, and unloaded that night, or the next morning, and there's four of us for that; another couple of hours to bag, tag, and store it; then it can sit till we ship it. I'll have time.

Personally, I think it will work out well. That will keep Di busy so I can study. Our dads and moms will help with the kids; and probably with the deliveries, we don't outright ship. We'll just have to work out a schedule. Besides, it's just turning winter. The crops won't be ready for a few months. We can do chicken and beef till then.

I have beef ready to go—you can help with that—and we can buy the chicken; and, other than feeding, the ranch is in its down time. No hay has to be cut, or baled; It's the perfect time to start. If I work hard, I can get a year of classes done by the time the baby gets here," he talked it out as he thought it.

"You're actually serious?" Danny looked at him like he had four heads, "did your dad put you up to it?"

"No. God called me. I said yes. Now, I just need to learn how." Frankie felt complete assurance of the calling, and it came out in his voice. "Maybe I'll practice on you guys."

"Oh, no," Danny said. "Keep that stuff away from me. I'm no church guy. I'll just let you boys do your thing, and I'll do mine." He looked very uncomfortable, just hearing Frankie speak so casually about being called to preach. *Geez. What was happening to his friends?* He felt even more distance opening between them, as the tormenting spirit filled his with repulsion.

They let the subject drop after that. Nate watched the look of disgust on Danny's face, and the look of disappointment on Frankie's, and decided he'd let Frankie practice on him. He wanted to support what God had called them to do, 100%. He felt a tug on his heart, that he too needed to get right with God. He decided to stay and talk to Frankie after Danny left.

They rode back a little quieter than they'd been during the first leg of the trip. They had to make a couple more pit stops for Diane, then they were back at the ranch. Danny left without a lot of talking, and Nate asked if they could stay for a little while.

"Sure, come on in. When do you have to pick up Will?" Frankie was relieved.

"In a little while, but I'd like to talk to you." Nate looked troubled.

"What's up?" Frankie asked.

"I'd like to hear more about what your dad said about repentance. I believe you, Frankie, and it feels right. I knew when I researched the freeze-drying module that it felt like I was drawn to it, and I knew you were supposed to be involved. As soon as you told me this morning, it's like it was a confirmation, and all our dads paying to get us started, just felt like it's supposed to happen. I'm not sure why, but I know Danny's not supposed to be as involved, also. I didn't understand that last night, but today it's just something I know.

If it's a 'God thing,' as my mom would call it, then I want to be able to be called too. I've known for a while, and especially since Will was born, that I needed to get right with God and start reading my bible. I want to be the kind of dad that my dad was. He said he raised us the way God told him too, just like yours did. Would you tell me what I need to do?"

"I repented today too," Diane told him. "I feel like we were all called to do this. I don't want anything to come between us."

"Then I want to, too," Candy nodded. "We've been together too long for us not to do this thing totally. I know I don't always think ahead like you three do, but I've been listening with Nate to the podcasts, and listening to his dad. Everything he's said was coming is what we're watching happen to this nation. My dad says the same stuff. I'm in."

Frankie told them about the bible study at Professor Johnson's house. "My dad is calling him to see if we can come. I'll ask if you can too. It'd be nice to have someone to discuss all this with. And if we're going to be working for God, we'd better get to know him, and his word. That's what Jesus said I need to do." He looked around at them all; his wife, his best friend, and Candy. They'd all been friends for as long as he could remember. He teared up at how supportive they all were.

"Thank you. I'm doing this with, or without, any of you; but I'd much rather know we're in it together." He placed his hand palm up in the middle of the table and Diane placed hers in it. Candy put hers over Diane's, and Nate rested his on top. Frankie spoke of the magnitude of the task, his determination to do it, then told them more details of the vision and about the things he'd seen in God's eyes; how it'd completely humbled him; then began to speak about true repentance.

He simply recounted what he and Diane had learned that morning from their dads, then they walked Nate and Candy through a simple and sincere prayer of repentance. Then, they all thanked Jesus for calling them and opening the door to make it happen. Nate and Candy looked happy and at peace, and Diane and Frankie were grateful their best friends would walk this new journey with them. They all hugged; then the Scott's went to pick up their son, and share their new-found salvation and Frankie's experience, with their parents. Frankie went out to feed his cattle, and Diane climbed in the recliner and went to sleep.

Their guardians were rejoicing with all of heaven. This had been a monumental day for them all, and in his heavenly throne room, Jesus smiled. His will would be done on earth, in spite of all the hateful determination of the enemy.

The enemy, on the other hand, were seething at four more humans escaping their clutches. They dreaded going back to headquarters. They didn't know about all that had happened, because Jesus had shielded the knowledge, but each had been forcibly kicked away from the group by their guardians as soon as the decision to follow Jesus had been made. They'd lost any legal right and had to leave. It was infuriating.

A couple, though, left the group. They'd realized that Danny's resentment and jealousy had given them a giant opening into his heart and mind, and they were about to stroke the flames of fire as high as they could get them.

New Beginnings

Chapter 33

INA WAS NOT HAPPY as they pulled up to her home. She'd lived most of her adult life in this home with her husband, and she'd raised her son and her grandson in it. It held almost every precious memory she cherished. *How am I going to just up and leave it?*

But she'd do anything to save Erwin, and after what she'd seen today, she knew the threats against their lives were very real. She wished she could tell her husband what was going on, and verify that she now knew everything he'd told her was the truth. She was sick that he'd gone to his grave knowing she didn't believe him, and she couldn't help but wonder if Gene would have lived if he'd been better prepared.

If together, they'd taught him the unvarnished truth, and lain a foundation of prayer and what his authority in Jesus was, maybe he would have rebuked the demon the way that Erwin had. She hadn't wanted Sherman to talk to him about any of it. Keeping her head in the sand had possibly contributed to his death, and now her continued silence had allowed evil to once again brush up too close and get it's hooks into someone she loved. *Never again*, she decided. *Never.*

She got out of her car with steel in her spine and a smile on her face. She would accept Dan's generosity, and get Erwin out of this house. If it meant leaving her home and never leaving the ranch again, that's what she'd do. She worked in town at a local bank during the day, but possibly Dan might have a need for help as well. He'd already told her she'd be targeted and he didn't want her off the ranch for a while either. She was going to make a brand-new start. It was time to push back evil and stop living in the land of 'everything is normal.'

Normal wasn't coming back, and she knew that in the depths of her soul. She'd read on a cup recently that 'Normal isn't coming back, Jesus is.' The Holy Spirit had been whispering to her about prophecy fulfilling for months now. It was time to work full-time for the Lord, and help the team fight, to eliminate the destruction of the people in their area by evil-doers. She hadn't planned on retiring so soon, but living at the ranch meant expenses would be way down.

Erwin looked at her, concerned that she'd change her mind. He couldn't leave her here alone, and he knew he couldn't stay. He had seen too much, and participated in too much. If he were ever going to escape being drawn in further, it had to be now.

He dreaded what Billy and Wolf would do when they found out; and the other guys in the group were the only other friends he had, except for Homer; and Homer was more of a mentor than a true friend. He wasn't close at all with the others, but he felt a pang of regret over Billy, and tamped it down hard. He'd seen too much to turn back now, and knew Billy was dangerous.

Dan instructed his crew to wait outside for a few minutes, to give Ina privacy, while he went in with her and Erwin. "Ina, I know it's hard, but we need to be brief today. I'll bring you back out to get more, and you can tell the guys what you want and we'll bring it all, but for now please pack like you're going away for a month, and make a list of your most precious items.

I'll help, and when you're ready, we'll bring the boys in and you tell them what you want today. I have two more on their way with an enclosed trailer. We can take everything today, if you want, but I want your most precious things in our personal trucks so you know where it is. Let's start with that. You too, Erwin.

Ina surprised them both. "I need my clothes, and my picture albums. The rest: dishes, furniture, books, all of it; have them pack it up. We can put it in the barn you offered while we stay with you, and move it into wherever you have for us later. I can't stand to leave it here, but I'm going to be making some hard decisions before we move it into the new place.

I may just call a used goods store and sell the bulk of it. I've been hanging onto 'stuff' because it reminds me of my husband and son, but Dan, stuff won't bring them back, and I don't need to be reminded of their lives or their love. It's inside me. I have Erwin, and that's enough.

I don't know if you have any need for a bookkeeper, but if you do, I can quit my job and neither of us will need to leave the ranch for a while. Maybe they'll think we moved off. I'm not ready to do that, but after what I saw today, I can believe they're capable of all that Sherman told me, and most probably more. It's time to act like they are who they are: servants of Satan. I've sugar-coated the truth for too long. It's time to call a spade a spade.

If you told me a serial killer was after us, I'd take every precaution. According to Sherman, they're that, and more. It's time to live like it's real, because it is."

"Well said, my friend. Well said. Get what you want. Do you want me to help, stay out of your way, or call the boys in to start loading?"

"They can start with the furniture. I can load my clothes in my car. I'll put my most treasured photos in there too. Erwin, what do you want?"

"Gran, I don't have much. I was so busy working and being Billy's lackey that I really haven't acquired a lot of things. I want the bible you gave me, my clothes, and my books." He looked at Dan. "You can have them throw away the entire gaming system, including the programs. If one of them wants it, they can have it, but they can't ever bring it around me.

I'm not too sure if you've ever really been involved with gaming, but it's all crime, sex, nudity, and selfish murder and destruction. You win games by destroying other people, just like the coven. I'm through with it all. I don't want anything to suck me back into that life."

"Erwin, I'll help you acquire the things that matter in life. Gaming is for kids. Life is for adults. I told you already, I've let you, Gene, and Sherman down. I'm done with that. Life on the ranch is hard, I won't lie, but it's turning winter, and we don't have near as much to do. I've got a huge library, and I'll personally instruct you in the bible, and teach you to ride, and how to operate a ranch.

Ina, I do need a bookkeeper. Since Jane passed, I've been making a mess that keeps me in trouble with the CPA. I think it's a good idea for you to not travel back and forth alone for a while. If you want to go somewhere, me, Matt, or Rusty will take you.

We can go to Dallas or Houston if that's what it takes to keep you safe.

As soon as they realize you're out of their reach, the retaliation will be swift and hard. It's not our first time dealing with their wrath, but it's hard on everyone. We'll need to double the guards and patrol the property lines. Every alliance family will be put on notice. If you don't know how to shoot—both of you—we'll start that tomorrow. You don't go anywhere unarmed, or alone. Not even on the ranch. And Ina, I mean it. I've seen what they can do to a man or a woman. It's not pretty."

Erwin nodded, "Let's get started. I've seen a lot too. Gran… please hurry… I've got to get out of here, and you do too."

Ina heard the fear and urgency in his voice, and walked into her bedroom to start the process of leaving her home. Erwin grabbed a box from the pile that Dan's guys had put on the porch, and Dan told them to come on in, giving them instructions.

Then, hearing a scuffle of some type out back, he went to the kitchen and standing sideways from the window, he peered out and started a slow evaluation of the back fence area and tree line. He immediately grabbed his phone and texted Rusty, his right-hand man under Matt, bringing the trailer.

Get here fast. Come in hot. Be ready. There's some movement in the tree line. Call the boys out front. I'll protect Ina and Erwin. Get Matt over here, asap! He copied the message in a text to Matt.

Got it boss. Five minutes out. Matt right behind me.

Dan slid under the window to the other side, then checked out the opposite side of the back of the property. There were no less than five wolves standing just inside the tree line, two more fighting over something, and he could make out something taller, but not what it was. He could see the top of the head though, and nothing out there should be that tall.

The hair on the back of his neck stood up. He slid back down, and all but crawled to the door, then stood and quickly walked to Ina's room. Erwin's door was straight across and he beckoned him to come over to her room with them. He filled them in on the situation, and Erwin's face lost all color, knowing who it was, and what he was capable of, "What do we do?"

"First, we pray," Dan led them in a prayer for protection. He asked God to thwart the enemy. Just before he ended the prayer, a long lone wolf howl began to rise. It went on for an impossibly long time, then other wolves joined in.

Ina, in a calm voice, said, "Dan, we're safe here. I've anointed the entire property line many times. I've seen evil outside the fence on more than one occasion. God has this. Just watch."

Dan stepped to the front room. "You boys, ok?"

"Yeah, we're ready. We can have the trailer loaded in no time. Let's not leave anything for them to destroy." Rusty was as rock solid a man as Dan had ever known. He'd been around long enough to know exactly what was about to happen, and he'd never backed down from a fight in his life. His eyes met Rusty's with a silent exchange. He nodded. He understood far more than the others, and he'd be ready.

"Dan, you better come out here;" another ranch hand stuck his head through the door.

"Coming." He stepped outside and followed his employee to the end of the porch. "Look," he was instructed. He peered around the side of the house and saw the black fog swirling around the back fence. It looked like a miniature tornado, but was strangely shaped, twisting and turning. As he was watching the phantom entity, the truck and trailer arrived, with Matt coming up the road behind them.

He rebuked the evil thing, and watched it melt back into the ground. The wolf howls and scuffling sounds intensified, but stayed in the forest.

Matt walked up, and assessed the situation, having witnessed the entity while arriving. "We've got to get this done asap and get out of here." He turned and instantly created two-man teams from the workers. He assigned each a room. "Get everything she wants. Be careful to not damage anything, but don't waste one movement. Let's get this done and get gone."

"Come on Dan. Let's help Ina."

They walked back in and Ina met them with two suitcases. "Here, put these in my car please." She handed them to Matt. "I need you a minute, Dan." She turned and walked back to her room. She had a box filled with photo albums, and another one with framed pictures from the wall. There were two more sitting in the hallway. "Please put these in mine or Erwin's truck. I can't bear to lose them."

Dan looked, and it was her wedding portrait; Gene and Shannon's wedding portrait; and in the top of the box, he could see shots of all the family at various stages of life, and all Gene's and Erwin's school pictures. He nodded, walked over, picked up the largest box, and took it straight out, putting it in his own truck. He wasn't taking any chances with those.

He came back and carried the others to her car, one by one. He noticed on each trip that the sky was getting darker and the wind was picking up. There wasn't supposed to be rain today, and it was only around 3:00.

Ina was packing shoes in two other boxes. She showed him one for her car, and said the other could go in the trailer. They were summer or occasional shoes that she wouldn't need for a while. There were another two boxes with summer clothes.

When her room was empty, except for the furniture, she motioned Matt and Dan to come close. "We need to go to the shed. Just us."

"Are you sure you want to go out there?" Matt asked. The shed was about ten feet from the fence and very close to where the wolves were.

"Yes. We need to get something I can't leave. We'll need a sturdy box." Her eyes met Dan's, and he understood.

Dan had known Sherman a long time, and had an inkling of what they were after. "I have something better in my truck. Hang on." He walked outside to his truck, flipped up the tool box lid, and reached in for an ammo can he kept there. He poured the screws it held into the box he'd grabbed as he came out, and set them back into the toolbox, then turned the can upside down and shook it.

He met Matt and Ina by the back porch. "Ina, if you'll tell me where, I'll go get it."

"I'm not afraid of them, Dan. Come on." And she started walking with her head held high across the yard she'd walked for over 30 years. The closer they got to the shed, the more the wolves howled. Dan was amazed at her composure.

Ravens and hawks began to circle above them, and the wind sharply increased, and it too, began to howl. Ina's blonde hair was whipped around her head, and they could hear a strange growling sound from the woods, but she never broke stride. The men could hear her prayers begin to rise as she neared the shed. They started praying too, and as the sky continued to darken, Dan wondered if a tornado could appear out of nowhere.

She reached to grab a shovel from the lean-to, and a sudden movement from the ground made Matt grab her and yank her back. A rattlesnake strike just missed her knee as he pushed her behind him. He grabbed the shovel out of her hand and hit at the snake. It, rose up in anger, and began to weave back and forth, preparing to strike again.

Dan slipped around the other way and grabbed another shovel and a garden hoe. There was a second snake, and then he saw a third. The lean-to was suddenly alive with movement, as at least 15 to 20 reptiles began to slither across and around one another, disturbed and mad.

Rattle snakes didn't usually pile up in dens in these numbers. Usually, it was only during mating season. Now it was close to hibernation. It wasn't natural at all. Most of them began to move toward Dan, which was also unusual. Usually, they would try to get underneath something or get away.

But these behaved differently, and a few began to challenge Matt and Ina, too. Both men drew pistols from the holster on their hip. Each began to shoot the vipers, and at the sound of repeated shots, three of the ranch hands, including Rusty, came running, pistols already drawn. One had a look of horror on his face as he saw the tableau in front of him. He hated snakes, and it looked like they were going to win.

The three newcomers got as close as they could, while maintaining the distance needed to avoid a strike and to stay out of range from stray bullets. All began to shoot, and snakes began to be 'shot to doll rags' as Dan's dad used to say. Chucks of them flew in all directions as the bullets hit them. Hawks began to swoop down and grab the chunks and fly off; one even picked up a live snake and flew away, with it twisting round and round the bird, tying to bite it.

The hawk finally dropped it, then swooped down to watch it die, picked it up once again and took off toward the forest. One, that had lain still along the edge where the blocks held up the building, unseen because its coloring mixed so well with the soil, suddenly shot out at Matt, fangs extended; he lowered the shovel with his left hand, just in time for the fangs to meet the metal, instead of his leg. It hit the shovel head-on, so hard one of the fangs snapped off. It was close, and a cold sweat broke out all over him. He shot it with his other hand, watching it twist in rage, trying to crawl closer, even as it was in its death throes. *That was way too close. Thank you, Father.*

A horrible stench, mingled with the acrid smell of Sulphur from the gunpower, made them gag. The wolves were going nuts. One acted like he was going to jump the fence. He was snarling with anger at the humans a few feet from him. He was huge.

Ina, still unflappable, said, "Come on. Let's do this."

Dan motioned for Matt to accompany them, while Matt ordered the men to keep a watch for anything; snake, wolf, hawk, or person. "Just watch our back for a few minutes." He warned them to not get close to any snake heads. Even unattached, the deadly venom could reach them if the fangs scratched them. All three took up a stance that only ex-military could in under a second.

Matt, Dan, and Ina walked around to the other side of the shed. "Here," she pointed toward a solid pile of blocks holding up the corner of the shed. "The one painted blue. It's not cemented. Move it, then it's 10" to the right, and 1 foot back under the shed. Be careful."

Matt and Dan took turns moving shovels of dirt for a couple of minutes, then Matt's shovel hit metal. It rang like a bell as he did. They slowed down, but kept removing scoops of soil, then seeing the box, they began to carefully excavate it. Dan recognized it as one he'd give Sherman a few years before he passed. He knew exactly what was in it now.

He hooked the edge of the hoe under the metal handle and carefully picked it up. Neither of them wanted to reach any further. He gently moved the box out from under the building, and carried it several feet into the yard before setting it down in the grass, but hidden from anyone's ability to see, except theirs. He noticed the lock and decided to leave it on. He placed it inside the ammo box he'd brought. "Are there any more?"

Ina grinned, "You know Sherman; but that's the easy one. We can come back for the rest. She then turned toward the tree line and addressed the wolf pack. "All of you evil creatures: This land has been dedicated to Jesus Christ, and he protects it. You cannot come in. In the Name of Jesus, get away from me and my family. We are servants of the living God, and we have His protection. Get your evil serpents out too!" They heard a crashing sound as something large retreated into the forest.

Dan looked at her in complete respect and not a small bit of astonishment. No wonder she'd turned him down so many times about moving to the ranch. She really knew God would take care of her, and he'd seen grown men that would have already gone running, while she still stood there so fearlessly.

Matt carried the box to Dan's truck, and locked it in the toolbox. Dan and Ina followed him, and the ranch hands walked backward, pistols still pointing toward the shed and tree line as they retraced their steps to the front yard, then holstered their weapons and went to help finish the job.

The other guys were struggling with a refrigerator, and with the added manpower, easily rolled it into the trailer.

"Can we come back for the tools in the shed, when it's colder?" Matt asked.

"Yes, or just leave them."

A wind gust whipped through the pines growing all over the yard and just outside the fence, sending pine cones raining down upon the group. They hit hard, and specifically hit people, but not the empty spaces between them. Scratches began to appear on bare skin and blood began to ooze from the deeper ones.

It was like they were being thrown by unseen hands. The wind picked up the dust and flung it into the workers faces; some got an eyeful and began to try to blink it away. Nature herself, it seemed, was making an all-out assault on the movers. More dark birds were appearing in the sky, malevolent and seemingly unaffected by the currents on the ground.

The men all got busy loading the truck. Ina, Erwin, and one other man were packing boxes as fast as the others could carry them out. Ina kept praying, and soon she looked around at her empty kitchen. She'd have sat a moment, but they'd already carried her chairs out. Maybe it was for the best. It eliminated the sad goodbye she'd have had otherwise.

BOOK 1: "PREPARE FOR THE END" SERIES

The attack had stirred up her anger and she'd used the adrenaline to get the job done. With the number of men Dan had pulled off the house cleaning job and the fence building project, they'd made short work of it. She waited until the house was empty, then asked Dan to stay with her for a minute.

She closed the door, walked into the kitchen where she'd cooked for her husband, and stood there, while he hugged her from behind. She leaned into his strength, wondering how to let her home go, but loving Erwin enough to do it. She bowed her head and let the memories chase through her mind, while Dan held her, whispering that he understood, knowing how hard it was.

Finally, she kissed her fingers, gestured around the room, and smiled. In her heart, she thanked Sherman for the years he'd loved her in this home, and apologized for her unbelief, then turned to Dan, who hugged her tightly; holding on until she knew she'd be ok, then looked up and nodded.

He tightened the hug one more time, holding her solidly against him for several minutes, and kissed the top of her head, then they walked back outside. She was finally ready to move on, and nothing the enemy would throw at her could take away the years of love and happiness she'd experienced here, but she knew God had something new elsewhere.

They all climbed into the various vehicles, Dan placing Ina and Erwin between him and Matt—wishing he'd just had her ride with him—with the trailer carrying their furnishings in the front. Another skirmish had been won by prayer and determination.

Erwin's phone rang as he pulled onto the highway. He glanced and saw 'Billy' on the screen. Tears sprang to his eyes at the years of shared times with him, but he'd also realized that most of the good times he thought he'd had, really had only been seen through the rose-colored glasses he'd worn for too long.

He was horrified at how he'd let Billy run his life, order him around, and all the things he'd been drawn into; and embarrassed over at the sudden memory of how Billy had treated girls, including Missy.

He looked at the back of Matt's truck and knew that he'd never treat a female that disrespectfully; instead, Matt would move hell and earth to help a lady. He wanted to be like Matt, instead of like Billy. He wondered again if Billy already knew he was supposed to kill him.

A sense of safety came over him as he realized he'd be living with this group. He'd felt alone for most of his life. Gran had always been there, but he'd missed out on siblings, parents, and a true male figure to pattern himself on. He couldn't wait to have them teach him what it was to be like them.

He had no idea how infuriated the coven would be, and it was just as well, because he was experiencing a peace that would very soon be shattered.

The Reality of Bondage

Chapter 34

RANDY WOKE UP IN pain, unsure where he was. As his eyes focused, he saw a doctor with a mask across his face, a surgical hood, and a white coat, walk over to him. He could see his eyes only, intense and watching him. He looked like he was about to go into surgery, only the room behind him didn't look like a hospital. Randy tried to sit up, but the pressure and pain on his back, and the intensity lower on his backside made him groan and wince, and he dropped back down.

"I repaired the damage," the doctor stated, with a detached voice, slightly muffled by the mask. "You had two large lacerations in your rectum. That's where all the bleeding was coming from. One was rather jagged and took a lot of stitches. You'll be fine, but it will take a few days to heal enough to sit comfortably. I also stitched up some scratches on your back. I'm no plastic surgeon, but the scars should be minimal. Are you hungry?"

Randy tried to answer, but his throat was dry and his voice came out weak and raspy. "I need water." His head was pounding and he was still disoriented.

"Of course. Let me get you something cold." The doctor left the room and returned with a bottle that he opened, then raised the head of the bed enough that, with his help, Randy could drink from. He gave him small sips, but Randy wanted more and more, and ended up drinking the entire bottle. "Let me get you another one. You need the fluid. I've had you on IV, but your body needs to replenish the blood you lost."

He drank the second bottle more slowly and gradually his need slackened. "Where am I?"

"In a safe place. We couldn't take you to the hospital, but it's ok. I have everything I need here. I assessed you at your house before moving you. I didn't think you'd want this on your medical record." He was brief, but thorough with his answer.

Who are you?" Randy asked.

"That doesn't matter for now. Waya called me, and I took care of your injuries. Let's get you a little more hydrated, and, if you can eat later and have a bowel movement, I'll take you home. Do I need to call your place of employment and have you excused from work for a week?"

A queasy look came over Randy's face. His hands gripped the sheet across his body so tightly it twisted on both sides, sliding up until his feet were exposed. The cold air made him pull them back in quickly. "I'll get fired if I don't call in, but I can't let them know why I can't be there."

"I can say you had emergency surgery for a twisted bowel. There's no shame in that. I'll let them know you'll be off for a week, and that you're at a relative's home for recovery. It's not an uncommon condition. I'll tell them know we forgot to give your phone back, and had to mail it to you. I have a Stamps.com account. I'll make an overnight envelope, with a label addressed to your home for you to open and leave in your living room.

If anyone asks why you didn't answer the phone, you can show it to them. I'll send a bill to your insurance company for my services so they won't question it, but it won't go through the hospital. I own an out-patient surgical clinic. Of course, I'll write your part off." he said in that same detached manner.

Randy was embarrassed that he had the injuries he had, and wondered if the doctor knew what caused them. "Will there be any lasting damage?" he was worried. He didn't remember the entire ceremony, but he remembered enough to know that he could be very injured.

"Not this time." The doctor leaned against the wall and folded his arms across his chest. "Sometimes there are. I'd be careful for a while, and not get involved in anything of this intensity."

Randy still wasn't sure how much the man knew. He wasn't even sure if he should be asking questions. He reasoned, if the man was operating on him outside of a hospital, and doing it at Waya's request, he had to know something. Possibly he was a part of the group Waya belonged to. He'd wanted to join that group so badly, but now he wasn't so sure.

He had a sudden memory of the kind of entity that had caused his injuries, and a wave of weakness came over him, accompanied by an instant nausea. He started dry-heaving, then the water he'd been drinking decided to come up. The doctor grabbed a basin and held it until he was finished, then wiped his mouth. "You'll get used to it," he stated, correctly surmising the cause. "It's not always like this. Let's get these sheets changed."

He walked to the other side of the room, opened a cabinet, and removed a folded-up package. He began to unwrap it, and Randy saw that it was a set of sheets enclosed within a pillowcase that had been wrapped tightly into a square bundle and stacked neatly on the shelf. As Randy's eyes followed his movements, he took in more of the room.

It was about 15' x 20', the walls were grey, and it had other medical equipment. He saw an x-ray machine, several pieces of lab equipment, and more cabinetry, both on the bottom, with additional ones hanging on the wall above those. It looked like an exam room in a clinic mixed with a lab. There were two more beds like the one he was in, but they were empty. It was cold like a hospital. He could smell the antiseptic smell most medical facilities had.

"We'll go more slowly with the water." He untied the wet hospital gown, and threw the sheet into a bin, "Here, roll over so I can get these off, and put the new ones on." Randy did as he was instructed, gasping in pain as he did, and soon the sheets were replaced with fresh ones. The doctor then went to another cabinet and came back with a fresh hospital gown. He helped Randy change, and he was exhausted when they were done, while the pain in his rectum was increasing by the minute. He groaned and fell back, then shifted to get the pressure off the area.

"I'll give you something to take the edge off. Let me hang a new IV bag too, that way we can get you hydrated faster, and keep you hydrated until you can keep the water down." He changed the bag, adjusted the machine, and then took a syringe and medication vial from the drawer beside him. He drew up a dose, flicked the needle with his finger, then shot a small portion out to remove all the air. Randy wondered what was in the vial, then had a moment of fear; he'd been helpless, still didn't know where he was, or who this man treating him was, and he realized he could have given him anything while he was out, and still could.

His pain was such, though, that he welcomed the medication as the doctor pushed it into the port in the IV line; He watched the color move through the tubing, and in seconds he could feel himself slipping back into sleep. As he was fading out, his thought was, *they wouldn't waste the time and drugs if they were going to kill me.*

He became aware sometime later that someone was doing things to his body. Pain mixed with pleasure, each vying for top place, took his breathe away. Even with his eyes closed he realized there were too many hands and body parts touching him for it to be one person. He fought to open his eyes, but was drugged with something. He finally cracked them open enough to see two women and some men surrounding him.

Some were doing things he liked, and some were hurting him badly. It was mixed up in a weird, dream-like medley of movement and sensation, and fear began to creep in as he caught a glimpse of the doctor standing by the wall watching it all with an intense look on his face as he took in the scene. He looked like he was watching for something particular to happen.

Randy tried to move away, but he was trapped between the bed and the people. His mind retreated in horror, while his body responded to the stimulation. He was being used for something, and his brain was too sluggish to figure out what. He couldn't stop any of it. He was immobile and passively received what they offered, both good and bad. He tried to focus on the pleasant feelings, but as soon as he was lost in them, the pain would grow in intensity and overwhelm him.

He felt the internal stitches tear and the hot flow of blood that followed. He tried to scream, but a low moan was all that came out. Just as he thought he could take no more, a dusky-skinned woman with long black hair climbed up and took over. He looked into her eyes and they were the blackest, largest eyes he'd ever seen. They all but wrapped around the corner of her face, highly slanted and unusual. They looked deeply into his own, and the pain receded as she moved.

The pleasure rose with each movement, along with a growing sense of him being enmeshed with the woman. A look of surprise came over her face, and he knew she felt it too. As they merged into one mind, he became aware that he was feeling not only his own sensory input, but hers as well, as if his mind was attached to both bodies at once. He felt his release, then felt it as it rushed into her body as if he were her.

He knew the moment that conception took place, and they both knew immediately that each individual sperm had joined with the corresponding egg, and multitudes of zygotes had been created. She felt a union with this man such as she'd never experienced, in all her jaded past. Her master screamed with delight. She heard his triumphant roar of satisfaction in every cell of her being, and knew she'd completed what she'd been sent to do.

The shock caused her to jerk with surprise, as parts of their psyche fused in that moment, and neither would ever be the same. They experienced the zygotes becoming sentient and an overwhelming desire to protect each one flooded them.

He stayed still as their eyes met. Neither understood fully what was happening, but both instantly knew this was the purpose of the entire encounter. As their eyes met, their souls further fused, and with their shared knowledge they silently vowed to protect whatever had just been created. He heard the voice of the demon whisper in his mind…well done, my servant…well done.

He caught a glimpse of the doctor nodding in satisfaction, and it was if he knew what had silently transpired between them. He closed his eyes and instantly passed out.

Much later he suddenly jerked awake in the hospital bed, smelling the dried blood and other fluids that stiffened the sheets. He looked around for the other people, but the only person there was the enigmatic doctor, who sat in a chair against the wall. He was watching Randy with an amused look in his eyes.

"They give good dreams, don't they?" he smirked. "You'll get used to that too. It's one of the perks that makes the rest worth it."

Randy stared at him, confused at his words. He knew the incident had been real. *Hadn't it?*

They went through the sheet changing ritual again, and he was given both water and broth, helped to use the urinal, then

was gone again seconds after the doctor pushed another drug into the IV.

I'm Struggling With That

Chapter 35

ERWIN WAS SHAKING. He hadn't realized how much he'd been drinking, or how dependent he'd become on the alcohol and drugs. He'd never taken the harder stuff Billy used, but he suddenly found himself craving that too.

He lay awake wishing he'd indulged in one more ritual with the beautiful pagan women. He didn't even know their names, and had never seen most of their faces, due to the masks, but he found himself thinking about them constantly. His body longed for what he was used to, and he was remembering lots of things he'd enjoyed about them. He liked the ranch, and he liked being free from Billy's control. He even enjoyed the bible study with Dan, Matt, Clayton, and Rusty, but it seemed like he'd given up everything he was used to. It was a ceaseless refrain in his mind.

He knew his grandmother was enjoying being on the ranch; and her friendship with Lupe, the housekeeper and cook, was growing closer. She and Dan spent of lot of time talking, sitting on the veranda, and laughing. He hadn't seen her so happy since his grandfather died.

He felt so much guilt about his overwhelming desires, and knew she'd be so disappointed in him, if she knew. He wasn't even sure why he still had them. He felt like that should have been gone when he made his decision to turn his life around, and when the demons were cast out. Guilt increased, as he felt like such a loser, he couldn't even get salvation right.

He needed a cigarette. He'd borrowed a pack from one of the other ranch hands, and he'd given him a lighter too. He got out of bed, and quietly made his way through the house, going out on the veranda to smoke, and think about what he wanted.

He'd been out there a short time, when Dan walked out to join him. *Apparently, I'm still being watched. I've exchanged one controller for another.* He looked up at Dan with angry defeat and Dan remembered Sherman looking just like that after his deliverance.

"Can't sleep?"

"Something like that."

"I told you I want to make up for what I should have been doing all along. Will you allow me to speak to you like a father speaks to his son?"

Erwin shot him a look that Dan fully understood, in all its intention, "I'm not even sure how a father speaks to his son, but you're not him, and I'm not a kid."

Clayton had walked out just in time to hear the last remark, and watched his dad to see how he'd handle it.

"I know. Erwin, I was out here when my dad talked to Sherman when he was right where you are. I was younger than Clayton, and sitting right where he's sitting. Son... I know I'm not your father, but I'd like to be his representative for you. Sherman was my best friend, and I also know what he went through, and he was just about as resentful as you are right now.

You don't have to talk if you don't want to, but let me tell you what he went through. You may be surprised. It's been my observation from reading the Word of God, and historical novels, and history books, that people don't really change all that much. What we did then, is what we do now. Technology and the amount of information we receive may have changed, but the human heart has not.

The enemy of men's souls doesn't have all that many tricks in his bag, so he keeps using the same ones he's always used. Sherman's not the only person I've known who was mixed up in that either. As we've spoken about before, people who've gotten out have shared a lot with us, so let me make some educated guesses, ok?"

Erwin took a drag on his cigarette, blew out the smoke, glanced over at Clayton, wondering how much he knew; and how he'd see him if he knew the extent of his involvement, and all he'd done the past few years. He looked at Dan and shrugged, "Whatever."

Dan grinned, knowing Erwin was trying to be callous so he wouldn't know how much he was hurting, and so Clayton wouldn't see him as inferior. He knew what kind of man he was from Homer and dealing with him at the hardware store for the ranch, and this wasn't it. *It can't be easy to make such drastic changes in so short a time.*

"Ok, we're all men here, so I'm going to talk like one, and address a few subjects that may make you uncomfortable with me speaking about them. Erwin, when you get to the level with pagans where you're brought into a ritual of that magnitude, you don't get there overnight. I also know you've been groomed since before you were ten years old.

Son, I know how they do that. They ply you with alcohol, then drugs; give you freedom not granted to kids until they're much older, or adults. Most brought in that young, have their virginity taken very soon after, while under the influence, far too early for them to be able to handle it emotionally. It helps start you keeping the secrets, and needing what they offer. All of those things can be addictive.

Bodies of any age, once that desire is awakened, keep wanting to have what they're used to. Sherman had a hard time with withdrawal from all of it. They sent what we figured out was a succubus, that drove him almost insane. He couldn't even sleep without feeling it wrap itself around him, making him want what he didn't need.

Erwin looked at him, and he saw it in his eyes before he even asked, "What's a succubus?"

"It's a particular type of demon that comes to a man at night, in his bed. It desires to have sexual relations with him, and seduces him until he gives in, and many times forces it on him, even when he doesn't want it. Men get so addicted, they can't function in the daytime, from either sheer exhaustion, or desire to stay in bed with it.

The male form that comes to women is called an incubus. The origin, according to extra-biblical pagan literature is that Adam was married before Eve to a woman named Lilith. She'd mated with an archangel named Samael—one of the names used for Satan—and left the garden and refused to return. Succubus' have always been known to be associated with the devil.

It's another form of torment he uses to try to steal the blessings God gave us, and pervert them. In the bible it's called a screech owl or night monster, and the origin of the term nightmare, as she was referred to 'riding' the men. I don't believe Adam was married before Eve; that's the pagan version, but I do believe it's a higher-level demon sent to enslave through sex.

God gave us marital relationships to procreate and bring comfort to one another. It's intended to add an additional level of intimacy between a husband and wife that they don't, or aren't supposed to get, anywhere else, and binds them closer together. The devil uses those needs and desires in wrong ways to destroy people by destroying families, making children that don't grow up in loving families, and to make what God intended as good, into something cheap and tawdry.

That's why a lot of rituals have a free-for-all in that department, and why they tend toward what happened in the one you just went through. It's a depraved version of God's plan, and it's my understanding that the higher-level demons demand that form, just like in Sodom and Gomorrah. The closer the demon is to the serpent, the more they crave it.

Sherman wasn't in any of it as long as you have been, and he was almost grown when it started, but he still had trouble with the desire to continue having what he'd grown used to. Coven girls often draw a young man in with sex, as do the young male members, with girls. They're instructed to target someone they want to take down, or someone in a family they want to take down.

They've caused many to turn away from the way they were raised and God's rules, and many a person is bound for life by sharing a child with one of them. Corruption has always been a part of Lucifer's attack on us. Have you had issues with that subject, or something that seems female coming in the night?"

Erwin looked at Clayton again, embarrassed, while lighting another cigarette; and Clayton said, "I'll go back in if you need me to, but I'm a young man too, Erwin. You don't have to be in it like you were, to desire things. Especially in our generation where its normal to indulge in sex, or have it shoved in your face all the time; or where you're treated like there's something wrong with you if you aren't active.

Even listening to the ranch hands talk about their dates can sometimes get to me. One reason I don't date much, is woman all seem to think that's part of a relationship now, and I want to do it God's way and bring a cleanness to my marriage, when I get that far. My mom's been gone a long time, like yours, but I remember how she and dad were, and that's the kind of marriage I want; and I don't want a girl that's been around everywhere, and I'm not going to give a woman a man that's been around either. I'm sure if I'd been involved in that since I was a kid, I'd have issues too."

He nodded, "I'm having problems in that area. It was very regular, and it's almost like it's been that regular my whole life. But that's not all. I guess I drank more than I realized, although I seldom did unless Billy was in town. Tonight, I just got to wanting a beer, or a joint, or both. I couldn't get away from it, and I'm shaking all over. It's probably some form of withdrawal, and Nicotine helps take the edge off, but not much.

Dan, I guess I thought that deliverance and salvation meant that part of my life was over, and I wouldn't want to even go there again. I have also been having dreams where it feels like a woman is in bed with me, and I'm not even asleep. I'm not going out to find anybody, it's coming to me."

He looked at Clayton again, "I wish I was like you, more than you'll ever know, but I can't undo it, and I'll never be able to." His eyes filled with tears, and Dan heard his anguish, "I'll never be as good as you all are, and I've ruined so much that I'll never be able to fix. I think maybe I drank so much, in part, to cover up how guilty I feel, and how disgusting I really am. I wish I'd never met Billy."

"Did you find Sherman disgusting?"

Erwin looked at him, surprised by his question, "No. You know what kind of man he was. My grandparents were like you and Clayton's mom."

"And yet, he sat right here on this veranda, and told my dad the exact same thing. Erwin, it's not going to be easy, and you may fight the memories, and the desires, the rest of your life, I know sometimes he did; but he got free, and you will too. If you want to.

I was married to one woman in my life, and she was sick for quite a while before she died. That was 15 years ago, and I still miss not only her, but that part of our relationship. At first, it was excruciating, and I'd wake up wanting to be with her so bad, I'd have to get up just like you did. I'd come out here, and for years I used nicotine to deal with it. And sometimes whiskey.

Clayton was young, and that's not what I wanted him to grow up with, and it wasn't what I grew up with either. I knew the enemy could pull me into things I didn't want for me, or him, if I continued. I know it's not the same, but it was hard to give up anything that comforted me. For you, it's not just comfort, it's addiction, and escapism.

It's going to hit you hard for a while. You'll deal with a lot of things that Sherman did, too; from loneliness, losing your parents, and being in a certain way of life since you were a child. It's going to take everything you have to let it go. The first seven days you're off alcohol, it's acute. After that, its straight up habit. Sugar is the same.

What helped Sherman was he began to keep a little notebook with him, and he'd write down when he craved alcohol or drugs the most. He'd write down what he was feeling and what was going on around him when it hit, and when it was the worst. If he was upset, or someone was hassling him, or just plain up bored. He did the same with nicotine.

I worked with him, and we figured out the pattern. When he was stressed. When he was lonely, especially when he needed sex. When he felt judged, or inferior… and a lot of things ignited his sense of inferiority at first. The demons seem to hit you hard there; even Janie went through that from something in her past.

He found there were certain times of day, or the week, or month, that he craved it more. He usually lit up after meals, or when he got in his truck, or when he finished a job, and was sitting and thinking about what he needed to do next.

After we figured out the pattern, he tried not to do it at those times, so he could break the pattern. He'd come and get me and I'd talk to him, or we'd go riding, or swimming, or cook something, or play cards. Anything to distract him from the craving. Eventually he stopped."

"Was that all it took?" Erwin looked hopeful.

Dan grinned, "It all helped, and we became best friends in it all, but the plain truth is," he started laughing, "he didn't get completely done with it until he fell asleep in the barn, smoking, and the barn caught on fire. I saw it, and got him out; but it burned the entire barn, the hay stored in it, and a calf we couldn't get to. We got the rest out, but he never got over losing that one to his addiction."

Erwin stared at him, "My grandpa burned the barn down?! What did your dad say?"

"Erwin, my dad was as human as the rest of us. He had a temper like Matt's, and had a screaming meltdown; but he loved people, and he loved Sherman. He'd done some stupid stuff when he was young too, and regretted it. He made us both help build the new one, and while we did it, he talked to us a lot about choices, and where they led, and consequences; some of which you can't undo.

With such a dramatic example, it was the last thing he needed to let it all go. I'm not saying he was perfect after that, or that I am now, but he made better choices. Erwin, he was the one in Randy's place; and they hate your family line, so the physical damage was extensive, and he never really got over what the demon did to him inside his body, or his mind. Ina was the best thing that ever happened to him, and working here was a close second, but the only thing that saved him was giving his life to Jesus, and letting all that go.

You know he seldom left the ranch or your house. That's why. It scarred him in ways I'll never forget. I was one of a handful of people he ever let get close, or trusted. Matt's dad, Zach, was another, and Jake's dad, and all of us were close. He eventually let Bobby and Mason in, but not as much. I don't want that to happen to you too. Would you let me be your dad, and Clayton be your friend like I was for him? Will you let us help you through this? And maybe be the family you've lost?"

"I'm surprised you want me anywhere near Clayton. I might corrupt him."

Dan grinned, "Clayton gets himself in enough trouble without needing you to take him there. Just be responsible for you; he can be responsible for himself. Erwin, you're one of us now. Please don't be suspicious of my intentions, or my thoughts. I'm an open book, son. If you want to know what I think, just ask me.

If you have something you want to say, there's no censorship here. We discuss hard subjects all the time. You and Clayton are grown men, and you can come to me, Matt, or Jake, anytime, and we'll hear what you have to say, and give you our best. Rusty can help too. He has his own story. You will be loved here, son, and mentored, unless you refuse it."

"Dan, what if I can't change? I wanted a dad, but he was gone. Billy was all I had, except for Gran. I didn't like a lot of stuff Billy did, but I've never made friends easily. I don't know how to be a cowboy or how to be a Christian.

I don't even know how to be a friend, except in the context of my relationship with Billy, where I was always in last place. I have issues with even knowing who I am, but I'm realizing I'm far behind being who I should be by now. He suppressed me no matter what I tried to add."

Clayton pulled his seat closer. "Erwin that doesn't matter here. I'm already your friend, and I appreciate you. You made such a difference when we were in high school and I don't think you even realize how much it helped.

You don't have to be Albert Einstein here, and you don't have to be under our feet either. You can stretch and be all you can be. You just learn to be who you really are, not who Billy, or anyone told you, you have to be. If you have an idea, say it. If you don't know, or don't understand something, ask. The only reason I know what I do, is I asked Matt and Dad about a kazillion questions growing up. Matt used to pay me ten cents a minute to shut me up."

Dan grinned and started laughing again, "It never cost him much, cause he never shut up much."

Erwin started laughing too, relaxing his guard a bit, "That's how it is at the hardware store. Billy always wanted me to quit and go to work for him, but Homer treats me like I'm intelligent and capable. I'm in charge of things and he trusts me to do it, but I can go talk to him for help, or just to hang out anytime. If I have an idea, he'll let me do it, or we discuss it and make it better, then we do it. I miss that."

"Erwin, you have the option to go back if you want, but for a while I hope you stay here, so we can keep you safe. You'll be treated like that here too, you just don't know us, yet, like you do him. And if the ranch gets a little tight, I have a helicopter. Clayton can take you anywhere you want to go, and you can explore other places, and broaden your horizons a little. You're not in jail here. Let's just get you a little more past this first, ok?"

"Erwin, I wasn't going to tell you this, but for Sherman, and others we've helped, there were usually multiple deliverances before they were finally free. And most of them became students of the word, and students of the war between the two kingdoms. I'd like to get you completely free before you leave the ranch. Can we work on that first?"

"Dan, is it too late to be a righteous man, and learn to be who I really am, and recover my life? I just feel so embarrassed, and so hopeless."

"Let me answer that, Dan." Rusty was walking up the outside steps of the veranda. He'd been sitting lower down, where he couldn't be seen, and heard the entire discussion. He sat and told Erwin some of his story. Erwin was surprised. He'd never seen that in the rugged kind man that worked so closely with Matt, to keep them all busy. "Dan, why don't I take them for a ride and talk to Erwin so you can get some sleep. I know you're going to the meeting in Dallas in the morning."

"Sounds good to me. That ok with you, Erwin?"

Erwin looked to Clayton, who said, "I'm up for it. I can't sleep either. It must be catching. Let me run in and put some jeans on, and grab a sandwich. I'll make y'all one if you want to go get dressed too."

He agreed, and when they went in, Dan turned to Rusty, "Do you think he'll recognize you?"

"Dan, there's no way. He was never in anything important, and I don't look nothing there like I do sitting here, anyway. You know I don't talk about it much, but I'll tell him enough to help him. You and Matt saved my life, and my sanity. You still do. I'll pay it forward. Let's just get him entirely free, and keep him safe.

He'll be ok. He's young, and Clayton will help him. Sherman had you. I have both of you. He has all of us, and Jake. The only way he can fail, is if he wants to; and if he does, none of us can prevent it. You already know that. We'll teach him about ranching and help him grow up and be who he's meant to be. If he's anything like Sherman and Ina, he'll be a good man. We may need to find him a wife sooner than later though, when he's past it."

Dan grinned, "Clayton too; although you, Matt, and Jake, aren't setting too good an example in that department."

"Well, it wasn't because we didn't try, now, was it? Have you looked at your own example? I know you did it right the first time, but that was while ago too."

Dan chuckled, knowing he was right, "I know. I just couldn't deal with the thought at first, then dating was a disaster, and Clayton and all y'all needed me. I may think about it again. Too bad they don't have mail order brides still. I'd order us all one."

Rusty laughed, "Oh, Lord, Dan. I'd rather pick one out myself than to see what you'd order."

The young men came back out, and Clayton handed Rusty a bag, then a thermos of coffee. "Here, if we find too many, it may take a while. But with this, we can stay out as long as we need."

"Thanks. Come on, the fence isn't going to fix itself, and I know of at least three cows that are about ready to drop their calves. We'll check on them too. Erwin, this is what I do when I have issues with sleeping. You can go with me anytime. Just text me."

He nodded, "Thanks. Right now, anything helps."

They walked down, got in his truck, and Rusty talked to him a lot as they worked, knowing Clayton was probably surprised as he did. He didn't know a lot about Rusty's past, and Rusty was careful what he shared, but still wanted to give Erwin what he needed.

They got back around 3 AM, and all slept late. Dan was ok with that. He may run a cattle ranch, but his chief business was the Master's work, and healing his boys would always take precedence. He decided to ask Matt about ideas for them all to take a trip soon, and just hang out with them all, maybe hunting up north.

He sat in the kitchen with Matt, drinking coffee, and teasing Lupe and Ina, content for the time being, and glad she was there. "Ina, you look good in that apron. I should have hired you a long time ago."

She grinned, while Lupe pointed her spoon at him, "I'm not enough for you, boss man? You need more help now, just because you moved in a pretty lady?" she went off in rapid Spanish and Matt cracked up, "That didn't work like you meant it to, did it?"

Dan grinned, "Not really. I may need to give her another raise now."

Rusty walked in, yawning, listened to Lupe for a few minutes, then looked at Dan with his brow raised, "What did you do to her?" he knew more Spanish than Lupe realized, and he got tickled. "Ina, I better get my own coffee, before she boils you in something."

Ina rolled her eyes. "Y'all, leave her alone. She likes me being here."

Lupe suddenly grinned, "It's ok. He can hire you. I have more aprons. He can give me a raise too, tho, since he can afford two house keepers. I'm ok with that."

Everybody laughed. "Lupe, tell me what you need, and I'll get it for you. You know that." Dan and Lupe had a close family relationship. Dan was good to everyone on his ranch. He'd always wanted more family, and when his wife died, he'd just adopted them all and made them family. They all knew it, and would do anything for Dan.

"I need a husband. Can you get me that?" she grinned, and Rusty cracked up. "Don't encourage him. Last night he was talking about ordering us all mail order brides."

Matt looked from one to the other, "I have things to do. I'll see y'all later." He was laughing as he went out though.

They Are Here

Chapter 36

MAGGIE SAT STRAIGHT UP in bed, her heart pounding with fear. Adrenaline rushed through her body as she 'heard' hundreds of thousands of people screaming. The dream was heart-crushingly real. Multitudes of beings, not quite human, were everywhere. They were like evil children. She didn't know how, but she knew they'd just been created. She'd seen them in her dream. Large black alien eyes; slanted at inhuman angles.

A strange dusky color that was also somehow pale. She'd never seen that shade of skin before; somewhere between cream and grey. Straggly, stringy hair; sparse and coarse on the misshapen heads. Large feet, and hands that didn't look quite right. Malevolence seeped out of them and permeated the air. They had zero compassion, hurting and killing humans without compunction. It was like an army created in hell, sent to destroy every human on earth. The smell of death surrounded her even now.

Then, there'd been others. They looked entirely human. They'd intermingled with society, worming their way into homes and businesses. You couldn't tell they were the same by looking. They were some of the most beautiful children she'd ever seen, and were far more subtle in their approach, but did their damage just the same, manipulating families or groups against one another.

Lying, hurting others; all the while with a huge smile upon their face, as they 'just wanted to be honest about what they'd seen.' It was as if a narcissistic devil had taken on the form of an 'angel of light;' she shuddered at how easily people had trusted them, simply because they were so attractive.

They'd shown up as orphans whose parents couldn't be found; or as children of men who hadn't known about them. Or had known, but never acknowledged them; their very presence causing pain and anger in the home, as wives learned their husbands had been unfaithful in earlier years, and were now being forced to raise the product of the adultery.

It was as if someone knew the secret sins of men and women everywhere, as even children that had been secretly given up for adoption were coming to find the parent who'd relinquished them.

Lawyers had presented them to the fathers or mothers, or to entire families, as nieces, nephews, or grandchildren they hadn't know about after a sibling or child had died, with signed paperwork and birth certificates; or being delivered by policeman who'd brought them to the only people whose name the children knew.

Of course, people accepted responsibility for them. She'd seen the world decimated and an unbelievable amount of people dying. Good people protected orphaned children everywhere, hoping to rebuild. There were lots and lots of orphaned children, as parents died of the vaccine or the growing violence.

Multitudes of children had died as well, and people were devastated at the loss. They'd slipped in among the real children in all the chaos she'd seen, coming from God knows where, and had instant acceptance. She'd seen them letting the other ones, who were so malformed, in the homes at night. Collaborating with them as they murdered their new families.

She needed water, but didn't want to turn on a light or walk through the house in the dark. She was disturbed in her spirit in a way she'd never been before. It was another warning. She was sure of it.

She grabbed her phone to check the time, 3:00. It was both too late and too early to call Jake, but she found their texts from earlier and hesitated only moments before hitting the send button. This was too big to carry alone, and they'd called one another tons of times around this time. She sat up in bed and wrapped her arms around her knees, hugging herself, while alarm bells went off inside, rising with each unanswered ring.

Jake always answered by the third ring; but a fourth, a fifth, a sixth…on and on, until it went to voice mail. The fear notched up a level. *Where was he?*

She waited five minutes, then called again. It went through the series of rings, and again went to voice mail. *Did he leave his phone downstairs? Was he sick? Was he gone, and his phone in his car?* That conjured up thoughts she didn't want to think about. Again, she wondered what would happen if he found a girlfriend or a wife. *Is that it? Is he with someone?*

She began to pray, calling on God to help her with these dreams and visions. To give her the strength to carry the knowledge and the understanding of what to do with them. Should she warn people? Would they listen? Would it keep them from caring for the real children who desperately needed mothers and fathers and families?

Should she not tell? Then more people would die, simply from not knowing the danger that was coming. She had no idea when it would happen. She realized she needed to capture every single detail while it was fresh in her mind. She started shaking as she realized she'd have to relive it in order to do that. As she sat there, she continued to pray for the people who would be on earth when this happened, and for Jake, as she was starting to worry.

Annie, feeling her tenseness and fear, squirmed up beside her and wiggled her way onto her lap. She hugged her, glad she was there, and didn't feel so alone. She knew Annie would bark at the first noise she heard, and her fear went down a notch, knowing she was safe for the moment. She turned on her bedside lamp, went to the bathroom, got a tumbler of water, and then grabbed a notepad and pen from the drawer by her bed, getting back in bed to document the dream.

She closed her eyes and purposely went back through the dream, seeing it play out in her mind exactly the way it had the first time. She carefully recorded each detail. These types of dreams were so detailed and vivid, and that was another way she always knew it was a prophetic dream; it was so different in quality. Each one she'd had she could recall in its entirety. It didn't dissipate upon waking, like regular dreams.

Each one etched itself into her memory.

Watching it like a journalist taking notes helped her stay more detached, but it was still such an awful attack upon humanity, that she was shaking just a few moments in at the evil transpiring. She wrote the word 'attack' at the top of the page, then the spirit of the Lord spoke to her:

"It is an attack. It's an attack against humanity itself; not only their life, but the DNA that makes them human. It is coming. It is here. It will very soon be 'as the days of Noah.' Wickedness will rise continuously. People will die in many ways. Men's hearts will fail them with fear at what is coming upon the earth. Nephilim are being created in many combinations, and 'pure bloods' will be hunted by many types of evil creatures.

All humanity is targeted for destruction, but my people most of all. Satan is furious because he knows his time is short. He will do many of the same things he did before the great and terrible flood that cleansed the earth the first time, but far worse. Bring everyone that you can to me. Know this: It will a time like none other. He knows this is his final season before being locked in the Abyss for a thousand years.

Maggie, be vigilant. Watch for the signs I give to know who you can trust, and who you cannot. Don't go by names, appearances, what they say, or how they present themselves. It is an age of deep deception. You will know them by their fruit. Share this with your partner without delay."

She wrote the last word, added the date December 15th, then jumped in fear as her phone rang. It was Jake. "Maggie, are you ok?"

"Yes. No. I just need you for a few moments. I'm sorry to wake you," she replied.

"I was already awake. What's wrong?"

"I had a dream. It was a warning. Oh, Jake, it's awful. Then the Holy Spirit spoke and authenticated the warning, and said 'tell my partner.' I don't know if we're supposed to warn others or not."

"Put on coffee. I'll be there in a few minutes. And… Mags… I'm bringing someone to meet you."

Her mind began to spin. *He really was with someone. He was bringing the person to meet her, at,* she glanced at the phone screen, *4:00 in the morning?! And he'd already been awake? Oh God. Who was he with?* Her body went totally still. Then she spoke, calmly and detached, in the old dissociation from her pre-healed days; "Of course. I'll be ready."

He hung up and she was sick wondering who he was with, and why he was bringing the person to her house. *He knew she didn't share these dreams with very many people. If it was Sharon or Rachel, or one of his brothers, why didn't he just say so.* She didn't want to share the dream with him while someone else was there. Their being called and tasked together was intimate between them. The thought of him being with another woman, and...OMG...bringing her to Maggie's home in the middle of the night made her sicker.

She had no claim on Jake. He was his own man. She realized he probably had many other people in his life she wasn't aware of, and it was perfectly ok. She'd never told him how special he was to her. She hadn't even realized for sure how much, until recently. She needed to be happy for him.

But it was really unlike Jake—and the character and integrity she knew he had—to be with a woman in the middle of the night.... *unless it's you, staying over...* she reminded herself, then ruefully smiled. Maybe she wasn't the only one who did that on occasion. The thought hurt more than it should have, and she put it away to deal with at another time. Jake was coming, and he was bringing someone for her to meet. That was the reality she needed to face right now.

She climbed out of bed, dressed, combed her hair, pulling it back and clipping it up, then went to the kitchen. She made coffee, setting out three cups with saucers, cream, sugar, and honey. She had some pastries she'd bought at the bakery yesterday, so she set out three dessert plates, with napkins and silverware.

She had no idea who was coming, but she was determined to be gracious, no matter what. She'd just have to adjust to not contacting him, or being as free with him as she was used to. She'd deal with her feelings about it later.

She heard his truck pull up and schooled her face, as she pulled herself up into her full dignity, then walked to the door. She peered through the peephole, making sure it was him, then opened it. He was getting out, then went around to the other side, opening that door, and pulled something out and shut the door, carrying it as he walked toward the house.

She watched the other side of the truck, waiting for the other person to get out, but no one did. She wondered if the woman had decided not to come after all. She moved aside, realizing he was carrying a box, and let him in, shutting the door behind him. He followed her to the kitchen, looking confused when he saw the table set for three. "Is someone else coming?" he asked.

"You said you were bringing someone for me to meet," she replied evenly, being careful with her words as she looked at him, waiting to see what he would say.

His grin spread across his face, as he stood there holding the box. He watched her face for a moment, "Who exactly did you think I was bringing at 4:30 in the morning?"

"I had no idea. You didn't say."

"I wanted to surprise you."

"I was surprised," she looked at him, trying not to show the hurt she felt.

Jake looked at this woman, who was so much a part of his life, and realized that she was upset, but not sure why. He was instantly sorry, and wished he'd just told her. He'd wanted to surprise her and wasn't even thinking about her thinking it was a person, or who that person might be.

He sat the box on the counter. "Come here." He began to opened the flaps, and then reached inside, pulling out a sleeping puppy, "Meet Beniah. He's who I wanted you to meet. I'm sorry I confused you. I just wanted to surprise you."

Maggie's eyes flew to his face. *A puppy? He'd been talking about a puppy?* Instant relief went through her and it showed on her face. "When did you get a puppy?" She moved closer to examine his new friend.

"Yesterday. I was going to invite you out tomorrow, but then you called. I was outside with him doing potty duty, and then rocking him back to sleep. He's cried a lot since it's his first night away from his mother, so I haven't slept at all. He's only six weeks old, and it may take a few nights before he settles."

"I didn't know you wanted a puppy."

"I got to thinking about everything, and what we know is coming. It will be increasingly dangerous, and I decided we need a watchdog. I know you have Annie, and she'll bark, but she won't deter an intruder. We need a larger dog for that. So, I started asking students, and watching the papers. I found him yesterday, made the deal, and picked him up after class. I'd have brought him by, but I knew you were having your Narc Abuse Class," he explained.

"What did you say his name is?"

"Beniah. I named him after one of David's mighty men. I call him Ben for short," he smiled, "he'll be my mighty man, helping to keep us safe." He glanced at the small bundle of fur in his hands. "Eventually," he added.

"Let me hold him." She loved puppies and reached for the sleeping dog. She'd just gotten him, when Annie, coming into the room, erupted in loud barks, startling them all, including Ben, who began to cry. It was chaos for a few minutes, while they introduced Annie to the baby. She was distressed by his whimpers and examined him all over, then eventually began to lick him, and he quieted, easing everyone's distress.

She instructed Jake to bring their pastries to the living room, then settled into her recliner with both dogs. Ben, missing his mother, responded to the attention of Annie, snuggled close to her, and went back to sleep. Annie watched him anxiously for a few moments, then moving to keep him between herself and Maggie, lay down to guard them both, and promptly fell back asleep as well. Maggie sat there with a lap full of dogs, letting Jake serve her, and was entirely content, almost forgetting why Jake was there in the first place.

They drank coffee, ate pastries, and visited for a short time, then Jake asked her about the dream. He saw the distress on her face as she closed her eyes, reliving it yet again. She didn't want to disturb the dogs to go get her notepad, but didn't need it anyway. She described the entire awful thing to him, and was relieved to not have to carry the burden of knowing what was coming alone.

He was very bothered by what she described, making notes on his phone. "Maggie, I'm sorry you had to see these things, but it truly is a gift of God to have the heads-up. We read Genesis and Revelation, trying to understand what it was like, and what it will be like, but we've never understood the truth of evil at that level and what it was really like for people then, and how bad it will get in our time. Very soon, I'm thinking."

"That's what the Spirit said."

"I don't think people, even the church, are prepared for the supernatural realm invading our world in a more tangible way. We need to do more study on the days of Noah, the Nephilim, and the events that prophecy says is coming, and really try to envision it, so we can be as prepared as we can be."

"I think that's a good idea," Maggie yawned. The warmth of the dogs, and the safety of Jake's presence, were lulling her back to a state of rest. She'd only slept 2-3 hours before the dream.

"I think we need to share the vision with the bible study group, and the alliance group," he added; then yawned too.

"Yes." Maggie leaned back a bit farther. "That's a good plan, but for now, let's not just shout it everywhere. People will think we're crazy."

Jake slipped his shoes off. "Mags, rest a bit. I think I will too. Do you mind if I sleep here on the couch for a couple of hours, while he's quiet?"

"That's fine," she mumbled, as her breathing deepened and she fell asleep.

Jake smiled at her, seeing the mother in her as she unconsciously put a hand on Ben as she shifted to a more comfortable position. He grabbed the couch pillow, stretched full-length on the sofa, then, having had no sleep while tending to his new companion, he closed his eyes, and was soon snoring softly.

They slept till Ben woke them; whimpering, hungry, with Maggie's pants wet, as he hadn't yet learned how to hold his urine; so, he was also protesting the wet spot he'd created.

"Here, let me take him," Jake took both dogs out, while Maggie went upstairs to shower and change. She came back down to Jake heating milk to mix with some of Annie's dog food for Ben, while Annie was eating her favorite dog cookie and peanut butter rollup. She grinned at the scene, then taking eggs and sausage from the fridge, she began to prepare their meal as well.

It was comfortable being with Jake, and he knew where everything in her house was, just as she did his, but underneath she had a pang, realizing how quickly this could end if he began to date someone. *I wonder if it really was just Ben tonight? He was completely dressed, and didn't look like he just threw something on for a quick trip to show me a puppy, and talk.*

For a long time, they'd studied and taught together; driving to group meetings together, and sharing their lives. Tonight, had shown her how quickly that could change, and she couldn't help but wonder what her place would be if he met someone; it would affect every part of her life. *What would that be like?*

She'd be a third wheel, and she realized immediately she couldn't do it. Her relationship with Jake would have to end, and she might need to reconsider selling her home and moving in with them all. She couldn't live there with him and his wife, seeing him interact with a woman he loved, while she was relegated to family friend status.

She'd cared for Jake for a while, and in that moment, she knew she loved him; but had no ability to tell him, knowing it'd make him uncomfortable, and she'd lose even his friendship. She felt a pang of the loneliness she'd carried her entire life, but managed to carry on as if nothing were wrong. It was a trait all abuse victims had—the ability to hide the pain and pretend that all was right—when inside, you felt your world crashing in. Again.

As they ate, they talked about the weekend. All of them were supposed to meet at his house for target practice on Sunday, and to plan more for the move. They'd planned a shopping trip as well, to add more berry plants if they could find any left, and more food and other supplies.

It would be a bit harder with a puppy, but Jake also wanted to look for a couple more. He thought they would need more than one dog as it became more dangerous, and he wanted to get them all now, so he could train them together, and they would grow up like litter mates.

He remembered Matt had said Dan had a litter so he called him around nine, and was invited to come on out to take his pick. They left around ten, taking Ben with them, as he was too young to be left with Annie. He fell asleep as soon as the truck began to move.

Maggie was too quiet, but Jake chalked it up to missing sleep, and the aftermath of the vision. He too was tired, and after going through and getting her a tea, and him a coke, they drove out to Dan's without saying much. It was unusual for them, but all in all, still ok.

After being stopped briefly at the gate, they drove up to the house, parking just as Dan, Ina, and Erwin came out. Maggie put Ben down into the grass to explore and do his puppy thing, while Jake shook hands with Dan and Erwin. Ina came over and they walked a short distance from the men, staying close to Ben.

"I'm so glad to see you, Maggie. I appreciate you and Jake, and what you did for Erwin."

Maggie smiled and hugged her. "It's what we do, isn't it? I'm afraid we're going to do a lot more of it in the coming days," she said, "and a lot more people will probably need it then we'll be able to rescue. When will you be moving to the ranch?"

"We're already here," Ina responded.

Maggie was a little surprised, but glad. "That's good. How is he doing?"

"Fairly well, all things considered. We just got here two or three weeks ago." She told Maggie about the events while they were moving. "We've gotten the attention of the coven, no doubt. It may get messy before he's completely free. Sherman said it took several rounds of deliverance before everything was gone.

I hated to leave my house, and I'm not really scared for myself, but … for Erwin … I am … it's going to be a big change for him, and they will do all they can to draw him back in. Maggie, will you help me learn the things I should have learned while Sherman was doing his best to tell me? I need to take up the fight with you, instead of getting in the way."

"Of course. I can drive out once a week for a while so you don't have to leave the ranch. Will Erwin join us, or will it be just us?"

"Matt and Dan are going to be in charge of training him. He needs a father, and they need to do what they feel like Sherman and Gene asked of them. It will be good for all of them, but he barely remembers what having a dad was like; and I can't help but wonder if the teenage rebellion that he was too reluctant to take out on me will come out with them.

He's not used to a man being in authority over him, except for Homer, and he really wants to break away from being a lackey, like he was for Billy. I'm going to stay out of it as much as possible, but I expect it to get interesting. I remember Sherman and Gene almost coming to blows a few times. I didn't help much, always taking Gene's side. I probably caused it to last longer than it should have. I'm not making that mistake again."

Maggie laughed, remembering her own kids' rebellion, although she'd left before they'd gotten over it. "It may get interesting, for sure. He's a little old for teenage rebellion, but he hasn't really grown into himself yet, so it could happen. Dan can handle it, he had Clayton; but Matt...now that part may get fun...he's never had a child of his own, and I suspect he really would have liked to.

He's had a little practice with Tucker and Clayton, but they both had fathers that took the brunt of it, and he was the 'good guy,' so he may 'over parent' a bit. It will probably actually be good for all of them." She smirked the way only one woman can with another, as they discussed the way men acted amongst themselves. "Call me if you need to get out for a break, or just need to vent."

Ina grinned too. "Or if I need someone to yank me back, and remind me to stay in my lane?" she asked.

Maggie's grin got wider, "Yes. I can do that too; only don't shoot the messenger."

Ben was finished with his business, and he began to whimper, thinking he was alone, having wondered off a few steps. Maggie picked him up and they walked back to the men, and Dan said, "Come on. Let's go find him some buddies. What kind is he?"

"Great Pyrenees." Jake answered.

Dan shot him a look. "Dang. Those are good dogs, but don't they run about two grand or more?"

"Usually; but He's mixed with a Golden Labrador. I have a student whose parents raise both types. He got in trouble for letting them breed when he was watching the place, while they were gone for the weekend. They get top dollar because they are known for their pure bloodlines; and he was tasked with getting rid of them, so they didn't have perspective clients ever challenging their dog's pedigree.

He was desperate and begged me to take one, and as I'd already decided I needed some guard dogs, I graciously took the last one off his hands. But," he looked slyly at Dan, and with great delight shared his secret, "he didn't know that, so now, he owes me one." He and Dan both laughed, and Dan slapped his back in the age-old acknowledgement of a deal well done.

Ina shook her head at Maggie, "Men. And their deals."

"…and keeping score for the future…" Maggie added. Both women snorted, amused by the story. "I swear, they're always boys at heart, vying for top position, and getting one over on somebody."

Ina laughed again, "Isn't that the truth."

They walked to a small shed behind the barn. It had a lean-to, and that's where the dogs were. Dan mostly had blue-heelers, which were fantastic cattle dogs; but a few years back he'd rescued a German Shephard who turned out to be a wonderful guard dog as well, getting on well with his heelers, and he'd never gotten around to getting her spayed.

His litter were also a mixed breed, but should be fine with Ben, and her mixed pups had always turned out to be good dogs. He had six left and they were just the right age to leave their momma.

Maggie sat Ben down to see how he'd react to the rest of the puppies. He held back for a bit sitting on her foot, but a couple of the others came to check him out, and soon he was rough and tumbling with all six. They played for a while, then went to their mother for milk.

He followed them over, and after she smelled him for a few minutes and licked him all over, she put her head back down, unconcerned about an extra mouth. He pushed his nose in, found a spigot, and began to nurse.

Maggie was touched by how animals cared for orphans, while so many humans abandoned their own children. She had a brief thought of the dream. *That will change; but not for the good.*

She noticed one puppy, smaller than the rest, brown with black splashes, that seemed to want to stay near Ben. She pointed it out to Jake, and after they were fed, he picked it up and flipped it over. "Maggie, this one is female."

"You could name her Abishai, and we could call her Abby. That's another one of David's Mighty Men."

"With the emphasis being on 'men,'" he reminded her.

"They don't have to be all boys," she countered. "After all, we're in enlightened times now," she argued her point. "Women can be warriors too. That's what you call me," she reminded him.

"Seriously?" he said with total affront. "You want me to shame David by naming a girl one of his Mighty Men's names?" he hadn't quite thought that one out before it left his mouth. Now he had both women on him.

"If you're getting them for guard dogs, you can't go wrong with a female," Ina huffed. "They're some of the most protective animals in the world. They can be ferocious. I think Abby is perfect."

Dan decided to stay neutral, "If you're planning on having them around for whatever's coming, it wouldn't be bad to have a female. If something happens to some of them, you may want to breed more. And if you see the need for protection, other people will too. It may become a source of income later or have a high trade value for pups; and if you do that you can't rely on just one female, you may need a couple.

But, if you're determined to get all males, these four are male," he pointed to the lighter ones, with the blue spots from their heeler heritage.

Even Maggie had to admit, they were cute too. But she held fast to 'Abby' and wouldn't budge. "If you don't take her, I will."

Knowing they'd be in the same house, Jake gave in, but not very gracefully. He grumpily picked up one of the males and played with it for a minute, while secretly grinning at Maggie's fiery spirit, thinking no one saw it. It yawned hugely, peed on him, then fell asleep against his shirt, claiming his territory in the first encounter.

Dan turned his head to hide his amusement at Jake letting Maggie have her way, and him being wet on, but his chest moving up and down, and the muffled sounds as he cracked up gave him away. He was still laughing when he turned around. "Well, I guess he has to be one of the three: Josheb, Elea'zar, or Sammah. He ain't takin crap off nobody."

Erwin watched the older people closely. They argued good-naturedly, but without true anger like he'd experienced from Billy for years. He noted the ability to speak up, without trying to dominate; and the way you could lose an argument, but retain the relationship. It was fun and enjoyable when no one had to win. He liked what he saw, and filed it away for future reference. It seemed he had a lot to learn, and these were exactly the type of people he could learn it from.

He felt safe in a way he hadn't since his parents died. But just as he had that awareness, an uncomfortable feeling began inside him, and he couldn't seem to shake it. Something felt 'off' and he had the thought that maybe no one was really that good, or nice. It would bear watching, to see if they stayed the same, or were just putting on a show. Something inside said to not trust so easily. Afterall, that's how he'd become Billy's flunky.

"I know it's a lot of mouths to feed, but don't you need another female?" Ina asked. "Dogs tend to pair up, and two males with one female will most likely lead to fighting over her. That will divide their loyalty, and if you do want to sell or trade them, like Dan said, you may eventually need more than one. You just as well raise them together."

Jake, knowing he'd been out-maneuvered, looked at Maggie, who was smirking. "I do agree, but I don't think they all need to be brothers and sisters. I have one more source to go see." He looked at Dan, "If they don't have what I want, I can always come back. And just for the record, this one just earned the title of Elea'zar. Eli for short." He tucked the tiny dog into his shirt, and started back to his truck. Everyone laughed at that, with Dan grinning at Maggie, as he saw her kiss both Ben and Abby, as she followed Jake, smiling at them both.

When they neared the house, Dan invited them in for a glass of tea, but Jake declined. He had a lot to do today, including building an enclosure for a pack of dogs. He'd only intended to get one or two at first, but now it seemed he'd be raising several. He didn't know if they'd keep each other company at night, or if he'd now have a chorus of cries to deal with. Maggie looked happy as she cuddled Ben and Abby, though. *That was worth the extra trouble,* he decided.

They put all three puppies in the box that sat between them. Maggie had to fasten the top down this time, and hold her arm over it, because Eli kept wanting to climb out. "That one may be more trouble than he's worth," Jake remarked.

Maggie smiled at him, with her eyes twinkling. She loved smart dogs, and these three were very intelligent. They would be fun for Jake to train. But, for a good while, it'd be like...well...what it was...herding puppies. He'd have his hands full.

They made one more stop, after a long drive, where Maggie immediately fell in love with a chocolate lab/mutt mix. Labs have long ears anyway, but she may have had some basset hound in her. Her legs were a bit shorter and her long floppy ears were ridiculous. She kept stepping on them and tripping, yelping each time.

She instantly dubbed her Sammy, a form of Sammah, and short for Samantha. Jake agreed, loving making her happy; so now they had four of David's Mighty Men...sort of... and Annie. She smiled, picturing Rachel and Sharon's faces. Rachel would love them. Sharon... not so much... He stopped at a farmer supply, leaving her to watch the puppies, while he ran in and bought the last of the berry bushes, one of each garden tool, puppy chow, and several collars, leashes, and feed bowls.

They drove back to her house, picking up take-out he'd called in from the local BBQ place, and put all the dogs out back to play. They ate, still tired, talking awhile, then Jake left; and she did her housework and laundry so she would be free for the shooting practice the next day. She was very troubled though, and thoughts of Jake dating someone wouldn't leave her.

Every time she thought about it, it felt like she was being punched in the stomach. A couple of times she thought about calling him, and just telling him she cared for him, but her old fear of rejection made it impossible.

On Sunday, she found herself alone with Sharon while Jake and Rachel went to get more ammo, and she casually asked her if Jake was seeing anyone. Sharon, thinking Maggie was wondering if people realized she and Jake were an item, decided to tease her, while setting her mind to rest, "Oh, yes. Of course, he is."

Maggie went instantly still. The pain Sharon's words brought almost cut her in two, but as usual she hid it, and kept a pleasant look on her face. "Is it serious?" she asked, wondering why Sharon had never mentioned it before, and why she'd never met the woman.

"I've never seen him more serious over a woman in my life." Sharon was still talking about Jake's feelings for Maggie, misinterpreting Maggie's stillness as mortification that anyone had caught on. Jake and Maggie were both very private about their relationship, and Sharon and Rachel had watched them a long time; and while they'd never shared with them that they were a couple, both could plainly see that they were deeply committed to one another, and had waited years for them to make it formal. And all Jake's brothers were taking bets on how long it'd take Jake to finally ask her.

"Do you think he'll every marry again?"

"I'd bet my soul on it; he's already making plans for when she moves in," Sharon confided, winking at Maggie, with a smile. "A few years back, I'd have said no; but this time, he's totally all in. So yes, I think he will. In fact, I'm sure of it; and it's probably soon; we'll love living with her here."

She believed Maggie was also wondering if Jake would ever pop the question, and was feeling her out to see what she thought. She wanted to reassure her that Jake really would eventually get around to it, without giving away that she knew about them. It never occurred to her that Maggie was thinking down an entirely different thought line.

Jake and Rachel came back with the ammo, and they all reloaded. Maggie fired shot after shot, straight through the circle drawn over the heart on the cardboard cut-out, never missing, but said very little. She was quiet through dinner, and after playing a few hands of UNO, and watching the puppies play, she loaded up Annie and went home, pleading a headache.

It was really a heartache, she acknowledged as she drove. She was sick at what she'd learned, and embarrassed at how much time she'd spent with Jake; how much she'd opened herself to him, and the times she'd talked to him almost all night long, when the whole time he'd been involved with—and planning to marry—another woman.

And, while he'd looked at his cousins and smiled when he said not all would be his brothers coming to live there, he'd never indicated it was someone he was about to marry. Then she got mad. *How could he? Why didn't he bring his girlfriend out in the open? Why did he always take me with him to events, rather than her. How could he lead me on this way?*

Then, the tears came. It was just like her ex. She'd been thoroughly married, while he'd had girlfriends in nearly every town, he did business in. Her heart, which had been slowly healing for years, froze up, shut down, and locked itself for business. There was no way she'd move in with them. No way she'd spend time with him again.

She had no idea if she could retain the relationship with Sharon and Rachel either. She felt so betrayed, and such a fool. She wondered how many people knew, and how many laughed at her behind her back. *My god... as close as he and Matt are, he and Dan would have to know... and yet Dan hadn't said one word today, or ever... or Levi... I can't believe he didn't tell me...*

Once again, she'd lost all she cared about. Her marriage. Her kids. Her home. Her life. Now Jake. And she couldn't do the bible study anymore either. So, add that to the loss side of the ledger. She was the loser in every area, while someone else got the gain. She wondered how many times she'd spent the night with him, Sharon, and Rachel, and how many times they'd spent time with Matt and Rachel like she and Jake had so many times.

At this point she didn't even want to know who it was. She almost vomited at the thought of being invited to his wedding. She wondered how soon it was, and when he'd been planning to tell her. She remembered him saying he wanted to tell her something, he should have already told her, but he was trying to figure out how.

She almost wrecked as the pain went through her. *Why had he invited her to stay the other night?* She wondered why he'd asked her to go with him today, too. *Why couldn't she have gone to pick out the damn dogs? ... before I fell in love with them too...*

She got home, showered, and went to bed, only to face a long sleepless night of memories. Jake laughing. Jake explaining an intricate subject. Jake playing with Annie, then the puppies. Jake with Rachel and Sharon, and laughing with Matt, or his brothers. All of them spending their vacations together at the lake, where she was always Jake's partner in everything. Jake cooking. Jake hugging her when she was finally able to tell him how she lost her babies and at the recent deliverance. Jake, taking up the calling of God with her; the two of them meeting for coffee so often; and the endless phone conversations.

None of it made any sense, but it haunted her, and each memory ratcheted up the pain in her heart. She already missed him, and the closeness they'd shared. She missed her kids. Tears soaked the bed, and around three she gave it up, went to sit in her chair, and picked up the word of God. It opened to the verse in Genesis: 'And the LORD God said, it is not good that man should be alone; I will make him a helper comparable to him.'

UGH. Not what she needed. She flipped further to the back of the book, into the New Testament. 'Neither was man created for woman, but woman for man.'

She flipped back to Proverbs. 'He who finds a wife finds a good thing and obtains favor from the LORD.' Then one more time, only to find Psalms 68: 'God sets the solitary in families.'

It was a sign; even God thought Jake was doing a good thing. Where did that leave Maggie. *Without even the support of God,* was the thought that whispered through her mind. The enemy was behind all of this, and if she'd been in her right thinking she'd have instantly seen that, but she'd been triggered into a reaction caused by old wounds, and the fear the dream had generated; and she was too distraught to think, so could only swim in the pain, unable to extract herself.

She was easy pickings in the hands of the unseen ones, that were given more and more latitude to torment her, as she lost faith in everyone, including her maker. She finally did something she never thought she'd do. She hurled her bible against the wall and broke down, sobbing out the pain, the loss, and the unfairness.

BOOK 1: "PREPARE FOR THE END" SERIES

Around 6, she woke to her phone ringing. She picked it up, and it was Jake. She said something she hadn't said in over 20 years, and hurled it to the wall, where it impacted hard, cracking the glass, then fell hard enough to knock a piece of wood out of the baseboard, then silent to land on top of her bible. She began to grab books off the shelf, throwing them each against the wall.

She stomped into her bedroom, picking up her favorite picture of him, and threw it at the bedroom wall, taking pleasure as it hit, and then went to the bathroom, picking up the perfume that came from him, and threw it hard against the shower wall, comforted by the sounds of the glass shards as they fell tinkling back into the tub. The smell enveloped her, and she sat down on the toilet seat and cried, as shattered as the glass; needing him more than she'd ever had before.

She was done with it all. She went back to her recliner, too upset to function.

She fell back asleep, not waking again until 8:00. Annie was nudging her with her nose, needing to go out. She pulled upright, still tired, and tried to orientate herself. She finally managed to stumble to the back door and open it long enough for Annie to walk through, then closed it, and pushed the button on the coffee maker. She stumbled down the hall to the bathroom, then back to pour a cup, add honey, let Annie back in, and finally made her way back to her chair.

She yawned as Annie jumped up beside her. She had her cookie in her mouth, and apparently wanted to eat it lying in Maggie's lap. She wiggled into just the right position, then flopped down, chewing loudly on her breakfast. The aroma of damp dog rose to Maggie's nose. "Good grief, Annabelle, it's morning. Did you have to get stinky already?"

Annie thumped her tail at the sound of her voice, and kept chewing. Maggie lay back and flipped up the footstool. She took a drink of coffee then drifted back to sleep once more, with fresh tears on her face. Annie finished her cookie, snuggled in, and both dropped into a more restful sleep.

At ten, she crawled out of the recliner. She didn't have any appointments today, so the time didn't matter so much as the state of mind she was in. Now, she didn't even have a phone to work with. She'd have to remedy that first thing. Her phone and computer were the tools of her trade, and she was usually very careful with both.

She picked up the broken halves and put them in her purse, hoping the phone tech could rescue her contacts and texts.

After getting the new phone, she decided she needed some fresh air. One thing about her trade, she could work anywhere, and since the covid lockdown, she did mostly zoom or phone meetings anyway.

She decided on the spot to go to Galveston to the beach for a few days, to decide what to do about the move, and get away from everyone while she pondered how to handle this new information. Hating herself, she downloaded another picture of Jake and saved it with his number.

She was still shocked, appalled, and hurt beyond belief, that Jake, or even Sharon and Rachel, had not mentioned Jake's girlfriend. No one else had either. She couldn't imagine why he'd not had her in the bible study, at the very least; or what she thought about Maggie staying over. *Maybe he was keeping as much from the other woman as he was from her.* Unbelievable. It's like he was a totally different person from the man she'd thought she knew.

She took Annie to Hank, her neighbor, who kept her when she was out of town, then took off, distressed, and needing to just run away. She hadn't done that in years, and it was as if the healing years had never taken place, she was so upset. She got her daily tea, turned up the music, and hit the gas. It was time to grow up and stop dreaming about starting over. No one could be trusted. It was time to accept that.

Distracting the Warriors

Chapter 37

JAKE WAS TIRED. The puppies played well together, and slept in a pile, comforting one another, so he got a little more sleep, but all were about the same age, and missed their respective mother and litter mates. He saw the wisdom in getting more than one, but it was still going to take some time. If one wasn't whimpering, someone else was, and then all joined in.

Someone would wet or soil the box, and that would make them all cry, too. It was surprising the volume of noise four small dogs could make. And the mess. He'd never seen so much feces generated so fast in his life. His nieces and nephews hadn't been as bad. *Of course, diapers were easier than cleaning the box,* he reminded himself.

He was heating milk to mix with the dog food, and he picked up his phone to dial Maggie again. She'd been very quiet yesterday, and he was concerned that the dream had scared her more than he realized. It rang and rang, going to voice mail. *She must have an early appointment, or was on a company webinar.* She'd call when she got out, he knew.

He fed the puppies, laughing at the way they acted like they hadn't been fed in a week; standing in the bowl and stealing bites from each other, wrestling over the green pieces, falling, then crying because they were covered in food. "Ok, you guys; stop playing and eat. You have all day to play, but I have to go to work."

He let them eat until their bellies dragged; then put them all in the bathtub for a cleansing. Then, it was time to take them all out again. He set them in the yard, then went to change the newspaper in the box, and put in a clean towel for them to crawl under, or lie on. *I wonder if this is what it's like to have an infant. Endless tasks, making sure they're fed and clean, worrying when they're in the yard alone.*

I always wanted to be a father. Maybe having all these mutts will fill something inside me that I missed and didn't know it. When he went back out to check on them, Eli had fallen into a fresh pile of steaming excrement, while trying to bite Sammy's tail; and had to be bathed all over again. *Well, you asked for it.* "Get over here, you little bugger. Stop aggravating everybody." He bathed him again, while they played in the bathroom with the door closed, then put them all back in the box, to fall asleep. *At least they're not crying.*

He glanced at the clock and realized he'd have to rush to get to class on time. Rachel was coming by to check on them in a few hours. She'd agreed to check on them a couple of times a day until they were older. *I can always count on Rachel. I always could.* She was planning on bringing a few things out on each trip and he would pay for her gas. It would help each of them.

He turned the radio on so they would have the sound of voices, then left for work. He tried to call Maggie again, but still got no answer. He texted, but she didn't text back. *She must be with a client. It never takes this long. I hope nothing's wrong.*

He tried again at noon, and again got no answer. It was puzzling. She usually at least texted back. He sent a short message, saying he was free at 3:00, if she wanted to grab coffee and a piece of pie. No response.

Rachel called with an update on his fur babies, and he asked if she'd heard from Maggie. She hadn't, but reminded him Maggie was a professional, independent woman, and she was probably busy. She left for a house signing and didn't think anything about it. *I know she's right, but Maggie always calls me back.*

Meanwhile, Maggie was miles into her trip, enjoying the drive, but greatly troubled at heart. *I can't believe he didn't tell me he was dating someone. I must have looked like a complete fool to him. Always available. Treating him like he was 'mine' when he clearly has never made the slightest declaration, or showed the slightest inclination to ask me on a real date. What's wrong with me that I couldn't see he wasn't fully disclosing everything?*

She stopped for a meal and a rest; sitting too long, playing with her food, and mad every time she saw Jake's name and face pop up on the phone screen. She put it on silent and turned it over, but she saw the light come on twice while she ate. *I feel like I've lost my best friend.*

She'd tried to wrap her brain around Jake with a wife, and somehow, she just couldn't get ok with it. She kept picturing him laughing and teasing this unknown woman; cooking with her; praying with her; ministering to others together; telling her about his students; or mad at some inane thing the government was doing. She thought about him wrapping his arms around her and hugging her when she was scared the other night, then saw herself replaced as he hugged someone else.

As stupid as it sounded, she felt completely betrayed, while telling herself she had no reason to feel this way. She'd grown more distraught through the drive, while rationalizing that it was perfectly normal for a man his age to date, have friends, and lots of people in his life. Sometimes he was unreachable, but he'd always been 'counseling a student,' 'in a staff meeting,' 'shopping,' 'outside working,' or 'with a family member.' She'd never thought a thing about it. *It never occurred to me he could be on date.*

It was still surprising he hadn't said anything, or introduced her. She told herself Jake was as private about his personal life as she was, but they usually talked about everything. Except now she wondered what else she didn't know. And Sharon and Rachel...she just couldn't understand why they'd never said anything. *How can I trust them ever again? Especially, Rach... she knows....*

.... Oh God.... Did she tell him, and that's why he hid it from me?

She felt her eyes get wet, and she turned to look out the window while she got herself under control. She saw a couple about her age walking hand-in-hand to their car, laughing and smiling at one another. They looked like they'd been together for decades. *That's what I wanted in my marriage. I did my best, but it takes two, and he refused. I wonder what it's like to be that close to another person? To know that they love you back? To not have to question their loyalty, or if they'll walk away. I thought Jake and I were that close in a lot of ways.*

Then she saw a young woman about her daughter's age, carrying a baby, and holding a small child's hand. An older woman, who could only be her mother, got out of another vehicle, walked over, and took the child by the hand, kissed the baby, and hugged her daughter. They had an easy comradery as they entered the restaurant, working in tandem to get the children settled, as if they'd done it hundreds of times. *That should be me and Kasey. My grandkids should know me like that.*

A knife went through her middle at the loss of her granddaughter. It was a wound that would never heal. Two women, both older than Maggie, walked in and joined the small family, and before long the words 'Grandma,' and 'Auntie,' drifted across the room. She watched them, again wishing she had an extended family like that, and again feeling the absence. *I hope they know how lucky they are, and never know what if feels like to be alone. I gotta get out of here.*

She left to continue her journey, but loneliness ate away at her, fueled by the unseen creatures who hurled fiery darts at her mind and emotions, making her mental state even more tenuous. *Who am I? Why am I always on the outside? What am I going to do?* She'd grown used to being with Jake and his family members. She'd begun to feel like one of them, when in reality it seemed she was just a casual friend, who didn't even qualify to meet dating partners.

She checked into the beach house she'd rented; glad it was off season and she'd been able to rent it immediately, while getting a huge discount for a week's stay. She put away the groceries she'd bought along the way, and sat in the reclining beach chair on the veranda, holding her bible in her hand as she watched the waves endlessly coming ashore.

She'd always loved the ocean. It soothed her in a way nothing else did. She felt small against such a force of nature, but it made her aware of God's power, since he'd spoken it into existence. *How nice this would be with a husband or a family. Thank you, Father, for your presence; but I need people too.* She repented for throwing her Bible against the wall, and sat and prayed, asking him to help her know what to do.

She changed into sweats and beach sandals, went down to the ocean, rolled the sweats up to her knees, and walked for at least a mile, but possibly two, as she meandered; sometimes in the surf, sometimes in the sand, smelling the salt and the fishy aroma. *I wish I could do this more often. If money wasn't so tight, I would.*

Her hair blew everywhere in the gusty wind that was steadily picking up; but she kept walking; watching the small pieces of trash and sea oats swirling into the air, until she was finally ready to rest a while, sitting on a pier that jutted out into the water.

It was peaceful, and she felt the peace, but it stayed outside her. Her heart wouldn't let her absorb it. She was once again in a bubble, removed from society and feeling like an outsider to humanity; abandoned, rejected, and replaced. *The waves could sweep me away, and no one would know. Some people might miss me for a while, but it wouldn't affect one single person's daily life. Before yesterday I would have said, at least his daily life would be affected. How wrong I was. How did I live this long and not generate that in another person?*

Tears flooded her soul, and escaped from her eyes. Endless, silent tears, created from a place deep inside her that she'd thought was healed. She didn't cry loudly. The salty liquid just kept coming, dripping down her face, and falling on the hands clenched in her lap. A black cloud rolled in, dropping rain on her, and it was if nature itself cried with her. *Good, now if anyone sees, it'll just look like rain, or ocean spray.* She was comforted that some part of creation understood, and shared her grief.

She sat and cried in the chilly rain for a long time, knowing she shouldn't stay, but unable to move; eventually her shivering was bad enough she had to go, and walked slowly back to the rental, completely drenched, and going straight to the shower. She was depleted, but the tears kept silently dripping as she pulled up her computer to check her schedule.

She had a light week. She'd meant to have dial time today and set up more appointments, but now she was glad she hadn't. *I can't work right now. I don't have it in me. I just have to be alone for a few days.* She hadn't taken time off in over two years. This time she'd take care of Maggie.

443

She had two whole days before she'd have to talk to anybody. Right now, just breathing was all she could manage. She remembered her early days with her support group and being instructed to 'just breathe and stay alive. Do just one thing. That one thing could be to get dressed or comb your hair; maybe make a phone call. Nothing big. Just one thing.' She'd done that by taking a drive and walking. Now, she was done.

She curled up, unable to even read. *I never thought I'd ever feel this much pain and anger again. Is there anyone anywhere I can trust? Where are you, Lord? Why? Will it always be this way?* She just stared out the window at the ocean, listened to the endless waves breaking, cried, and held on to whatever had carried her this far in life; a dauntless courage and determination that refused to give up, even if she'd taken another devasting blow. She'd just breathe, and not die. That was enough for today.

People always tell me how strong and courageous I am. That's bull. If I don't die today, I'll have to get up and do it all over again tomorrow. That's not courage, or strength. That's sheer survival. She finally fell asleep lying on the bed, but not under the sheets, while her phone light cycled on and off numerous times, still on silent, as Jake grew more concerned by not being able to reach her.

He was worried about her being sick; worried about the coven retaliating, and just worried in general. *Where is she? Why isn't she picking up? Did they get her on her way home last night? Do I need to call the group? Are they going to pick us off one by one? Am I just over reacting?* He felt an uneasiness in his spirit, that told him something was wrong. It wouldn't go away, and he couldn't get peace, even after praying.

While she slept, he stayed up all night, praying and worrying; calling every hour, on the hour, afraid he was being over the top, but unable to stop himself. At 5, he drove to town, more concerned when she didn't answer the door; knowing she was gone when he realized Annie wasn't barking.

He shined a flashlight into the small window in her garage door, confirming her truck was gone, and drove back home, upset. He had no idea where she'd gone, or why she hadn't told him she was going. He fed the dogs, dealt with their other needs, put them back to bed, then fell into a restless sleep on his couch.

The unseen ones cackled with glee. They'd be rewarded by the Master for separating these two. The hated words 'where two or more are gathered together' were known by them all, and it was counted a great coup to divide people and pit them against one another. Lies, half-truths, hurt feelings, misunderstandings. It was low-level demonic harassment 101.

People never changed. What worked from the beginning still worked today. 'It is not good for man to be alone' was another one for which they used kindergarten oppression tactics. Alone they could be tormented by loneliness, rejection, and unmet needs. This made them vulnerable for addictions, fornication, and anger at God.

Starving people would eventually eat a substandard sandwich from anyone, and women were especially vulnerable to flattery from a man. These two minions of the dark kingdom had tripped up many a human by sending in their counterfeit 'significant other' after creating friction between friends or lovers. "We can send one of ours to distract her and make even more confusion."

"Yes." The second demon clapped his hands in glee. "We will have a promotion for this. Oh, I can't wait to mess this budding romance up."

And they had even more reason for a great reward. They had heard Maggie speak out loud her decision to stop teaching the Bible study with Jake. That would disrupt the entire group, breaking the unity, and causing more friction and division; while stopping people who relied upon others to feed them, from getting the spiritual nourishment they were being given. Weaker people were often derailed and turned from God after a split in a church or a home group.

"We can get into the minds of the group members as they divide on who to support."

Cackles of demonic laughter rang out in the spirit world as they planned many evil things to divide the group further, and lead people into directions they couldn't before.

They had a particular vendetta against these two humans. They had been instrumental in costing them a sacrifice that had been planned for years; even casting out multiple demons that had been attached painstakingly through the years; freeing their victim, and breaking the powerful hold they had on his mind, soul, and life. The first demon thought evil thoughts even against his partner. *I'll find a way to take full credit for this one alone. I'll be on top. Wait and see.*

When these two stood side-by-side and ministered, there was a strength and power created that was formidable. The supernatural realm could see them covered in intense light, and powerful warriors of the Most High, guarded them, making it hard for the demons to harass them; but, when they were apart, upset, or distracted, their fiery darts sank deeply into their hearts and minds, disrupting the spiritual flow.

The twisted creatures could tap into humanity's carnal nature, created from Adam's fall, and attach themselves; but when people knew who they were in Christ, and joined together in prayer and fasting, Bible study, and ministry, it was harder to reach them.

Evil spirits know exactly how to target any flaw, hunger, or wound to inflict the most pain; but spirits who were cast out had extreme punishment, and if they allowed these two—and the groups they led—to flourish, it would cause the kingdom of darkness great setbacks.

These arrogant individuals knew how to detect their presence, and order them to leave. They knew how to free others and teach them who the fallen ones were, and the greatly hated truth of how to reach and trust the Father Himself. The Master had big plans for this area, and servants of the Most High had to be eliminated...one way... or another...

They filled Maggie and Jake's minds with horrid dreams. They built upon fear and rejection. Maggie and Jake had both experienced loveless marriages where they were badly hurt, and both had trust issues. That was a crack they could dig their long, ragged, filthy claws into; infecting them in the places that were the most vulnerable.

Jake cried out in his sleep as, in the dream, he once again saw Maggie in the vision from the deliverance. He couldn't escape the images he was forced to watch; then the scene changed, and he saw her with a good-looking man, having dinner, laughing, smiling, and the man resting his hand on Maggie's.

They left in one vehicle, and Jake saw him kiss Maggie while holding the car door open for her. The man looked right at Jake, smirking, letting him know that Maggie was now his. It tormented Jake, and he tossed and turned with the changing scenes, asleep, but not resting.

Maggie slept deeply, as if she were in a drugged state, but her mind was already in turmoil, so her nightmares were dreams of Jake with his girlfriend. She could never see a face; but the trim figure and long blond hair tossing in the wind, or with Jake's fingers running through it as he held her, haunted her.

She saw Jake's family members all looking at the happy couple with smiles of approval; and joy that Jake had finally met the woman of his dreams. Each of them, in turn, cast looks of disapproval at Maggie, indicating that she was trying to stay too close to Jake, and needed to back off.

She woke with tears still seeping from her eyes, the pillow soaked with them. *I can't watch that. I just can't.* She ate sliced bananas and cheese for breakfast, then went out to the veranda. It was still a little gray outside, but the rain had stopped. The gusty winds from the night before were now a gentle breeze, comfortable against her skin.

She watched, mesmerized by the movement of the water, the screeches of the sea birds, and everchanging colors of both the water and sand, as the sun broke through in spots; illuminating areas for long moments, before disappearing as the cloud movement closed up the opening. She inhaled lungsful of the unique Gulf of Mexico smell. It wasn't quite the Atlantic Ocean, but close enough for today.

She watched as ships, small to her sight by the distance, traveled from right to left, and left to right; hauling their freight, fewer in number in these strange times. It almost seemed normal, but nothing in her felt normal. She had to get herself together, and create a plan to survive the coming days alone. She felt small and helpless as she watched the world around her, knowing it was all coming to pieces. She felt as stunted as she'd been in her pre-healed days, when she hadn't yet known or accepted the wonderful woman she'd always been. *I can't regress to that either.*

As she felt the power of nature grip her, she was reminded of a poetry piece she'd written in her early healing days. It was called 'Force of Nature' and was written during her healing journey, as she began to own herself, letting go of other's opinions of who she was. It had strength and courage, and Maggie had memorized it. She could still recite every word:

Force of Nature

There's no way.... to describe....
the wildness of the sea
.... or even find the words....
for that place inside of me
that rises up
 .... responding....
to a force
beyond myself
oh, how I wish
 .... I'd known....
   .... when I was young....
.... the warrior chick....
 .... I've always been....
   .... suppressed....
    .... beneath his gruff....
a queen upon a stallion
a pirate on a ship
climbing sky high mountains
 .... leveraging....
  .... my grit....
I watch the waves
come crashing
relentless
in their quest
 .... traveling for miles....
   .... to end in rolling crest....
breaking
in a crash
spreading on the sand
white foam

.... flowing back....
.... to do it all again....
something in the pattern
used designing me
attaches straight to nature
.... calls me to be free....
letting go.... of.... doormat....
.... accepting who I am....
creates an excitement
.... and.... I don't give a damn....
who likes it
.... or who doesn't....
.... it's simply who I am....
the world is there before me
calling out my name
.... if I embrace my courage....
.... and never.... again....
.... be tamed....

Maggie smiled sadly. She'd grown so much in the last few years; realizing that she was capable of much more than anyone, including herself, had ever given her credit for. A lot of that was due to Jake's friendship and belief in her. She'd always appreciate him for that, but she couldn't keep him in her life, knowing he'd lied to her, even if only by omission. And, as used as she was to being the second half of a pair with him where ever they went, she couldn't become the third wheel. She had no idea why God had called them to a shared ministry while knowing Jake was about to be engaged. It seemed cruel.

As she pondered on it all, she was surprised to see how much of her life was knitted to his; and his family, as well. She couldn't put her finger on just when that had happened. It would be a great loss. She wondered if she should just move away, but realized, in today's changing world, that would be foolish. She had other friends in town, and a thriving business, even as reduced as it had become in the last couple of years.

She wished she'd had a chance to kiss him. She'd wondered what that would be like for years. She'd just have to come to grips with the new reality, and be the woman of grace she'd chosen to be so long ago. She wasn't running away from her life a second time; she'd just have to do some trimming of her acquaintances as the situation required.

She decided to go to town for lunch, and found a small place on the beach that had fresh seafood. She ate shrimp and french-fries, with a wonderful side-salad. She was enthralled with the sparkles on the water from a ray of sun that had broken through, when a voice interrupted her solitude.

"May I sit with you?" a deep male voice inquired. *Who is this guy, and why is he interrupting me?*

"Excuse me?" she wasn't sure what he wanted, as she was dragged from her internal thought world.

"May I sit with you?" he asked again. "This seems to be the only table on this side that isn't dirty, and has a direct view of the Gulf."

Maggie was used to talking to strangers in her line of work, but she wasn't working, and really preferred to be alone, but she didn't want to be rude either. *Maybe he needs a sunshine break as much as I do. It would be terrible of me to refuse him that.* "Of course. I'm almost done."

"Don't hurry off on my account." he said. "I've been holed up in my hotel room for hours working, and I just needed a sanity and nature break, along with my lunch." *She seems nice. I wonder why she's here alone.*

She smiled. "Me too. I came down here to work as well, but the beauty brought me out. It's lovely, in spite of the weather." *Maybe him sitting here will distract me for a while.*

"Yes. I watched the storm last evening from the window. The waves were huge, and the lightning spectacular."

"Yes." Maggie agreed, without mentioning that she'd watched it from the beach. *He'd probably think I'm a nut.*

"What do you do?" he asked, then took a huge bite of his fish taco.

"I'm an insurance broker," she answered. "How about you?"

"I'm in Real Estate." He replied, after finishing chewing. *Among other things.*

"I actually do a lot of mortgage protection, so I have relationships with several Real Estate Brokers. My business starts with people buying homes, and several friends are in Real

Estate, and it's good to have people who refer me to their clients." *If he's a professional, he can't be too bad.*

"I'd like to have someone to refer my clients to," he admitted. "Some of them get some real winners for agents," his sarcasm was thick, reminding her of Jake's.

"Yes. I've had many, many clients who've had a few of those," she agreed. "It makes my job harder, but I'm known for taking care of people, so I get a lot of referrals." *I hope that doesn't come across as arrogant.*

"Do you live around here?" he asked. *I really don't need a local in my business.*

"No. I live a few hours away, but I can do zoom meetings from anywhere. I'm actually licensed in several states, and do lots of those."

"Do you have a business card?"

"Not on me."

"Would you be willing to meet me here tomorrow and bring me one? I'm Mark, by the way. I can send you a ton of business, and it would be nice to have someone to send my clients to."

"Actually, come to think of it, I have a box in my truck. I can give you a stack. I'd appreciate the referrals. I'm Maggie." She reached across the table to accept the hand he offered, shaking it as they officially met, and made a business arrangement. *I really didn't mean to get that involved, but it would be nice to have some free business.*

"I'd take of few of yours too, if you have them. I always have clients who move in from other states, and they ask me for lists of people all the time. I have plumbers, electricians, roofers, and real estate agents, among the many others. I have agents in my area, but sometimes they don't want to stay and I have people in several areas I refer to them. What area are you located in?"

He looked slightly uncomfortable for a second, but covered it quickly. "Oh… around Dallas, mostly."

Maggie hadn't meant to put him on the spot, and realized she hadn't said the exact area she was from either, and it wasn't on her business card, just her phone number, "that's close enough." She let him off the hook, "I have lots of people who move over there. It will be great to have someone to refer them to."

They finished their lunch; sat and made small talk while watching the birds play, then each went back to their own agenda. Maggie watched him walk away, for the first time realizing how attractive he was. *Only you, Maggie, could meet a good-looking man, and not notice.* He'd been so friendly and easy to be with, that she'd felt comfortable, but hadn't scrutinized him.

She felt something was a little cagey about him though, and was glad he'd left. They'd sat on the same side so they could enjoy the scenery, and she'd been so into her thoughts as they ate, that she'd just watched the water most of all, but something inside was troubled.

I just don't know the rules of society, anymore. I've gotten too used to Jake's family, and how they behave, and I've never really explored how others interact that much. Maybe I've been too myopic and that's why I didn't see what was right in front of me. Maybe I need to get to know people outside of my area. She drove back to the beach house, parked, walked up the stairs to the veranda, sitting there for another fifteen minutes, then decided she was going to be ok.

She went inside to do some paperwork, and then picked up a book she'd been planning to read about the Dead Sea Scrolls. It was fascinating, and she read for a long while, until the sunshine, now pouring through the window, drew her back to the beach. *I need outside air. I'm at the beach. I'm going out.*

She walked straight into the ocean, as cool as it was, going out far enough for the waves to try to knock her over with the tremendous force of each incoming surge, but not far enough to get too wet above her knees. A few times the spray caught her, but with wave after wave, she was able to withstand the pounding without falling into the water.

Right now, I feel invincible. It's silly; not being knocked over by waves doesn't make me invincible, but right now, I'll take anything that makes me feel strong, or even like I'm going to be ok. She felt strong enough to conquer what she needed to, as she withstood the force of the waves. The piece of poetry went through her mind again, and she began to own her strength and courage with each victory. *I'm a survivor. I'm becoming a conqueror. No man, or his family, is going to take that away. It's time to just face it and move on.*

She decided to walk down the beach in the opposite direction from the evening before, going farther than she meant to. She saw larger houses, and wondered if she was in the private beach area, but she hadn't seen a sign warning against trespassers, so she kept going. Once she saw a weathered post leaning at a sharp slant, but it held no sign, so she ignored it. *What are they going to do, arrest me? At most I'll apologize and move on.*

She kept walking until she was past all the houses; then she found a lonely place with a craggy rock that jutted into the sea, nestled within several high dunes, and sat on it for a while, pondering; praying; making decisions she didn't want to make, but felt she needed to. It seemed as if another era in her life had come to an end, and she wasn't sure what came next. It'd be a part of her life that would be as hard to let go of, as being a mother.

She just knew that she had to move forward, no matter what. *Maybe I need to move to the beach. I'd love a place like this; where I can just sit here and think and pray every day. But...I don't think I'd like the hurricanes.*

She decided she had time to go a little farther, and was enjoying the late afternoon, lost in her thoughts, but finally noticing the greater piles of debris. She had just realized this part of the beach was out of the area where it was kept cleaner for tourists, when she noticed something red in the sea oats and driftwood on the deserted stretch of beach. *What's that? I wish people would stop throwing out trash and ruining everything.*

Curious, she walked closer to investigate. It almost looked like a shoe. As she neared, she saw it was indeed a shoe, but as soon as she was sure of that, she saw that it was attached to a leg. She ran over, thinking someone was hurt, but gasped as she saw the person. *Oh, God. What happened to her?*

It was a woman, lying in an unnatural way, and she was clearly dead. Her clothing was ripped and it was apparent that she'd been assaulted. Maggie didn't have her phone with her, and had no idea how far she'd walked, and it occurred to her that she was in a very lonely part of the beach, with no houses visible. *How foolish I was to come so far from the main area.* It was far from the beach road, and the dunes were much higher here.

She had no idea how long the woman had been here, but Maggie felt her anxiety rise, as she realized someone may come back to hide the evidence, or they could still be here. Just as she had that thought, she heard a noise behind her, but, before she could turn around something hit her head, and she felt herself falling. '*Help,*' her mind screamed. She opened her eyes, and with blurry vision saw a man with dark hair lifting a chunk of driftwood, bringing it down on her head again. Her world went dark.

From the Author:

Here, we end the first book. You've met the main characters, and the people around them.

Maggie and Jake, the bible study group, some of Jake's family and students, and Louise's employees.

Missy and Amy, along with some of the diner patrons; and experienced the easy comradery there.

Billy, Erwin, Waya, and the guys in their group.

Frankie, Diane, Nate, Candy, and Danny, and some of their dads.

Dan, Matt, Ryan, some of the ranch hands; and Gregg.

Matt's family

Dr. Stella, Rachel, Sharon, Pauline, and Homer.

You've gotten a glimpse into many lives and the character of each person. Some people you've heard about in passing; such as Clayton, Erwin's grandmother, Jenny, and people from our characters' past. I wanted to let you begin to understand who each character is, and how they are so inter-connected; what has shaped their thinking and their character.

What will happen going forward? As the story unfolds, they will be challenged in ways that will either break them or grow them. I'm currently writing book ten, and it's been a wild ride so far. Where will it continue to go? No one, knows, not even me. I write as God gives it, and sometimes even I'm surprised. As for the next ten books:

Will Maggie be rescued? Who has her?

Will she and Jake realize they are 'one' already, or will they allow the influence of hell's denizens to force them apart through misunderstandings?

Will Matt and Missy become a family?

Will Billy ever escape his heritage?

Will Erwin be free?

What about Randy?

We have three unborn babies. Will they be human, or something else. Who are these beings that were created between Randy and the mystery woman in the ritual while he was drugged?

What is Waya's true calling, and how far will he go to fulfill it?

Was Frankie's 'dream' real? Will he and his group feed multitudes? Will he become someone who leads many others to Jesus? What about his family, and Diane's? Will they help, or hinder the calling? What forces will oppose them?

Who else will we meet as we focus on how people respond to the changes in our nation and the world around us? What else is coming?

Are we really in the final days of history before Jesus comes? What if we are? What is your role? What if we're not? Then what is your role?

You've seen into the supernatural realm as well. How the forces of good and evil around us affect our lives daily. I have taken some license in this area, while trying to stay as much into the things we know biblically as possible. I've spent much time and years studying the Word of God. I've spent about as much time speculating on what is really going on in that dimension we can't see, and how it affects our own dimension.

I've spoken with many people in my area who have seen the supernatural with their own eyes. It seems they are getting bolder, and are being allowed to come into our dimension with an ever-growing boldness. What will we see before it's all over? Do you know how to deal with it, if you see something (or someone) from another dimension? Read the Word. It's in there. It's a primer on fighting evil. Learn it as if your life depends on it. It does.

Individuals and groups choose whom they will serve. Many others lives are affected by our choices. Some choices can't be undone. It sets us on a path that we can't seem to escape from. Sin takes us farther than we ever meant to go, and keeps us longer than we ever meant to stay. If you have been on the path to destruction, it's not too late. Change sides. Call upon God to free you. Ask for His forgiveness, and give Him your allegiance from this day forward.

Study. Grow. Find those who don't just attend a church. Find the true body of Christ, who follow His will daily. They are the remnant. Prepare for the enemy to try to crush you and bring you back into their kingdom, by wooing, or by force. You are both the pawn and the prize in this great tug of war for the hearts, minds, and lives of humanity.

God's path frees us. We become more like he planned for humanity to be. We love. We help. We grow. We teach. We build. We make an environment rich for others to grow. It promotes unity and joy. It protects. It leads us to a future where we will once again reside with Jesus and be his family.

Satan's path is the opposite. It enslaves. It damages. It cripples. It kills. It promotes hate and disrespect. It diminishes people and draws the demonic beings from the second heaven, and even the air around us becomes 'charged' with evil. It brings the mystery of iniquity. It leads to a path of destruction and everlasting torment as we are punished in a place that was created for Satan and his angels. It was never meant for mankind; we go because we reject God's free gift of salvation.

RINA LYNN

But, as we've seen... people who know who they are in the Lord; who are willing to take up their cross and do the work God has tasked us with; can take authority, take back an area, dispel the demonic hoards, and free people around them.

Which one are you?

We live in strange times that were prophesied about. Demonic activity is rising, and the church has become complacent. This series is, in part, a story of good and evil, a teaching of the truth going on around us, and a call to rise up, take the mantle God is trying to hand to you, and fight the good fight.

I challenge you today:

Make bible study your daily desire and activity.
Ask the Lord to show you what He is calling you to do at this time.

Learn what the bible (and supporting documents) such as the book of Enoch, the Dead Sea Scrolls, and the words of the ancient church fathers have to say about the great tussle between heaven and the kingdom of darkness.

Time grows short. Decide today which side of the battle you are on; then take up the fight.
As for me and my house... we will serve the Lord!

I invite you to join us as we further
explore this microscopic view of the
battle in our characters' lives.

I've created a website for the series. (It's new, and it's a lot more fun to write, than build a website, so don't judge. Technology is not my thing!)
Please pray and help this woman push back the lies of the enemy with truth.

https://rinalynn.com/

Read the books; give them as gifts, and promote them on your social media; and pray for me as I reveal more and more of the story.
These characters are fiction, but they are based on the experiences that real people face every day.
Please go to where you bought the book and **leave a good review** so that more people can learn about the battle of the ages. As the story progresses you will see hurting people, growing people, people in pain, and people healed on so many levels.
They are human and make many mistakes, but watch how they repent and move forward, or what happens when they don't. As they make decisions you don't agree with, ask yourself... what would I do in this situation... who knows what you may face before the end

About the Author:

I have held many positions in my local churches through the years. Sunday School teacher from the age of 16; Board Member, Woman's Ministry Leader, including being an invited speaker to other women's groups, and at the District Level; Mission Treasurer, Mission President, Church Office Secretary; Work & Witness trips. Written many skits, programs, and whatever was needed for the current ministry. VBS; Helped in teen departments, children's departments, and nursery worker. District Builder's program; Delegate to District functions; Children's Quizzing Director.

I attended Brannon House's very first Leadership Academy. It was at a Worldview Weekend event that I met Norm Geisler, and he gave me his PowerPoint and notes for 'I Don't Have Enough Faith To Be An Atheist,' which I've used to teach apologetics ever since. I sang for "The Witness" in Hot Springs, AR, Choir, and special singing… all my life….

Painted for a year and a half at Cathedral Heights Church of the Nazarene in Texarkana, in the new children's wing… bible stories coming alive in art; some rooms were 8x16 walls, some 4-wall wrap-arounds; a long hallway with 16 'glimpses' into biblical history. It was wonderful to give the kids such a visual reference to the bible history we taught in the class rooms.

God has taught me many things to prepare to write this series, and when He laid it on my heart to do so, it has brought so many blessings; in the people I've met, the ones I've ministered to, and the ones who ministered to me. We're all growing and serving, while awaiting His arrival.

Writing is my passion, and the story never gets old…

A SAFE HAVEN